Finding Myself

By the Same Author

Adventures in Capitalism
Beatniks
Corpsing
deadkidsongs
Exhibitionism

Finding Myself

TOBY LITT

HAMISH HAMILTON
an imprint of
PENGUIN BOOKS

To Mum and Dad

HAMISH HAMILTON

Published by the Penguin Group
Penguin Books Ltd, 80 Strand, London WC2R 0RL, England
Penguin Putnam Inc., 375 Hudson Street, New York, New York 10014, USA
Penguin Books Australia Ltd, 250 Camberwell Road,
Camberwell, Victoria 3124, Australia
Penguin Books Canada Ltd, 10 Alcorn Avenue, Toronto, Ontario, Canada M4V 3B2
Penguin Books India (P) Ltd, 11, Community Centre,
Panchsheel Park, New Delhi – 110 017, India
Penguin Books (NZ) Ltd, Cnr Rosedale and Airborne Roads,
Albany, Auckland, New Zealand
Penguin Books (South Africa) (Pty) Ltd, 24 Sturdee Avenue,
Rosebank 2196, South Africa

Penguin Books Ltd, Registered Offices: 80 Strand, London WC2R 0RL, England

www.penguin.com

First published 2003
1

Set in 10.5/16.5 pt Monotype Times New Roman
Typeset by Rowland Phototypesetting Ltd, Bury St Edmunds, Suffolk
Printed and bound in England by Mackays of Chatham plc, Chatham, Kent

A CIP catalogue record for this book is available from the British Library

HB ISBN 0–241–14155–9
TPB ISBN 0–241–14156–7

VICTORIA'S MANUSCRIPT,
EDITED.

FROM THE LIGHTHOUSE

~~FINDING MYSELF~~

by

Victoria About

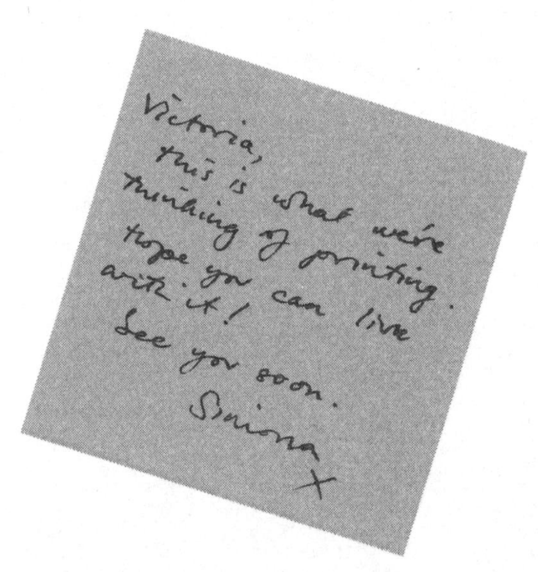

Victoria,
this is what we're
thinking of printing.
Hope you can live
with it!
See you soon.
Simona
x

This morning, after long discussions with my Agent, I sent Simona Princip, my Editor, the following:

I can't write this in neat, organised sections – you know how I am. So I'm just going to blather it out whichwise-whatever, and let you on that basis make up your mind.

FROM THE LIGHTHOUSE

What I'm proposing to write won't be a novel *per se* (not like my previous ones, anyway). Instead, it will be a novelisation of something that really happened. Not something that *has already* happened, but something that *will* – because I make it – one day, one month, August most likely – *happen*. Half my job in writing it (the docu-novel, the true-life story, call it whatever you like) will be to control the actual events.

My idea: You pay me a sizeable advance, with part of which I rent a large house by the sea (within sight of a lighthouse, preferably). I then contact a number of my friends – hereafter referred to as 'characters'. What I propose to *them*, roughly, is this:

> You can come and stay, completely free, for a month, in this lovely seaside house I've rented. (Good food and plenty of alcohol will also be provided, *gratis*.) *But* you must allow me to write up the events of the month in a semi-fictionalised form, afterwards. (In other words: you promise not to sue.)

> My publisher's lawyers have sorted all this out. Disclaimers and that sort of thing. Copyright issues. However, at the end of the proposed book, you will get three full pages (approx. 1,000 words) to say exactly what you like. If you think I've distorted things, told outright lies, etc., you can contradict me. And I, for my part, promise not to interfere editorially with your text in any way. Even if it is, as I suspect some of it might be, libellous of me. I am inviting ten other people along, as well. Some of them you know; some of them you don't.

I would select my characters very carefully: a couple of couples, a quartet of single bisexuals, an egoist or two, the odd drama queen, someone suicidal, someone eccentric, someone older, at least one other professional writer (less successful than me). Mix together. Slosh in the alcohol. Sprinkle a pinch or two of magic dust on top. And – *voilà* – cocktail time.

Plus, once everybody has confirmed, I will sit down and write a Synopsis. This will be a ten or so page prediction of *exactly* what I think will happen when all my characters get together. When finished, it will be sealed, notarised, given to you, and published at an appropriate point in the book. Then people, by which I mean *readers*, can see: How wrong or right was I? Do I know my friends as well as I think I do?

Of course, I won't be able to change a comma of the Synopsis – once it's in your hands. (I may need to add an addendum, however.)

Finally, if you're worrying that *nothing* at all will happen and you'll be left with a no-goer, I can promise that at least one major thing definitely will. Unfortunately, I can't say what. You'll just have to trust me.

The cost to you? Well, I'd usually say make me an offer of the sort that my agent would call 'quite interesting'; but with an idea this good, I think you might even have to stretch to 'very'.

This afternoon, Simona replied:

> Victoria, you are such a genius!
> Count me in, as publisher and participant.
> (Can William come, too? *Please*. He's dying to.)
> 'Very' is a lot, but let me see what I can do.

*

I think I deserve a treat, don't you?

MY HOLIDAY DIARY

June. Athens does traffic very well. About as well, I'd say, as anywhere else in the world.

Shoes – shoes – shoes. The overwhelming, all-consuming fascination and importance (to me) of shoes.

See note overleaf. →

Hotel Stanley. X lies diagonally across the bed. We went out to a ritzy restaurant last night and drank too much ritzy plonk. All this morning X has been in the bathroom, puking like a kitten on a new rug.

Port of Piraeus. Mainland Greece. Sun hangs in bright sheets. Awaiting a jetfoil. X has gone off to buy us a couple of bottles of water. Note: The marble statue in the square, with its patented 'National Liberator moustache'. One sees the same thing all across Europe (I include Russia, I include Lenin). The moustache disappears when one hits Mao-country, but the statue stays roughly the same. Stiff. Male. Ridiculous.

The only word I understood in the entire Greek-language 'Welcome on board' message which came over the Tannoy just now was 'katastroph'.

Island of Naxos. Honks, bangs, shouts and whirrs. I know it's a cliché, but they're so *passionate* round here. Our room is halfway along the well-known *Street of Cataclysmic Argument Daily at 3 O'Clock Sharp*. Dustbinmen go psycho.

I know how you hate footnotes, but we probably shall *have* to insert one here. Your readers are going to want to know why you are calling one of your main characters 'X'. My suggestion is that you insert a small note to say that, at a certain point in the proceedings, which they will reach soon enough if they read on, 'X' withdrew his permission for you to use his real name. He was, you can say, ~~one of the~~ the only one of the guests that you trusted enough not to have sign the Agreement your thoughtful publishers had drawn up. You felt that it would be, in your own words, 'like I'd be requiring one of those awful Hollywood-type pre-nuptial agreements'. You might also add, although this is *entirely* up to you, that on this matter you now realise you should have *listened to your editor's advice*. The only other solution to the problem of 'X' is to give the character another name, an invented one. I can think of quite a few, and I'm sure you can, too. Some of *them* we might not be able to print, however. But, you know, I do like the romance of anonymity granted by 'X'. Although, of course, if anyone has read a gossip column or, in fact, a front page, in the last year, they will know *exactly* who the mystery man is, or was.

Tip to budget travellers: Brightly coloured clothes and an elaborate hairstyle are wonderful ways of expressing your lack of personality.

We arrived on the smaller Cycladic island of Iraklia late yesterday afternoon. I felt like a small valise that had been used for baggage-handler soccer all the way from Reykjavik to Delhi, including connecting flights.

Finally, the beach. What I'll be writing, *From the Lighthouse*, will, if it comes out right, be just the *best* beach book in the world, ever: naughty, gossipy – with just the right ratio of tittle to tattle. (You know what I mean, darlings, and don't pretend you don't.) Virginia Woolf's letters (here in the string bag) are all very well, but they don't exactly make one *throb*, do they? Unfair: they make one throb, but higher up rather than lower down. And when I'm basting nicely on Sun Mark 8, factoring in my Amber S (or the wonderfully named Piz Buin – who he?), I need something with a bit of oomph, something with a bit of pandering to the baser. Otherwise, I lose interest, start watching windsurfers, wondering how ever they manage to stay up – and go so fast – and why they bother in the first place... etcetera. (Can you tell I've been playing truant from my Woolf to X's Wodehouse?) I wish I was Bertie Wooster and had a Jeeves – so does everyone who reads him, I bet. *Servants*... What a fantastic idea! We can have servants in the August House. A butler and a cook. Or a maid and a cook. Or, if that's too expensive, a maid who can cook. Maybe if I make enough money from *Lighthouse*, I'll never have to write anything else ever again: I can just move somewhere very all-year-round hot, and learn to windsurf.

Casting I. I've been thinking about who I'm going to invite. At the moment the list is as follows: X; Cecile Dupont (of course); Simona Princip and her husband, William; Cleangirl, her husband, Henry, and her child, Edith (those are the two couples); two single women (one, probably that bisexual model X vaguely knows – she'll be a drama queen, too, no doubt; the other, that eccentric stylist I met whilst researching *Join-the-dots* – immensely mmmm), a single man (much harder to find, but probably Alan Wood – aka the less successful writer), or maybe two single men (one can be the suicidal one), and finally a representative of as many minorities as I can find (Simona insists we 'at least make an attempt to reflect the diversity of Britain today'), and that's enough for now, isn't it? Don't worry. I don't expect you to take in all those names at once. A little later, when I'm more in the mood, I'll do a few short (promise) character sketches of those I hope *will* commit. Any that don't, I can cut out later. To make things a little less monotonous, formally, I'll intersperse them with my impressions of the small picturesque Greek island of Iraklia and its colourfully eccentric inhabitants – bum! No, instead I'll write a lot about having wondrous sex with X – that'll definitely keep you reading.

I have often, in reviews, been accused of creating unsympathetic heroines; this, I have been told, is a grave fault. Whether or not people are going to find me, as narrator if not as heroine, sympathetic is beyond my control. I won't suck up to them, nor will I lord it over them. Instead, I will take the original – or maybe that should be 'conventional' – approach: I'm going to be honest. Let people see me as I am, then make up their minds.

Enfin, I hope, in the very end, that people will come to regard me as deliciously wicked or wickedly delicious. Not as an interfering, manipulative little bitch. Why? Because I give them such pleasure they can't bring themselves to hate me.

Niceness is all very well – but what people really want is fun: if it's a battle between *nice-but-dull* and *nasty-but-what-the-bloody-hell-happened-just-then?* I know whose side I'm fighting on.

Wondrous sex with X – after which I slink off into sleep, like a black cat down a back alley.

I assume some time has passed between this and the previous entry – a day or two? Shall we put in something to indicate that? Here.

See it clearer now. I'll be the villainess of the piece. Perhaps no-one's going to like me. Perhaps it will be the end of me, fictionally. Perhaps something nasty will have to happen to my character. But that's the price to pay. To you, dear reader, I make this sacrifice of sympathy. By those who understand me (through this gesture), I will be cherished; by those who don't, ridiculed.

One's – 'one' – that sounds good, doesn't it? 'One's in-laws'. For once, the unapologetic voice of the upper-middle and lower-upper. Let it speak. Let it ring. No mockney translation: instead *one* will speak of oneself, queenly, as 'one' – as one usually would. In letters. For this, one will take courage from Virginia. Her suicide gives special retrospective pleading for her feyness. (She *meant* it.) But all along she risked, knowingly, the accusation of irrelevance. (The Twenties and Thirties – Marxism and the McSpaundays – the General Strike, for Christ's sake.) With anxiety, but with grace, she stepped aside – allowing the brown wave gushingly to avoid her shoes. 'Step into the road!' came the inviting cry. 'Join the march!' they implored, grubbily. 'You can help!' they meagrely cozened. 'Thank you very much for your kind invitation,' came the definite response, 'but no.' With real anxiety, Virginia confronted, in letter and diary, the things she knew she couldn't do – fictional and otherwise. (Of course this, her fret, only became public after her death; during, however, during everything, her response must most probably have appeared glibly, unanxiously High.) I myself will make it overt from page one: One is *here*, not all over the place; one is what one is, not something more massively palatable; one must – being here, being what one is – be either taken or left. The moment now approaches, it is here, it is now, when the takers must grab, the leavers depart... p.t.o. (politely turn over)

And now They have left (the others, the *hoi* – the ones who aren't 'one's), and We are quite alone together, just as We used to be, We can amuse ourselves thoroughly – though not at Their expense. That isn't why We have disposed... or rather have set free, blessedly released, the not-Us (the non-U). No. It is so that We may more intesely, nakedly, domestically be *Ourselves*. (Come into the garden, Maud. Come out of the *Guardian*, Claude.) For too long We've run in fear of being considered 'posh' – well, damn 'em all to hell and blazes, as Daddy used to say. We'll be Us, together, militant. We'll have our own Slogans: 'You and Me, the Bourgeoisie! Me and You, the Nearly-New!' And we'll have our old needlepoint maxims: 'Have nothing in your house which you do not know to be useful or feel to be beautiful.' (Isn't quotation subversive, sometimes?) The newly militant upper-middle – and I intend to be in its very vanguard: I shall be the Mean mean machine, the comedian of the Median, the most modish of the Mode!

X now almost totally indifferent to pertly naked breasts on the beach. (N.B. *almost*.)

I find that hard to believe.

Have been so lazy, after initial spurt haven't written anything for days... Self-disgust.

When one has nothing to worry about, one starts to worry about nothing.

X and I have reached that delightfully terrifying stage of mid-holiday intimacy where we no longer exchange more than, say, 300 words per day.

Errr-morning. Sleep okay? Oh dear. Do you want to tell me about it? Yes, it kept me awake, too. I'll just... shower. Breakfast? Ready whenever – Look at the shutters on that building: beautiful colour... Yes, it's a bit stale, isn't it? And the jam here's terrible. I think I miss a good cup of tea most of all. And e-mail. The beach, definitely. We can always do 'the walk' another day. I've got the sun cream. Don't go out too far. I worry about you, darling. Of *course* I do. I *do*... How was it? Really? Don't look now – it's that *man*. From the – yes, *him*. If he told another racist joke I'd have – well, you didn't either, did you? This? It's not nearly as good as her last one. Too wordy. No sex. I wonder what those two over there are arguing about? Oh, an ice-cream would be just heavenly. Do you want some mon- Oh, you are a sweetie. Thanks. All down your chin. Just snoozing, you know. Ouch. Well, does it look like sunburn to you or not? Hotel? Same place as last night. Can't be too adventurous. Thank you – and you look lovely, too. And could we have some still mineral water, please. Well, you always forget. You *do*. No, I *wasn't* making eyes at him – he's far too muscular for me. Oh, I didn't mean it to come out like that. Yes, it's a bit stale isn't it? I think I miss e-mail most of all. And a good cup of tea. The beach, definitely. We can always do 'the walk' the day after. It's not as good as her last one. No sex. I'll have the baklava, and don't call me a pig – I'm on holiday. Yes, you did. You called me a pig. Don't look now – it's that *man*. Yes, him, again. Good evening. Yes, lovely. Oh, couldn't organise anything, could they? Yes. And you. Christ, I thought he was going to sit down. Look at the stars! I was *not* eyeing the waiter up. Mmm, I *love* your muscles. Oh, I love the stars. Home-again-home-again-jiggety-jig. No. *No*. Just a bit tired. Tomorrow morning, we'll... Sleep good dreams. What?... They haven't started again, have they?

(N.B. I have excluded pet-names, which initially comprise around 90% of holiday couple-conversation but which thereafter decline to around 10% – reaching an all-time low during the homebound flight.)

Was that 300 or more? I can't be bothered to go back and count. I spend my life doing wordcounts. (I wish this notebook had wordcount.) It's too hot here. The hottest June in decades.

A small child (female) singing to itself on the beach: endearing-annoying-endearing-annoying-endearing-SHUT UP!

I'm going to treat myself to a character: Cecile. I first saw Cecile Dupont in Borough Market on a Saturday morning at 11.30 or thereabouts. If you haven't been to Borough, you are missing one of London's greatest joys. It's like the delicatessen of your dreams housed within a wrought-iron Victorian railway terminus. The whole place drips with atmosphere, and dirty-oily water. When I'm in there, I feel a bit overwhelmed – by people, by odours. You can buy herby olives, meat of all sorts (including ostrich sausages and cuts of wild boar), the weightiest bread in the world, energy-giving smoothies, anaemic-looking anchovies, bright white and orange scallops, wonderful vegetables (pink cauliflowers, sunset-coloured squashes), dried fruit, coffee-beans, cheeses, flowers, cakes. It is middle-class heaven. Amidst all this, Cecile was sparsely small, very well dressed (though I can't tell you exactly how – this is one of her mysteries: her clothes are so apt one seems to forget what they were); her face drawn with a few bold lines. Even now, I still don't know exactly how old she is. Somewhere between... no, it's ungracious to guess. Cecile is no longer in her forties, more I can't say. At the moment I saw her, I was staggering along like an overloaded scarecrow; no make-up, sloppy clothes; two full shopping bags dangling from each hand. She, having not yet seen me, walked almost into my chest. (She is short-sighted, but hates wearing glasses.) Yet the moment she *did* take me in, she realised it was she, not I, who would have to step aside. This she did with the swift, *suave* grace of a ballet teacher – almost as if the whole movement were a curtsey. At the same time she brought off the most fantastic smile: friendly, distant, forgiving, humorous. Swifter than a Siamese cat slinking back through the almost-shut door of a forbidden room, she was round and behind me. And I thought: ***I have** to know you.* So I did something I've never done before (except with boys at University): I pursued her. As it wasn't in me to announce myself plain and simple, I turned and followed her; followed her to the cheese stall, where she gracefully and without a hint of impatience was just joining the three-long queue. (I'd already bought cheese from here, but I so wanted to meet this woman I was prepared to face the embarrassment of a return.) It was almost as if Cecile were delighted to find herself in a queue, for it would give her time fully to consider which cheese she was going to buy. One of the people in front completed their purchase, turned and walked off. I decided that I would get another quarter of stilton: X loves to destroy his breath with the stuff. Having made up her mind what she wanted, Cecile looked benignly around for something to distract her – whilst still keeping enough of an eye on the *fromager* to be sure of knowing exactly when he came free; Cecile looked around, around, and of course caught sight of yours truly. I couldn't be certain whether she remembered me or not (from almost having bumped into me); nor did I know whether I wanted her to. Subsequently, I've never asked. 'Oh, my dear,' she said (meaning *oh, ma chère*), 'why don't you put your heavy bags down?' I hadn't done so because I was still thinking I might not go through with it; might turn and scarecrow wobblingly off in the other direction. 'It's terrible,' I said. Cecile glanced around, and it was as if she had said, 'Unaccompanied?' The question was voiced so clearly it was all I could do not to answer it directly. 'I'm going to get a taxi home,' I said, 'though it's not very far.' At which point, Cecile came to the front of the queue. For an instant I was allowed to think that that was it; I'd missed my only chance. Delightfully, however, Cecile lifted up a hand to the *fromager*, fingers spiralled, 'One moment...' it said – or rather, 'Take a moment... I understand you've been working hard. Slow down. I don't intend to hurry or harass you. I shop in a very different way from everyone else here: I shop as if shopping were festival.' Then she turned back to me, 'I'll help you,' she said, and smiled. And before I could refuse or say thank you, Cecile had begun to discuss, in detail, the merits of a Roquefort – in which exact set of caves, she wanted to know, had it been stored? This may seem extreme, but I'm now sure she would never have asked had she not been certain the young man behind the counter would know the answer; and be delighted that she'd asked. She only bought a single piece of the cheese, and it wasn't large. Wrapped in white greaseproof paper, she opened her handbag and slotted it neatly inside – as if the bag contained a compartment intended especially for slices of blue cheese. Clumsily, feeling thirteen all over again, I asked for a slice of the same, of a similar size. I didn't like Roquefort at all – but had on the spot resolved to retrain my tastes. Cecile picked up two of my bags just as I finished. 'Is there anything else?' she inquired. 'No,' I replied, though I had still to buy bread (putting it off until the end because the loaves are so heavy). 'Then... let's go.' The walk to the road was enswathed in a mist of chat: good chat, not chatter – alluding to the imperative survival of Borough Market. From it all I remember only one word, 'planners', spoken by Cecile with philosophical disdain: as if Man had concocted nothing more evilly pointless in life than to sit around all day *planning*. It took fifteen minutes to hail a cab. (We couldn't face the walk to London Bridge.) During all this time, Cecile waited with me: it wouldn't have been genteel not to. 'Do you need a lift?' I asked. 'Oh no,' she replied, 'I can walk – it's hardly any distance at all. We're practically on top of it as we are.' I told her who I was and a little of what I did; she introduced herself, and said that she did, 'Nothing at all,' and laughed – but I knew she was lying: I knew she did and saw and knew *everything*. And by the time we parted, she had given me neither her telephone number nor her address, but the single piece of information I most needed: 'I'm always here on Saturdays, at eleven thirty, or thereabouts. We'll surely see one another again.' (With this utterance, London became what it has hardly ever been – a village, where meetings can be both accidental and expected.) And we did, see one another again – soon; and we were both, I think, pleased; and one weekend we had coffee; and also the next; and then she was invited to dinner at mine; and by then, I'd say, we'd become friends. But that was all, for the moment, for the future. On the Saturday I met her, Cecile hailed me a cab, helped me put my bags into it, kissed me lightly on both cheeks (what perfume could that possibly be?) and left me – speeding away – with the distinct impression that I was Cinders having just met her Fairy Godmother.

This spindly pen is about to run out.

To be honest, I've always found sunsets rather boring: they go on for far too long – and the end isn't exactly a stunning surprise.

The thought of marriage and children is unbearable but the thought of no marriage and no children is unbearable.

I'm a writer. I love words – and judging by how well they've rewarded me the feeling's mutual. Singing to myself yesterday in the shower, I had a fantastic revelation. Because I've gone non-fictional, I no longer have to hide behind some semi-inarticulate narratress; no more must I deny myself a word merely because it wouldn't be in *her* vocabulary or would but wouldn't be used by her in that *exact* context. If I want to, I can grab my lovely battered old Mr Roget and just ravish him completely: orchidaceous, multunguous, trepan, scher-wing, kookaburra, scunge... Swinging high, swooping low; any way I want to go: slangy or snobby, yahoo or yobbo. It's the literary equivalent of being let loose on Manhattan with someone else's credit card; someone very rich and very much in love with you. I write this on the beach, on a Greek island (Paros – had exhausted the delights of Iraklia) on the most beautiful, sunniest, bluest, white-picturesque cupolaed churchest June morning the Mediterranean has ever seen. X is off, snorkelling. (Which must be one of the top 10 comic loan-words in English. Up there with *anorak* and *karaoke*. Just try dropping it into any conversation, in a demi-Swedish accent – you'll get a laugh, I promise.) And because I'm working – inscribing these few stray thoughts into my notebook; because of all this, the whole think I mean thing is unmistakably, delightfully and fully tax-deductible. (Repeat to myself the guilt-freeing mantra: You *deserve* it. You *deserve* it.) Five novels in six years – gosh, do I deserve it. Perhaps you've read a couple of them? Or maybe not. If this little baby is as cooed over as I think it deserves to be, I should pick up shedloads of new readers. Hello you and you and *especially* hello you. Anyhunch, for the latecomers, here's a bit of a recap. Name: Victoria About (my name is pronounced Abut – an illiterisation – of Arbuthnot; or so I choose to believe.) Age: twenty- what shall I say? nine. If I say that, you'll know what I mean, won't you? 29. (I should warn you, I'm going to idealise my character, just a little. My character must be marvellous. Please forgive me, it's probably the only chance I'm ever going to get.) Someone once joked that I was born in East Wittering. Actually, it was Chelsea. I am, strictly, a Chelsea girl. I was started off with the nuns, then went to school in Westminster, at the school where girls from Chelsea who go to school in Westminster go. After that, *Must* College at *Must* University (i.e., I *must* I *must* I *must* a. lose my virginity, b. get a boyfriend, c. get another boyfriend, d. avoid boyfriend 1 meeting boyfriend 2, e. be successful). I live in Borough, SE1, and did so long before it (or I) became desirable. Marital status: Well, X. That's almost all you need to know. Weight: 110 lbs. (Idealised.) Hobbies: clothes. Really, I dress *very* well. My first novel, completed in the two years after I left my musty old university of Must, was called *Join-the-dots*. It was defiantly un-autobiographical. A year later came *The Sweet Spot*, the follow-up. After that, annually, *Incredibly Well-Hung: A Satire of the Art World. Looking the Other Way* and my latest, *Spaciousness*. I write at the very upper end of what has sometimes recently been called 'chick fic'. I am greatly traditional. My favourite English writers are Jane Austen, George Eliot, Henry James. My favourite writers, though, are all French: Laclos, Flaubert, Sagan. My private life was, up until the success of *Well-Hung*, exactly that: mine, private and really a life. I did, for a while, date an actor. We all make mistakes. Since then, I have been interviewed over 200 times but I have never written a confessional newspaper column. I have been on Woman's Hour but I have never won a literary prize. (I'm not bitter.) (Am.) (Am not.) (Am.) (Am not.) (*Am.*)

Sitting here with a cold wet towel across my heat-rash back: almost pleasantly painful – like people turning twig-ends round against my shoulderblades.

I can't resist doing a little more about Cecile. I do love her so... She sounds like she belongs in a textbook, *Basic French for the 1950s. 'Alors! Qui est cette jolie femme là?' 'Cette jolie femme là est Madame Cecile Dupont.' 'Et qui est Cecile Dupont?' 'Cecile Dupont est la femme la plus chic du monde. Voilà.'* As far as I know there is nothing particularly noble about her background. If I could, I would invent for her some utterly fabulous name with at least one *de* or *de la*, one hyphen, several obscure accents and apostrophes, two *nommes de grandes familles*, and the implication of at least three *châteaux* – if not now owned then once occupied. She has such a wonderfully animated simplicity about her – she has manners; manners which can, in a word, *cope*. There is no social

She does have a 'de', in case you hadn't noticed.

situation with which Cecile couldn't deal. She (I infer from various hints) has buried two husbands, and has delicately declined to consider a third. It is not, I like to imagine, that she has exactly *killed* them, more that they have found themselves unable to live with the idea that she may predecease them. I have seen before the bitterness of widows – worse, I have sensed it. Yet somehow, by some trick of character that I'd like to believe could be taught, but ultimately don't, she has managed just to sidestep this – as one would, if one were nimble enough, the puddlesplash of an arriving taxi. Her moral shoes are never dirtied. Too *petite* for modelling; too delicate for acting – unless a theatre had been reduced in size to accommodate her. (It would have to be a proper theatre, with gilding and a proscenium arch; otherwise she simply wouldn't have fitted.) The silver screen is the only otherworldly place in which Cecile might have belonged – ~~appearing halfway through that argent epitome *Les Enfants du Paradis*. (Too ripe. Cut.)~~ Of all my female friends, the bulimic and the anorexic, Cecile is the only one I can imagine daring to stand beside ~~Audrey.~~ Hepburn

Otherwise the reader looking back might get confused between this Audrey and Fleur's cat, Audrey.

X has been lying in bed next to me all morning, snoring and letting off Boxing Day farts. I feel in desperate need of an infidelity. If I don't have one soon, I'll end up being really unfaithful (i.e., not telling him about it afterwards, as per our agreement) – and that would be awful, for I do love X so. When we get back to England, I'll have to do something practical about it. Henry Snow? I'm sure X is feeling exactly the same way. We both need a holiday, each from the other.

A glimpse, possibly, is perfect; intimacy acknowledges irritation.

Dialogue. Great Lines of Our Time. X says blah blah blah you're looking lovely blah, to which I reply, 'Don't try to placate me while I'm being unreasonable. It really annoys me.' Wondrous sex afterwards.

I'm getting very concerned: none of my friends seem to be having affairs. None that I know of, anyway. And how can that be? – how can I not know? For I surely can't believe that none of them are *having* affairs. Statistically, it's nigh on impossible. Yet they all seem to be so embedded in each other (and themselves) that I have difficulty even imagining for them the reciprocated office-crush, the business-trip grope... My friends do jobs that are too interesting for that sort of thing to happen, perhaps. In their twenties, it was all mess; in our forties, what with the inevitable divorces, it's sure to be messy once again; but now, right now, everyone seems silently to have agreed that our thirties are to be the years of decorum. I have several theories why I don't know about the few affairs that *are* happening. 1. I'm deluded. They're really and truly not happening – not a single one. 2. My friends don't trust me. They know if they tell me anything juicy, it will end up in print. (True.) 3. People are having affairs, but they're over so quickly that they don't really register – even for the participants. 4. They are having affairs. Really serious ones. Having sex while their partner is in labour, or the next room – that sort of thing. But they're putting enough thought and effort into it (i.e., they still love and respect their 'official' partner enough) not to allow themselves to be caught. And it's boring. I make my living recasting the splurge of my friends' emotional lives into the symmetry of fiction. I mean, where have all the bastards gone? There used to be some really good ones around. If it carries on like this, I'll end up having to write about suppressed passions in religious communities or delicate flirtations during fell-walking holidays. Even my single friends seem to be married; married to their careers, to their pets, to the comfort of their re-re-done-up flats, to their lush, sterile gardens.

A glimpse has the possibility of perfection (because the glamour of the moment idealises); intimacy, real intimacy, always comes at a cost – knowledge hence boredom hence irritation. And so, I've been thinking quite a lot about dumping X. Not however for anyone in particular, but instead for the memory of a well-cut suit two steps above me on the escalator; for the harsh side of a face seen in a pulling-away London cab; for hands – hands doing things in an undemonstratively expert way (oh, doctors – doctors); for the mere idea of a world-class pianist; ~~for the edge of a Coutt's card bisecting an immaculate K2 of cocaine;~~ for, I have to admit it finally, romance with not only a capital R but capitals OMANC and E, as well. But I don't think I will. Dump, I mean. I am equally afraid, whatever I may elsewhere say, of the empty horizon and of the empty bed. (Though the latter often seems far further off than the former.) Perhaps X would be prepared to share me on a more long-term basis? I don't think he's the type. Perhaps that's been the problem all along – he's my type, definitely, but he's not *the* type: the type that both does and doesn't. ('Does and doesn't what?' I hear you ask. If you do ask, you don't; if you don't, you do (and don't).) Oh, if you want the truth I just want him to stop all this messing and ask me to marry him...

You owe me for this one.

Sufficiently brown, sufficiently bored. Sorry if I didn't write enough about picturesque Greek island/eccentric characters.

Home-time.

JOURNAL

July.
London.
Four weeks to go.
I know where it's going to be set! Not exactly, but almost. It was the title gave it to me, as always happens. *From the Lighthouse* – and the only town in England with a lighthouse? Southwold! It's perfect. X and I are taking a trip up there this weekend to scout for locations. Staying at the Swan, eating at the Crown – which is the *only* thing to do.

We found two suitable houses. One is in town, one about four miles to the north. Neither is perfect. But I've had a few further thoughts. If I put everyone in the centre of Southwold, some of the necessary intensity would almost certainly be lost. Whenever an argument happened or a love-tryst was about to take place, people would be able to absent themselves. And I don't much like the idea of that. We have to be all higgled and piggled on top of each other, for the whole month. Hothoused. Then interesting things are *bound* to happen. The houses outside town are also cheaper. X found the northern house. It would do, at a push. But it didn't exactly make my heart sing. I suppose I imagine something like the house in *To the Lighthouse* – something that, in some way, smacks of New England as well as Olde. Or *Howards End*, with the witch tree in the garden. Or Garsington. Or what's that other place? Monks' Hall. So, I think we'll have to keep pestering the letting agents. We've only got three and a half weeks in which to find it (and then equip it). The house has to be dead right; if it isn't, all else fails.

Southwold itself is fantastic – the sort of place where the tourists walk faster than the locals.

Casting II. I know I'm going to be criticised in the reviews, etc., for only casting media-trendy London people. But, honestly, I mean, I don't know any blacksmiths or coal miners – and nobody I know knows any, either. (Unless it's their parents, whom they've chosen to forget.) One has enough difficulty these days finding a plumber let alone a real manual labourer. In fact it's getting pretty hard to locate someone who both a. speaks English (a requisite, I think you'll agree) and b. gets dirty when they work. Everyone it seems – whatever they 'do' – sits in front of a computer and spends their 9-to-5s tap-tap-tapping away. Why the government doesn't massively increase our GNP by putting typing on the National Curriculum, I have no idea. Anyhunch, everyone interesting in England ends up in London eventually. (By England I mean Great Britain/the United Kingdom, etc., whatever you call it – so don't go getting uppity.) However, I am myself working hard to get some representation in the more *important* stroke *interesting* categories of gay, black, disabled and poor. All my feelers are out, and believe me when *they* get going I make the Creature from 20,000 Fathoms look like the Inchworm. These will have to be pseudonyms. The originals (and I've pleaded) won't either of them allow their names to appear in connection with this – and I quote – 'infamous project. I suggest Emilia Dimp and Issy Squidge, or something similar.

All the invitations have gone out. The final list is: 1. X, 2. Cecile Dupont, 3. my Editor and 4. her Husband, 5. ~~Aurelia Dumfries~~ and 6. ~~Sigmunda France~~, 7. Sub Overdale, the director, 8. Vong Po, the actor, who has agreed to allow his real name to be used, as long as it is categorically stated that he never for a moment entertained the idea of taking part. 9. Alan Sopwith-Wood, 10. Cleangirl, 11. Henry, Cleangirl's Husband and 12. Edith, Cleangirl's Daughter. There will also be 13. A Maid and 14. A Chef (not a Cook, I've decided).

Here is a key to the invitations. 1 and 2 you are familiar with. 3 and 4 I must be careful in speaking of. Very much so. 3 is a darling, especially after having written me that massive cheque. 4 I have ~~problems~~

~~with. 3 has problems with him, too. 4 and I have never really got on; but then, we've~~ only met a very few times. I'm sure he's lovely, too. 4 is a high-end copyright lawyer; 4 sues people for large amounts. 3 and 4 live in a lovely, massive house in Highgate; views, garden, envy. 5 is my guarantee that someone will at least have sex with someone. She swings both ways (as do 6 and 8). There's a real possibility of three-in-a-bed – or even four (7 might be persuaded). 5 is also a model, so people come on to her all the time. She doesn't mind. It's probably why she became a model. That and Daddy's roving hands. 6 is so incredibly needy that she's bound to want a faux-boyfriend for the duration. My money would go on either 1 or 7.7 is most likely, as he would be very good for her career. 7 himself will drink a great deal, and sleep with any woman who offers herself. 8 has bedded enough people to be bored with the mere bedding bit. What he wants now is the full Valmontian challenge. Which guarantees he'll make a play for either me, 3 or 10.9 is in as sort of ballast. As for the sexual interplay, I've always had a sneaky suspicion he'd go for my Editor – seriously go for her. Which would liven things up no end. 10, 11 and 12 are a unit. 12 is 11-years-old, so will be flirted but (I pray) not slept with. The only danger comes from 8. I will give him strict instructions not to go beyond getting her into a pash. 10 and 11 are so Scandinavian that if they ever did see other people, they would sit down and discuss it over schnapps and fondue. With the other people present. And the other people's partners. And *their* lovers, too. However, I've never been sure about this – their relationship. (10 once said in an interview that they always had sex once a day. But that was during her modelling days, and it was in a men's magazine, so I'm sure it was an exaggeration – meant to make her look 'up for it'.) I don't think either of them have ever been unfaithful, but I detect cracks. I would like to see if they open. 13 and 14, as I've said, will hopefully be old enough to be taken out of the sexual equation. I don't want romance between above and below stairs. It's been done to death, and I don't want to be caught interfering with the corpse.

I hope I haven't given too much away. When I come to make my predictions, they will be far more accurate than this little sketch. And if anyone decides they don't want to come, the whole thing will have to be changed.

As expected, I've had my first confirmations. Alan Wood is definitely in. I was expecting this: he used to be in love with me, and still does whatever I ask. He called up to say yes, and to ask who else was coming. I thought about it for a moment, then gave him a rundown. 'So, no Fleur,' he said. 'Definitely not,' I said. 'Right,' he said. 'Why do you ask?' I said. 'Because she's your sister,' he said. 'I naturally thought you'd invite her.' But I knew it was because he was hoping for a second chance with her.

Next confirmation was Cleangirl, via e-mail. As I've got the afternoon free, I'll do her character; and maybe her husband Henry's, as well. I met Ingrid (Cleangirl's real name) at school. She was the most beautiful of floaty blonde apparitions. No-one else in our class came close. Prairie girl meets Mädchen – Heidi from Ohio. For a while, until she started to age a little, and to play up her imperfections, boys were simply too scared of her to ask her out. And virginity didn't add to her attractions. She shone, brightly and whitely. The effect wasn't very sexy. Sexy is tarnish, is scratches, is chips. (That's how I've always consoled myself, for being such a cracked and chippy old pot.) I have one main question about Ingrid: Who scrubs her? One can't look so fantastically buffed (not buff, she's not *muscular*) without someone doing it for one. Someone professional. Or several professional someones. It's like the first time I turned up for a proper magazine photoshoot. A young woman stepped out of the location van, saying, 'I'm your skin,' and a young man followed her, saying, 'I'm your hair,' and then another young woman emerged, saying, 'I'm your grooming.' My theory is, Ingrid has herself secretly accompanied everywhere she goes by a team of beautician robots. As soon as she leaves people's sight, they descend upon her to cleanse, tone, moisturise, etc., removing dirt, unclogging pores. (God, does Ingrid even *have* pores? I'll have to check next time I look.) Put it this way: she could work in a shop selling fluorescent lights, and *still* look flawless. Her clothes are impeccable; her grooming, yes, fantastic. She has brought up Edith from an early age always to be sick on someone else's shoulder (thrice, mine). She claims – believe me – to look as good as she does merely by washing with soap (that's s o a p) and applying no-brand cold cream before she goes to sleep (that's s l e e p). Ingrid and I have these bizarre conversations, in which I attempt to prick the perfection. 'But I have problems,' she claims, 'just like anyone.' (Which comes out as 'just like you poor mortals do'.) But I wouldn't be surprised one day to go down to the beach and catch her strolling out across the breakers, Jesuswise. Of course I hate and envy and worship and adore and hate and envy her. Who wouldn't? I won't tell you about her marriage, it's too awful. I'll just say two words: wedded bliss. My mother always used to say to me, 'Victoria, you're always finding fault with every little thing.' And, yes, Mummy, you were right; I do. I want to find the fault in Cleangirl, in freckle-fresh-face girl. I can't allow myself to believe that anyone is that impeccable. (Implication: I'm not.) In summary, Cleangirl seems, and has always seemed, too good to be true. But I'm going to explore the deep blank blonde interior; I'm going to seek her inner Oscar-winner – the sobbing, cool-blowing wreck of neuroses; I'm going to find her spots; she has spots; everyone has spots; the spots upon her soul. (First to find her soul...) My plan: to set Sub Overdale up to seduce her. My theory: she will be attracted to her polar opposite – sleaze. ~~(As a bonus, he may even offload upon her one~~

Mr Overdale denies that he has, or has ever had, an S.T.D.. We both know he's lying (you, I believe, from personal experience), but the lawyers don't think this is safe.

~~of his rare venereal diseases (collected whilst whoring his way across the five continents); perhaps a choicely florid genital wart, something in green, pink and yellow; or a gooey discharge, a cumulo nimbus of thrush.)~~

X and I went up to Southwold again this weekend just gone, and almost immediately found the perfect place. It's a lovely crumbly old Georgian house about two miles north of the lighthouse; very close to the beach; almost enough bedrooms for all (if some are – oh no! – forced to double up); and the owners are happy to vacate. It'll cost several bombs, perhaps even a nuclear one, but it'll be worth it. The place has all the atmosphere one could desire. I kept expecting Virginia Woolf herself to waft round the corner, silk gloves in hand. Must now start negotiations with the Owners; Simona will be useful in this.

Have begun re-reading *To the Lighthouse*, and also Woolf's diaries, from the very beginning.

Visited the surveillance equipment shop – so exciting. Hard to keep a straight face, though: the salesman was ex-services and wore a navy blue jacket with rows of gold buttons and a crest on the pocket with a phoney Latin motto. Give Mr ~~Strang~~ his due, however, he was very efficient and asked no awkward questions. (I found out about him from the back of *Private Eye*.) When I confessed what I wanted done, he assured me it was entirely routine; a slightly larger job than normal (a slightly larger house), but something they wouldn't have any trouble coping with. He talked technicalities to me, but I couldn't be bothered to listen. What's important is, I'll be able to see and hear *everything* that goes on inside the house. I asked how long it would take to make the preparations. 'A day and a half,' he said. 'Could you do it in one very very long day?' I asked, charming. 'Yes,' he said,

He'll sue if you use his real name, or give any details that might identify his company. How about Mr Smith?

charmed. We agreed terms. I gave him my credit card. Coming out, I couldn't believe it had been *that* simple – and legal, too.

I'm so glad I've had the idea for this now. In a year or two' s time, all my friends will be sprogging, and are likely to become less self-aware (self-obsessed?) – in fact less plain interesting. Ask someone with a two-year-old what the last serious book they read was. Then mime cracking your upturned prayer-palms open at the spine, to help them remember just *exactly* what a book is. Trash, maybe. Thrillers and such. Romances. But History or Philosophy or Politics or even Popular Science? The poor darlings – after beddy-byes for baby-bunkins – hardly have enough strength to pick up a paper, let alone the concentration to pick up anything therefrom. They spend the next fifteen years deliberately being boring, for the children's sake. When they finally *do* return to taking some interest in themselves, it's only to have the sordid, flabby affairs of forty-five-year-olds. Not a subject matter I'm particularly looking forward to handling. Though, I suppose, like the affairs themselves, it *has* to be done. And so, by having this idea now, I catch my characters (the love-interest ones) at *just* the right moment – thirty or thereabouts. When the question of whom they will sprog with (or who will besprog them) is all still a-dangle. And in doing this, I intend to do a bit of dangling myself; dangling myself in front of Henry and then pulling myself away before his jaws have a chance to snap. (What a strange image! Dogs again. I hope this isn't going to be another dog-haunted text. The exploits of Rex in *Join-the-dots* were too cutesy for even the Cruft's freaks... Why do I always end up making animals crucial to plot?) This is the moment; these are the questions – how brightly before it is extinguished will burn our *St Elmo's Fire*? And – afterwards – how nippy will our *Big Chill* turn out to be?

Virginia is so naughty; I'm surprised people let her get away with it. What about this: 'The poor have no chance; no manners or self control to protect themselves with; we have a monopoly of all the generous feelings – (I daresay this isn't quite true; but there's some meaning in it. Poverty degrades, as Gissing said.)' That's from Thursday 13 December 1917. And this, from the page before: 'The women said it was a splendid speech; sentences that melt into each other impress them.' Tuesday (11 December). She's such a snob, thank God! I'm getting so close to her now, in some ways, that I'm almost hallucinating her. I see her, Virginia, Mrs Woolf, setting out across Bloomsbury Square of a frosty morning, with her hat, her shopping basket, & her gloves & her immensely confident-seeming fragility. What a darling; I want to keep her from harm, & from all those who would misunderstand us. Delicate as a lifted eyelid; intense as white heat – she's, I've just realised it, my *Muse*. O Virginia, bless what I'm doing; if you're still in the business of handing out blessings. I expect you're not; I expect you're worrying about the servants. (So am I.) This is how I pass an idle hour, these days: going slightly potty, on paper, for my own amusement. And like her I worry that I'm more scatter than brain. (I've never actually *been* mad; though I've been close; I think – that time just after university – whatever it was, it was at the very least severe depression. One doesn't find oneself in a bathroom with a wide selection of razorblades when one's mental health is unthreatened.) Cutting remarks, cutting generally. ~~Cut this~~. No. I like it. Gives your character some much-needed depth

Wonderful news: we have our important Other categories covered – Alan Wood has a friend of a friend who works with a woman called Marcia; and can you believe it, she's a – wait for it – poor black disabled lesbian who hasn't had a holiday in seven years! There may be a few arrangements to be made, *vis-à-vis* spazz-ramps between the rooms, bath facilities downstairs – but once I've met her and given her the once, everything should be easy. I've sent

Alan a thank-you e-mail, just now. The little love. Oh, I'm so happy. We are now representative! (-ish.) ~~Note to self: Better take out spazz-ramps when I revise this~~. *No. I don't think so. Plus, there's a later reference to them.*

All arranged with Owners. Simona was magnificent in dealing with them, especially him; fox *and* Rottweiler.

Disaster. It seems that a group of the invitees got together, in Soho late last night, and decided – collectively – not to come. (How did they know each other? And how did they know which of the others I'd invited? I told everyone to keep it secret. Which was probably a bad mistake: if I'd told them to tell everyone, they'd have kept silent just to annoy me. I blame e-mail.) They are/were ~~Aurelia Dumfries~~, Sub Overdale, ~~Sigmunda~~ France and Vong Po. Which leaves me with huge gaps and just three weeks to fill them. I'm in an utter gloom. X tried to console me, just now. 'You must have a B-list,' he said. 'But I want the *A-list*,' I wailed. 'The B-list are the B-list because they're not so good – and I don't really want them.' He opened a second bottle of wine. 'Who's on the B-list?' he asked. 'It's only in my head,' I replied. 'Tell me.' 'Well, we could have one or two fewer people.' 'Of course.' 'Which might be a good idea,' I said, 'It was thirteen or fourteen before – assuming Marcia comes.' 'What's happening with her?' 'We're meeting next week.' 'Which leaves only one slot to fill.' 'Or two.' 'So, who's on your B-list?' I gave him a couple of names. One I'd already approached, and they'd already said No. The other I knew was going to be book-touring America in August. 'And, well,' I said, 'there's always my *sister*.' 'Didn't you want to set her up with someone a while ago?' 'I tried. It was Alan Wood.' 'Try again,' he said, 'invite her.' It would take too long to explain *why* I didn't want this to happen. Alan and Fleur had seemed a predestined couple: Mr Clumsy meets Ms Mumsy; the Heffalump meets the Frump. But when I had them both round to dinner, they hardly even looked at

I wonder whether you still think this, now it's all over. I think we were very entertaining, actually. B-lists are always more interesting than A-lists.

one another. It was one of my biggest failures, matchmaking-wise. I don't want to have it repeated, and also have to write about it. However, I still believe deep down there is the possibility of something between them. X is right. My sister is there to be asked, as a last resort. I am drunk and am going to be a complete bloody failure if I don't come up with some interesting, sexy characters pretty bloody soon. I've left it far far too late. I should have been planning all this at least a year in advance: house, guests, everything...

Things don't look as bad as they did last night. Even with this stunning hangover. You know when you squint because the sunlight's so bright – like X and I did on the beach when we had no sunglasses on – it's like that, only inside my head, and I can't squint inside my head. Things in the real/fictional world look better because: a. I had too many characters anyway; and b. X is right, it might be fun to have Fleur along. First, however, I will check with a couple of people who only just failed to make the A-List. Maybe their summer schedules have changed.

Servants arranged with agency: Maid (40ish) and Chef (25). Latter unsatisfactory (too young, too attractive), but all they had available. *Don't you think your readers would like to be able to visualize the maid? I know what you were doing by not describing her, i.e., keeping the servants in their place.*

I need to catch up with doing my characters. If you feel like skipping this, and looking back later to see what I said, that's fine. For now I think I'll do... Edith, Cleangirl's eleven-year-old daughter. Edith is more than pretty; in fact, more than beautiful. If she were merely pretty, merely beautiful, I should envy her, and I don't: I worship her. Each and every time she enters the room, I think of advertisements and annunciations. She is blonde, and will clearly stay blonde for ever. Already I can tell that she will be one of those old women whose beauty is not diminished, only

But as she does start to play her small part, later on... It needn't take much. How about this? 'The maid is 41, with a pleasant roundish face, pink forearms, hennaed hair and a charming Eastern Counties accent.' (I've tried to imitate your style.)

desiccated. She will turn from a lovely meadow into an equally-if-not-more-lovely desert. She dresses – I think *dresses*, rather than *is dressed* – so well; she's almost French about it. And she has the ability that certain *jeunes filles françaises* have – of turning her grandmotherly name (after Wharton not Sitwell or Piaf) into something *trés trés chic*. It's almost as if by naming her so clumsily, her mother was setting a double-dare: to herself, to have produced a daughter capable of this difficult denominative transubstantiation; to the daughter, to fit her name so simply, effortlessly, shamelessly, that the question of the double-dare never publicly occurs. Imagine the disaster if it hadn't come off; witness the triumph, now it has. Because of all this, Edith is cherished by everyone; she entertains, just by being there. Over the coming years, it will be an experience almost sublime to witness Edith's indifference to the male hearts she will vaporize, and is already – not heartlessly but thoughtlessly – vaporizing. Old men look at her and wish they were but five years her senior; young men look, wince, and look away, losing heart at the very moment they lose their hearts. In this, she is like her mother. It is sublimely terrible. The only men Edith might ever love would be her own sons, should she have sons; and, if she had daughters, she would pass on to them the intensity of her, and her mother's, indifference to men. Daughters, a daughter, would be catastrophic. If this went on another generation, it would become a curse. The only hope, the only salvation, is for her to suffer an early crush, opening her own heart up to hopelessness. Otherwise, during her and her daughters' lives, the hopelessness will only ever be upon the male side. Yes, that is what I feel when I myself gaze upon her: hopelessness. But I have a plan, which I shall tell you now, rather than saving it for my Synopsis. I intend to turn Edith into one smitten-kitten. I have an instinct about her and X. I know how to make it happen. It will be necessary to make X glamorous to an invulnerable heart. To do this, I will have to render him bereft, grief-stricken. And this will be his state, definitely, a week in – on the second Monday: for that is the day I intend to dump him. (That was my promise to Simona – that something big would happen. This is it.) I'll do it right in front of her. I doubt Edith will ever have seen a grown man so distraught. Or so attractive. He loves me. He really does.

I do have a P.S. to add: Edith has badly chewed-up nails. This may not seem very significant now, but one day it might. That's always been one of my tests of my own fictional characters: *Do I know what their fingernails are like?* If I do, then they've passed the reality test. Edith isn't perfect; no-one is.

One week to go.

Went and bought ten copies of *To the Lighthouse*. I've decided it would be fun to do a reading group, and have chosen this as the obvious book. I had to go to five bookshops to gather together enough in the right edition – all up good old Charing Cross Road, then pikey Oxford Street. It was only when I finished that I realised I could have got X to order them for me over the internet. Still, I was able to check on their stocks of *Spaciousness* and my other titles. A little disappointing I must admit, but most of them stock some of them.

Met Marcia. She's perfect. Wheelchair-bound but very energetic. (It's polio, Alan said.) Bedroom arrangements (~~see Map Below~~). Marcia was already getting the ground-floor bedroom, even before I heard she was disabled. I explained this to her, that there was no prejudice, and she said that she was fine with it. She speaks very good English. Not, perhaps, as colourfully as one might wish. Maybe when she relaxes a little she'll start to sound a bit more Jamaican. (I think that's where she's from. Somewhere in the Caribbean.) Perhaps I should invest in a patois dictionary?

Here's her character description: Marcia Holmes, 30, Education Worker, West London. In a relationship at the moment (her girlfriend, I gathered, is able-bodied), but wouldn't go into detail on this. I sensed tension. Very pretty face; not great complexion. She seemed very serious, but I'm sure she'll laugh and bring sunshine into our lives once she's got a little rum in her belly. I think that'll do for now.

This is so horrendously crass that I can hardly believe you thought it, let alone wrote it. It stays.

In all of this, connecting it together, all my characters, I have come to realise that they do have at least one thing in common: more than merely interesting or fascinating me, they profoundly perplex me. I want to know how it is they manage to do what they do, be who they are, or, at least, seem as they seem. And of no-one more so than Cecile. If I could choose to be any of my guests, she it is – despite her age, or maybe even because of it – that I would be. (To be her, and younger! Imagine!) It's not hard to tell, is it?: I'm infatuated with her. She can turn placing a piece of cheese on top of a piece of biscuit into *cuisine*. She can make even a *beret* look original. I have cultivated her in hopes that she will cultivate me. Whenever I'm with her, I know that if I follow what she does I will be doing the correct thing. I do want to be better bred; it's a very unfashionable, snobbish thing to have to admit. Social aspirations – didn't they croak around the time of the Brontosaurus? But I *do* – I do. I want to learn the art of entering a room: not a grand entrance, not a movie star's – just a proper, definite, fully achieved arrival. I have tried to ask her what it feels like to *be* her – with her gifts and accomplishments – but, naturally, she puts off the question. She *isn't*, she is without the business of is-ness. She slots as neatly into her place in the world as that slice of Roquefort into her handbag. I remember once, when I turned up to have my photo taken for some magazine – Japanese *Vogue*, I think – a woman glanced at me from the other side of the room; she then went over to a clothes rail and picked from it three outfits that fitted me to the millimetre. Cecile is like that: she sees, she knows, she acts. My only wonder about her, and her slottedness, is simply how she can *stand* to live in grubby old England. There is the suspicion in my mind that, *chic* as she is, the boulevards of Paris know expanses of the demure beyond even those of which Cecile is capable. If that thought terrifies me, it must utterly harrow her.

My alternative A-listers have let me down. Fleur it is, then. I don't doubt that she'll say *yes*. She's been after an opportunity for revenge ever since I fictionalized her as Dotty's dowdy sister Fuschia in *Join-the-dots*.

As Fleur doesn't have e-mail, I had to call her up to ask. Couldn't waste any more time. It took her about five minutes to get to the phone – she was probably off praying or milking cows or something. She'd heard a little about the project already, via Mummy – whom I'd had to tell in order to explain about not visiting her in August. 'I suppose someone dropped out at the last minute,' Fleur said. I couldn't pretend that she'd been in the plan all along. 'I was very wary about involving family,' I said, 'It might be too much.' 'I'm not "family",' Fleur said, 'I'm me.' You're too much you, I thought. 'But perhaps *I'm* too much,' she said. 'Look, will you come or not?' I asked. 'I would love to,' said Fleur, very slowly. Which is her feeble way of trying to sound menacing. We talked for a while longer, then I asked, 'Would you like to know who else is coming?' I wanted to tell her about Alan, to gauge her reaction. 'No,' she said. 'I'll let it be a surprise. If they're friends of yours I'm sure they'll be... like friends of yours always are.' I refrained from firing back; we didn't need to have that argument again.

Drugs.

The para I've taken out was so libellous that I'm not even letting the lawyers look at it – which is why I've cut it out, with scissors.

Alan, in complete contrast to this, never touches anything but prescription medicines.

In the idler of my moments, I've been thinking up usable pseudonyms for my main characters – should any of them legally insist on being disguised. (This isn't going to happen simply because I won't let it happen: if they're not in, then they're not in.) But it's amusing, and a way of seeing the whole project translated into farce. Of course, as always, I've been able to come up with hundreds of aliases for my big sister. Being the younger by two years, name-calling was always my first and ever since my best form of vengeance. So far I have 'Faye Lear' (not bad, say it out loud), Jean Poole, Ms R. E. Guts, Ms R. A. Bullcow, Sally Fallowfield (cruel but *trés amusant*) and my own so-far favourite, Hester Sump (merely descriptive). Aside: You may be wondering if I'm worried what sis'll think when she reads this in manuscript. Well, I'm not. You can read her reaction at the end – in the Responses. But please, I beg you, don't pique me by peeking. I suspect she'll first shrug, then cry, then console herself over tea and going-to-seed cake with the thought of how infinitely superior as a moral creature she is – and has always been – to me. She may, if I'm successful, turn to Alan and say something that just fails to be cutting. An extra trip to the village church might even be in order, to pray for the strength to forgive me. Fleur, believe me, don't bother, I'm not worth it.

I realise I haven't done a character for Henry, Cleangirl's Husband. But that's partly because I'm not even sure if I know him; not *really* – even though we were at university together, and I did introduce him to Ingrid. He's a theatre producer and sometime director. To me, physically at least, he seems such a catalogue man: designer stubble (when he doesn't shave) and designer wrinkles (when he smiles or feels pain – both rarely). Maybe when I get to see him a little off-guard, I'll learn something more. (Maybe, in other words, if I succeed in seducing him.) He's gone completely grey, now. Fatherhood has made him a good deal more haggard than X. He has lovely hands – intelligent, and as expressive as English hands get; male ones. I imagine him adjusting the posture or costume of a pretty young actress – though I believe he's a lot more hands-off with his productions than before he married Cleangirl.

Two days to go. Call from Mr ~~Strang,~~ the security man. They got into the house without problems (I'd passed the keys on to them after the Owners sent them to me). Access to the attic was a little trickier, but they found the padlock key after a couple of hours. They've fitted cameras in all the bedrooms, also in the kitchen and living room; not the corridors or outside, though – it was getting too expensive. Everything will be ready for when I arrive – I'll just have to switch on and watch. However, I've made a resolution: I'm not going to use the surveillance equipment for the first week. (I am asking X to make sure I stick to this.) During that time, I'll rely entirely on my intuition. In fact, I may not use the cameras at all. I may complete the project *au naturel*, but only if I feel that I'm getting everything I need through the Suggestions Box and the Confessions – plus my own observational gifts.

X just told me he wants to *ride* up to Southwold on his motorbike. I told him no. If he has it there I'll never be able to keep him inside the house. He'll keep ripping off on 100 m.p.h. jaunts to Cornwall or Aberdeen. Also, he mustn't have such an easy escape for when I tactically dump him.

Having left it to the last minute, I now have to do a character of my sister. I don't want to do one of those long perceptive ones, just a physical description. Basically, she looks like a sheep, and when she puts on make-up she looks just like a sheep in make-up, but when she takes it off she looks like a sheep who *needs* make-up. Facts: She lives in a farmhouse near Hereford. She was married, once. It went wrong. I'm sure there'll be reason to tell you about that later. I thought her husband was alright (Clive, he was called); better than she deserved, really.

SYNOPSIS

It's Day Zero. X and I arrive to make final preparations. I cry a lot, and tell him everybody that's coming hates me. He consoles me, and tells me that if they didn't love me, they wouldn't be coming.

There are 10,000 last-minute hitches to be sorted out with the Staff. 'It's got to be perfect, you understand – perfect!' I scream at the Maid until she, too, starts crying.

Later in the evening, I seek her out in the tension of the far end of the garden, and apologise. She says that she knows I'm under a lot of stress. She tells me she read one of my books, before she even thought about applying for this job. (It was *The Sweet Spot*.) She laughs as she remembers it, saying she never thought she'd meet me. I thank her sincerely, and praise everything she has so far done in preparing for the guests' arrival. We bond. I borrow one of her cigarettes, aware that I may be smoking 60-a-day again by the end of this mad project. We bond some more.

Back in the house, I go from room to room, more relaxed now, full of delightful anticipation. As I walk through the emptiness, so soon to be filled, I think about all the things that may or may not happen there; things that, if it weren't for me, would never get the chance to happen.

X joins me, and I share a little of what I'm feeling with him. He immediately accuses me of megalomania. He says I shouldn't get too caught up in the power-trip aspect of it. 'Power,' I say. 'Of course it's about power. Everything's about power. The W.I. Annual Cake-Decorating Competition is about power.' He calms me down, as always. Tells me that all I need do is sit back, relax and wait for things to happen. The hard work is over, what remains is the reward, etcetera. I tell him not to be so bloody patronising, as I know that already.

We go upstairs to bed. He gives me a long back-rub. He makes gentle, tingly-touchy love to me. He tells me he loves me and rolls over to give me half the bed and three-quarters of the duvet.

The world is once more peaceful; outside the window, the sea sings lullingly; and I sleep not a wink.

Week One, Day 1

I get up early, virtuous and Puritanical. (*Lord, I may, in the past, have sinned, but I don't intend to today, not so far as I can help it, anyway* – that's roughly my sentiment.)

The butterflies in my stomach feel as if they've been netted, pinned, and put on display under glass in heavy wooden frames; they're not dead, though – oh, no, they're still flapping around: I can feel the corners of the frames, stabbing my insides.

Without asking me, X gives the Chef a break and cooks us a Full English Breakfast; more, in fact, than a Full English: a Total English – black pudding, grilled tomatoes. He says that, what with everybody arriving, I might not get the chance to eat again before evening.

As soon as I tuck away the last bite of toast, I feel sick. I feel very sick. I dive to the sink and I *am* sick.

I feel better.

I'm sick again.

I go for a quiet walk around the garden to calm myself down. The garden: it is so growingly full, so beautiful, so English. The air is cool, but will heat up later. Morning is the best part of the day, out here. I feel strong. I feel ready.

I go into the toilet and try to make myself sick; I fail. I know I am ready.

I have a sip of orange juice to take away the last of the taste. To make double-sure, I brush my teeth. A car draws up outside. I am sick all across the hall carpet. But it isn't a guest, only a bunch of flowers – sent by Simona to wish me good luck.

Deliberately so as to annoy me, Fleur makes sure she is first to arrive; she takes the early train up from London (where she has stayed overnight with a Christian friend), and phones from the station. X and I have a mini-argument over who should go and pick her up. He loses, but I go anyway.

Just as she's walking towards me down the platform, I have a pulse of *tendresse* towards Fleur. In her bad clothes, she looks so Holly Hobby and all alone in the dangerous world. I remember how she used to let me play with her dolls, and how I always found ways to break them, and how she forgave me, and how angry with her I was for being such a *nice* person.

We kiss in the About girls way, as our mother taught us: once on the chin, once on the lips, once on the forehead. This intimacy of past-knowledge embarrasses us. I ask for recent news of our parents, and Fleur is still giving me details of Mummy's various illnesses as we get into the car. I refrain from telling my sister which of them I think are imaginary (about 90%): I know that there is an argument here to be had, whenever I want it.

As I drive her back from the station, Fleur gives me the latest news from her village. If someone has died in a particularly gruesome way, I am stimulated; otherwise, I am preoccupied with anticipating Fleur's reaction to the house. I know she'll think it a fake farmhouse, and will say she would have preferred the real thing. (Wuthering Heights, perhaps – complete with a heap of dead rabbits on the kitchen table.)

We drive up the drive, and Fleur surprises me by saying something unexpectedly generous. I become tearful and almost crash the car blindly into the bushes.

X comes out to greet the first guest.

I show my sister up to her room, and leave her alone in intimate confab with a suitcase full of floral prints.

Then come... Cleangirl *et famille*. They tumble out of a vast German estate car, miraculously well-tempered after their five-hour drive from Brighton. Ingrid stands and look at the house, monumentally – like some statue of gigantic Soviet Motherhood. She has such presence that I become terrified that she's about to steal the whole thing from me, by dint of sheer blonde charisma. Henry kisses me hello, and I hold on to his shoulders for a moment or two more than necessary – a mini-linger, in preparation for ones later and longer. Edith is full of enthusiasm for the house; she will very soon fall in love with it. She notices the strength of X, as he carries their suitcases into the hall. Perhaps he has hugged her, too – and she is still giddy from such intimate, all-out-blotting embrace.

Cecile has already told me that she won't be able to come until the second day: I think this is so that she can make one of her *entrances*. I wish I could be half so grand, rather than – as I'm sure happens – being Mrs Tiggywinkle welcoming visitors to her humble hole in the ground.

Then arrive, in no particularly important order, my Editor,
wonderfully (or perhaps I should put awfully wonderful?)
Simona, and her awful husband, William, and then Marcia, and then Alan Sopwith-Wood. Yes, I expect Alan is the last. He, again, I have to pick up from the station. (The others have cars, even Marcia.) But I *want* to be the one that brings him back to the house. This ensures that I am there to witness his first (second) meeting with Fleur. Since I told him that she wasn't coming, I've conveniently neglected to tell him that she is. The more I've thought about it, the more I'm sure there was the possibility of love between them: something went wrong the first time they met; something didn't happen which might've. X was right: if I put them together again, flustered and unaware, it might all suddenly click. Fleur, as I've described above, was quite resolute in not

wanting to know who else I'd invited. Annoyingly so, because I wanted to tell her about Alan – gauge her reaction.

Chef arrives and begins to cook.

At the end of the first day, we all sit down to a marvellous dinner. I make my little spontaneous speech of welcome, the one I have been drafting and redrafting ever since I thought up this mad idea. We go to bed, well fed and full of anticipation.

WEEK ONE

I don't expect a huge amount to happen; the fireworks, I leave for Week Three.

Days Two to Four

This is the period of settling-in. The guests are finding their way around the house. I have given a great deal of thought to putting everyone where they will feel most comfortable, and so I don't anticipate any problems over the sleeping arrangements.

~~To save time, and as a handy reference, here is a map of the house, and who is going to be where.~~

There's no need for expensive artwork.

There is one spare room, the daughter's, which I am setting aside for Simona, if and when she leaves William. (See below.) ←

I am leaving these references in, generously

Doubtless I have not foreseen every single requirement of every single guest. There are special foods to be added to the Chef's shopping list; likes and dislikes, allergies and intolerances to be taken account of.

During the first couple of days, the guests find their way into Southwold; make small forays there and back. It is a lovely place, and I expect them to thank me for having brought them there.

There is some initial resistance, generally, to my ban on television – most of this comes from Edith. Anticipating trouble, I will have had X remove the TV from sight; not into the attic – they might try to storm the place in order to get at it. And we can't be having that, can we? No, it shall be hidden away under some blankets in the daughter's room.

This might be an opportune moment, when the TV is being missed, for me to mention the Virginia Woolf reading group, and to distribute copies of *To the Lighthouse* among those who express an interest.

Strategic alliances begin to form. Cecile and I spend a great deal of time together – just as we have always wanted to. X, with a little prodding, attempts to get to know Edith. Marcia and Fleur become firm friends, bonding over victimhood – there is sexual tension between them, though; Fleur's secret Sapphism, about which she'll never actually do anything. (Joke.)

Simona and William turn in upon themselves, weathering each other's storms. Cleangirl and Henry treat us all as baby-sitters, having long lie-ins every morning. (Yes, it takes a while for the two couples – the one secure, the other insecure – to divide; allowing the individuals to savour again their individuality.)

To begin with, Alan and Fleur are a little shy of one another. There is some embarrassment at finding themselves thrown together, for a whole month. But they are both secretly pleased; Alan may even take me aside to thank me.

Only gradually do they work their way towards one another. They are both immensely clumsy, as emotional people; and so their love – when finally it happens – shall be a fumbled, dropped, chipped and fingerprinted thing. For the first week, I doubt if they want to be seen talking. (There is always the possibility that Fleur won't allow anything at all with Alan during the entire month; restrains herself, and delays even their beginning until afterwards. My sister has always loved to thwart me, mostly when she thinks I'm meddling.)

Fleur probably spends much of this early period in an Alan-related sulk. If the weather is decent, she haunts the garden and the beach; the house, due to its association with me, is her anathema. But she quickly-quickly begins the rebound, as she always does, towards forgiveness.

Of course, as a separate issue, my sister is inevitably attracted towards Edith. A child, any child, however unpleasant (and Edith is about as far from unpleasant as a child gets), has Fleur's utmost devotion. There is a big scene, early on – bound to be – in which my sister makes full use of this devotedness, and the reason for it. She attempts to turn people against me; she may even succeed, for a while.

A few days in, I begin my flirtation with the lovely Henry. Ever since university I've always wanted to test out what he felt about me. I sometimes think I was a little in love with him then; I sometimes think I still am. It was only when he married Ingrid that I saw how terribly attractive he had become. I can't help but wonder how we would have been, together; this month gives me a chance to find out – harmlessly, of course.

He likes to spend hours on his own, and I catch him during one of these; not going into their bedroom – that would be too much, and scare him off. I show a greater interest in, and respect for his work than does Ingrid. This is difficult, she is so thoroughly devoted, but with my eyes and my words I am able to manage it. I am very tactile with him.

By the end of the first week, Henry has been brought back to life as a sexual hunter. He shall be magnificent again, just as he was when I so briefly had him at university. Yet in finding himself stirred, he feels great marital and parental guilt. Not wanting to show this to Ingrid, he starts to avoid me. It may be necessary to have a scene or two in which I am alone together with the two of them. The presence of X, clearly, would make the *frisson* run even more ravishingly down the spine.

At the same time, X begins to flirt with Ingrid. They have always done this, mildly and from a fairly safe distance. But I know that X always likes to have another object of sexual attraction, in addition to me. Ingrid is really the only serious option – apart from a toy-flirtation with Edith.

If I see that nothing is happening between X and Ingrid, I shall force them together: sending them off on errands, asking each of them to find out what the other is thinking and feeling. I'm sure this won't be necessary, but it can always be done.

Ingrid enjoys the male attention, and doesn't straight away feel any guilt.

All of this I discuss with Cecile, in some detail.

I can't at all see where Marcia is going to fit in, unless as friend to Fleur. Is there anyone she finds attractive? I know so little of her, it's very difficult to plot her in. Perhaps, if she doesn't do anything worth while, I can edit her out entirely.

I have a number of events planned for Week One (and for the other Weeks, too). On the evening of Day Three or Four we play a few getting-to-know-each-other Truth Games.

At the end of each week, on Sunday night, we have a large ceremonial dinner. The menus are already planned. The Chef must outdo himself.

The Rest of Week One

Overall, an unclenching takes place; a fist releasing a flower, miraculously uncrushed (because filmed backwards and played forwards).

By Day Five, Edith is very taken with X, and the idea of X, but hardly dares speak to him. Subtly, I find ways of bringing them together – just once or twice, alone. Or perhaps it would be better if they teamed up for something. Board games. I should buy some before we go. If she is to develop a crush, it must happen crashingly quickly.

Fleur wants to take long walks along the beach and down country lanes; in this, she probably finds a partner in... Henry? (I don't know who else there is that walks, willingly.)

Simona and William have their first big argument. Arriving at the house and being with other people keep them civil for a few days. His viciousness cannot be withheld for long, though.

I'm cutting this as it's one of only a couple of references in the Synopsis to the spy-cameras, and as such it seems rather inelegant. When I read it first time, it really struck out.

WEEK TWO

~~At this point, I am finally able to turn the spy cameras on. It will have been desperately tempting to go up into the attic and find out what the guests are doing when I'm not around, when no-one is around. But I think, with X's support, I will be able to resist.~~

About Week Two, I am going to try to be a little more specific.

Days Eight and Nine

I strongly believe an important event takes place on the first day of the second week. No idea why I think that – perhaps only because after the guests have been in the house this long, they must start to reveal their true selves. It has all been best behaviour up until now, but around Day Eight this becomes bad behaviour – or at least, truer behaviour.

My suspicion is that it is William who precipitates the tumble into honesty. Simona spends the first week restraining him; he spends the second rebelling. In doing this he may try to form a male clique with X, Henry and Alan. Alcohol is his currency. He says things like, 'Look, we're on holiday – what's the problem with us relaxing, for once?' By relaxing he means getting drunk; and on at least one occasion, he becomes outrageously, publicly pissed. In this state, he is aggressive towards several of the women in the house – those he feels most threatened by/attracted to; specifically, myself and Ingrid. ~~If this happens during the afternoon (William is a lunchtime pubber) we shall have to keep him away from Edith~~. ~~We can't have her memories of this month haunted by a lechy, bearded, shabby, raving man~~. Secretly, I am grateful to William for breaking things up a bit – letting Dionysus out for a run-around. His disgrace is a much-needed reaction against the nicey-niceness of Week One.

> This goes too far. You can say you think he was going to leave me, but not accuse him of anything horrendous.

Henry now seeks me out. These are the tender early days of our affair – an affair that is to be terribly thwarted. We go for a walk together, and it is all he can do not to bundle me into a hedgerow and brutally *take* me. (At least, these are the sort of thoughts that go through his head; a kiss that only half-hits my lips is the more likely outcome.)

Cecile and I are together for much of the time. We are completely relaxed in one another's company, and talk with absolute freedom about anything we feel like. She tells me all the intimate secrets of her life, the great tragic romance that broke her heart.

Marcia gets on very well with the Maid and the Chef, perhaps; they talk about... things in which they are interested: food, sport. (Help.)

Simona and William's marriage, already perilous, begins, around Day Nine, to collapse, self-destruct. We have already, Simona and I, on a number of occasions, discussed what she should do – how she should go about leaving him. This August away from home offers her the best opportunity she's ever had. What prompts the final split? I'm not quite sure. Perhaps one too many evenings of William coming back pissed from the pub. With my encouragement, Simona slowly gains the strength to confront William, to tell him what she feels, to leave him.

~~Simona is torn at this point between a desire to maintain her dignity and a wish for *From the Lighthouse* to be as sensational as she possibly can. To begin with, she contented herself with being a minor character; as the days go by, however, she discovers in~~

I wasn't at all attracted, you silly thing. I always knew exactly how I wanted to come across.

~~herself the desire to be the star. She realises that having a horrendous break-up from William would guarantee her a high wordcount; she is attracted by this notion.~~

William, ~~more straightforwardly,~~ wishes for a simpler, quieter life. He'd like to be a Hobbit. (He looks a bit like an elongated Hobbit.) This month is, as he sees it, a small step towards that. I doubt that he expects such a short period of time is enough to take him the whole way – he is too middle-aged for that. His War of Expectations is in the process of being lost; but his War of Temptations rages on.

Around this time, Alan and Fleur are concentrating on the day-to-dayness of their relationship. Beneath their slightly dull surfaces, Romeo is scaling castle walls and Juliet is making a pet of her Nurse.

On Day Thirteen, I strategically dump X. He is expecting this, I think. He surely knows that I need a back-up plan in case everything goes wrong and nothing happens. He also knows that it isn't really a *serious* break-up. If it were that, he would have to leave the house. What I want to do is grant him a temporary freedom – to roam; to roam through hearts, both young and old, and perhaps also through bedrooms. (I am thinking of Ingrid, not Edith; even I am not perverse enough to set him about seducing a pre-pubescent. A little horseplay on the sofa wouldn't go amiss, though.) This, I would say, is the last time I shall do this, for a long while. By the end of the month, he must have proposed marriage to me. After an infidelity, he is always incredibly attentive – in a shamefully typical male way. That is why I do not rule out letting him loose again later on in life; in order that, once spoused, we keep each other in perspective. The last thing I want is for us to transform into those distorted monsters of monogamy one sees everywhere: mouths turned into broken zips by the frantic tugs of sexual fury; eyes gone basilisk with the furious attempt *not* to look, *not* to see. We shall not bicker on the stairs in the theatre; we shall not fall out every time we get into a car. No, no – it shall be a matter of entering and departing from other people's lives, glamorously – it shall be the sharing of intrigues and the laughing at mistakes – it shall be a choice of one's lover's chocolates or of cocoa at the homey hearth – it shall, in fine, be the subject of such magnificent envy that neither of us need ever do anything remarkable again (though, of course, we shall – much, many, most). But that is for the future; for now, X must be rendered seductively abject. Unless otherwise required, during this period he still sleeps in my bed and brings me coffee in the morning. This is part of his abjection. (Sexual slavery may also be required, in the unlikely case I do not manage instantly to subjugate another.)

WEEK THREE

is a week of high tension for Edith. Her crush on X is, by now, a bruise in full bloom – bright, sore, pride-inducing. She places herself where he might pass; there are interludes of the most delightful flirtation. Ingrid's attitude to this is ambiguous. She cannot, as she wants to, ban her daughter from spending time with X – that would be explicitly to confess her feelings of jealousy. In fact, Ingrid can hardly prevent herself from copying her daughter. Henry, too, is jealous – jealous of another man occupying Edith's affections, jealous of Ingrid's preoccupation with their daughter. He probably sees how Ingrid is trying to prevent herself from wanting to spend time with X. In reaction to this, Henry begins to woo Ingrid. Subtly at first, but then – realising public displays are what she requires – increasingly dramatically, Henry makes love to his own wife; and she responds, how could she not? Henry converts his ardour for me into demonstrations of marital affection. He finds himself powered forwards by the guilt he feels having been unfaithful, if only mentally.

Simona leaves William. I can't be sure exactly when, she has delayed so many times before. With my encouragement, though, given during our Confessions, she moves into the kept-free daughter's room. William is distressed. He pleads with her to return to the marital bed. *Never*, she says, *I have taken enough abuse. No more*. There is a terrific stand-up row, which everyone hears. (Edith is stunned; is this how grown-ups talk to one another?) Simona finally brings out all the horrors of their relationship, and William – shamed, defeated – gets into their car and drives off. (Probably only as far as the nearest pub.) Simona spends the night in floods. Cecile, who is marvellously good at this sort of thing, helps console her.

The next morning, Simona sleeps in late – and when she comes down to lunch, no make-up on, she looks fifteen years younger. She is beautiful – purged of all bitterness and fury. Gently, she takes my hand, squeezes it and says, *Oh, Victoria*.

The reading group, I think, takes place on the Wednesday or the Thursday of this week. We have an extended discussion of Virginia's masterpiece, all secretly examining the parallels with our own relationships.

By the middle of Week Three, Alan and Fleur have started spending a great deal of time together. They awkwardly change subject if happened upon alone together. There may also be secret meetings, trysts. I shall have to watch for glances at the dinner table, the licking and flicking of their eyes. I am unsure whether consummation occurs whilst they are resident in the house. My sister may be too proud to allow me that gratification; Alan may be too shy altogether of letting their romance become known. I suspect, though, that their attraction may attain an unexpected power – it may be that their scruples crumble. I would be so happy to see them happy – coyly aglow in post-coital knitwear, strolling loose-jointed along the unlonely beach. Yes, I'm going to be daring, and assume that this *does* take place.

WEEK FOUR

Of course, the later in the month I anticipate, the harder it gets to predict what happens.

With William gone, the house feels larger, freer. Simona continues to blossom – spending time with Edith and feeling that she, too, has a whole life to look forward to.

Alan and Fleur have overcome their shyness and are quite the happy, public couple. They are almost certainly to be observed kissing and holding hands. ~~The spy cameras confirm that their intimacy goes yet further than this. (I turn the screens off, although I feel I have something of a right to observe a consummation which is, in a way, as much mine as theirs.~~) The rest of the guests rejoice in their love – there may even be a small, spontaneous party to celebrate. I, too, receive the guests' gratitude. I'm not expecting an actual engagement: Alan is unprepared for that.

This is shameful – if quite funny.

X tries to come back to me. He is repentant; he is completely hangdog-ish. Yet I do not take him back – I make it clear that he must demonstrate his affections *extraordinarily*. He can be in no doubt what I mean. One day, he disappears in the car – no-one knows where he has gone. That evening, he returns. All embarrassment ignored, he asks me – in front of all the suppering guests – to marry him. And I agree. Delight at this turn of events is not universal. Edith's little crush is crushed, but she learns by it – perhaps not immediately, her melancholy is too deep right at this moment; in a month or so, she looks back at her first great love, and realises that men have the power to hurt her just as much as she has the power to hurt them. Henry, too, feels betrayed. But by what? He realises that almost everything that he thought *happened* between him and me was in his imagination. He realises also that he has nothing to feel guilty about – very quickly, he converts what didn't happen (our affair) into what he heroically resisted (his own unruly passions). And because he has put so much effort into re-wooing Ingrid, and because she has reacted against her and her daughter's attraction to X, they are in sympathy as they haven't been since their wedding day.

The month culminates on the evening of the 27th. This, the start of our last night together in the house, is the occasion of a fantastic feast. I have decided to recreate the famous meal served up in *To the Lighthouse: boeuf en daube*. In this, I shall probably be assisted by Chef, but I intend to be the *chef de partie*. Everyone in the house (after the reading group) is by this time familiar with the culinary allusion; there will be laughter, applause. I make sure that there is a great deal of alcohol in the house, which I insist we finish up. Alan and Fleur sit side by side, touching unselfconsciously; Simona looks at them and anticipates a true love of her own (arranged, almost certainly, by myself); William is imagined standing bitterly at the bar of some skanky London pub, cursing Simona, me, the house, everything; Henry and Ingrid are closer than ever, having seen their marriage, like a car engine, dismantled, cleaned out, put back together, returned – they shall purr; Edith is exhibiting the first signs of teenage melancholia: her failed crush on X has begun to make her more empathetic; Marcia laughs and brings festival into the room; X and I are also wafting on clouds of candied bliss – he, revelling in the success of his marriage proposal; I, delighting in the success of the stratagems by which I got him to propose; Cecile smiles across at me, and that is blessing enough.

Final Day

We pack and go home.

Satisfaction is the overarching emotion of the house. *Together, we have accomplished something quite extraordinary*, that's what the guests (mostly) feel, *merely by being ourselves we have been entertaining, moving, thought-provoking. All that remains is for Victoria to be faithful to the material with which we have provided her.*

AUGUST

Wednesday

Day Zero

The house was looking most splendidly something something, that fine summer day – tall brick chimneys red against the blue sky.

(I think an opening passage like this will probably be necessary – though I don't really feel like doing it right this moment.)

Notes for description: boxy Georgian building – tree-shaded gravel drive up to an oval grass roundabout – 16 white-framed windows at the front – ivy, of the dark-leaved, white-edged variety, running all up the left half – very gentleman-farmer farmhouse-looking, and not in an estate-agent way – a real sense of history, atmosphere and plot-potential, or is that just me? – I think there was birdsong audible; not 100% certain but I'd better put some in anyway – maybe some bumblebees and butterflies, too (or would that be overdoing it?).

Walked into the hall – greeted by the Maid who said Chef is shopping in Southwold for the bulk of our first week's provisions – he'll be back around 4.

I'm in my study (actually, the Master Bedroom), tapping away on the laptop – it really is very nice here, light and clean – good-size *escritoire* in the corner – I'll have to keep reminding myself to sneak off and make lots of notes – if I don't have the computer, I'll just have to jot them on whatever's to hand and type them up later – anything else about the house? – all the beds were made, sheets stretched tightly across – maybe I should start with X and I motoring up the drive? – 'Victoria laughed gaily, though not without a certain nervousness' – that sort of thing – shopping list – Maid has taken care of toilet paper and everything practical – I think we need more flowers – haven't yet spoken to the gardener – must phone

Owners, tell them how lovely it is – I'm feeling at home here, already – can't wait for people to arrive and for the fun to start.

Spent the late afternoon reclining on the sofa in the drawing room with my head on X's lap. It was here, only a few weeks back, we sat and talked terms with the Owners. How long ago that seems! And now the place is ours, for a whole month! They, the Owners, went off on Saturday, to stay with friends in Tuscany. I'd been wondering what they were *really* like, and have been having a snoop around, before the guests arrive: trying to find out as much as I can. (I feel as if I should be able to list the contents of every cupboard, drawer, tea caddy and matchbox in the house.)

I think they must have rented this place out quite a few times, because, while being quite welcoming, it's also quite impersonal – apart, I have to say, from the daughter's room, which is, no other word for it, spooky. We're not meant to go in there – but I have found a key, and unlocked the door shortly after we got here. It's one of those 'Everything's been kept exactly as it was on the day they died' rooms. I don't think the daughter's *really* dead. (It didn't come up in conversation.) More likely, she just went off to boarding school at an early age, and they never got round to redecorating. It's exactly the same with the nursery, where Edith will sleep: hasn't been touched in a decade, at least.

From what I've gathered, looking around the house, the husband is the less interesting of the two. He fancies himself a bit of an old salt. There are many books on sailing: *100 Stories of Adventure on the High Seas*, *Yarns from a Suffolk Boatyard*. (I'm not just attributing these to him: on the inside front cover, he has signed and dated them all.) Very ungrownup. This explains the slight ship-in-a-bottle feel of the downstairs hall. One fantastic book he has, *The Pusser's Rum*, is of sailor's slang.

The wife, sadly, longs for romance – of the tawdriest love-on-the-plantation sort. There is a bookshelf in one of the spare bedrooms entirely filled with fruity fat volumes – covers featuring a muscle-bound hero clutching a hardbodied heroine, whilst a purple tempest lashes behind them and their clothes begin to rip spontaneously. Lots of other more demure love stories, too. (Strangely, she also had copies of all my novels. I expect she bought them when I got in touch about renting the place – checking me out, no doubt.)

Putting the romances together with the Sea Yarns, I'd say unhappy marriage – but I could be wrong.

I went through a few of her books, looking at the final page: they all had the same last line. 'And when he took her in his masterful arms, she knew that she would be safe for ever with him to hold her, in his masterful arms, and keep her safe.' Approx.

After this, I went and found X; with a bit of encouragement, he masterfully held me in his masterful arms.

X and I had a quiet evening in. Chef impressed us with scallops and bacon fried in butter and sherry accompanied by a salad of intriguingly bitter leaves. No one will complain about the food, at least.

My God, I'm sounding like a hotelier, when I'm meant to be coming over as Ottoline Morrell. In the final draft, I'll make sure I come over as incredibly suave and confident:

'The Hostess (or just "Victoria") awaited her guests with no more trepidation than was to be expected. She knew, in her heart, that her project would be a glorious success.'

No, that won't do either – the tone of this thing still eludes me. I shall have to experiment for a while. First person, third, etc.

I love everything about this house: right down to the coat hangers: they are thick, wooden and give low glockenspiel klicks and klocks as one flicks through one's frocks.

Thursday

Day One Week One

Awoken by the dawn chorus, lovely, so lovely. The pitch of the birds was little short of angelic; a soar and sweep about it, never shrill. Sound in which to drown.

Last night I had an anxiety dream so clichéd I don't think I can bear to record it; suffice it to say, a Biology exam and nakedness involved.

When we were allocating the bedrooms, X and I made sure we got the nicest. Two long floor-to-almost-ceiling windows decked with spiky ivy leaves look directly out over the back garden. The decor inside is a little florid – it's not how I'd do it myself. But it does make one feel as if one is staying in a very exclusive hotel. The king-size bed is the most comfortable (and we've tried them all, in various ways). More importantly, there is a square hatch in the ceiling which gives access to the attic – which is where I have had all the spying equipment installed. There is a pole with a funny-shaped hook upon it, to pull down the attic ladder. Once I'm up there, the hatch shut behind me and the pole with me, I am undisturbable. X will be the only person in the house to know about the cameras. (Even Simona doesn't know.) He is sworn to secrecy. On his life. If he gives any hint of it, I have promised to bite his balls off – and not in a nice way, either.

Ahem.

The attic is large, dark, dusty, and full of atticy things. I shan't be spending too long up there, I hope. Spiders – eek!

Back down in the master bedroom – we have bedside tables which, when we arrived, were piled high with middle-class classics: *Corelli*, *Birdsong*, *Wild Swans*. All, of course, half-read. There are two large empty *armoires*, of which I occupy one and a half. A sink and shaving mirror mean we don't always have to queue for the bathroom. Except to use the loo, and the shower.

I don't suppose anyone will resent our having all this. What they're getting is perfectly nice, for what they're paying – which is absolutely nothing.

The bed (back to the bed again) is a large Elizabethan affair, with fantastic red velvet drapes that can be closed – muffling out the world. In summer, no doubt, this might be a trifle stifling. But we're determined to try. It worries me only slightly that by closing the curtains I won't be able to hear anyone midnight creeping along the upstairs landing. Perhaps I should have had some special sensors put in. But the whole gubbins was becoming far too James Bond anyhow.

X thinks the room excessively feminine. He doesn't like flounces and frills of any sort. He insists that ornaments and knick-knacks are always a sign of ravaging loneliness. He called the ruched curtains 'menopause flags'. I think he would have us all John Pawsons – living on light and concrete, everything at right angles and nothing comfy.

~~Sometimes I think about what a very different place the world would be, were women exclusively in possession of it; I think that this would be nowhere clearer than in the field of interior decoration. I don't really even know if we'd have recognisable houses anymore. I think it's likely it (the world) would be something much more like a huge mansion, with rooms that one could trespass through at will – without it being trespass. One wouldn't have street names; in order to find out where one was, one would have to talk to the people around one. Location would be to do with relationships, not map references. Perhaps what I'm trying to say is this is (or may be) my utopia – attempted utopia. But I don't, of course, want everything to go right; I need, in fact, things to go *wrong*. Not dreadfully wrong. Just emotionally a little haywire.~~

Hello, Germaine – and goodbye.

~~My grandmother always loved emergencies; the Second World War was her absolute heaven. I think I take rather after my grandfather, who liked to mend the things (and most particularly the friendships) she, my grandmother, had broken. 'They make me feel properly alive,' she used to say – meaning emergencies.~~

~~(Cecile, I think, feels the same way. She once said to me, 'Routines – they're death, aren't they?' And this from the woman who shops at Borough Market every Saturday at eleven thirty exactly.)~~

It's mad. I'm worried – already! – about my ending. And the whole thing's hardly even begun. The problem is, not everyone is certain they can stay until the end. Several (Cleangirl's family, for instance) say they may have to leave a week early. No real reason given. Surely, for me, for the book, this will mean anticlimax: diminuendo enforced by other people. A trailing-off rather than a whopping great blow-out. And I can't bring new characters in, so late in the action. Or can I? I shouldn't have let the Cleangirl clan come in the first place. Oh, I'll just have to do what Mummy always said: 'Wait and see.' But Mummy meant sitting demurely on a chair at the edge of the ballroom, hoping to be spotted by the Handsome Prince. (But *quel* Handsome Prince she ended up with, demure as she always was – dear dead Daddy.) I can hear someone coming up the drive. Better go and see.

Fleur has only been and gone and brought her bloody *cat*! (After I specifically told her not to.) I have to admit, it's no common or garden moggie; it's a full pedigree of some sort – rare breed, and is probably the most expensive thing she's ever owned. It itself is a she, and *she* is called Audrey, and Audrey is the most marvellously glowing grey, just like a cat-version of a Weimaraner. *Svelte* beyond words. If one were to say that a cat could be *chic* then Fleur's cat is so – which surprises me entirely. I'd expect her to have some ginger-white minger that leaves hanks of fluff and piles of squishy delight all over everything, and everybody. Audrey is far more the kind of cat I'd expect Cecile to have.

At least by arriving first, Fleur fulfilled one of my predictions. But there was no scene at the station, as I'd expected: she had driven up from the farm, in her banger of a Saab.

She honked cheerily as she chugged up the drive. I went out to meet her. We gave one another the About girls' kiss, then Fleur opened the car-boot and fetched out a large balsa wood box, of the sort that usually contains tangerines – but this, instead of containing tangerines, contained about one foot by three foot of green grass.

Without explanation, Fleur had me lead her to the kitchen, strode up to the sink and ran the box quickly under the tap. Then she left it there, dripping on the draining board.

Back to the car; Audrey out in her carry-home from the passenger seat. Grass partially explained.

Then, from the boot, the Grudging Gift: Fleur had brought me a huge bunch of pink roses.

I *hate* pink roses. She knows I hate, and have always hated, and shall always hate, pink roses. They're so ugly. They look like the upturned snouts of hungry little piglets. I put them in a vase on the window-ledge in the downstairs loo, where hopefully no-one will notice them.

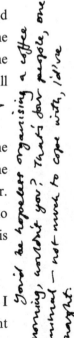

1.00 p.m.-ish. I'm finding it hard to keep up, what with all the arrivals and arrangements. No sooner is someone installed in the kitchen with a mug of coffee than another is knocking at the door. So far we've had Fleur (and cat), Ingrid, Henry and Edith – who behaved very much according to the Synopsis. All we need now is Marcia and – hang on, that's the phone again.

You'd be hopeless organising a coffee morning, wouldn't you? That's four people, one animal – not much to cope with, I'd've thought.

3.00 p.m. That was Alan, calling from the station at Darsham. I drove over to pick him up. And, wouldn't you know it, *he'd* brought his bloody *dog*! (After I specifically asked him not to.) It's a whomping great Dalmatian, called Domino. He apologised. 'The kennels I booked – they said they'd had an outbreak of something or other horrible. Foot and mouth. Kennel fever. I couldn't find anyone who could take him at such short notice. I tried my mother. I tried my father.'

'It's all right,' I said. 'Don't worry.'

'I'll get rid of him in, uh, a few days.' I was thinking: I made a special promise to the Owners that there would be no pets in the house, and now I've got two. (No children, either, they'd said. I made an exception for Edith. At eleven she's hardly a *child* any more. I'm sure the Owners meant puking infants.) Have to deal with this later, I thought.

Dear old Alan certainly seems to have dressed for the occasion, in full melancholic pale-blue linen suit, strategically stained. He is so tall and scruffy he somehow manages to create vertical wrinkles, four feet long.

We put Domino behind the back seats, drove off. It was still a lovely day, with the sun through the leaves of the trees above us dappling and dazzling the windscreen. (Perhaps description not necessary here.) We talked: 'Lovely day,' etc. When he asked who had arrived already, I decided it was best to bring up the subject of Fleur. 'Oh,' Alan said, lugubriously, 'really... You didn't mention her before.' After which, he didn't say anything much at all. I noticed he started to pick at his cuticles, and they were fairly red-raw already.

Alan's curiously affable-smelling BO filled the car – always forget this about him; always find it half-pleasant half-unpleasant to be reminded. His hairy Adam's apple, too – such a long neck he has. He doesn't seem to have shaved today; his stubble is mostly white, although the hair on his head is brown. Which makes me wonder if he dyes it. That would be odd.

I was there when Alan and Fleur saw one another for the first time. Alan dumped his two falling-apart suitcases in the hall, then followed my directions (right at the end! not that door! left!) into the kitchen. I had Domino with me, frolicking about on the end of his lead – glad to be uncooped. Fleur was leaning back against the sink, having a coffee with X. I wonder what they found to talk about. Perhaps Audrey, who had tied herself into an elegant knot beneath the kitchen table. At the sight of Domino, however, pussikins sprang to her feet and formed her back into a gothic arch. But I was at that moment concentrating most of my attention on Fleur. I saw her take in Alan; and, yes, I definitely saw the spread of her tell-tale blush. At which point, Domino made a friendly lollop towards Audrey – intending no harm, only play. Out the back door and zinging straight across the garden lawn went the terrified grey streak of a cat, with Fleur whompling afterwards.

'Welcome to the Madhouse,' said X. (I had a word with him afterwards about this. It's not called the Madhouse, I said. If you're going to do dialogue, at least make it something I can use.)

'Shall I let him off the lead?' I asked Alan.

'Better not,' he said. 'Not right now.'

By quarter to four this afternoon the hall was jagged with luggage, as yet untransported up to rooms.

Simona and William have arrived. Fleur has yet to come back.

Day One conversations: all journeys and journey times, criss-crossing. 'How did you get here?' *'Good trip up?'* 'By train. I don't have a car.' *'Not bad.'* 'Really?' *'How was the traffic?'* 'I love travelling by train.' *'Not bad. Getting out of London wasn't too bad.'* 'So do I, but we couldn't, this time.' *'I tend to avoid the M25 whenever possible.'* 'How did you come?' *'Oh, it can be pretty awful, when it chooses. How was your journey?'* 'We came by car. We thought it best. With Edith. A car gives you a lot of... flexibility, doesn't it?' *'Not bad.'* 'I don't know – I've never had a car.'

A polyphony of banality, but I'm confident things will soon improve.

4 p.m. Confession. Didn't happen today, obviously. But Simona sought me out, anyway. (I was at the *escritoire* in the master bedroom, typing the above.) She tells me, quickly, how proud she is of me. I get the feeling she knows exactly how she wants to come across in the finished book. (Of course, she will have some influence upon that. The editing process is going to be very interesting. I wonder what she'll object to. Will I have to take anything out?~~ For instance, if I mention that little one-night stand of hers, at last year's Frankfurt Book Fair. And I'm sure she wouldn't let me say anything about her two teenage abortions. Nor her recent personal-hygiene problems. But if I tell you that~~ I've never had a better, more sympathetic and supportive Editor...

You can say that again.

Half an hour's respite, while the guests unpack. I realise now that I've completely forgotten to do a character of Alan. Alan Sopwith-Wood. 37, teaches film studies, very tall, very clumsy; a gentle giant. He is writing a book on Woody Allen's most gloomily unfunny films: *September*, *Another Woman*, *Shadows and Fog*, *Alice*. Occasionally, he has identity crises in which Alan and Allen become confused. My favourite remark of his: 'Most of my students think, um, post-Modernism is a Modernism correspondence course.' Said deadpan. Alan is the most miserable person I know, and the most deserving of happiness. He would hardly need anything much to make him content, which is lucky because Fleur is hardly anything much. (That sounds like a firm of solicitors, doesn't it? Hardly, Anything and Much.) Alan would probably think himself fulfilled if he had someone to sew leather elbow patches onto his yellowy corduroy jackets. I once asked him if he'd ever slept with one of his students. (This is the man who teaches an entire course on 'The Cinema of the Erotic'.) He said, 'What do you mean? Of course not.' And I said, 'Well, what other use are they?' And he said, 'They're nice to look at – some of them. They talk. Ask questions.' His voyeuristic tendencies are well known; though I don't think he's ever asked a couple if he can watch. As for God – an important subject for Fleur – I think Alan is persuadable. He wouldn't look out of place in a provincial pulpit, reading one of the lesser lessons. ~~(Insert this earlier.)~~ works better here, I think.

Note: I did once, very briefly, go out with Alan. It was a relationship entirely sustained by neither of us knowing which of us was the more embarrassed by the relationship. He bedded me like tulip bulbs in November – deeply, and at regularly spaced intervals. He's really quite a lot stronger than he looks.

5.20 p.m. We've just finished having tea and cake. I feel a bit stupid, rushing off all the time to type things up. And Fleur still hasn't come back to the house since bolting off after Audrey. We know where she's been, however: on the beach. Edith went for a walk there, by herself. I assured Cleangirl it was safe. Strangely, Edith had never met Fleur before today. I think they said hello whilst I was collecting Alan, or before. Anyway, when Edith came back from the beach she said she'd seen a woman there, holding a cat and crying. When she got closer, she saw it was Fleur. Wisely, Edith left her alone. Fleur must be upset about the dog. She's bound to blame me, even though I did my best to prevent both dog *and* cat. I will have to tell Alan to go and explain the situation to her. Get them together again. (I realise that I'm not writing very elegantly, but I'm feeling a bit rushed for time. This cat–dog drama is a bit trivial, and unexpected, but it does at least get some momentum going.)

6.30 p.m. Still no sign of Marcia. Called her at home. Answerphone. Perhaps she's wimped out?

11 p.m. Evening. I'm going to make my first attempt at third-person novelisation.

It was a wonderful meal. Victoria stood up after everyone had finished, and made the speech she had been thinking of for at least two months. Her eyes glittered bright with excitement. She spoke softly but perfectly audibly: 'I'd like to welcome you all. I'm very glad that each of you decided to take part. Hopefully, most of the time, things round here will be pretty informal – and as natural as possible, under the circumstances. But there are one or two unusual features...' There were smiles. 'Obviously, I'm hoping that some of you are going to do interesting things while you're here.' Victoria realised that she was using the words *hope* and *things* too frequently. 'But there's no obligation to feel that you have to play up to any pre-conceived notion of Action.' Fleur made a small farting noise with her lips, pooh-poohing Victoria. 'What I want is for you all to just be your wonderful selves. Leave the rest up to me.' Victoria paused, for a sip of red wine. She was less nervous than she'd anticipated. In the soft candlelight, she looked warmly radiant. 'One of the unusual things I'd like to mention, however, is that from four o'clock onwards, every day, for half an hour – tea-time – I am going to be in the little parlour off the front hall. If any of you feel like popping in for a *tête-à-tête*, to make some suggestions for the house, to discuss how you're feeling or just to talk about the weather, then I'll be more than delighted to see you. Please form an orderly queue – or make a reservation in advance.' Victoria was gratified to hear a deep laugh pass around the table. 'Otherwise, there is going to be a Suggestions Box on top of the fridge in the kitchen. If you want to communicate with me anonymously, then *that's* the way to do it. I've already had one or two little requests: one of which I think is, for me, physically impossible – unless I have surgery and work very hard on my suppleness (but thank you for the kind thought).' Victoria looked at the note-writer, Fleur, who had been careful not to disguise her handwriting. 'The other, a heartfelt plea for some tomato ketchup, I have already passed on to Chef.' Victoria looked at Edith, who smiled back a thank-you. 'Speaking of whom, how about a round of applause in appreciation of the food.' The table obliged. Chef bowed from the kitchen doorway. He was, Victoria noticed, quite obviously eyeing up Cleangirl. 'I think that's just about it from me – apart from saying Welcome, once again, and wishing you a delightful and relaxing month's stay.'

The Writer sat down, to an encore of warm applause. That had all gone very satisfactorily.

I found it quite difficult to keep up today, what with the arrivals and everything. I'm wondering what it will be like if things start to happen really rapidly. I shall have to take notes, write them up after everyone's gone to bed.

Cecile should be arriving some time tomorrow. If Marcia turns up too, the house will be full. If...

Friday

Day Two Week One

Dawn chorus again, round about four forty-five; beautiful, but wish they'd keep it down slightly. Got off again when they quieted.

After lunch – 3rd person. Victoria had a decent conversation with Henry, in the garden, on deck chairs, on the lawn, in bright sunshine. She found out what it is he's doing at the moment, workwise. He asked her not to include any mention of it in the book, because it's at a delicate stage – and might still be when *Lighthouse* is published. But Victoria couldn't see how he'd mind her writing just a little about it; it'd be good publicity after all. He is working with a playwright called Hector Furnace on a highly ambitious staging of *A Midsummer-Night's Dream*. What happens is this: there are two productions going on simultaneously – one of *A Midsummer-Night's Dream*, the other of a play written by Hector. (They haven't quite decided upon a title for this, as yet. It may just be called *Night's Dream*. Or favourite is *Summernightdream*. Or *Summerdream*.) The set of one play backs onto that of the other – so that when an actor leaves the *AM-ND* stage as, say, Oberon, they enter the backstage-stage as whoever they are in the other play. It's all immensely, hideously complicated. The timings will have to be exact to the very second. And, of course, the more major a character is in *AM-ND*, the less they are onstage in *Summerdream*. There is a real off-off stage; they had to decide on that early – because of the children in the cast, the fairies; Moth, Peaseblossom, etc. It's against union law to have them working too long or too late. *Summerdream* concerns a great deal more than the usual actor-y shenanigans. It's a little like Stoppard, Henry said. And a little like Ayckbourn. And Pinter, too. And Mamet, in parts. Of course, for the audience to get the full effect, they have to go one night to see *AM-ND* and the next to see *Summerdream*. The best thing, Henry said, would be to go after that and see *AM-ND* again – because then you'd be able to see the backstage tensions being played out onstage. The whole production can't help but be a triumph, though exhausting for the actors.

Henry was so brilliant. Victoria found him unbelievably attractive. Always had. And despite his marriage to Ingrid, perhaps in some ways because of it, she had continued unwaveringly to lust after him. He was a lot more conventionally good-looking than X, really. It was a case of the catalogue man (Henry) vs the wall-eyed but handsome man (X); Cary Grant or Henry Fonda as against

Jean-Paul Sartre or Serge Gainsbourg. X had that same slightly glazed Parisian look about the eyes; Henry's were brown or green, depending on cloudcover and wallpaper. Victoria had always been very taken with people who were distorted versions of other people, and through them she could glimpse herself as another version of herself – as Hepburn (Katharine) to Henry's Grant, as Charlotte to X's Gainsbourg.

Victoria had begun the conversation by asking about daughter/Ingrid, about how she was settling in. She now tried to ask Henry the same question again, but he just repeated, 'Oh, she's fine.' He then stood up, excused himself, walked down the garden and out onto the beach. No joy, no flirting.

Ingrid had spent most of her time so far with Edith – doing Victoria didn't know what exactly. They had gone into Southwold together, that very morning.

(Note to self: Need to insert a description of the garden before this scene.)

The garden wasn't terribly big – from the middle of it one could see all of it. There were high walls, left, right, and along the bottom, secluding us in a delightfully selfish, English way. Beneath these were wide, interesting flowerbeds. A gardener dealt with all of this, letting himself in the green garden door and opening up the shed with his set of keys. Victoria had had no reason to speak to him, and if she did it would only be to congratulate him upon keeping the place in such a fine state. There were three apple trees growing in the lawn, over to the left as one faced out from the house. These were old and about as large as apple trees get. Their blossom was already long gone; blossom would have been too much to ask for. At the moment they just had normal-sized fruits upon them; but by Autumn, no doubt, they would have grown into huge double-fisty cooking apples. The lawn sloped gradually downwards towards some steps at the bottom of the garden.

I should say more about the flowerbeds, but I really don't know what's in them. That's one of the drawbacks of being a city girl, born and raised in flats – and never, like Fleur, having gone country. I don't know the names for all these things. Really, though, they're very colourful. Yellows and pinks (unfortunately) and deep, deep violets. I don't think there are any red-hot pokers like in *To the Lighthouse* – I think I'd recognise them. Nor pansies, daffodils, chrysanthemums. These must be the kinds of lovely flowers that grow in the kind of soil they have here, near the sea. Oh dear, maybe I should speak to the gardener. He'd be able to tell me all the names, and a few quaint stories about how they got them. People like that kind of detail. If I don't do enough of it, they won't think this is the seaside idyll I want them to. I'll try: towards the fronts of the beds are lots of low mossy plants. I think, at other times of the year, these would have flowers upon them. Small yellow or red ones, I'd imagine.

At the very bottom of the garden was a door – wooden with faded green paint – in a high, brick-flaky wall, through which one walked out directly onto the sand dunes behind the beach. (Which is what I'm going to do right now...)

Settled again. The sea itself, depending upon the advance or retreat of the tide, was either thirty or forty metres away. It didn't go in and out all that much up here in Suffolk. The waves curling to crash sparkling on the tinkling sands were a lovely sight – so lovely that it soon became tiring, trying to maintain one's impression of its loveliness; and after a while one began to resent this relentless loveliness of scene, hoping a black cloud would pass, if only to vary the relentlessness for a moment by introducing the notion of degree.

The dunes were Victoria's favourite part of any beach: scraggy like the scruff of a mongrel dog's neck, with plenty of places harmlessly to hurl oneself into space, and plenty more places to hurl oneself dangerously into the arms of someone inappropriate, someone not one's special one. (Where has Henry hidden himself?) The sea was the sea was the sea was big and wide and far and one would love to say blue but even being the kindest one could possibly be would still in all honesty be blue-grey, grey-blue, grey with a tinty-hint of bluishness.

To the right, as one stood with one's back to the house, Wherewithal, was Southwold. The lighthouse itself rose above the town, ludicrous were it not for the number of times one had already seen it upon postcards and tea-towels, keyrings, on menuboards outside pubs, in snowdomes. There were shops in the town which seemed to subsist entirely upon selling scale-model lighthouses to sentimental tourists.

(I will leave describing the town until another time: the sun has given me a bitch of a headache and I must go back to the house now to get some paracetamol. Also, the people walking by and spying me upon the dunes tapping away on the laptop make me uneasy. I couldn't bear the thought of it being pinched: it has almost everything on it, and not just to do with *Lighthouse*. I save to disk, incessantly.)

4 p.m. Confession in the front parlour. Tray of tea-things. Simona came ~~and told me a lot of things I don't really want to include.~~ If ~~she's attempting to use me as a way of getting back at her ex, I'm not interested. And so I won't include her descriptions of the end~~ of ~~their marriage (now over ten years ago) in the finished novelisation~~, ~~or even write them roughly down here. She is very reluctant to talk about leaving William, changing the subject whenever I try to bring it up. He had, this afternoon, taken himself off to one of the local pubs. He does drink. Alan also came, but went away very~~ quickly when he saw I was with Simona. 'We'll be done in a moment,' I said, glad of the out. 'No, no,' replied Alan. 'I just came to see what was going on.' He looked flushed and full of emotion – ~~I felt annoyed Simona had prevented me from finding out why~~. He

Eight and a half years, actually.

has been very quiet even by his own silent standards, this past twenty-four hours.

5 p.m. Cecile made her entrance this evening – called from the station and X went to collect her. She brought me a lovely bunch of elegant, beautiful, wonderful, fantastic flowers. All right, yes, I admit it: they were roses – pink ones. But they were of an *entirely different order* to those brought me by Fleur. These were tall and delicate, not fat and piggy. Their colour was so delicate as to be almost not pink at all. They made me quite change my mind about roses and about the colour pink, and about the combination of the two.

I was stunned by Cecile's luggage: for now, she has brought only a pair of slender calfskin suitcases, a hat-box and a handbag. I expect the rest of it will arrive later (a trunk?), having been 'sent on'.

Oh, how I worship this woman. I hope living in proximity with her isn't going to be a let-down. I'm sure she's going to hate me – if only for having a sister like Fleur.

Of course, Cecile will say *but she's adorable*; what she'll mean is *once we get back to London you will never see me again. I would never be able to see you again without thinking of this Lump.*

About fifteen minutes after she had arrived, Cecile came downstairs into the kitchen and asked, 'Is there an iron I might borrow?'

'I'll have one sent up straight away,' I said. 'And an ironing board?'

'If it's not too much trouble,' said Cecile.

'Of course not,' I said.

'Thank you,' said Cecile, and retired again to unpack.

I took the iron to her myself, hoping to get an early peek at the contents of the calfskin suitcases. But the door to her room opened only wide enough to admit the ironing board; a distance clearly too narrow to be mistaken for an invitation.

Yours truly had a sharp moment of disappointment, alone on the upstairs landing after her door shut. But then I thought, 'No, it's wiser altogether for me not to see the clothes in their uncrumpled post-travel state. And we have a whole month to explore one another's wardrobes. I needn't worry. The door will open for me – will open wide as Cecile's experience of life.'

I think I shall go and try to find Cecile, right now. Protect her from the vulgarities that are all around. I shouldn't have invited her, should I? But she seemed quite keen to come. I wonder why.

7 p.m. Small chat with Cecile. Not quite as intimate as one would have wanted, but at least a start.

Dinner. I'll have Chef do me a list of menus, so I don't have to keep writing them down here. Conversation was pleasant enough. Fleur is sulking about everything: about being Fleur, I expect. Edith chattered on and on, very confidently. Cecile was, I could see, charmed by her. Cleangirl noticed, was proud. Henry refused to make eye-contact with me – he was being so obvious about it that X may guess at an affair.

10 p.m. Marcia finally turned up. I went to answer her furious knocking at the front door.

'Hello,' I said.

Without a word in reply, she bumped her wheelchair over the threshold and accelerated down the hall.

'Turn right, then left,' I said, and she swept round the corner – straight into the drawing room.

I closed the door and ran after her.

'You're paying for everything, aren't you?' she said to me, pulling up alongside the nearest sofa.

'Yes,' I said, after a pause.

(We had all by now noticed it.)

'You can pay for my petrol, then.'

'Of course,' I said, 'It's lovely to see you.'

(We none of us wanted to be the first to mention it.)

'My luggage is in the boot, which is open.'

X slipped discreetly out.

'Everyone,' I said, 'let me introduce Marcia.'

Marcia saw us all examining her. Her left eye was blackened; sealed almost to a slit.

'Do *not* ask,' she said.

'Of course not,' I said. 'Would you like a drink?'

'You have whisky?' she said.

'Double?' I said.

'Oh yes,' said Marcia. 'Big as it comes.'

X staggered in with a large blue suitcase with fat straps.

'Why don't you go and unpack?' I said. 'We'll have your drink ready for you when you –'

'I'll have it now, if you don't mind,' said Marcia.

'Yes,' I said.

'And maybe another one quite soon.'

'Good idea,' said William.

Edith looked at her, trembling with the desire to *know*.

'Bed-time,' said Ingrid.

Edith put up no resistance; though I could tell that – later in the month – she might. She did, however, say one small thing before she went to bed. 'Has everyone arrived now?'

Marcia downed her whisky in two gulps, separated only by a sigh like a cat hissing at another cat.

'Yes,' I said. 'Everyone's here.'

'Oh,' said Edith.

'Why?' I asked. 'Did you think someone else might be coming?' Of course, I could see that she had been hoping for a young man; someone of her own age who might fall in love with her, or whom she might fall in love with. As if to confirm my suspicions, Edith blushed when I said, 'I'm afraid it's just boring old us. Is that so terrible?'

'No,' she said. 'It's really not terrible at all.'

She disappeared quickly, looking a little more upset than I'd expected.

Conversation continued whilst I listened to her – her footsteps tripping lightly up the stairs, her footfalls banging along the landing, her bedroom door slamming.

'I wonder what that was about?' said Cecile to me, as an aside. She had been the only one, apart from myself, to notice Edith's huff.

Marcia let out a long, deep, rather ostentatious sigh.

Though it was rather difficult, we attempted to keep talking as before. The subject had been *How Nice the House Is*. We moved on to *How Convenient for the Beach*. Took a quick detour through *How Clean the Beach Is*. Then came back to the more refined *How Nice the Bedrooms in the House Are*.

When she had finished her second whisky, I showed Marcia to her room, even though it was only back through into the hall.

She mellowed, somewhat, when she saw the arrangements I'd made for her.

Note on Marcia's speech: It's not really Jamaican at all, except when she comically puts on a Jamaican accent. I'm a little disappointed by this, though I suppose it saves on the colourful apostrophes. Her main idiosyncrasy is to emphasise half a word at the expense of the other half. Hel*lo*. Peo*ple*. *Wel*come. *Never*. Like that.

In bed. About 11.30 p.m. The house is now at that stage novels often reach: everything's assembled, nothing's decided. One is poised on the precipice, blindfold, and one doesn't know whether it's a cliff or a ski-jump. One doesn't even know whether one has skis on one's feet. All that one can do, at such moments, is trust to the fact that one has done similarly mentalist things before, and survived. But that argument doesn't work when one is aware that although one has done similar things, one has never done anything half so extreme. I've put my reputation on the line by predicting what everybody is going to do. I haven't shirked: the Synopsis is there to be read. So far, I seem to have been fairly accurate.

2 a.m. Jazzed. Couldn't sleep. I can't stop thinking about Cecile's luggage. Does she really intend to dress herself for four whole weeks, using only two small suitcases? I am desperate for a sniff around her room. I have even considered breaking my one-week purity promise and going up into the attic for a look on the screens.

The house is very quiet at this time of night. I like it. I love it. Not that it's been particularly noisy during the day, so far; there haven't been any arguments that I've been witness to: Edith hasn't even slammed a door.

I am writing this sitting on one of the armchairs in the corner of the master bedroom. X is snoring warmly: I hardly had a chance to speak to him, all day. He seemed happy enough. The light coming from the screen of my laptop brilliantly and bluely matches that of the moonlight coming in through the window. The moon is almost full. With the top of the window open, I can hear the sea. The waves from this distance sound very like the moment one drops the lemon slice into a tumbler of really fresh gin and tonic.

At times like this, I'm glad I am what I am and do what I do. It's so beautiful to be alone, here; alone, in a manner of speaking. As I'm 100% certain there will be no bed-hopping this early on, I can relax. I'm not missing anything.

I really feel like going for a walk on the beach.

2.30 a.m. This is divine.

I've bought the laptop with me. I'm sitting here on the sand, cross-legged, in the middle of the night, with the sea in front of me, the house behind me, the moon above me, typing.

Typing words that are one day going to form the basis of a book; sentences that might, this one even, go straight in. First person to third to publisher to reader.

Sometimes, truly, it is an age of wonders.

Oh, and off to my right I can see Southwold lighthouse, four red flashes, a pause of twelve beats, four red flashes.

I close my eyes, and look at the eyelid traces of Southwold by night: like X-rayed teeth, conifer-shaped, in red, upside-down.

The waves spread out across the last, flat, sandy part of the beach, like white sheets drawn across a mattress.

Saturday

Day Three Week One

4.45 a.m. Awoken again by the dawn chorus. How I love it, still. Just. By the skin of my. By a hair's.

Despite the lack of sleep, I felt wonderfully refreshed when I woke up this morning. I stayed in bed until twelve; X brought me up tea and toast.

I don't think I missed a great deal. The guests had had breakfast – about which they were all highly complimentary. I told them their thanks should be directed towards the Chef, and that I'd been asleep while the preparations were being made.

'Will there be a breakfast like that every day?' Marcia asked.

'Of course,' I said, 'and a dinner, too. For lunch, I'm afraid we have to picnic. But as it's not a formal sit-down affair, I thought people would prefer to fend for themselves.'

'I should think so,' said Fleur.

There were a few grumbles about the absence of a TV.

Weather today not very good – quite bad, actually. Very low grey sky, a thumping wind and everywhere the idea of rain. Reminds one they have winter here, too; *real* winter, not muggy London winter.

1 p.m.-ish. Oh dear. I was in my study (the Master Bedroom) just now when there was a knock upon the door. I answered, and I found it to be Cecile. I was delighted, of course; the idea of her coming to seek me out, wanting a *tête-à-tête*... But then, lurking behind her, I saw Edith. 'May we come in?' asked Cecile.

'Of course,' I said, and stepped back. I have been very wary of allowing anyone into the Master Bedroom, *à cause de la* hatch, painfully visible, in the ceiling.

Edith looked incredibly glum, as she has the whole past day; ever since Marcia's arrival, in fact. I hadn't consciously linked the two things – apart, as I said, from believing she might be disappointed I hadn't invited a boy of her age.

'We'd like to talk to you,' said Cecile, 'about the sleeping arrangements.' Stunned – what could they possibly have to say?

'I'm not a child any more,' interrupted Edith, with a sob, 'I'm bored of being a child. I thought I was going to be treated *properly*.'

'You shall be,' placated Cecile, 'I'm sure.' She put her arm around Edith, and they sank back onto the counterpane – making hardly a dent. 'You'll have understood by now,' said Cecile, 'I'm sure someone as sympathetic as you can't fail to see the problem.'

This had me for a moment, then I realised. 'Look,' I said, 'it's Clea–, it's her mother that decides when Edith goes to bed. I don't think it's really in my power to interf–'

'I don't *care* when I go to bed,' moaned Edith, quite passionate, 'I really don't care at all – I don't want to sit around with all your boring talk and your being superpolite. But I'm not going to sleep in a *baby's* room.'

Cecile was looking at me, a little shocked that I hadn't managed to decipher the problem. Honestly, how could I? 'Edith would like to be moved,' said Cecile. 'We understand there is a spare room. We've had a look at it.' (It was true: I had foolishly left the daughter's room unlocked.) 'Edith likes it. She'd be much happier there.'

'There are toys on the shelves and silly wallpaper and the bed's too small,' Edith wailed. It took me a moment to realise she was still describing the nursery.

I turned away from them, stalling. ~~The spare room for Simona – for when she finally made the break from William. It would give her refuge, for a night or two, before he left, and she moved back into their room; or (if that pained her too much) someone else moved into their room, and she into the room thus vacated. This rearrangement not only ruled that switch out (would Simona be prepared to move into the nursery? wouldn't that be ceding all the dignity to William? wouldn't that be capitulation rather than triumph?), it also put into the daughter's room someone who was quite likely to rearrange and damage things.~~

This may read a bit unsmoothly if we don't put something in to replace it. I suggest something like, "I had given the Owners my promise that no one would sleep in that room; plus the fact it was a child, and I'd promised no children. What could I do?"

I turned back, about to say no. But Edith looked so beautifully upset, and Cecile's big eyes were turned towards me in what was, for the moment, supplication but which, in a moment, could become defiance. If Victoria were to stand a chance of the intimacy with Cecile that she wished, it was clear that here was a concession she was going to have to make, etc.

'Of course,' I said, 'you can move in there whenever you like.'

Grief to joy can be the shortest of steps, when one is young. She beamed, herself like a little lighthouse. Cecile smiled, too – remembering, no doubt, how small things had for her, once, bulked so large they blotted out all light; remembering the relief of their quick removal. 'Thank you,' said Edith, 'thank you thank you.'

'Well,' I said, 'you didn't have to get all miserable about it; you only had to ask.'

'I'll move in straight away,' said Edith.

'And I'll tell everybody you've moved,' said Cecile.

'One thing,' I said, 'the Owners of this house...' And I explained. Edith listened with comical solemnity. I think she'd have liked me to make her take some sort of vow, a pledge to defend the daughter's bedroom against all damagers. To gratify her, I asked, 'Do you promise?', and she put her hand on her heart, she really did, and said, eyes closed, 'I *promise*.' And that was that.

'Thank you,' said Cecile, as they left. Her eyes were still glistening. She took my hand and gave it a squeeze. I'd hoped she might now stay for a chat; acknowledging the lack of perspective in Edith's *naïf* world-picture; a gentle confidence or two, about how we remembered being girls ourselves – the passions felt, insults suffered – that was all it would have taken. But she went out with Edith, and within a few seconds I heard them opening the door to the daughter's room.

Standing listening for another five minutes, I held onto the hope that once Edith was installed Cecile would return. She didn't. I heard the door to the daughter's room close. No footsteps departed. Clearly, Cecile was at least temporarily as installed in there as Edith.

All this fuss and I don't know for why. The Nursery is perfectly nice; a little childish for Edith, I'd have to admit – the ballerina wallpaper, the letters-of-the-alphabet curtains. Wall-shelves filled with children's books; an almost complete set of Enid Blytons. On the mantelpiece, about a hundred Whimsies (small brown animal china collectibles – simpering squirrels, doting doves and such). A large painting upon one wall, of a doe-eyed Indian squaw. The bed in the corner beside the door is single and narrow; as if Edith were going to need anything else! The wardrobe has hearts cut into the top and diamonds cut into the bottom. In fact, the whole room has a Wonderland feel to it: if I were to sleep there, I'm certain I'd wake up every morning murmuring, 'You're nothing but a pack of cards! You're nothing but a pack of cards!'

Edith does not wear and never has worn an Alice band. She's one of the unSloaniest children I've ever met. I think she's able to fix things with her hands, knows how the insides of other things (which she can't fix) work – in theory. Her mother has brought her up to be a good little boy. Which, I suppose, is why she took so violently against her girlish prison.

Mind you, the spare room isn't all that different. Instead of the Enid Blytons, there's a full set of Jilly Coopers (*Imogen, Polly...* etc). This was the room the Owners' teenage daughter occupied, before she left for boarding school. The wallpaper here is indeed Laura Ashley; it's altogether very 1970s soft-focus. Colour-scheme is faded peach. The bed has a flouncy Spanishesque valence, and the curtain-strings are ended with village fête pom-poms. The paperbacks are faded and on soft pulpy paper. I feel I could sleep in here – sleep very well, and have very erotic dreams about teenage boys. The carpet is thick and orangish, like a shaggy wool thing that one might make at school, or a puppet from an old Children's TV programme. There is a dressing table with three mirrors in front of the window, which looks out over the front drive. There are decal stickers on the glass, faded almost to white: ponies. And the thumbtacks in the walls bear witness to what must once have been a serious collection of *Horse and Pony* centrefolds.

There is a stable halfway up the drive, and a large field in which the Owners once kept their daughter's horse. It died about two years ago, they told me. (In fact, they told me a great deal more about the horse – Lilac – than they did about the daughter.)

The daughter's room has a fuggy atmosphere, and feels overheated even when it's cold. The furniture is all in pine. I can't see how Edith could find it in any way attractive. The wardrobe is full of the Owners' daughter's out-grown clothes. When she moved away, her mother must have moved them all back in. In hopes of what, I have no idea; for surely no one is ever going to wear them again.

On the dressing table is a silver framed photograph of a pretty girl with flicked blonde hair. She is about ten and has braces on her teeth.

Help! Just now, Marcia asked to have a look round, *upstairs*. Alan offered to carry her, on his back; she accepted. So, wherever they went, I went with them – to show them around, the temporary lady of the house.

As we entered each room – the daughter's, Cecile's, William and Simona's, Henry and Ingrid's, the nursery, X and mine – Marcia absolutely *raped* it with her eyes. She knew this was probably the only chance of a look-see she was going to get, and she really did take *everything* possible from it.

By the time we got to the Master Bedroom, I was quite terrified. She would spot the hatch! She couldn't fail to spot the hatch!

I opened the door, Alan carried Marcia over the threshold. It was like a party game: Marcia gets two minutes of observation, after which she has to name as many objects in the room as she possibly can.

I thought I'd got away with it, but no: her eyes groped their way up to the ceiling. 'And that?' she said, pointing towards the hatch, 'What's up there?'

I was ruffled, but it didn't show. 'You know,' I said, 'I'm not really sure. I think it's just an attic.'

She looked at it, longingly. I was worried that getting up there was about to become a challenge in inverted commas, and you know how disabled people are when faced with a 'challenge'.

'It's padlocked,' I blundered.

Marcia looked at me, with all the rough penetration she had previously reserved for the bedchambers.

'So you've tried it then,' she said.

'Of course,' I said, 'Wouldn't you?' I thought this was a gaffe, but Marcia quickly said, 'Oh yes.'

Luckily, that brought us to the end of the tour. Alan carried Marcia downstairs again. 'Thank you,' she said, 'Now I feel I really *know* the house.'

Was I wrong, or did she look directly through me when she said those words? X-ray vision, for that second, didn't seem too bizarre a voodoo for her to have mastered.

Note on Marcia: A while before this we had a brief chat, in the hall. I was curious to get to know her a little better, and eventually to turn the conversation to her black eye. Her friendliness was of the politely evasive sort, however – she has brightened up considerably since her wrathful arrival: she *loves* the house. As for the guests, from what I've seen she gets on best with Fleur. Did I predict this? I think I did.

Because of the bad weather, because everyone has stayed inside, the drawing room has been occupied by the men; the kitchen by the women (apart from Chef, who mysteriously seems never to be there – apart from the hour before dinner).

Description: It is a very comfortable kitchen of the kind that anyone who liked cooking would be happy to cook in. There is a colour scheme throughout, dark blue and off-white: dark-blue Le Creuset, dark-blue Aga; off-white plates, off-white walls – all somewhat seventies. One imagines the food that comes out of here as being, for the most part, wholesome, fat-sliced, thick-sauced. It is a kitchen which doesn't hedge, when it comes to calories. Modernity intrudes in the shape of a large microwave oven, pushed back upon one of the work surfaces. It doesn't look as though it's ever been used, and Chef, I know, thinks it anathema.

I think it's the table and chairs that drew us (the women) here in the first place. (By 'the women' I mean Fleur, who seems definitely to be avoiding Alan – which is a good thing; it shows he can still stir emotion in her. Marcia came to join Fleur, and the others, including myself, flocculated around them.) It is a large deal table, which has had years of being used as a worksurface, and is chopped and rubbed soft as granny's hands. It is surrounded by eight Windsor chairs, looking like strange mutations of very delicate cartwheels: some have higher backs than others, and I'm still trying to work out whether there is a pecking order as to who possesses the most thronelike; or whether, as one might expect with women, there is in fact an inverse pecking order, where possession of the throne is seen as vulgar and the lowest, meanest seat is the most desired of all.

Each of us has her habits, her ways. When Marcia sits at the table, she removes all her rings (she has about eight, mostly silver and thick) – as if she were going actually to cook, to knead dough for patties or slice up some saltfish. She arranges them in a semi-circular pattern in front of her, which I can only – I am ashamed to say – assume symbolises a rainbow. There is indeed something of the hippie-come-lately about Marcia: the kind of woman who joins environmentalist organisations just before they close down due to incompetent management (taking her sub with them; spending it on a round of commiseration organic real ales).

Fleur, perhaps self-conscious about the wedding ring, which she still wears, twists it incessantly. This is the sort of detail which, in my fiction, I would find hackneyed – it has been used too many times to suggest anxiety, loneliness, in women; I would pick something else – I can't think of anything right now.

Of us all, Cecile makes most use of the arms of her Windsor – leaning back with her hands gracefully disporting themselves upon her lap, in the air. Her gestures are as expressive, as elaborate, as refined, as her background would lead one to expect. If style is perfectly assimilated affectation, Cecile has style. She can take something as simple as the *moue*, and turn it into *une chose* entirely her own. Her shrug is beyond compare.

Ingrid has the remarkable ability to make of sitting both pose and total lack of pose, like a cat: one can't really accuse her of playing up to any idea of herself, but neither can one throw the charge of naturalness at her. Of all of us, it is she, I think, who is most consciously sitting in a way that acknowledges that the only people in the room are women. She is attempting, I would say, to appear feminine, receptive, *sisterly*. It doesn't quite work, for her beauty – as I'm sure she's aware – does all her rebuffing and smarming and crushing for her. None of us feels comfortable sitting beside her, as we all know the invidiousness of comparison. Without admitting it, we prefer to sit opposite her – as if we were in a gallery with benches and she were a painting we'd come a long way to see.

The only non-avoider is Edith, who is quite prepared to allow her appearance to be tested against that of her mother. Instinctively she knows that, time passing, the benefit will accrue upon her side. Whatever her mother possesses and is losing, she too possesses, plus youth. However, Edith's preferred place is anywhere she can observe Cecile. She is already adopting a *repertoire* of entirely French gestures, which are comic (as sophisticated beyond her understanding); unless gestures *themselves* bring understanding, in which case her learning curve is vertiginous.

As for me, I have no idea how I appear. I slouch, I think – but that association may merely come from my proximity to a surface around which human beings may gather to eat. During my adolescence, I believe my father addressed more dinner-table remarks to my backbone than he did to me. (Keep.)

A small amount of smoking goes on in the kitchen, but those doing it stand by the window over the sink – one of the ones looking out over the garden; and when they are done, they douse the evil red circle under a whoosh of tap water.

The room smells fragrantly of the first few Edinburgh-fresh puffs, not the dreggy gray Liverpool smog-smell of ashtrays.

What do we talk about? Well, I'd like to record some specific conversations, but I can't be bothered; nothing all that interesting has been said. A great deal of the time, so far, we have talked about different kinds of food; the weather; the garden; the beach; Southwold; what the men can possibly be talking about in the other room; holidays; our journeys up there; the house itself; other houses with which it bears compare. (Cecile does not join in with this last topic.) There have been casual intimacies but no real confidences; those will, I hope, come later.

The drawing room is large, oblong and full of greenish light coming through from the garden. At one end is the long dining table, able to accommodate all of us at once; at the other is a countrified fireplace, around which the male inhabitants of the house naturally gather. Three sofas, with gaps between for entrance and exit, surround it: three deeply squishy sofas, which match – they are all dark red velvet. They are wonderful – I would like to steal one of them at the end of the month, have it carted back to London: these sofas seem to be ready to suck up all secrets that are uttered on them, they are so acoustically dense. The atmosphere they create is one of wombic cosiness, which must be why the men like it so much – big babies that they are. Alan was first to colonise them. The chimney breast is of raw brick, and there are – I have to admit it – beams visible in the white of the ceiling; though they have not been Tudorised – they, too, are raw: a wood that is dustily light. The walls are whitewashed. Blah. Paintings. The Owners' taste in art isn't too bad, really. I think there's even a Bomberg somewhere, or something very like it. The floor is flags, millstone-smooth, carpet-like; so smooth one almost wants to be a child and caper on them. In the mornings, however, they can be dagger-cold.

The drawing room is a room that doesn't make one feel guilty about smoking. (I've had one or two; cadged off William, I confess.) In fact, it makes one feel that smoking is one of the two or three main points of life – talking whilst smoking.

Already, the men all have acknowledged sofa-places. They sit and talk, about almost nothing as far as I can make out. They are competitive, in that pointless male way, but I don't think any decisive battles have yet been fought out between them. Masculinity is so tiresome, and it takes up so much time – time that could much better be spent being interested in other people, and in what they have to say for themselves. X, as my partner, and as an all-round Alpha Male, has a certain precedence. But there are other hierarchies to be considered. Henry is the most comparable masculine article. William is the eldest, has most hair, and hates to be seen taking anything from anybody. Alan forces himself upon no-one, man or beast. How it will all work itself out, I have no idea at present. It's not what I'm primarily interested in – *that* is the intersexual relations; which, in turn, is the only reason the men are here. Without a mixture of the sexes, there may be *élan* but there is no *éclat*. Women will be the emotional structure of the house, men the decoration.

~~No, I don't know if there's anything interesting going on between the men; I don't know if there's ever anything *that* interesting... But they fascinate me, in a strange way: when I look at them all together, in a group, I feel like I'm watching a Nature Programme – they seem so stylised. As women, we advertise our fragility (because we're not really fragile; we're a lot bloody tougher than they are); we add little glissandi to each of our gestures – our hands move through the air in arabesques and sinuosities. For the men it's all hunched business-as-usual; they can't admit grace – grace notes. Which makes me wish we had a gay man here. I should have made sure to include one. (It's not as if I didn't try.) At least camp brings with it a certain expressiveness.~~ Either this or the next paragraph must go. Take your pick.

The men in the drawing room seem to be having a plain-speaking, plain-thinking competition – as if they were all American plainsmen. Although we *know* they couldn't kill and skin a buffalo, they have to pretend that they could. They're effete European Englishmen – women have spent centuries domesticating them, their species. Yet they still bring with them a whiff of the wild; or of game – they smell gamey. Often, I feel sorry for them: all those little things we had to force them to invent; all those deceptions we had to perfect – like the notion they had in some way spent history oppressing us, rather than being our hapless slaves.

The drawing room is the room in the house (despite the men) where one most wishes to stay. If the weather is good, however, the garden will inevitably draw one outside: the garden is inexorable; and once in the garden, the garden says, 'You will only appreciate me fully after a walk on the beach.' And so to the sea, which makes one look back at the house and think how lovely it would be to be inside, away from the vertigo of the wet horizon – imagining the sailors being churned around, and the miles of no culture, no decent words, only grunts and rope-burn.

Early afternoon. I've been naughty – bad-naughty – I've been trying to find out who carried Cecile's suitcases upstairs. I'm sure it wasn't *her*, as she came straight into the kitchen where she talked to me; and by the time, a few minutes later, she went to unpack, they had already been taken up. I never saw her thanking anyone for doing this, though no doubt she did. Detective-like, I set out to find out whodunnit. X, I was able to ask directly: *No*. For William, I asked Simona – she said ~~he hadn't even helped with her suitcase, let alone anybody else's. (He is such a beast.)~~ [she was sure he would have, if he'd been asked, but he wasn't, so hadn't.] With Henry, I made a joke of it, 'You've turned into a proper little bell-boy...' I said. 'But I've hardly carried anything at all,' he said. 'What?' I said. 'Not even those tiny little things of Cecile's?' 'Not even those,' he said, and went back to his book, the Arden *A Midsummer-Night's Dream*. The Chef, I was able to confirm by various timings, had been all along in the kitchen.

Of the men, that left only Alan – and Alan it turned out to have been. I managed finally to certify this by observing, out in the garden, just before dinner, while he was smoking, what an interesting thing it was, comparing everybody's luggage: how much about them one could tell. After a little more flimflam, I said, 'Cecile's suitcases, for instance, are so perfectly tiny.' I was going to say, 'One wonders how much they weighed.' But Alan said, promptless, 'Not um heavy, though. I carried them upstairs for her. They hardly felt like they had anything inside at all.' 'Really?' I exclaimed, unable for the moment to appear calm. I was schoolgirl-frenzied in my curiosity. 'I expect she's having the rest of her stuff sent on.' '*Sent on,*' said Alan, 'can you still do that?' 'If you're rich enough,' I said, 'you can do anything they did in the past.' 'Is Cecile rich, then?' 'Vastly,' I said, allowing myself to be possessed fully by the gossip-voice, 'I think she was once married to someone incredibly wealthy: an Italian film director, somebody like that.' 'Really?' said Alan. 'Well, you know her a lot better than I do. She doesn't strike me as particularly um affluent.' 'That's taste for you,' I said. 'Real wealth, deep wealth, is very hard to spot.' 'I suppose we'll find out eventually,' said Alan. 'Don't ask,' I said, panicked back into being the hostess. 'I may be um a little crude,' said Alan, 'but I don't go round asking people what they earn, or are worth.' I think I offended him, a tiny bit.

A message in my Suggestions Box, signed by six of the guests, requesting a 'House Meeting'.

Although I've been trying to resist Studentiness, in whatever form it raises itself, this petition had undeflectable momentum. Hence, we gathered in the kitchen at 4.30 p.m. – rumour having brought those direct invitation had missed. This, incidentally, included the Maid and the Chef. The petition had obviously been put together by the first two signatories: Fleur and Marcia.

After simply saying that I hoped everyone was still enjoying themselves, I gave them the floor.

'It's this,' said Fleur. 'We're unhappy,' said Marcia. 'With the cooking arrangements and whatever,' completed Fleur.

So *that's* what they've been talking about. I looked amusedly at X: they were quite the double-act, weren't they?

'So what we'd like to suggest is...' 'Is that once a week we give the Chef the night off...' 'And cook for ourselves.' 'Marcia and I would be happy to go first.' 'On Saturday nights,' said Marcia. 'Starting tonight,' said Fleur. 'So, we better get busy,' said Marcia. 'We thought,' said Fleur. 'But it's only a suggestion,' they said together, like Shakespearean servants.

Everyone looked at the Chef, who did his best to look chuffed rather than smug; failed. 'Sounds good to me,' he said. Then everyone looked at me.

'It's a wonderful idea,' I said, 'I just wish I'd thought of it myself.'

There was one of those general murmurs, with which groups of middle-class people swathe an agreed-upon idea – the non-Westminster equivalent of the MPs' jowl-wobbling *hear hear!* No one uttered any comprehensible words, they just made noises in the key of D major.

'Well,' I said, 'if that's it...' Of course it wasn't. I should have been expecting an ambush. Underhand: Saturday dinners had been the hand, we were about to see the under.

'We're not happy about being cleaned up for, and babied, and generally pampered,' said Fleur. 'It's not right,' said Marcia.

Those with the better manners among us were mortified. Cecile, however, was dignified enough to appear perfectly bland – I cannot imagine the social-psychic effort this must have cost her. If this were a subject to be raised, then certainly the servants should not have been present. The Chef hid his annoyance behind an amused-seeming smirk; the Maid looked to the flags of the floor, burning.

'Washing-up, for example, should be done by the people that created the *mess* in the first place,' said Fleur. 'And it's no trouble, really, to make your bed when you get up in the morning,' said Marcia.

'Then what would you leave for Elsie?' I said. (Elsie was the Maid's name; I felt referring to her as 'the Staff' wouldn't go down very well.)

'Everything else,' said Marcia. (*Else does everything else*, I thought.) 'Everything reasonable,' said Fleur. 'We could have rotas for what we want to do,' said Marcia.

'We don't have rotas,' I said, 'we have servants. We have Elsie.'

'These are not servants,' said Marcia. 'These are free human beings, just like us.' More smirking from the Chef, more blushing from Elsie.

'No,' I said, 'unlike us, they are being paid, in cash, for being here.'

'And you?' said Fleur. 'You're not being paid?'

'I'm working, too,' I said.

'That's not good enough,' said Fleur.

'I'm afraid,' I said, 'that being pampered is a torture you shall just have to learn to endure. I have deliberately tried to arrange things so that everyone in this house has as much leisure-time as possible. With the best will in the world, Elsie is not my subject: *you* are – all of you. And I have no wish to write about you doing the washing-up. Subject closed.' I smiled, hostess-like. 'Is there anything more?' There wasn't.

It was good that I was firm with them; but they didn't half mutter amongst themselves as they sidled off.

A Saturday-night cooking rota has been agreed upon, during a post-Meeting meeting in the garden. (I saw it was starting up, ran out so as not to miss anything.)

Rather than trying to avoid the chore, as most sensible people would, there was wide competition between the guests to ensure that they got to labour.

The order is this: Marcia assisted by Fleur; Cleangirl; Edith assisted by Cecile; X and I.

Why? After all I'd said to the contrary. Why? Well, I had to be seen to join in; I felt it necessary to intervene.

'Surely,' I said, 'the final meal should be mine to make?'

Almost everyone agreed. (Fleur, what a surprise, thought it should be something cooked by all the guests, collectively.)

Since she arrived here with that ridiculous piece of turf, I can't help but notice that Fleur has turned into a complete parody of all the worst aspects of herself. If it were intended satirically, it would be a vicious caricature. One wonders why – perhaps sheer and simple self-hatred. Her censoriousness is ceaseless: she can turn closing the curtains into a morality play. Every other thing has to be a good lesson for poor Edith – who must be thinking she'd be better off going back to the convent.

Confession. Still no takers. Hoped for Cecile; she didn't come.

4.10 p.m. Marcia and Fleur, out on the lawn, smoking, were earlier observed in deep confab about ingredients; blue biros scrawling on scrap paper. Ever since the Meeting, they have been in a total frenzy about tonight's meal – although the Chef said he was quite happy to postpone his night off until tomorrow. This, at least, would give him time to get something organised. They insisted, however, and sent him home – with nothing to do. I wonder if he has a girlfriend. He is very good-looking, in that slightly criminal way of chefs. I wonder if Cleangirl has noticed this; he has certainly noticed her. He made biscuits earlier this afternoon. She doesn't eat biscuits. Nice try, though.

Shortly after 7 p.m. The kitchen was Hades when I went to have a look in there just now.

'Pepper – the cayenne pepper!' Marcia screams, as I glide through the door.

'I'm sure we bought some,' says Fleur, reasonably.

'I'm sure we did,' laughs Marcia, 'but where has it hidden itself?'

'Hello,' I say. 'Can I help?'

'Find the cayenne pepper,' says Cleangirl, who is at the sink, washing rice. So she's in on this, as well. Isn't that cheating?

I look around, helpless. 'I'm sure the Owners must have some somewhere,' I say. 'Isn't there a spice rack?'

'Good idea,' says Marcia. She is slicing peppers on a chopping board resting across the arms of her wheelchair.

'Here it is,' says Edith. She had been standing so quietly, I hadn't noticed her there before.

'Fan-*tas*-tic, *mar*-vellous, wonder-*ful*,' shrieks Marcia.

'Which is it?' asks Fleur. 'Is it the one we bought?'

'I think so,' says Edith. 'It was just over here, behind the salad leaves.'

'It doesn't matter at all, at *all*,' says Marcia, 'put it by the stove.'

'Can I help?' I ask again.

Fleur looks desperately at Marcia. 'How about you make us some drinks?' she says.

'Oh goodie,' says Edith.

'*Not* you, she meant,' says her mother.

Humbly, I take drinks orders.

10.20 p.m. Supper was late but, Victoria had to admit, delicious. Banana fritters – which were for a starter. Jerk chicken with rice and peas. Something on the side approximating to ackee and saltfish. Such colossal portions! The guests drank Red Stripe at first, then moved on to rum.

The guests were all still at the dining table, bloated and trying not to burp, when Fleur started up – completely, for once, unprovoked:

'I've been thinking a lot about it, Victoria, in the last day or so,' she said, in a fake-gentle voice; but the sharp singing-ringing tension in it – like a saw being played with a violin bow – made everyone shut up to listen. 'And I've decided I'm not going to help you at all. I've brought some novels with me, ones I've always wanted to read – and, if the weather's good enough, I'm just going to sit out in the garden and read them. And that's *all* I'm going to do. At night, I'm going to eat some lovely food and then go back to my lovely bedroom – on my own – and sleep – on my own.' She did *not* look at Alan. 'So, try to get some material out of that.'

'Well,' Victoria said, 'you're being an absolute gift right now. All this is going straight in.' This remark garnered some laughs, and some slightly ashamed smirks.

'I'm going to stop being a character in your little power-project. From now on, I'm going to be boring-boring-boring old Fleur, who never does anything – with her life, with anything. You're paying for a nice quiet holiday for me, I think you owe me that, at least – after everything else.'

This was either a reference to Victoria's having stolen Charles Sweded, an early boyfriend of hers, or to Victoria semi-fictionalising her divorce, in Chapter Twelve of *Spaciousness*, or to that other thing, which will surely come up again later.

'Oh, Fleur,' Victoria said, 'can't you see what a *cliché* you are? What a *cliché* your life has become?'

'Well... can't *you* see how inhuman you are these days, Victoria?'

'I'm not your doll any longer,' Victoria replied.

'I don't even understand why you take the trouble to hurt me, these days. I mean, it's not as if I'm anything of a threat to you – even out here, with you doing your best to turn half your friends into instruments for popular amusement – and, in the process, turn them entirely against you, I've no doubt. I've done nothing to harm you, have I? If I have, tell me what it was. Did I lock you in cupboards or pull your hair? Why do you insist on constructing me as some kind of nightmare Victorian Governess, some kind of mutant Brontë sister? I'm not out of a book. I do really live in the real world. A realler world than yours, in any case. You wouldn't believe some of the things I have to cope with. And you're certainly incapable of making them up...'

'May I speak?' Victoria said.

'No,' Fleur replied, 'we haven't had an argument like this in years, have we? Not one where I stood any chance of winning. Up until now it's all been your snidey letters arriving a few days after Christmas and Easter – giving me no real way of responding. They're an onslaught of rain, a wall of rain, a rain of words, which is intended to leave me drenched and without shelter. You're never more eloquent than when you're being bitter; and the bitterer you become the more eloquent your writing becomes, and the fewer readers you have. Doesn't it hurt you to think of that? The larger your readership, the worse your writing. Your masterpieces have been masterpieces of spite, and I'm the only one who has ever read them. I've burnt them – I burnt them as soon as I'd finished tearing them up. Oh, I know you'll have been narcissistic enough to have kept copies. But they're not the real letters. They are unpublishable, unformed. In your soul, you rant: just like I'm ranting now. I can't express myself as well as you, and I'm glad I can't because somewhere along the line – the line of my life – I have to put what I can't express into love for the people around me, the children I teach. I *hold* them, I don't trap them in my plots. I simply put my arms around them, no doubt in a *clichéd* way, and I tell them everything is going to be all right, even though that's a *cliché* too, and I know that everything is *not* going to be all right, that it's going to be *nowhere near* all right, that it will be bloody awful for a long time if not for ever – and I do this for them, with my arms and my words, and do you know what? it *means* something. In my small, one-to-one, human way – which no one's going to remember when I'm dead, and no one reviews in the papers or discusses at dinner parties – and even the child will probably never remember (but might just feel a little more secure as an adult, without knowing why) – in my way, which isn't as "important" as yours, I try to contribute to other people's lives. Not in easing them through the evening's commute with a rip-roaring page-turner, but in really loving them. And I know you think it's amusing I don't have a husband to love, and that I can't seem to get one, but I have loved men, and some of them have loved me. But this – my life – isn't permanent. Neither what I do nor what you do will *really* last – not long, not so it matters. I think it's how people are feeling that's important. So, mock me, mock what I am, but never mock what I do – or what I try to do – what I believe in doing. Because I really do believe it, you know. I'm not just putting it on for effect. If it's a *cliché*, then I'm a *cliché*: Love is the most important thing in the world. It was a good enough moral for James Joyce, and it's a good enough moral for me. But perhaps you're better than either of us. You certainly seem to think so. Thank you, God bless and goodnight to one and all...'

'Finished?' Victoria asked, calm, so calm.

'Finished,' Fleur said, and got up from the table – out the door she went, slamming it behind her. Her final word echoed in the social Grand Canyon that was now gaping in the middle of the dining-room table. It echoed and echo-cho-choed; the tumbleweed blew; the vultures hopped closer. And then, the corpse (Victoria) unexpectedly spoke up. 'Ladies and gentlemen,' she said. 'My sister.' Never had Victoria known a silence like it. A glance at Edith showed her how thrilled, and appalled, our youngest guest was. 'After that performance, you will probably be sympathising with her – and thinking me a total bitch. Which isn't at all the case. By the end of next week, I predict, your sympathies will be equally divided; by the end of your stay, you will start to find her almost as frustrating as I do. Much as I love her, and I *do* love her, she's as mad as a stick, and twice as brittle. There are reasons for this, which I'm sure she'll tell you, if you ask; but only ask if you've got the whole afternoon free. What she'll say is mostly truthful – though if you'd like a little perspective, some outside or inside knowledge, then come to me: I *know*. Fleur has had a tragic life; at least, according to Fleur, she has. I would argue, on the contrary, that Fleur's life contains elements of tragedy which, because they happen to Fleur, and are reacted to in the way Fleur reacts to things, are deprived of whatever grandeur or dignity they might otherwise have. For others they would be debts, these events, they would be chunks gone missing from their hearts; for Fleur they are collateral – a whole Fort Knox of woes that bankrolls her against any further involvement or pain.' She looked towards Alan, who was using his teeth to do yet further damage to his cuticles. 'All that it's necessary for you to do to get her to invoke this wealth is yourself to pain her in the slightest, even unintentionally. If you do, she will immediately draw a large cheque – and buy whatever she can of you: your sympathy, your pity. It will be a takeover bid; if necessary, a hostile one. And the more time that goes on without you asking or paining her, the more interest her capital accrues. I'm in the bank, myself; I went in there a long long time ago – every tug of the hair, every cutting word; somewhere in the credit or debit columns – though it is always hard to tell which is which, as the things which one deprives Fleur of become her choicest possessions. If I wasn't the first to hurt her, I have certainly become the most consistent of her tormentors. However much I try to assuage things – for instance, by asking her along here to this – Fleur uses me merely as a source of new riches, of massive woe, an America, an Indes. Do you think, knowing what I know, and what I've now told you, I would have let her anywhere near here if I hadn't been prepared to put up with behaviour of the sort we've just witnessed? And so will you. You'll find out very soon – the only relationship Fleur allows anybody to have with her is betrayer, is Judas; unless she changes. If you think you're becoming good friends, watch out – anything, any incident, could give her the excuse to cash you in. If you don't believe me, don't – all I ask you to do is wait and watch: Fleur will claim her first victim – I should say "second victim", shouldn't I? this evening makes it clear I'm the first – the second victim will be claimed by the end of next week. And that's all I have to say.'

The table broke up in silence. Victoria went upstairs and typed, in tears. X comforted her in a slightly distant way.

Must keep going. Cecile wore... two outfits today. This morning, a simple pair of blue trousers with an artist's smock. This evening, a white cashmere twin set with khaki slacks and alligator-skin loafers.

Marcia sent Edith up to see that I was all right. Very kind.

I think Fleur is partly angry because she's missing Audrey, who cannot be persuaded back into the house. She greyly haunts her tangerine box full of grass, down towards the bottom of the garden. I see Fleur, taking her bowls of milk. A blanket bed has been created for her in the shed. Alan has promised to do something about Domino; investigate kennels.

Sunday

Day Four Week One

Woke up with a huge sheet-crease down the middle of my face: the older I get, the longer these take to go. This one, I think, will remain until lunchtime. I wonder Cecile doesn't come downstairs every morning with a face like a relief map of the Lake District.

Cats are doing us a noble service by killing so many birds: if they didn't, we'd all be deaf. The dawn chorus this morning was like God's tinnitus; quite unbelievable.

8 a.m. Terrible. Fleur has persuaded everybody to accompany her to church. I didn't know about this until about five minutes ago.

'Fleur said she thought you wouldn't be interested,' said Edith, casually.

No time to think about it now. I must go. Will report back later.

10.20 a.m. Wasn't as bad as I'd thought.

I've found out now how it started: After Fleur stormed out last night, Marcia went to talk to her. Fleur mentioned her intention to go to church, Sunday morning. Between them, they decided to make a proper excursion of it.

Cut to today. Apparently Fleur suggested it first to Cecile. Over breakfast. Or rather, she asked Cecile if she ever went to church. (As far as I know, Cecile has no religion – apart from *la mode*.) The conversation turned to what she and Marcia were intending. Local church. Picturesque. Cecile, good-mannered as always, said what a marvellous idea, and asked if Edith would be coming? Fleur wasn't sure, so went to ask. Edith, apparently, was quite keen, too; despite going to a convent for her education. Then, as I said above, I heard from Edith. X said he'd amble along, too – though he gave no reason why. Perhaps Edith asked him, and their small flirtation has begun.

So, in the end, it was Fleur, Cecile, Edith, Cleangirl, Marcia, X and myself. I wasn't surprised that Alan didn't come; it was too much Fleur's thing for him to feel comfortable with it. No one had seen anything of Simona and William. They sleep late, and it didn't seem fair to wake them. Henry was – I don't know where, exactly.

We set off. Lovely clear-skyed day, unlike the bulk of yesterday.

To begin with, I was angry with Fleur: she seems to be doing a very good job of hijacking my characters. So far, *I* haven't been very successful in getting them to do anything. In the event, however, church seems a good place to have gone. Nothing happened, of course; nothing ever *does* happen in church. (Christenings, weddings and funerals excepted – and they're *ex post facto*.) But I was able to imagine us as an Edwardian weekend party, with all the romance and class conflict that entails. The problem is, we're meant to be the Bloomsbury set – who would *never* have been caught engaging in Anglicanism.

Edith looked very pretty, in a simply cut dress; her mother wore something very minimal which hung stunningly, pale grey. And while we were walking to the church, Cecile paid Cleangirl some elegant compliments, none of which succeeded in making her blush. One of the most terrifying things about Ingrid is that she seems to be without personal vanity. She takes a compliment to herself as if it were a compliment to the universe in general. 'Yes,' Cleangirl seems to say, 'isn't it good that there are at least *some* tolerably attractive people in the world.' ~~(Alternative: It is as if she were a chef, and one weren't complimenting her *per se* but her dish, her cuisine.)~~ Not necessary. I think your jealousy of Ingrid has, by now, been clearly established.

Of all her good features, Edith's eyes are her best. Her problem is, she can't quite, as yet, live up to them. They are blue at the top and green at the bottom – at least, that is how I remember them (sitting here in my Master Bedroom study). Looking into her gaze is like looking out across some fantastic Irish dreamscape. Hence, her emotions aren't really *emotions* at all, they are internal weather – she has sunny periods and storms, frosts and thaws. Her mother's eyes are pure eggshell, her father's, *corduroy* green or brown. How they between them came up with Edith, I'm not entirely sure; all their complications seem absent from her. Somehow, merely by existing, she renders them (the complications, not her parents) irrelevant – unimaginable. *All one need do is be nice – be nice, and the world will be nice back*. Most amazingly, for Edith, so far, this dictum has been a success. One wonders, though...

Fleur and Marcia walked and wheeled ahead of everyone else. Fleur, I think, because she was worrying that the bringing-together of such a large congregation was going to make her late; Marcia, to prove a point – that she wasn't slower than the rest of us. The odd passer-by stared at Marcia; because of her chair or her blackness, I don't know.

Deciding to make the effort, I caught up with them. 'Good morning,' I said.

They replied, then went back to their conversation – which, for some reason, was about turnips. (I had hoped it would be about black eyes, street crime, domestic violence, etc.)

The church was just what I would have wanted it to be: a high, handsome, flinty building surrounded by a green and grey graveyard. The service, too, with dreadful sermon and dreary hymns, did not disappoint.

The Vicar was a tall man, with white hair and black eyebrows – a trait I've always found suspicious.

Fleur came out bizarrely invigorated. I suppose this is because she felt she had done her duty, or some such Fleur-ish thing.

What felt strange afterwards, having wasted an hour worshipping a God one doesn't believe in, was how it gave one's whole day a sense of being longer – of having greater possibilities.

I couldn't churchgo regularly, I'd be a hypocrite if I did, but I have to admit it made me feel as if something, however small, had been accomplished.

Lunch. Has become a diffuse affair. Some skip it altogether; rarely are more than four gathered together around Chef's salads, platters and soups. Very good gazpacho, today: garlicky-chesty feeling all afternoon.

2 p.m. As there is nothing better to do, I've decided to allow myself a little speculation as to Ingrid and Henry's marriage. It has always been a glamorous object to me. Someone, a man, once described his own marriage to me thus: 'It's like an electric plug. I'm one wire, the brown, the neutral; my wife's the other, the live, the blue. The appliance to which we're attached, which is our lives together, our house, our kids – that's fine, as long as the two wires never touch. If they did – pow! – there'd be a flash, a bang, they'd fuse and cease to function. As for the appliance, that'd probably be f****d.' The reason I've given this as an example (~~and I'll have to check with Scott if he minds me using it~~) is that I think Ingrid and Henry's marriage is different in every single way. Unless they are touching, constantly, there is no energy getting through to their appliance. I've seen them go through periods of sexual *ennui*. (I think they're going through one now.) Ingrid has told me about it, and the signs of it have been visible upon Henry. He looks terrible: harrowed by his own faithfulness. I can't *tell* you how much I've wanted to *help* him. But something always sparks them off again. I suppose that's why it is, after all, a marriage: because, unlike a relationship (be honest, Victoria – 'unlike every single one of my own relationships'), it doesn't just die; it regenerates, it resurrects. What fascinates me most is how both of them cope with the knowledge that, for a while at least, they've been dead – to themselves and to each other. Doesn't that make them afraid that, one day, they'll simply fail to come back to life? Or does it, instead, convince them that their marriage is immortal (invisible, naught changeth thee – has been banging around my head ever since this morning)? Whatever else, there is certainly very little touching going on between them at the moment.

Domino is most often to be found in the drawing room, lounging along the edge of one of the sofas. He is one of the most steppableon dogs I've ever known; I think he enjoys it – which characteristic he shares with Alan.

3 p.m. 3rd pers. Victoria *did* want to do this; she'd had her doubts, but now she knew she did. The colours seemed so bright in the garden, when she went out there carrying a cup of good coffee that she hadn't had to make for herself. The general world was, she felt, heightened, because it was all there for her to take in; if she didn't do her job, then the matter of this creation was pointless. Not Wherewithal or Southwold or the North Sea *per se*: but these people, here, at this time, in this combination. She felt, for almost the first time, reassured by the simple fact of her project.

Victoria was just at this point reaching the height of her happiness when Simona came out to see her. What Simona said was trivial, but at least it was something going on; Victoria felt she had better record it, as it might turn out to be useful. Simona said that Fleur had confessed to feeling some remorse about last night's outburst. (My sister and I did not say anything but 'Good morning' 'How did you sleep?' 'Very well, thank you' 'Good' this morning.) Reconciliation, if Victoria wanted it, was possible. Many others in the house, Simona said, were intent on playing peacemaker – not least, Marcia. Victoria said *thank you* to Simona, who left her author alone. A good editor knows when to edit himself or herself out of the text.

You don't know the half of it, yet.

As she watched Simona drift away, Victoria's mood turned. All at once, she remembered the dream she had been having when she woke up that morning. It wasn't very clear, only an image remained: of a man, quite clearly mad, climbing over the edge of a cliff, going downwards, his only hand-holds pieces of cloth held to the cliff-face by drawing pins, going down a bit, and across, and then beginning, whilst upside-down, with a ballpoint pen, to fill in a form, attached – like the T-shirt cloth – to the cliff-face by drawing pins.

Victoria didn't pretend to understand what the image meant, or what it said about herself – but something of the atmosphere of pointlessness that suffused it wafted out into the afternoon sunshine. She crashed; she crumpled. Everything which before had been reassuring now became threatening, like a played-with softkitten suddenly slashing out with newly discovered claws. Victoria almost stumbled back into the house; if she hadn't felt it overly melodramatic, and likely to cause her internal humiliation and embarrassment (before the jury of myself), she *would* have stumbled.

I was just flopping down onto one of the sofas in the drawing room, perhaps for a cry, perhaps just for a whimper, when Alan came in, Domino at his heels, nails a-clicking on the flags. I thought about making some excuse, and going upstairs. But Alan seemed keen to talk. 'I'm glad to catch you, um,' he said, 'alone; I've been meaning to ask, you see – about this tea-time four o'clock thing.'

'You tried to come the other day, didn't you?'

'Yes,' he said, 'that was, um, a bit embarrassing. At the moment it all feels too formal and off-putting. If other people didn't know you were going in, you'd be more likely to go – I'd be more likely to come.'

'I'm sorry,' I said, 'but that's just what confession's like – imagine being some little Catholic girl with her mother and grandmother in the pews outside. Waiting. Counting the seconds. Estimating the sins.'

'What?' said Alan, and as he lifted his head to drain the dregs of the thought, I tried to imagine him as a Catholic girl; I found it disconcertingly easy.

It was only now that I realised I'd called it *confession* out loud, to one of the guests. What a mistake.

'Well...' I said, about to give some jokey explanation.

'No,' said Alan, having taken in as much of it as he could without choking. He was awkward, but then Alan is always awkward. He sat down. Domino came close.

'Did you have something you wanted, in particular, to talk about?'

'Oh no-no-no,' he said, too-too-too quickly. 'Not to talk about, I don't; but ask.'

We were getting closer, but the thing was still hidden from sight – in a bush, down a well. 'Ask *me*?'

'Um, yes.'

'Ask away,' I said. Domino's nose was permanently a-sniffing of Alan's fingers, as if he had found a stupendously interesting scent there; I wondered naughtily what it might be. Alan looked over his shoulder, towards the French doors. 'No one's around,' I said.

Alan lunged up out of the sofa and serio-comically said, 'Do you mind?' He checked the doors for lurking listeners; found none; collapsed back down. He took – he did, he really did – a deep breath. 'Has um Fleur come to "confession"?'

'Of course not,' I said, 'we're not speaking, as you might have noticed.'

'Why did you ask her here?' he said.

'She's my sister,' I said, 'and besides –'

'But you two don't get on...'

'And besides, I needed to make up the numbers.'

'You did?'

'I had some drop-outs. Don't worry – *you* were in right from the start.'

'Oh, well, um, thank you, I suppose.' I waited; the technique the confessionals had already taught me. 'So...' Alan eventually dragged forth, 'you asked me and then, at the last minute, you asked Fleur.'

And then the realisation came. He was still full of hope. ~~in, like a stray child in dirty wellingtons – welcome but likely to make one angry: Hope.~~

'That's right,' I said.

When Alan finally came to it, it was really quite predictable.

'So she didn't ask you to ask me?'

I reached out to stroke his hand, console. 'No one had any influence over who I invited, and certainly not my sister.' This, to him, was bad news. He cupped one hand around his eyes, darkening them; the other dangled, for Domino to sniff. But it seemed that, as soon as Alan's Hope was reduced, the hand stopped smelling so doggily interesting. Domino decided to sit down, and made as big a performance of it as possible: tail-chasing, turning, circling, changing direction, settling, re-settling; and all of this took place in what he probably didn't even notice as a profound human silence.

When Alan took his hand away from his eyes, he seemed more relaxed – as if for him solid issues had melted away into the general swill of atmospheres. He restated, one final loud time, the theme of what I hoped was going to be his overture: 'Fleur didn't ask you to ask me here.'

'No,' I said, 'she didn't know you were coming until she walked into the kitchen and saw you there.'

Alan stood up. This was rather scary, as he is so tall. Domino stood up, too; and even the Dalmatian's head was higher than mine. I stood up. 'Is that all you wanted to ask?' I said.

Alan was distracted: the beach, and striding out, and thinking – his head was filled with such. He mumbled a reply, then turned and – dog-followed – ambled through the French doors and down the lawn.

I can't be wrong, can I? Until our conversation, Alan's Hope was that Fleur had asked me to ask him here – because she remembered him from my dinner party, because she thought of him as a prospect. This is great news. I have half my romance. Alan, no doubt, is a gloomy giant; he's hardly going to caper when I tell him his hunch is wrong. But now I know how he feels about my sister, I can concentrate all my attention upon her. However, she's so resistant to anything – anything coming from me – that I feel inclined to exert myself in trying to keep her and Alan apart. This might be my only way of forcing them together. Obversely, conversely, perversely, if Fleur detects me doing this, she will thwart me any way she can. So I shall have to be extra-subtle. A reconciliation scene with her may be necessary, however.

~~It's terrible. People no longer seem to have time to be emotionally complicated – or complex (that's more polite, isn't it?) Not in the *old* way – the way of Jane Austen, Henry James, Virginia Woolf. Back then, people sat around all day, talking, taking tea and finding finer and finer grains of subtlety in themselves. This loss, and it is a loss, is very dismaying – particularly for the novelist. Humankind spends most of its energy nowadays in attempting to simplify itself. And so our contemporary fiction is nothing but action; and action, after a while, becomes so so dull – because, basically, it's obvious. One knows in advance that any given writer is going to be obliged to follow the path of most resistance (just as their characters must follow that of the least). If the 'it' can be cranked up a notch, it will be: people will be chased, tortured, murdered. So what I'm saying to myself right now, here in this house, is this: 'I don't mind that nothing is happening; or that only small, almost infinitesimal things, are happening. Because this is exactly what, in some part of myself (a higher-up part), I've desperately wanted. Despite having assembled such a complexity of characters, such a plethora of plotlines. I've wanted to take them away from *doing*, and have them, for a while at least, just *be*. That is the space that this house, time, project, is intended to create: an Austenesque, Jamesian, a Woolflike space.' With Alan and Fleur, it starts to develop, to ramify.~~

Pretentious beyond belief.

It has just occurred to me how little I've written about Marcia and her disabilities; the reason for this being, they've hardly been a problem at all. She's clearly been disabled for so long that she knows how to make it inconspicuous. For instance, she gets up early and uses the downstairs bathroom before anyone else has need of it. After which, she rolls out onto the verandah and sits there watching the sky. If she has a blanket, then it's round her shoulders not across her legs. The dinner gong, at the beginning at least, always caused a starved stampede. Marcia, though, made sure to be at the table five minutes early, having come to an arrangement with the Chef. Soon, the wiser among the guests were watching Marcia for any sign of movement towards the table: once she was off, dinner was on. I should probably say something about the wheelchair itself: it's none of your National Health grey-plastic and grey tubular steel; no, it's almost Porsche-like – so sleek and sexy that one almost wants one for oneself (without, naturally, the inconvenience of incapacity). Black, moulded, with dark blue trimmings – quite the thing. 'It's German,' I heard her telling Fleur, 'and it cost me I can't even bear to tell you how much.' Then she told her. And I was a little shocked. For that, one could buy a small car – a new one, even. On chairs, when she shifts across, Marcia has an Alexander Technique cushion to support her lower back. And that's it.

The pub has become, is becoming, a bit of an issue. The men, who haven't so far agitated for very much at all, feel they are being prevented from going there; which is quite true, they are. This is all part of their attempts to outbloke one another. It's an ugly and undignified spectacle; part-football, part-farmyard. The whole thing is centred around cool, around infuriating lack of affect. And there are so many levels to male *insouciance*. To win points, one has to be seen doing something well; better yet, to be doing it very well without making an effort; or even better, to be doing it fantastically well without seeming to be one iota aware that one is doing it at all. Hence the line, fine and forever being trespassed, between supreme excellence and showing off. (A vertical line.) And hence the other line (horizontal) between triumph and (as they delightfully and revealingly put it) making a complete and utter fool of yourself.

This evening I attempted conversation with Marcia. I'd hardly got beyond, 'How are you?' when she started, like this: 'Don't seek me out – don't try to draw me out – don't try to find me interesting – don't look upon me as some authority, as "representative" – don't patronise me with your attention. If I'm boring, let me be boring. If you don't like me, *say* you don't like me; or be polite, and avoid me, as you would with anyone else. Ask yourself if we'd be friends anyway, without the plus factors. If we wouldn't, then tell me to f*** off out of your house – like you would any other black intruder.'

'If you think I think that then why did you come here in the first place?'

'You're a gift horse, and I'm not going to look you in the mouth.'

My first thought... well, it was anger. I hate being sponged off, unless it's by an attractive good-for-nothing young man. (That I'll forgive. That's my weakness, not his.) My second

Interrupted. I had a second thought, but I can't remember what it was. Frustration, maybe.

Depressed at Marcia. What if she refuses to speak to me? I strongly suspect that Fleur is turning her against me. What to do? I must make an effort. Charm. Subtle.

Dinner. Quiche. Much male muttering about pubs.

8.45 p.m. X just came in to tell me that everyone is gathering in the drawing room for a spontaneous party. No work to worry about on Monday morning is the general feeling. Just time to put some perfume on, join the grown-ups.

oh these peoplge i've inbigtted to this houjse are gjust so wondefful-lly lovelllypeople im glad they'r all here we"ve been having a little drinky or two and now itt's time fot bedddybyes bu t someone's in the bathgenrom now and ihav e a minute or two of typing to thype this in the dark an d to dsay – i"m go so gland i inivited who i dood d it' ds clll goin g to be gbe all riihhght!!!!!!!!!!!!!!!!!!

\\ps someone told me dsomthing very strange important who9ch i hvene' ttime to wrtupe down now but i shall tolmorrow. oh the sgossip here is just fjust fantasticallyt fuantasticQ!!!!

pps Cecilb;e wores somthingb reddish

Monday

Day Five Week One

Slept through the dawn chorus!

However, worse was to come – a great deal worse. These are the present contents of my head: every dentist's drill I have ever suffered or suffered nightmares about; the brass alarm clock I had at university whilst taking Finals; a carnival of woodpeckers; the Grimthorpe Colliery Brass Band; Snow White, hitting her high note over and over again; the Seven Dwarfs, trudging back and forth with sandpaper on the soles of their boots; a wedding disco; someone randomly firing off a staple-gun; a gypsy violinist or two; a sloth sliding slowly down an infinite blackboard, trying to cling on with its claws. I've had hangovers before, but never like this.

To recapitulate: We stayed up talking until four this morning, drinking wine; and when we'd run out of wine, whisky; and when we'd run out of whisky, vodka; and, when we'd run out of vodka, gin, neat; absinthe followed, for those still conscious. We sat in the kitchen and told jokes of which I can't – of course – remember a single one. It was a wonderful night. (William produced the whisky, Cleangirl the vodka, Fleur the gin, and Marcia the absinthe.)

When Victoria had a look back at her mistyped rambling from the night before, she could see that 'someone told me something very strange'.

She could remember hearing something very strange; she could even remember who told her it: Henry. But she couldn't couldn't couldn't remember at all at all at all what it was! And she wasn't sure if it was the sort of thing she could ever ask him to repeat. She felt that it was probably a one-off, work up your courage, splurge into someone's ear *confession* – of the 'I really fancy you' variety. But she didn't think it was that. It couldn't have been that. Could it? No, Henry wasn't in love with her. Henry loved his wife, didn't he?

It was very frustrating for Victoria. She usually had such a good memory for secrets, even when drunk.

One more reason, she thought, for staying sober-ish for the rest of the month – which was something she had just then decided; and this wasn't merely hangover remorse, she meant it.

Something I haven't recorded. A couple of mornings ago, I was just coming out of the Master Bedroom when I almost stepped through William; he was naked – entirely, ~~rotundly, wobblily~~ – apart from a damp towel slung waiterwise over his left shoulder. *I saw everything, everything I didn't want to see.* I don't know what he was thinking. He must just have had a shower in the bathroom. ~~(I'm sure it's him that clogs up the plughole with black hairs.)~~ He was

strolling along, whistling, as if happy – which I'm sure was an erroneous impression: Simona has never once mentioned the possibility of joy or delight in relation to her man-weight. He smiled and said, 'Good morning, Victoria,' quite the ingratiating Headmaster, gayly walked into their room and closed the door. I stood, shocked, immobile – possessed by the final image of his spotty buttocks. What was I to do? Surely no-one would believe that I'd been flashed in my own (rented) home? It was the kind of thing that the others – along with toilet paper runouts and light-bulb purchases – would bring up at a hastily called House Meeting. But I don't want to come across as prudish. What if Edith should see him? I'd be sued. I've read the contract; I'm responsible for practically everything that takes place in this house. Damage to property, injury to persons. Was I obscurely stirred? Do I secretly desire William? Oh, I hope not; no, surely not; I don't; no, I don't. He's – to put it basely – a slimy git of the lowest order. (Though that has been my type, heretofore – starting with university boyfriends. Who didn't so much two-time me as syncopate their way through an entire year's worth of rivals.) I've been shy of recording this – out of embarrassment, I suppose. On the plus side, it does give me a greater insight into his character; makes him come a little more alive.

As an aside: Alan informed me that he hasn't 'been' since he got here, over four days ago. 'It's always like this,' he says, 'I take at least a week to settle in.' Today he lies on the sofa, now groaning, now fighting the stabbing pains, now frankly farting.

Later. About 12.30 p.m. After lunch has finished. Talk around the kitchen table turns to bowels – it does not return from bowels for about half an hour, despite my attempts to steer it toward topics more suitable.

Alan's problem is variously diagnosed, and an even greater variety of cures are offered. (All of which Alan promises to try.)

'I have a friend...' said Marcia, as she always does. She is one of those people who value the anecdotal far above the scientific.

Cleangirl suggests he goes and sees his doctor, once back in London.

Alan stands, gangly, leaning against the Aga – a man who has bravely ventured into the Amazonian kitchen. We love him for this.

He dips his head into the conversation, like a chip into mayonnaise, then whips it out, like a chip heading towards the bite.

Fleur, I notice, for once does not run and hide. She listens to him, and I see her smile more than once.

It turns out that I'm far less lavatorially obsessed than almost everyone else in the house, even Cecile. The men started the toilet-talk craze, as an excuse for their constant farting. Now, they don't apologise for having done one, and no one else even laughs any more – unless it sounds particularly 'amusing'; like a duck or a creaky floorboard. Then the entire room collapses, as if in a hurricane of mirth. If the fart smells, and was silent, there are accusations and arcane rules. I can't be bothered to detail them, but they are far beyond, 'He who smelt it, dealt it.' At times like this the entire Project begins to feel ignoble. Living communally was always likely to be humiliating, but it is a disappointment to see how some people revel in their abasement.

2 p.m. A journalist came today from the local newspaper, the *Southwold and Walberswick Gazette*. (I'd asked the publicity girl in London to arrange this. A bit of regional press never hurts; they like to feel one's taking the trouble to talk to them. I thought it might help me get access to the Lighthouse – which is something I need to put more effort into.) I took her out onto the lawn, and we sat opposite one another on deck chairs. Henry, Cleangirl and Edith walked in from the beach as we were getting settled. The journalist noticed them, but said nothing. She was a mousy little

mouse who didn't have a tape-recorder. When she wrote on the pad, with her end-chewed pencil, I could see and upside-down-read her writing: no shorthand, either. She was so young and girly she still put circles above her i's. I felt at first as if I were talking to the school-magazine. But give her her due – she'd read all my books. I felt quite sorry for her, because she was asking me questions of this sort: 'What really happens to Roger on page 311, Chapter Eleven, of *Spaciousness*?' My answers to these were going to be of no use to her in constructing her 'Famous Author Rents House Just North of Town' story. Halfway through the interview, Alan came past – taking Domino out for a walk. The reporter noticed them, too. When she concluded by asking what I was working on at the moment, I merely told that it was a book set in and around Southwold. She did a mini-double-take, and I could see her regretting not having asked that question earlier – but I was already on my feet and a few steps towards the house.

As we were walking through the hall, she heard William practising scales in the parlour and saw Marcia wheeling out of her bedroom. The journalist's eyes went slightly wide, and she caught me looking at her, and was ashamed, so asked a question: 'Are all these people your friends?'

'Yes,' I said, unable to resist, 'I'm writing the book about them.'

'Did they do something together?' the girl asked.

'They're *doing* something together,' I said. 'They're living here – and I'm writing about what happens here.'

I didn't think there could be any harm in telling her; she looked so innocent, I'm sure she didn't really understand what I was saying.

5 ~~p.m. Simona came to a belated confession. 'I think I may do it tomorrow,' she said. Her *it* is, and has always been, leave William.~~

~~'Why then?' I said. 'Why not today? Why waste time? Why spend another day of your life with a man you don't love any more.'~~

'Because I do,' she said, 'that's what I came to tell you. I do still love him, despite everything.'

'You *think* you do,' I said, willing, for once, to challenge this supposed unchallengeable. 'What you actually are is dependent upon him, emotionally.'

'Not financially,' said Simona. 'I'm completely self-supporting.'

'I'm sure you are,' I said.

'In fact,' she asserted, 'I usually earn slightly more than he does.' She was talking through the tears, surprisingly eloquently.

'You don't have to stay in the house,' I said. 'We could just get someone to give you a lift to the station.' To be quite honest, I've been getting very impatient with Simona. I'm sure it never took me this long to dump anyone – even my first boyfriend, who of course I was at the time convinced was the only man in the world who'd ever come near me. (I was eight; he was ten.) Granted, I haven't actually been married; and I'm sure that makes one feel the whole thing will be headline news, for other people, from the start. There are parents to consider, and their sad hopes of marriages that will last (unlike many of their own). There are, in some cases, children, nannies, cleaners, gardeners too to be thought of. Simona has none of these excuses; what she has instead is a dead-loss of a husband – a bastard of the highest water.

I'm desperate to switch the spy-cameras on and have a look (and listen) in to one of their arguments. I've heard them, coming down through the floor into the drawing room. Perhaps I should have gone and leant on their door. But I know that I'd have been caught: their spats always end abruptly, with someone, usually William, storming out for a walk on the beach. Simona stays behind, weeping, and only emerges after reconstructing herself. The fragility of her emotions remains for all to see. William returns, his jaw slightly unlocked, his pupils slightly less dilated, and makes feeble jokes with the men about whatever happens to be going on. Even though they have heard the shouting and banging, the men readmit him, assuage him, allow him their fidelity. Surely they suspect the mental cruelty that is being practised, above their heads? Anyone who heard Simona shrieking like that would know that he had her by the hair. Men are disgusting: their inconsistency – sometimes leaping to judgement, sometimes reserving it indefinitely.

'I can't take too much more,' Simona blubbed. I realised that I hadn't been listening to her, for the past couple of minutes. 'So it's going to be tomorrow night,'

It was clear I hadn't missed much. 'Why night? Why not morning?'

'I don't know.'

'We could do it now. It wouldn't take much. We move your stuff into the spare room and I ask him to leave. No doubt he'd rant and rave a bit, but with X to help me, and the others to gather round and look disapproving, I'm sure he'd go.'

'I don't know – I don't know. Perhaps it's my fault.' I was bored of refuting this line of self-abnegation. However, in taking on the rôle of confessor, I knew that one of my main duties was to avoid at all times appearing uninterested in the repetitious griefs and peccadilloes of my penitents.

I gave Simona a good quarter-hour's soak in the aromatherapeutic waters of my sympathy; I washed her all over with soft, herbal, healing soap; I dried her; I oiled her; I spoke gently, told her to relax; I gave her a deep-muscle ego-massage. I was beautician to her very soul.

But still she made no promises.

This all goes, I promise.

This evening, I gave in to the men, and we all went to the pub – even Marcia, even Edith, even Cecile.

There are several ways to get to Southwold, from the house. Three, I've counted, so far. The first, and most pleasant, is to walk along the beach. This involves negotiating a few inlets and scooting through what may be semi-private property, but people are always doing it in both directions. If one has the time, this is the way to go: with the sea to the left of one, the Suffolk landscape to one's right, and Southwold ahead, lighthouse aloft. The second route is again walking but this time down some hedgerow-bounded, edge of field paths. (Yes, such things do still exist.) If the beach way is romantic, the paths are a sometimes brambly ramble. One needs to have been shown the route, probably twice if you're like me. A ball of twine would be useful, to find one's way back. I wouldn't recommend it, after dark. (It's so dark out here in the country, even with the lighthouse providing pulses of light.) The last route – which one can also take by foot – is the practical one: along the roads. But they are narrow in places, with blind corners, and one never knows when one is likely to meet an onward-coming boy-racer. (The Owners of the house mention this in their 'Hints for Guests' brochure, from which I should take some excerpts, as it is very funny. I doubt they'd give their permission, once they'd seen what I was going to use it for.) There *are* some guests prepared to risk road-death for fags or cayenne pepper. I prefer to drive, or be driven.

It was a warm night, so we were able to sit outside in the beer garden. I don't see why we did this, it entirely reduced the sense of going *to a pub* – it made it quite pleasant, in fact. There was no supersonic jukebox, no singalong locals, no wafts of ammonia every time the Gents' door swung open, no Australians behind the bar, no lewd city boys spilling beer on one another, no stripper, no quiz machines, no strange stickiness on the carpet, no packet of stale crisps lying disembowelled in the middle of a rockabye table, no injection-moulded horse-brasses, no olde-looking books. Even the drinks seemed unpublike – the gin and tonic fizzed, the wine made no-one gag, the beer tasted of beer rather than angry metal. I don't know what Edith thought of it all – she and Cecile did their best to look as if they fitted in, whilst I did my best to observe.

‘It’s delightful,’ said Cecile, ‘I really didn’t know such places exist. I *do* hope we can come here again.’

‘Oh, there are lots of others just as good as this one,’ said William, playing the local yokel know-all. ‘They brew beer round here.’

‘Well,’ said Cecile, ‘I think this shall always be my favourite, as it was my first.’

‘Your first?’ said X, smoothly.

‘Country pub,’ replied Cecile, plainly; then, aside to Edith, ‘in Suffolk.’ Such comic aplomb. Everyone – everyone who was meant to hear – laughed. And then everyone talked for a while, saying nothing particularly scintillating. We were on holiday, and to talk about that was enough. Soon, though, I felt things needed to be forced further, deeper. We were sitting around two longish tables; X, William and Alan had moved them, end to end. The people nearby us seemed quietish and not unrespectable: couples, lonely men. The farmers’ boys obviously sup their cider elsewhere. I knew we couldn’t play any truth-games, as Edith was present – and if whatever people had to confess could be said in front of her, then it probably wasn’t worth hearing. Closest to me – where I sat on the far right of the table – were X, Marcia and Fleur. I thought I’d break up the table-length chat, and start a proper conversation. It was also time to try to make peace with the twisted sister. ‘Do you remember,’ I said to Fleur, ‘when we went to that country pub, on holiday, when we were young.’

‘You mean with the bristles outside,’ said Fleur.

Others had been listening. I waited for her to explain; she didn’t, so I had to myself: ‘It was a bootscrape, next to the door to what I suppose was the lounge bar; and it had a rough upturned brush, fixed, to rub the dirt off your shoes. But we, being kids, didn’t know what it was. So, when we were safely sitting in the pub, we asked our parents –’

Fleur clanged in, with the punchline: ‘“What are the bristles outside?" Marcia laughed – a laugh that my sister had stolen from me. I was pleased, however, to see Fleur a little warmed by the memory. 'It became a joke for the whole holiday,' she said, 'if we went anywhere, we asked – "But will it have bristles outside?"'

'I wonder where we got the word "bristles" from?'

'Heaven knows,' said Fleur, laughing, relaxing more.

Oh, I hated this – playing at being sisters just because there were other people around. It was the only time we could draw together, and be as light and ludicrous as we'd once been. Together, alone, we were unable to stand face-to-face; it was back-to-back, ten paces, turn then fire. I missed the silly sausage that she'd been, once upon a time – back when she could teach me words like 'bristle'. Now, I realised, the situation was reversed; we were outside a pub with the bristles all on the inside. I sniggered; that was one joke I definitely couldn't say aloud.

Other people started to tell childhood holiday stories. Fleur and I looked at one another, smiled sadly. I gave up on trying to deepen the tone.

What else happened? Alan spilt beer all down his trousers, whilst getting the second round in. There seemed to be a lot more laughter, the guests seemed a lot more relaxed, at the other end of the other table. But when I insisted we rejigged, so everybody talked to everybody, and moved myself down there, the laughter had migrated, too.

I noticed that Alan and Fleur still seemed to want to sit apart, playing it coy, and Cleangirl and Henry, lovestruck, lovestuck, seemed not to want to be separated.

From now on, I shall have to be careful to sit in the middle of tables – so that I can listen to as many conversations as possible.

After the pub, we came home and had curry. The men had prearranged this with the Chef, without consulting me.

On the sofas, I suggested we play a few truth games. They were rejected as far too tacky.

Cecile wore a very thin black rollneck sweater, probably cashmere, and a grey pleated skirt, which should have looked outrageously schoolgirlish (and hence ridiculous on a woman of over 60) but which only succeeded in making all the schoolgirls of the world, ever, look overdressed. On her feet, she wore plain black shoes. I was clearly wrong when I told Alan she was having more clothes sent on. She seems to be dressing herself, for a whole month, entirely from the two suitcases. How?

A mouse – Marcia has seen a mouse in her room, zipping along the skirting-board, disappearing under the dresser. I'm sure it was cute, brown and an inch and a half long, top to tail, but to hear her describe it, the rancid ratbeast was slit-eyed, jet-powered, and had razor-sharp talons. 'I hate them,' she said, 'I hate them so much, you wouldn't understand. They might *get somewhere* when you didn't know.' One might think, with a cat in the vicinity, that this kind of thing wouldn't happen. Audrey, though, isn't exactly a mouser.

I've hardly spoken to X, this past couple of days.

Tuesday

Day Six Week One

Kept awake last night by the colourants in the curry. Chef had made chicken tikka massala, bright red, and it kept me speeding until about 3.30 a.m. As one does, I became frantic about not being able to catch up on sleep until the following night, and about underperforming throughout the whole of the next day. I should have stuck to the vegetable curry. Today I feel nauseous and headachy, and I have no idea why. I'm thinking of the chickens Chef cooked with: they died in squalor, I bet. I'm feeling as if I never want to eat meat again. I can't afford food poisoning. Is meat another thing I'm going to have to avoid in order to get through this next three weeks? The project seems to require me to give up something new every day.

The dawn chorus today. I thought by cutting down hedgerows, using masses of pesticides, etc., we'd been fairly successful in killing off these tweety little bastards. They all seem to have migrated to Suffolk, however – where pesticides are probably *passé*; the farmers round here having moved on to GM. The Chinese had the right idea: get everyone out from dawn till dusk banging on woks and petrol cans, until the flighty infestation dies of the tiredness of not being able to land. Then, shovel the huge feathery piles of them into the backs of lorries. Woken at 5 a.m. Back to sleep for 5.30. Awake again by 7.15.

Alan and Marcia seem to have formed somewhat of an alliance. I found out because first thing this morning I caught him lowering her onto the downstairs loo. (I'm not sure when this started: probably after Alan was the one to piggyback her around the upstairs rooms.)

He went into the garden for a five-minute wander while she did her business, and so, casually, I joined him. After the good mornings, I began with, 'You're helping Marcia, I see.'

'Not really,' he said, 'she doesn't really need any help. It's just, if I'm around, and I usually am, it makes things a little quicker.'

'Well, thank you,' I said, 'for becoming her unofficial carer.'

'Oh, it's nothing like that – it's not a chore. It's more like giving someone a light or a lift.'

The morning was delightfully chilly, making one feel as if one had just risen from a warm swimming pool into the cold air. Above us, the sky was a far pale blue, unclouded, and streaked distantly with jet-wool.

'What else do you help her with?'

'Victoria,' he said, 'it's private.'

'Oh,' I said, 'I see.'

He went back inside; 7.30 a.m., and I'd already succeeded in annoying one person, probably two.

The wallpaper in the downstairs hall, powder blue with golden acorns upon it – this is regal, and should be mentioned. On the consul table in the hall, a bowl of keys which have mislaid their uses.

Brief conversation with Alan: the curry has cured his costiveness – which shall be the last word on the subject.

~~Sometimes in order to get going with the writing it's necessary to just write and write and write like this until something comes and one doesn't know what that something is going to be until, suddenly, it is there: numinous, luminous, voluminous. (Cut.)~~ Agreed.

2 p.m. There was always a threat looming that this would turn into either a country-house farce or a country-house murder mystery – and now it seems to have done the unlikely, becoming *both*. The farce is that everything is farcically unfarcical. No question as to whodunnit, though – or what their collective motives were. It's like that Agatha Christie novel where it turns out that everybodydunnit. *Murder on the Orient Express*, isn't it? One of the clues is that there are multiple stab-wounds, one for each of the suspects. Well, the corpse of my career is lying bleeding on the drawing-room carpet, with ten deep kitchen-knife wounds in its back. Blood. Blood all over the place.

It's Fleur's fault. That little speech of hers on deliberate inactivity has inspired all the other guests. Since then, we've had two days of them doing precisely as little as possible. Agh! I hate her. They are parodying inaction in a quite extraordinary manner: they read books, flop about on deck chairs, go for quiet walks on the beach, sleep. Their talk, almost exclusively, is about food: what they had for breakfast; what they'd like for dinner. There's no appearance of intellectual play, no emotional exertion; no flitting as of butterflies, no fluttering, as of hearts. Fleur even knits, for Christ's sake! I'm dying. My Project is dying. And I know that, underneath it all, there are things going on. I'm *sure*.

X isn't any help – he has taken up sea-fishing!!! (And, unlike some people, I don't use multiple exclamation marks unless severely provoked.) He goes down to the beach all the time with Alan and Henry, even when I ask/order him not to. And this evening the men are planning to play poker.

Simona – ~~playing to type~~ attempting to assist me – is the only one who comes to Confession. ~~I can't really tell her to go away and stop boring me, because she's my best source of information about this conspiracy of do nothings.~~ (She warned me about the poker.) ~~When I ask her about it directly, however, she steers not so neatly away from the subject. Divided loyalties. She has refused any more to discuss leaving William. 'It's not going to happen,' she said. 'Why?' I asked, but she wouldn't say. She's afraid – afraid of what~~? ~~Being alone?~~

In the pub last night I wanted to stand up and scream *somebodydosomething!* I am starting to think up evil counter-plots: perhaps I could get Chef to put laxatives into the chilli-*sans*-carne. Or emetics. Then, at least, there'd be a little *movement* round here.

I am becoming madly anxious.

Cleangirl seems to have slightly disappeared from this diary; this is a habit she's always had. Never a wallflower; often wallpaperish.

She is still *there*, making one think that one's surroundings are delightfully attractive; she is more ambient even than wallpaper – she travels, she intervenes, she smooths in many places; but she shares its flatness and inoffensiveness. No, that doesn't work. Some wallpaper offends so much you want to call it out for a duel. It was bad wallpaper, after all, that killed Oscar Wilde. She doesn't *do* anything; she's just present for other people's doings – and because of the uncertainty principle, one can't be sure that she didn't have an influence upon their actions. It's very annoying. I knew she'd be very annoying when I asked her along. But I thought it might *pique* me into a competitiveness kick, in which my work and my looks would improve. Instead, she seems to have slumped into a holiday frump. Freed from total motherhood, she is dressing sloppily and seeking out opportunities to smoke. I should easily be able to entice Henry; with a little glamour, some flirtation and a smattering of laughter. But he, too, at some time in the recent past, seems to have middle-aged. They're both quite content to be here and to be done for, by others. I thought I was importing another pair of agents, of actors; I got a couple of layabouts. The Chef continues his seduction, without Cleangirl even as far as I can tell noticing. Perhaps she is preoccupied with X. She does look at him, occasionally. Henry avoids me – I even think he may secretly dislike me. So much for that prediction.

Became so desperate this afternoon that I had X drive me over to Southwold. We found a toy shop and bought a set of Cluedo. (They didn't have Monopoly – can you believe it?) With this, I hope to forestall the poker school. A good combative game of Cluedo might at least give me something to work on.

In the car, on the way back, I broke down. X told me he thought it was all going very smoothly.

'Exactly,' I said.

3.17 p.m. I come bearing a precious cargo: gossip. Cleangirl hates Marcia – can hardly stand to be in the same postal district as her. (And after what I said about her about an hour ago.) I first noticed this on Sunday evening, but couldn't be sure. After dinner, we were most of us still in the drawing room, and Marcia was telling a long story involving herself, axle grease, a tall staircase, and a man with a donkey. This was set in Jamaica. Marcia was just getting to the punchline, which involved two other people, one of them a transvestite, one a policewoman, when Cleangirl got up from the sofa and walked out through the French windows. I didn't go after her, couldn't. Marcia's story ended – as her stories always do – with a non-tragic outcome and a rich ripe cackle. Her moral is always the same: all one can do in a world as ridiculous as this is laugh.

When a break in the talk presented itself, I went out into the garden to look for the absconder. She was in one of the deck chairs beneath the apple trees, talking to X. It was magic hour: the sun below the horizon, the earth and sea still lit by the sky. X was adding to the magic by sending up curlicues of fragrant smoke from the tip of his cigarette. Cleangirl was as close to ranting as she ever gets. I approached from behind, and caught her end: '...going to be really difficult if it goes on like this.'

'And what are you two talking about?' I said. Both of them left the other to answer, the result being a silence of elegant rebuff. 'All right, then,' I said, 'I'll leave you to it.'

I turned and went back into the house, knowing that their embarrassment would cause one of them, or maybe both of them, to tell me. To be honest, at that moment I wanted X's cigarette more than Cleangirl's secret.

Today. 4 p.m. The Parlour. Confession. And for the first time, Cleangirl comes. 'I think you've guessed,' she says. It could be two things: Marcia or I'm in love with X.

'I have,' I say. 'When did it start?'

'I suppose when we got here, almost the first day.'

'And?'

'She's so... banal, isn't she? I mean, I know you're not meant to say that – because her position, politically, is so impregnable.' Cleangirl sniggered at the schoolgirlism. 'But, really, she talks too much – and what she says isn't all that interesting.'

'Now,' I say, 'why do you think you feel that about Marcia and not about my sister?'

'I have no idea. In fact, I'm lying to you by rationalising it at all. She's just one of those people who make me feel giddy with nausea. I've been feeling guilty about this ever since – well, ever since I met her.'

'You could tell, even then?'

'She's a victim, isn't she? A conscious victim. I find it very hard to relate to people like that.'

'I'm not quite sure what you mean,' I say.

'I mean someone whose strength is their weakness, or whose weakness is their strength; you know what I mean. Just because she's in a wheelchair and she's black doesn't mean that everybody should listen to what she says.'

'Do you think the wheelchair's more important than the being black?'

'No, not really. But you have to put them in some sort of order. I just wish there would be some general acknowledgement that she's boring, sometimes. I wish I felt I wasn't alone in this.'

'What did X say?'

'He quite likes her. He thinks she's amusing.'

'What did you say to him?'

'I told him to give it another week, then see.'

'Edith seems to like her,' I say.

'Yes, I'm glad about that,' Cleangirl says. 'I feel very mean-spirited.' That seems all she has to say, until: 'Please don't put this in the book.'

'Of course not.'

'It'll make me sound racist, and that's not it at all: I just don't like Marcia.' She gets up to go.

'Ingrid,' I say.

'Yes,' she replies, not yet at the door.

'If you're going to make a bad atmosphere, have a bust-up, whatever – do you think you could try and let me know in advance: I'd hate to miss it.'

Cleangirl comes over and kisses me on the forehead. 'I knew I could rely on you to be wicked about this,' she says.

Next was Simona, ~~But only~~ for a quarter of an hour.

So, when I came out of confession, dying for a pee, but dying also to see where Cleangirl has taken herself, what did I find? Her and Marcia, doing the washing-up together, snorting and chuckling and generally being best-friends-of-all.

This is how Cleangirl has always been. She is the most seamless actress. And for all I really know, she hates me far more than she's annoyed by Marcia, and just came in to talk to me at confession as a complex test.

But then, would she have left the room during Marcia's story if that were so? Would she have stage-managed it so that I caught her with X?

Her murkiness is so deep, underneath the clarity, that I don't think I'll ever fathom it.

And I'm sure she won't be out of Marcia's company for the rest of the day, if not the month.

I haven't had sex for a week. I realised just now. It's absolutely abysmal. And I've hardly missed it, what with all the house business. But what's worse – as far as I know, no-one else among the guests has had sex either. Not unless they snuck off during the

Wrong, oh so wrong.

afternoon whilst everyone else was out in the garden. The couple most likely to couple in this sly manner are Henry and Cleangirl. They, after all, must be very used to avoiding being caught by Edith. I can't believe I've missed them, though. When I turn on the spy cameras, I will learn the truth of what's been going on. I can't *can't* wait.

This evening, I will seduce X. Or maybe not. Maybe I should refrain entirely, in order to force him towards Cleangirl.

I've found out a little more about how Alan is helping Marcia. As I discovered this morning, he helps her onto the downstairs loo – this is, I think, because it's quite narrow; there is no room for her to shift herself sideways, after putting down one of the armrests of her wheelchair. The other main assistance comes at bathtime (I overheard them arranging it earlier this afternoon). Marcia, I would guess, finds it easier to be placed in there, and removed, than to do it all herself. This means the door must be left unlocked whilst she's in the bath. I think everyone knows about this, and has decided the safest thing is to avoid the downstairs bathroom altogether; take showers upstairs. Most of the time, though, you'd hardly notice that Marcia's any different from the rest of us. What she is very good at is sewing, darning, and she's a devil of a knitter. Down one side of her wheelchair (the non-flip-down side) she has an equipment satchel, containing make-up, wool and knitting needles, first-aid kit, reading glasses, rape alarm, and other essentials.

There has been some ludicrous studenty talk about setting up a rota for washing up. I've told people just to leave dirty mugs on the draining board, for the Maid or the Chef to do. But the guests are all being so egalitarian. Cecile's the only one who knows how to treat servants. She must be used to it. She's getting them to do *everything* for her – and because that means they're occupied, they love her. One can really see how well they respond to firm handling.

I myself have yet to master the art of mastering. Anyhow, people are also complaining that there aren't enough mugs to go round. I've offered to buy new mugs, but no one sees this as a solution.

Most of the things I'm getting in the Suggestions Box are of this order of triviality. I was expecting people to come up with marvellous ideas that would enrich all our lives. They haven't. Instead, they carp about toilet-paper distribution. (There has been somewhat of a problem with the downstairs loo. It seems everyone goes there, as no one can be bothered with the stairs.)

On another subject, I keep thinking of titles and ideas for murder mysteries: *Murder in the 'Murder Weekend' Hotel*, *Murder in the London Dungeon*, *Murder in Madame Tussaud's Chamber of Horrors*, *Murder at Scotland Yard.*

As dinner (halibut with new potatoes and *petits pois*; gooseberry fool) was drawing to a close, I blithely suggested Cluedo. The men were still set upon poker, but decided they could always warm up with a bit of amateur sleuthing. We helped the Maid clear everything from the table, then wipe it. I passed responsibility for running the game to X, who has nephews and nieces with whom he plays Cluedo regularly. The guests teamed up – couples decoupled: William went with Fleur, Simona with Alan; Cleangirl forced herself upon Marcia; Henry put his arm around Edith; I hooked Cecile. X put the cards into the envelope, and we began to play.

Characteristics soon reveal themselves. Marcia finds great difficulty keeping her deductions secret. Fleur is reluctant to share information, even with her playing partner. Cecile pretends not to understand the game, but was incredibly shrewd. William and Henry become competitive in a distressingly masculine way. Alan has to pretend to play worse than he knew how.

It was Simona and Alan who won the first game (Reverend Green with the Candlestick in the Ballroom). And the second game, set by the previous winners, went to... Cecile and me! (Miss Scarlett with the Dagger in the Library – which is surely the most glamorous combination of murderer, weapon and crime scene.) Everyone agreed that that was enough.

As gaps appeared around the table, the men spread themselves further out. Alan was shuffling the deck before the Cluedo board had even been folded up. Here, clearly, was a far more interesting game – for him. Surprisingly, Marcia asked if she could join in. 'Of course,' said Alan. The men didn't seem to realise there had been any gender divide on this. And then, far more astoundingly, Cecile made the same request. 'Delighted,' said Alan. He began to state the rules and regulations to the players: something about Texas and stud and what was high and what wasn't. Then they all turned to look at me. I confess, I had been stunned by Cecile's decision – one might even say her enthusiasm. Now was not the time to ask her reasons, however. 'I'll just watch,' I said.

I managed about half an hour; as expected, it was deathly dull. They played using matchsticks for counters, with low stakes. By the time I came upstairs to write this, Marcia had the biggest pile and Henry was down to almost nothing.

Cecile wore a purple blouse and skirt, with matching shoes! How she gets away with these colours, I have no idea. It's as if they've passed through some magic style mirror, and come out *chic* on the other side. I can understand her fitting all these clothes into her suitcases, just: but there is *no way* that she was able to bring all those shoes as well. Not unless she had a remarkably well-trained elephant with her at the time, to help sit on the suitcase after she'd put everything inside it.

Wednesday

Day Seven Week One

Dawn chorus seem to have acquired drills: yadda-yadda-yadda.

A strange encounter I had in the middle of last night (i.e., early this morning) with Cecile. An incident to be recorded in the third person, I think:

Victoria badly needed the loo. She felt as if her bladder was a Zeppelin, trying to propel itself out of her. I think, avoiding alcohol, she'd probably drunk too much mineral water at dinner. It was about 3 or 4 o'clock, and she didn't much fancy her chances of getting back to sleep again. She emerged onto the upstairs landing, and was feeling her way along the right-hand wall (it was almost completely black, and she didn't have a torch; outside town, one forgets how completely dark places can get – Victoria missed the constant orange-brown light of London). She was fumbling forwards in this way, like a blind person in a strange place, when she suddenly felt softness and coolness and cloth and skin beneath her fingers. She screamed, of course; as did the thing she had touched. Victoria almost immediately realised who rather than what it was; but the instant before the 'almost' had her believing something entirely different, entirely monstrous. '*Mon Dieu*,' said Cecile, breathing raggedly. 'It's me,' Victoria said. She was embarrassed, and glad of the dark; she had, she realised, touched Cecile's breasts – the material covering them. The door to Cecile's room was open, and suddenly they had the advantage of moonlight – it must have been behind a cloud, before. (Does this work? I think, perhaps, having gone out onto the landing and seen it so dark, I had closed my eyes, believing them useless, playing blind, trailing my fingers along above the dado and beneath the line of paintings.) 'I thought you were...' Cecile stopped. Victoria knew, somehow, what her friend had been going to say. 'A ghost,' Victoria said. 'Yes,' Cecile said. The moonlight seemed to grow brighter, perhaps the moon had come out from its final veil of cloud. 'Isn't it funny,' Victoria said, 'how that's one's first thought, in the dark.' 'You gave me a real *frisson.*' Cecile stood to one side, allowing even more light into the landing. The skin over her breastplate, open above the night-dress fabric, shone like a mirror. Victoria didn't at the time think it odd that her curtains had not been drawn, or had been undrawn. 'I was going...' she said. 'You go first,' Victoria replied. 'Can you see your way?' 'I can feel my way,' Cecile said, 'I've done it before.' 'All right, then,' Victoria said. She turned to go back into her room. And then the strangest thing happened. 'No,' said Cecile, quite loudly. Victoria stopped. 'Please,' Cecile said, 'stay where you are; wait until I come back. I'm scared.' 'But it's just me here,' Victoria said. 'I've been standing in the doorway for a quarter of an hour,' Cecile said, 'frozen there; trying to work up courage to walk into the corridor. Something was stopping me. A force. It only broke when you touched me.' 'Shall I turn the light on?' Victoria said. 'I think I can find the switch.' The whole incident had been so Gothic that Victoria had forgotten they had an easy solution to darkness; in her head she had been thinking castle, storm, candles-blown-out. (My sister and I used to play a game like this, called Ghostie, all around our parents' house. We played until we were almost teenagers. I think when we stopped playing it, we stopped liking one another in the light. What an odd thought.) 'No,' said Cecile, 'we don't want to wake anybody sleeping.' 'Of course I'll stay here, if you like,' Victoria said, deciding to ignore the reference to a *force*. Cecile did not reply, just went.

Victoria stood looking at the moonlight spill like slow-motion milk across the carpet. ~~She tried not to listen to the silence, then the~~

~~trickle, then the silence, then the longer trickle, then the longer silence, then the short trickle, the second short trickle, the silence, the splash, the silence, the flush. She was glad to hear the flush.~~

I'll save Cecile from this.

Cecile came out of the entirely black hole of the toilet; Victoria realised that she'd gone in and gone to the loo without turning the light on. Victoria supposed Cecile didn't want to hurt her eyes. Victoria wondered if Cecile would have locked the loo door, if they hadn't encountered one another; if Victoria had got out of bed a while later, she might have opened the door, turned round and sat down in Cecile's lap. What a thought!

Cecile came right up to Victoria, in the dark. 'Thank you, my child,' she said, and kissed Victoria on either cheek. She turned and walked into her room. 'Good night,' she said, without looking back. The door closed, leaving the upstairs corridor blacker than ever. The afterimage of the moonlight-milk on Victoria's retinas made it, for a moment or two, impossible for her even to see darkness. ~~She closed her eyes, and saw the devil – which is how retinal images always appeared to her: the laughing red face of Satan saying *I'm going to get you one day I am and you know I am.* Victoria shook him out of her head, saying, 'Devil thoughts.'~~ She went to the loo; she went back into the bedroom: nothing else happened. X was deep in sleep, snoring in an amusing way: his lips seemed to have stuck together, so when he breathed out through them it made a phut-phutting sound, like porridge cooking. Victoria was satisfied: she had seen a secret side of Cecile.

Jan's a loon.

Whatever else we share or don't share, we have had our magical moonlit moment.

7.30 a.m. Waking up in an old, cold house was wonderful; having to tiptoe around the ice-floored bathroom. It reminded Victoria of childhood holidays. (You can tell I'm desperate, can't you?) The windows upstairs in the house were all a-steam with the breath of the peaceful sleepers blah-de-blah. What is it? Do they hate me? Or are they just genuinely not sparking off each other? If things continue like this, I shall have to bring forward my mock-dumping of X. (Though I am seriously reconsidering this. Henry shows no interest in me – possible dislike; Cleangirl shows very little in X.)

Breakfast. Cleangirl's pursuit of Marcia continues: she is determined to mortify herself into liking her. Marcia's closest alliances continue to be with Fleur, her straight man (if I can say that), and Alan, her handyman. Henry, meanwhile, by laughing honestly at Marcia's jokes, has won himself a strong place in her affections. If she has something to show someone, he often comes first. She likes nothing better than to have people gather round her, unable to resist the attractions of the thing she holds, or knows. Her fantasy identity, I think, is siren on the rocks – there she languishes, bringing all sailors to the hilarity (for her) of peril. Edith is very self-sufficient for a child, but I think she misses company her own age.

11 a.m. Something romantic has happened! I got so desperate that I decided to go for a long walk on the beach, without telling anyone. Apart from my midnight jaunt a couple of days ago, I've hardly dared leave the house. If I did I was sure that I'd miss significant events. (Oh, there *was* the Cluedo-buying trip.) The guests would take advantage of the Narrator's absence to do what mice always do when cat's away. But by this point, I really didn't care. For all the good the place has done me, they might as well burn the house down. So I went for a solitary walk, heading northwards. The sea, I hoped, would help me put myself and my problems into a proper perspective; as it has done for Godforsakenly miserable writers since before the Classics were being dragged forth.

The clouds are the most fantastic thing of all, around here. One wishes to be even a despairing watercolourist, just to have a go at them – catching the look of half of half of one of them. As a child, I always used to wish that the world would turn upside-down – so that we could walk upon clouds and gaze up at the earth, fields, trees, as a sky. Now it's men I expect to make me feel as if I'm walking on clouds. Maybe, when I get older, and turn to gardening and going for walks across hilltops, I'll start to forgive them (men, not clouds) for letting me down so many times. It may very well be that this would work better the other way round: forgive the men first, then get rewarded with gardening and hilltops.

This being East Anglia, the landscape is flat – but off to the north it rises in what might almost be described as a ridge. The trees top this off as best they can. It's a little scraggy, a little scrotty. ~~But I think if I'd been born here I'd be grateful, because whilst I'd love my home landscape, I would always recognise that there were other more beautiful, richer ones out there the inhabitants of which would never appreciate – having never known paucity.~~

Trudging, trudging. Expecting nothing. And then – suddenly – up ahead – three figures: two human, one doggy. Something told me to slow down. I approached closer, recognised them: Alan and Fleur! Actually, I recognised the Dalmatian first – Domino; retrieving a stick that one of the figures – the male one – had tossed down the beach. They were sitting on the sand, looking out over the grey waters. For almost the first time this month, I felt the genuine jolt of a story. I remembered the scene in which Alan's Hope had been accidentally revealed – and now, maybe, it was beginning to find its justification. Hiding myself behind dune after dune, I got as close to them as possible. It was quite wuthery, so I wasn't able to hear what they were saying. But I could tell from their body language that the conversation was intimate. To me, it looked like one of those ripping-through-the-world confabs that soon-to-be lovers have when they've just met. I was wary of drawing any over-hasty conclusions; and of congratulating myself too early for successful matchmaking. However, it was with a small pulse of satisfaction that I lay down behind my dune. First, I knew I now had something substantial to write about: a romance, possibly. Second, if I beat them back to the house, I could see how they presented themselves. Would they, as I suspected, turn up separately; not wishing to give me any hint of their *liaison*? I was just about to hurry away when I heard my first snippet of dialogue. It wasn't particularly scintillating; at a distance of twenty yards, you wouldn't expect it to be. But it did contain the wonderful beginnings of something. Fleur stood up, abruptly. 'No!' she said. 'No!' Alan spoke, too quietly for me to hear. Then Fleur, turning towards where I sat, said, or rather shouted, 'You know *exactly* why not!' At this point, worried about being caught, I dropped down behind a clump of sea-grass. Fleur stomped past, not five feet away. For a moment I worried that our sisterly connection would alert her to my presence. Quite often, I pick up the phone even before it has started to ring: knowing that she'll be there on the other end. Hidden, I was so fiercely conscious of her that I found it almost impossible to believe she wouldn't sense that fierceness, that consciousness, and instantly become conscious of me. But she walked past, head down. I think there may even have been tears. I crept round the back of the sandy hillock, keeping it between us – even at the slight risk of coming into Alan's sight. As Fleur dwindled into the distance, I peered at the long-limbed man she had just left behind. He watched her departing back, gave a rueful shake of the head, looked down into his chest, looked out to sea. (This was marvellous stuff; just the sort of thing I was hoping for.) I allowed myself a moment's speculation. Most likely Alan had been too eager. Perhaps, if Fleur had reacted differently, I'd have been there to witness their first kiss. But Fleur was deep in sexual bitterness. Her little after-dinner speech had demonstrated that. Maybe that's what Alan had failed to realise. He wanted to start things right away, and she needed to be coaxed, wooed, seduced. He can be so clumsy, sometimes. There were other possibilities. Alan, perhaps, might have said something insulting about God. Or, though it seemed unlikely, they might have been discussing their pet situation. I had a great deal to think about.

However, there was no chance now of beating Fleur back to the house. It would be safer to go back by a different route – not along the beach. But then I thought that Fleur might ruin it all by deciding to leave. If so, I had to be back there to try to talk her out of it, and to observe the drama. The risk was worth it: I set off towards the house at a half-jog. Another jogger, a real one, overtook me: face like a spotted-dick pudding being steamed. It seemed unlikely that Alan was going to do anything worth watching – other than shake his head again a few times, and throw Domino's stick. (I'm so glad this has happened. All right, it's moving a little faster between them than I predicted it would. What did I say? Fireworks in the third week? I just didn't expect Alan to be such a mover.)

When I arrived back at the house, Fleur had retired to her bedroom. Cecile and Marcia were having a polite conversation in the drawing room. About clothes. Normally, I would have joined them. But I felt I had to try and get as much of this down as freshly as possible. I came up to the bedroom, but have kept – whilst writing this – darting to the window to see if I can spot Alan as he comes back. I wonder if Fleur is doing the same.

It makes me want to cheat, and turn on the cameras now. I was going to wait until tomorrow. Oh, hang it... No one's going to punish me, are they? I'm going to do it.

Horrors, someone came and tried the handle of the bedroom door. Luckily, I'd locked it. Telling myself it was probably X, I crept shakily down the ladder.

'Hello?' I said.

'It's me,' said X.

'Is anyone else there?'

'No.'

'Are you sure?'

'What's going on?'

I let him in. He immediately saw the open hatch, the ladder.

'I thought you weren't going to start until tomorrow,' he said, clearly alarmed that I'd started at all – especially without telling him. We are no longer quite so intimate as we were on holiday; he knows.

'Well,' I replied, 'they were always an option. Do you want to have a look?'

'What are people doing?' he asked.

'Nothing particularly bizarre, but it's fascinating anyway,' I said. 'Did you want something?'

'Only to give you this.' He handed me a copy of the local newspaper. I had made page five. A sweet piece. I skim-read it, then chucked it on the counterpane; it really wasn't important, in comparison. Not with the beautiful screens.

'Come on, then,' I said. I relocked the door, and we climbed the ladder.

When I first turned them on, of course, I had been dreading that the whole set-up – having not been used for almost a week – would fuse. I would then, somehow, have to get the repairmen in without anyone noticing: an impossibility, really. I had also been terrified that one of the guests would hear something, a hum, a click, and would realise that they were now being more closely scrutinised than before. But the whole thing, as promised, was silent, discreet, fascinating.

All of the bedrooms but one were empty, their occupants being downstairs; I turned my attention first of all to Fleur. She was sitting on the edge of her bed, sobbing. Her shoulders were jumping up and down as rapidly as if she were trotting on a horse. Not being entirely without sisterly feeling, my immediate reaction was to want to go and give her a big hug. Alan had clearly ruined her small dream of a slow romance. He was merely another man, only after one thing, etc. I think she must have been hoping to put him through a few churchy hoops before he got anywhere near. For several minutes, I watched her. Her crying did not seem to vary, neither peaking nor subsiding. It was bizarre. Perhaps I was right, and grief *has* always been Fleur's vocation. When it became clear that she was going to weep until lunchtime, I turned my attention elsewhere.

My first real discovery with the spy-camera in Cecile's room was that she has some sort of map pinned up on the back of the door. I'm fairly sure from the outline of the coast that it's the foot-shape of Cornwall. It jags around – yes, the more I look at it the surer I am – from Portsmouth to the Bristol estuary. Blue sea, I imagine; sandy, grassy land. The lines *on* the map are quite hard to make out because of the folds *in* the map. It is old, frayed. I found this amazing – without the cameras, I might never have known about it. (She just *doesn't* let me into her room.) But the knowledge seems quite useless. One can't exactly confront someone with, 'By the way, what's your connection with Cornwall?' On the other hand, it will begin to distort one's conversation in other ways: one will start being careful about not mentioning Cornwall – which is ludicrous. It's a little like being at a dinner party and knowing that someone at the table is having an affair with someone else at the table. One must be careful not to mention anything that might link them: not the exhibition where one saw them arm-in-arm, not the holiday one knows they secretly took. I wonder if Cecile's map of Cornwall is anything to do with an affair? A doomed affair with a Cornishman. (How could an affair with a Cornishman be anything but doomed?) Perhaps I shall be able to sit down with her, late one evening, and just get her onto the subject of, what? – say, regret... regrets. You can't have a map of Cornwall on your wall without it in some way being linked to bad memories. Maps in general are to do with grief and pain; making them, looking at them. Happy doesn't need a map.

I looked at the other screens. The empty rooms looked odd. Occasionally, in a film or a TV drama, one will see a shot of an empty room. But, because nothing is happening in it, and because something must happen in every shot, it will not be held for more than a couple of seconds at most. Half a minute, with informative music, if it's a French film. These fourteen televisions in front of me were breaking their own rules; merely by the fact of their being screens, I was expecting entertainment from them. I was confused. My position, now, was less couch-potato, more security guard.

1.30 p.m. Had to break off for lunch.

3.15 p.m.

I have become afraid of dialogue, and I don't know why. The reader enjoys dialogue; it gives them a rest from explication.

'What do you think, so far?' asked Marcia, seated beside the sofa.

'You mean the house?' said Fleur.

'Everything, I mean – this little set-up that she has here for us.'

'It seems fine,' Fleur said, with vestigial loyalty. 'Aren't you comfortable?'

'Oh, yes,' said Marcia, 'people don't usually think as much as this about how to put up with me. But I feel comfortable and uncomfortable at one and the same time, if you know what I mean.'

'I suppose I do. I'm not sure if Victoria really knows what she's meddling with.'

'It's a long time, a month. It's a long time to be away from home.'

'I'm sure she'd say she'd like us to make this our home,' said Fleur.

'Would she really?'

'She does go for the obvious, more often than not.' They shared an illicit giggle.

'It's such an intensely *arranged* house – I keep feeling I'm going to be overheard by someone.' Marcia glanced round the room, shoulders hunched down.

'The walls are fairly thick.'

'But there's lots of places to lurk – if one felt like lurking. Did Victoria use to lurk and listen, when she was a child?'

'Oh, all the time,' said Fleur. 'She was terrible for it – and always getting caught. What she could never do was keep what she'd found out to herself. It would always blurt its way out into the next conversation she had – she was too excited ever to keep a secret.'

Well, I thought, that's not going to happen now.

At which point, Alan walked in, and Fleur got up and left. 'Please,' he said, 'don't leave on my –' But she was already halfway to the bottom of the stairs.

Marcia gave Alan a very long, hard, *wise* look – I can't describe it any other way: owlish and yet full of sympathy.

'No,' he replied, 'I don't want to talk about it.' Just as if she'd spoken.

Marcia changed the subject to the garden exile of Audrey the cat, and Alan wasn't able to say he didn't want to talk about that either.

I said earlier that people are just deliberately lazing around. That wasn't strictly 100% true. They are also keeping fit. I have been loath to admit it, hoping it would go away. Henry does T'ai Chi under his tree on the lawn. X jogs, whilst yearning for competitive sport, for squash or badminton or fencing. Even Marcia has an upper-body exercise routine. The drawing room, at eleven each morning, turns into an impromptu power yoga class – led by Cleangirl. Cecile, I'm glad to say, does nothing worse than ballet exercises in the privacy of her own room.

All these conspicuous displays of health, it's making me feel ill: jogging, push-ups... The problem is, exercise may prolong life, but the parts of life spent exercising are very boring.

~~Sport is taking over society, and I don't like it. It's a plot, to stop everyone thinking. If all they watch the news for is to see the final score of Manchester United versus Hull Kingston Rovers, then~~

It really doesn't suit you, theorizing.

~~they're bound to turn into willing little drones who'll do anything you tell them to. I rarely feel political, but sport makes me so.~~

This evening, when I alluded to our midnight meeting, Cecile blanked me. I wasn't so careless as to mention it whilst anyone else was in the room. She had no reason, externally, to be embarrassed. I suppose she feels I've seen a side of her that I shouldn't – seen her as a frightened superstitious child. And this is obviously something she regrets. Cecile wouldn't want to be regarded as in any way lacking. One knows that the great have their foibles, their *faiblesse*, but somehow one always knits it in with their strength, thread through chainmail. It becomes, with them, eccentricity. What is my relationship with Cecile, now? The only feeling I can compare it to is that of the morning following a one-night-stand; that vertigo-inducing mix of intimacy and distance. What I haven't been able to stop thinking about, but desperately *do* want to stop thinking about, is her reference to 'the force'. Whatever could she have meant?

At about ten thirty p.m., I sat down on the sofa in the front parlour with Cleangirl. I thought we were just going to have a chat as we usually do, about Edith and what she's like this week, and what she'll be like when she grows up, and me, and children, and my children, and what they'd be like. But Cleangirl seemed to want to be more serious; for perhaps the first time since I've known her, I got the feeling she had what with anyone else you would call an *agenda*. 'Are you jealous of me?' she asked.

'What do you mean?' I said.

'Of me, and my relationship with Henry,' she replied.

Of course, I knew straight away what she was on about. She was thinking that I had instructed X to attempt to seduce her away from Henry, in order that I could seduce him away from her. I was amazed by her perceptiveness. Cleangirl hardly ever has an insight, and when she does it's almost always into herself rather than those around her. Occasionally she says something very intelligent about Edith, but it's almost always something that I myself have already long ago perceived. I did not delay in denying her accusation; my *façade* was seamless. To go on the attack immediately would be too obvious, so I asked her why she thought so.

'Because your relationship with X doesn't seem to be going too well,' she said. 'And because you've been seeking me out the whole time.'

This, again, was rather much for Cleangirl: paradoxes were fatal to her very essence. She was straight, that was her given position in the universe. If she attempted to be a thing as twisted and convoluted as myself, she would cease to be Cleangirl. I don't think I'd even be able to recognise her. Beauty is placed in the world for two reasons: to simplify things, for the possessor, and to complicate things, for everybody else. 'If you'd been avoiding me,' she continued by saying, 'I'd have thought the same.'

'If you think that, you can always leave,' I said.

'I'm thinking about it – about leaving,' she said. 'No, I really am. I don't know if what's going on here is good for you, for us, for anybody. I think there might even be something evil about it.'

This was more like it: Cleangirl is never happier than when infuriating me with morally absolutist talk. ~~She desires nothing more than to get to the point of mentioning people who work in prisons, and how often, when one speaks to them, they say that they believe in absolute evil – the kind of evil that one can detect whilst walking past the closed door of a paedophile's cell.~~

'If you thought that, why did you agree to come?'

She hesitated an uncharacteristically long time before answering. 'Because I didn't think that to start with. I thought it might be fun – fun in the way that things you do are often fun: fun with cruelty, yes; fun with an amount of spite; but definitely fun.'

'Is that what you think I'm like?'

'Of course I do. You know that.'

'Can I tell you something? Can I tell you how I see me, in relation to you.'

'Go ahead,' she said, 'though I have to warn you that I'm expecting cruelty and spite.'

'At school, I was your frame – your dark oak frame: sturdy and thick, to set off your glowing blue light. You were a pretty little Vermeer, and I wasn't even gilded. I resented being chosen second; being, in fact, in everything, entirely secondary. It seemed to me worse than being last, for I was forever within touching distance of first. But there was no way I could just improve; others must see me as having improved. A miracle needed to happen. And so I worked upon myself. I worked upon being interesting. I gilded myself. I was determined to be such a bright shiny golden frame that no one would ever bother to look at the picture it contained. Which is ludicrous, of course. People are trained never to look at frames; they don't expect to find anything of interest there. Things did change. Now, they saw me, took me in, were a little astonished, then did their best to ignore me while they gave you a close inspection. (By people, I mean mostly men – or boys; they were boys for us then, weren't they?) And I realised, after a while, that all I was doing by acquiring gaudiness was becoming an embarrassment – both to myself and to you. So, I waited. I let myself dull, be smoked over, tarnish. Eventually, no-one even glanced at me. But I watched. I watched how and who you were... No, I watched *how* you were *who* you were. And I realised that if I really wanted to, I could stop myself from being a frame. We went to separate universities, and I did become a picture. And I was my own kind of picture. Maybe not a Vermeer – too shadowy for that – but a Caravaggio; dark and discomforting. I found there were people who came to the gallery just to look at me. I wasn't as jewelled and brilliant as you were, but no one came to you to speculate upon shadows. The problem only arose when we were hung once again side by side – there's always a problem when we're hung that way.'

This is all P.B.B. (from now on P.B.B. = Pretentious Beyond Belief), but if you say you really said it, I suppose I have to leave it in.

She sat back for a moment, confused by unpacking my boxes within boxes of metaphor. But this was a speech I'd imagined myself making for years. I think I may even have come up with the idea of paintings whilst we were still at school together. Added Vermeer in the Sixth Form, etcetera etcetera.

'I never knew,' Cleangirl said. 'Why didn't you tell me you hated me so much?'

'I couldn't,' I said. 'If you'd been good about it, I would have hated you even more; if you hadn't, I'd have lost my best and only friend. And so, you see, you were so fantastically good already, in every way, I couldn't give you the opportunity to be perfect. And being good about being good would have been close to that. I couldn't have lived if it had been me that had given you that final push into perfection. At least you had the decency to lord it over people unconsciously. Your humility would have destroyed me.'

Cleangirl stood up. 'I'm going to have to think about this,' she said, 'and think about whether I want to stay in this house.'

She almost staggered out. I think this little talk, in the end, will be good for our relationship. She's always needed to know what I really felt about her, and now she does. If there isn't a relationship left there in the end, then there really wasn't much of one there to begin with.

I am relying upon Cleangirl's goodness, even as I attack it.

After dinner, Edith came in from the garden, aglow with excitement; she'd been lying on the lawn and had seen a shooting star. Of course, we all go out to try to see another one. Half an hour passes; nothing – as if the sky had never known drama. Some go back inside, William, X; then more, Simona, Fleur, Henry; then only four are left: Edith, Cecile, Marcia and myself. It is quite magical – the shimmer of the constellations, half in your eye, half out in the universe. Marcia sits in her chair on the verandah, the rest of us are on our backs, on the lawn. And then – a shooting star doesn't come; and again – that *wasn't* a shooting star; and finally – just when we've all breathed in, ready to utter a sigh and give up – a line of light comes zinging down from the top of our eyes towards the sea; it scintillates; we are scintillated; and then, before we've had time to look away, to look in congratulation at one another, a second and a third star fall, a fourth and a fifth; we coo, that is our communication at this point – as if bending over the cot of a new-born; a sixth; it's all too much; if we go in and tell the others about this, they won't believe us; still, none of us have spoken; and finally, to underline the moment, a seventh, longer and brighter than all the others, bisects the heavens. 'Wow,' says Edith, and for once the Americanism doesn't annoy me. It *was* a wow experience – there was no other word for it. The lawn-lying three stand up, knowing that we have surfeited; it would be an impertinence to ask the cosmos for any more. We reach out our hands and touch, clumsily, the forearms of those who have already reached for us. The bright doorway into the house has itself gone starlike, seen through the film of tears across our eyes. We move, in silent intimacy, into the drawing room. 'Any luck?' asks Henry, though he should be able to read our radiance. Edith nods, Cecile hems, Marcia smiles and I say, 'Oh yes.'

Cecile wore... No. More than that.

It seems as if everyone, of a single accord, has started to wear colours approximating to the sand on the beach: snub, flat, warm, grey. (I think there is a difference between grey with an e and gray with an a: I think gray is a lot colder, blacker. Gray is the colour of ashes in a grate; grey, of prize pigeon feathers.) Fleur's cat, Audrey, who continues to live upon fences, is grey, with bright blue and bright red in there somewhere, somehow. Of course, the most exquisite of the exquisite is Cecile, who has produced a garment I hardly know what to call; it floats around her, like an atmosphere; it is neither loose nor tight: I think one might, without going too far wrong, call it a dress; smock would be too frumpy; veil would be better, but would suggest it covers either rather less or more of her than it does. Anyhow, we have all started to fit ourselves in to the slightly bleached, driftwoody tone of the place; really, it's Whistler brought to life: a dash, a rinse, a wash of thin whitey-yellow, a blip of violet, a smear of green, a speckle or two of crimson – these set the grey off, and make it fulfil whatever profundity it has. I think the grey is a competition between the beach and the sea (the sea which, depending upon its mood, can be grey, gray, green, blue, pink, yellow, white; I particularly love it when, looking out towards France and Belgium, it goes conchy pink, the sun going down behind one's back; yes, that's a distinct advantage St Ives has over here: the sur-sea-sun-set. Though the lighthouse *there* lies to northwards). ~~Yet perhaps it isn't – the West provides a glorious burst of brash American-looking obviousness; the East, a melancholic gaze towards Europe, Central Europe, Russia. A mental step towards the steppe – for the sea is our surrounding tedium, just as grass is for the nomads.~~ When one watches the light washing away over the North Sea, from just north of Southwold, in East Anglia, looking eastwards, the sun going down behind one's back, it is as if one were watching a cinematic experience; a vision projected upon the wall of a cave – it is as if one really were in Plato's cave, with one's shadow running before one into the sea to frolic in the very last of the dying light; ~~the margins of one's being dissolving, not fading... like a teabag in the hot water of eternity...~~ this is where the rhapsody of the place enters one, and makes one feel as if all other experience were ersatz – because too clearly marked under the heading 'Experience' ~~because too edged in black to be anything other than cartoonish.~~ Here, where one's margins are so easily dissoluble, the effort to verify that the experience is really one's own, and not just an incursion of the landscape, seascape, skyscape around, before, above one – that is what gives that experience its special Suffolk pathos. ~~That and the sensation that, however far~~

Did you really think this? In these exact words?

one may try to isolate mood from moment, the two are really indivisible – and so, in a sense, which is a nonsense, East Anglia is really oneself as much as oneself is East Anglia. One doesn't come here to feel this way, one comes here so that East Anglia may feel itself, through one. When we arrive here, we all turn curlew – creaking out our lonesomeness (for there is something American about the sense of one's person in vast sky-down-battered space) towards the flat front-facing echolessness. Even so, there is modesty in one's relationship with the place. There are others, myself among them, through whom an even more powerful emotional symmetry presents itself.

(This is too much poetry to go all in the one place; I shall have to cut it into pieces and distribute it throughout the text; but it is one mood, not several; a mood picture but rather too large – if one includes too much of this kind of stuff, one will end up with one of those terrible things 'a meditation upon'. Mood pieces are all very well, as long as they are pierced by the incongruous – and pretty rapidly at that. What I've been saying here, though, is that, where we are, it's almost impossible to find incongruity: the picture arranges itself before one has even set one's canvas upon the easel – to steal a metaphor. Perhaps I should have known that coming here would leach all the blood out of my text – dissipating the colours like watercolour wash. Wide it slides out to either side, whilst I, monolith, sit, straight backed, wracked, fighting to make vertical all the sights I say I see. I'm not dealing very well with this. People will laugh, for the wrong reasons. Perhaps profundity is never going to be my stock-in-trade. Yes: cut this. Shame.)

Agreed.

The end of the first week; this, my mood.

Thursday

Day Eight Week Two

This Cecile-Cornwall thing, I realise that I'm going to have to pursue it or die of curiosity. Sitting here in the Master Bedroom early this morning, wearing the Japanese silk dressing-gown that X bought me last Christmas, with the pale light and the whoosh outside telling me that the sea is near, I am sure Cecile's secret – unlike those of most people here – will be worth the discovering. Glancing back over what I've written, in order to see what I've said about her; trying to remember whether she'd ever mentioned Cornwall in the past: I'm absolutely convinced that what she's hiding is romance – a great romance. She strikes one as so delicately cynical about love that one can't help but figure her, at some past time, greatly wounded by it. In 1960, Cecile would have been... in her very early twenties. I have decided, later in the week, whenever opportunity presents, to mention Cornwall to her. However, I have to be careful not to get caught using what I've learnt from the cameras; subtlety, in all things.

Edith walked into the kitchen at nine o'clock looking not so much white as off-white with a tinge of greeny yellow.

'I saw a ghost last night,' she said, then added, 'I did, last night I saw a ghost.'

Of course, she immediately had the attention of everyone in the room – which was the women, mostly: plus Henry; minus Cleangirl. Marcia's cookery lesson was quite eclipsed. She had been teaching us how to make a Jamaican breakfast, and kill ourselves with heart-disease in the process.

'Do tell us about it,' I said, thinking it might be *trés amusant*.

'Where was it?' asked Fleur.

'What did it look like?' asked Simona.

'Are you all right?' asked Marcia, knowing that if she could not herself be the centre of attention she might as well be seen ministering to the centre of attention.

'It was in the corridor upstairs,' said Edith, after she'd been sat down in one of the Windsor chairs, lifted up, hugged, sat down again. 'I was too scared to come out,' she said, 'before it got really light.'

Henry was leaning back against the Aga. I gave him an ironic look, expecting it to be returned – it wasn't. I think at that moment he truly believed that his daughter had seen a spirit of the dead. What a strange man he is. But she did seem entirely in earnest.

'What did it look like?' asked Cecile, repeating Simona's question.

'Well...' said Edith. She halted.

'Go on,' said Henry.

'No,' she said, 'I'm too embarrassed to say. If I say, you won't believe me.'

'I promise you on my soul,' said Cecile, 'that whatever you say, I will believe you.'

I don't believe anyone else could have coaxed the what-came-next out of Edith. 'It's stupid,' she said, 'but, all right... it looked like someone with a sheet over their body and with holes cut out for eyes.'

There was a huge relieved general adult laugh. I directed another ironic glance at Henry, and was delighted to find it pinging instantly back.

The only person to remain in the previous moment with Edith, the moment of green-faced seriousness, was Cecile. 'Was it moving?' she asked.

'Yes,' said Edith. 'It seemed to be floating down the corridor.'

'I see,' said Cecile, 'and did it make any noise at all? Did it speak?'

'It made a quiet moaning sound,' said Edith, 'like – whoo-whoo-whoo.'

There was another laugh, and total relief.

'I wonder who it was,' I said. 'Henry, was it you? Henry, you haven't been frightening your daughter out of her wits, have you?'

'No,' he said, seriously, 'what do you think I'm like?'

We laughed again.

'I hope you haven't been cutting holes in the sheets,' I said, enjoying the opportunity to flirt.

'Come with me,' said Cecile. 'I'm going to talk with you about this seriously – even if the rest of them will start to laugh at me, too.'

Fleur wanted to go with them, but Edith had seen her among the laughers. Upon this issue, Cecile was the only stony-faced person to retain her trust. They went together to Cecile's room.

I was desperate to go up to the attic, and listen in; but am aware that I have to be very careful about being caught. I waited for Marcia to finish her demonstration, then casually excused myself and strolled upstairs.

Disappointment followed: Cecile and Edith were not in either of their rooms. I later found out they'd only fetched their coats from upstairs, then gone for a long walk down the beach. Edith, it seems, hadn't wanted to speak about the 'ghost' so close to where it haunted.

Realised, belatedly, that I must have slept through the dawn chorus this morning. Perhaps I'm getting used to it, at last.

10.30 a.m. Alan's a very odd person. I walked in upon him in the kitchen just now. Without my asking, he began to explain what he was doing: 'Sometimes I like to make myself the worst cup of coffee I possibly can – stale instant powder, lukewarm water, long-life milk, three sweetener tablets, all stirred together with a plastic spoon – you know, with some of the granules not dissolving, just floating bitterly on the top...'

'Why?'

'I don't know – some form of self-punishment, I expect: nothing very exciting.'

Alan has been in therapy since 1983. He has other problems, too, besides the psychological. His mouth is the dental equivalent of immediately post-War Coventry, and he has terrible tinnitus. He went to one mid-'90s rave, to see what it was like – woke up the next morning and phoned the police about a car alarm going off in his street; only it wasn't a car alarm, it was the ringing in his ears – which hasn't stopped for a single moment since. He says being by the sea helps him not hear it.

After describing his intermittent yearning for crappy coffee, Alan told me that he'd phoned around and had found a kennel for Domino – quite nearby. Marcia is going to drive him and the dog over there, this morning.

The past few days, Alan has become more lugubrious than ever. He hangs around in the darker corners of the house, waiting for something to happen; something specific, I think, which he will not reveal to anyone else. He is like the man who hides under a lampshade in a vicars-and-knickers farce; he finds the oddest place in a room to stand, and then remains there a quarter of the day. He is so tall, too, that one has a tendency to walk straight past him when he's under his metaphorical lampshade – as a cartoon mouse would walk past the foot of a cartoon elephant. Sometimes, I feel I can't see his head for its being lost in the clouds: his hair is a fleecy tangle of thick black and thin white. It is as if he has suffered a bereavement, and yet refuses to let anyone know what it was. (Fleur? Fleur's refusal of his advances? The scene upon the beach?) He would be happier, I've decided, doing his most natural thing: lecturing. And so I've asked him one evening soon to give us all a talk. I expect he'll choose his specialist subject – the unfunniest films of Woody Allen.

Marcia and Alan back from the kennels; Domino happily – they say – ensconced. I wonder how long it will take Audrey to pad her timid feline way back into the house? Perhaps I should get Fleur to move the grass-patch nearer the French windows. Now she's here, I'm glad we have a cat about the place. Just saw Alan tickling her chin by the edge of the flowerbed – perhaps hoping Fleur would come along.

1 p.m. Lunch. Salads. The guests still talking about the ghost, all the time, all over the house, except when Edith is in the room. She is aware of this, I think. Everyone is being very kind to her; fearing perhaps for her sanity. Cleangirl, who only belatedly learnt of the visitation, has yet to leave her daughter's side. Cecile, too, is with her all the time. Whether because of this attention or in spite of it, Edith seems calmer than this morning. Henry also is more relaxed. I talked to him for ten minutes, without him running away. Maybe I can, after all, make my predictions come true.

3 p.m. Thinking out loud in the drawing room of nice things possibly to do, as a group, someone – Marcia, I think; though there is such a babble it might be any one of three – *a person* suggests going for a swim in the sea. Before I can put forward any objection (temperature, decorum, ludicrousness), half the guests are already in their bedrooms rootling for the cozzies they've all individually and unbidden decided to pack. As luck has it, I have packed mine, too; out of a similar illogic, probably: not that I expected to *wear* it, but that the idea of going on a seaside holiday without one seemed somehow wrong. We reconvene on the steps to the garden, five minutes later – then wait for Fleur, who's only just heard; and Marcia, who takes a little longer than the rest of us to get changed

We were coming to the seaside – of course we packed our cozzies, dumbo!

(for obvious reasons). Eventually, everyone heads beachwards – minus Henry, who at first seems to want to come but then decides to stay in the garden and read. Marcia is carried most of the way, piggyback, by Alan: she can make it to the bottom of the lawn in her wheelchair, but doesn't want to leave it (so expensive) there unguarded. There is a translucent-but-hazy sky with only one cloud in it, like an egg white containing a chick-placenta. The sun figures for a smear of left-behind yolk. It is, however, very very hot, and almost uncomfortably humid. Swimming-weather. As we cross the dunes there is banter: last one in's a... but as they can no longer be a cissy (not with Marcia thought-policeperson here), there is a halt, an embarrassment. Alan suggests 'a wet blanket' – which gets groans, for not working on any level. 'Spoilsport,' I say, but there is a rip of the wind and no-one seems to hear, so I don't bother repeating it. 'Scaredy-cat,' dares Edith, and gets cheers of congratulation. 'Yes,' everyone is saying at once, 'last one in's a scaredy-cat.' We jog the final few flattening-out yards, even Alan. Marcia, determined not to be last, is pulling the towel off from around her hips; Alan has his around his neck, and she grabs that, too – slam-dunking them both to the ground. 'Go on!' she squeals. 'Giddy-up.' Alan laughs, the soft sand under his feet giving way beneath their combined weight – causing him to teeter, her to slip, and them to keep veering, veering lop-sidedly. Others watch: will they make a sufficient depth of water before she falls? Spray bounces off Alan's knees and Marcia is shrieking with delight – out to the side, almost horizontal. He's in now up to his waist, and the drag of the water slows him somewhat. With a final effort, he tosses Marcia forwards – like a racehorse dumping its rider over a refused fence. She does half a somerset; just enough to land her flat on her back. Everyone cheers, and not half-heartedly as before: we feel ourselves genuinely united and delighted by their triumph. But now it's time to find the scaredy-cat. Those with towels and flip-flops drop them, without affectation, and jog in; those, like myself, more formally dressed, have to sit down to unbuckle and -lace. Soon, only Cecile, sensibly taking her time, and William, who has brought his trunks but hasn't yet put them on, are still (with me) on the sand. William is trying to hide himself with a towel as he attempts to step into the pant-like figure-of-eight, but he keeps missing, flashing the rest of us glimpses of a wholly undesirable nature. (After his earlier flash, I can't help thinking this deliberate.) In the end, he just throws the trunks down, says to himself more than anyone else, 'What have I got to be ashamed of?' and runs, completely naked, into the sea. The others notice, meercat-like, heads turning all at once. There is another, louder, cheer. How people surprise one! Cecile is now walking towards the water, making final adjustments to the pink floral-rubber swimming-cap she has somehow managed to pack along with everything else. She has astounding legs for her age. Looking at them, I forget the scaredy-cat contest until it's too late. I stand up and begin to trot after her. But not so fast that I will overtake her. She hesitantly makes her way into the surf, and I follow two steps behind her. 'Scaredy-cat,' Edith shouts at me. The others join in, as if this were a school playground. 'No, no,' Cecile calls on top of them. 'It was a draw! It was a draw! I'm a scaredy-cat, too.' I give her a bright smile meant to convey stupendous thanks. We swim. It is frighteningly cold. I think my heart is going to stop. Some – X and the other men, mostly – plough their straight furrows straight off towards the horizon. The rest of us stay within our depths, doggy-paddling, crawling, even butterflying (Simona). Marcia, though, is a very strong swimmer. She has a race with Edith – and although she doesn't beat her, she competes well enough to make the whole thing unembarrassing. Her huge shoulders keep her moving forwards, keeping her mouth out of the water. She loves it, though, and whoops louder and longer than everyone else. The sea is a great leveller; although Cecile, pinkly bobbing on her back, manages to maintain a greater decree of decorum than the rest of us combined. Alan does semi-underwater forward rolls; William whoops; Edith looks eight; Cleangirl stays close. It's like a party I went to once, where they had a bouncy castle in the garden. Staid grandmothers were suddenly flying through the air alongside giddy grandchildren. It was lovely. I look around at the various heads and backs and splashes and think, 'This is because of me: if it weren't for me, they wouldn't be here.' And for almost the first time since they arrived, I feel thankful. Then the Splashing Wars start: Edith vs. Cecile (no-one else would dare splash her; but with Edith Cecile doesn't seem to mind – is delighted, to tell the truth); Simona at first tentatively vs. me. This soon escalates into an all-out

Interrupted just then by something far less important, which I've already forgotten – but it took me down to the kitchen. Chef and something; menus. I don't feel like completing the description of the beach-swim, now. We stopped splashing, kept swimming, discussed the lighthouse, got cold, got out, waited for the further-off swimmers to crawl back, sat shivering, walked tenderfoot back to the house, made hot drinks. 'That was fun,' said Edith. 'We should do it every day.' O youth, youth which believes that if an experience is great once, it will be great when you attempt to repeat it. But all grown-ups know there is no return to the Halcyon Ballroom; once it closes its doors, a new dance-craze is what one has to find. Still, without innocence like Edith's, today probably wouldn't have been as special as it was. I'm still being called a scaredy-cat, and doing my best not to get annoyed by it. It makes me wish I'd sprinted past Cecile, dived under the waves; then no-one would be being called scaredy-cat. Certainly not Cecile. With her it would be equivalent to saying, 'You're old.' She is extraordinarily well-preserved, tip to toe. I'm sure it's down to never visiting a gym or worrying herself to death over modish health fads.

After the Explosion of Swim, I still have sand in various places about my body, places I'm not going to detail. My bottom feels deeply cold and damp, and will continue to do so until it's had hot water running over it for a long long while. The upstairs shower has been constantly occupied for about an hour now; I said I'd go last. Luckily, because it has one of those gas heaters which work on demand, we're never going to run out of hot water. That goes for the downstairs bath, too. I'm sitting here in the Master Bedroom in a towel with sea-sticky hair and skin feeling as salty as a French fry.

Shower equals heaven. Really, it was as good as Bach's St Matthew Passion, in hot bright falling-liquid form. A miracle: sunlight coming out of cucumbers.

Quick spy.

Marcia and Fleur, in the kitchen – pottering. After a lot of flim and a not inconsiderable amount of flam, they finally get down to it.

Fleur says, 'I hope you don't mind me asking –'

'No. Go on,' says Marcia.

'Wait till you hear what it is.'

'I'm sure I can take it.'

'– but when you arrived, you had a black eye, and well...'

'Oh, *that*.' Marcia gurgles richly, like a drain emptying of molasses.

'I wondered how you got it.'

Marcia strokes her forehead. 'It's almost gone now, hasn't it?'

'Yes, entirely.'

'Well, let me tell you what happened.'

Fleur leans back against the kitchen table, letting her face be licked by the tonguey vapour of her coffee-cup.

'I was at home, with my lover. It was the morning of the day that I was meant to be setting off for here. We were in the bedroom, and I was getting out of bed. My lover – she's called Mo – already knew that I was coming here for a month. I'd told her just as soon as Victoria asked me. (Which didn't give me very much time, at all.) And so, anyway, Mo starts pretending to be very logical, which is how she is when she starts arguments. I knew I couldn't stop her till she'd gone through all her moods. After the logical bit came the plea for pity. The logic was, I couldn't afford a month's holiday. Which was rubbish. What she meant was, I should be saving all my days and pennies up. She's set her heart on Africa, on seeing it with me. Then the pity, "You don't love me. How could you love me and then do this to me?" Then came stage three, silence. I had time to dress, start making coffee. I was in the kitchen when, bang, in walks stage four, fury. She didn't mean to hit me. She was just throwing her arms all about the place to show how passionately she felt. It's always like this with Mo. We've only been going out about two months, but before that I was friends with someone who went out with her. She told me all about Mo's little moods. Whack – whack right in the eye. And that's how I got it. Mo spent the rest of the day apologising, helping me to pack, waving me off.'

'Have you spoken since?'

'Oh yes. I called from a motorway service station, just to make sure she was okay. I didn't let her know how upset I was – the impression I was going to make: turning up here looking like some beaten-up boxer.'

'And have you made up?'

'She says she's planning a big welcome for me when I get home.'

Marcia gave a laugh, and Fleur gave one back.

Cleangirl spends much if not most of each day writing letters. When we arrived here, she began with postcards – most often of the lighthouse. But now she seems to be managing to turn out four or five quite wedgy envelopes, before teatime. A little routine has developed whereby anyone going into Southwold takes whatever post has been left upon the hall table. The guests are trusting enough to leave postcards there, readable by all and sundry. So far, I have resisted the wish to take the kettle up to my room, do some steaming. I have, once or twice, glanced over the pile, to see if I recognised any of Cleangirl's addressees. I did, a few: her mother, a Canadian friend who moved to Edinburgh, someone we were both at school with. At the moment I'm wondering if she's telling them about Edith's ghost; but if she wanted immediate advice, I'm sure she'd call them on her phone. She's said no more about leaving; we've hardly spoken since yesterday.

Spy.

William and Simona just now, on their double bed, *fighting*, really like a couple of kittens; managing somehow, I don't know, to look light-limbed – lightsome – and never likely to damage one another; but still biffing, faces and other parts, with what were less fists than paws; they *were* hitting hard, but without hurt – quite bizarre, and truly private and at the same time animal; if I didn't know better, I'd think they were putting it on, just for a laugh, just to freak me out. I was touched by this description. It's lovely. It can stay.

7 p.m. In the drawing room again, everyone was slightly *déshabillé*. We all felt a greater general intimacy with one another's bodies. Cecile sat upon the sofa, brushing out Simona's thick tresses – Simona who, in turn, was putting Edith's straight blonde hair into a Japanese bun, held together by a couple of felt-tip pens. This wouldn't have happened before the swim. It was such a success, I'm almost tempted to claim it as an idea of my own. I won't: I'm too honest for that.

Dinner began, without any falling-off of intimacy. Over moussaka and green salad, talk turned to *wonderful places we have swum*, and this led on, inevitably, to *wonderful places we have been*, and then just *places we have been*. It would be quite fun to create a complete list, as we seem collectively to have visited everywhere from Albania (Henry, on an Intourist trip) to Zanzibar (Cecile, to visit an anthropologist friend). Even Edith has been to France, Spain, Morocco, Venezuela, Germany, Belgium, Switzerland, America and Portugal – in that order (I hope I've got it right: she'll be annoyed if I haven't). There were some embarrassments, as people had to confess to having been to places with partners previous to their current. 'I never knew you went to...' 'Oh, yes, back in 1994.' 'Who was that with?' '1994 – that would have been...' I don't think anyone's feelings were badly hurt. Fleur mentioned Venice, briefly; but I was the only one around the table to know that this was where she'd honeymooned her first, failed marriage. (Alan, I saw, paid close attention to all Fleur said – whilst pretending to be absorbed in picking his cuticles.) Cecile hadn't travelled as extensively as I'd thought: she'd been all over the Soviet Union, 'as it was, but not since Yeltsin came to power', and Europe, but not Asia or South America. When it got on to favourite places, she said, straight out, 'Cornwall,' which I found astounding: I thought it was her most private thing of all. Fleur's favourite was Devon – and so the two weren't sure whether to feel closer or more rivalrous. My personal favourite was, 'A king-sized bed – I don't really care *where* it is.' When forced to pick a country, I chose France. This gained me a smile from Cecile, but it was a slightly pitying one. I should have thought more deeply: If she loved it so much, why would she have moved to London?

As I can't do a complete list of places visited, here is one of favourite places: X, Cape Town; William, Dublin – because of the pubs; Henry, Seattle – 'It feels so clean for a city'; Cleangirl, the Alps; Edith, the sea anywhere (Brighton); Marcia, Versailles; Simona, Barcelona – 'mainly at night'; me, sticking to Paris; Cecile, Cornwall; Alan, some temple-mountain in Japan, the name of which I couldn't possibly spell (A-ka-li-do); Fleur, Devon.

I had wondered, earlier in the day, whether there was going to be any trouble getting Edith to bed. Perhaps she would refuse to sleep another night in the house. But, curiously, she seemed quite eager to go. Daylight-bravery, maybe. At eight forty-five, she turned herself in. I am fairly sure that Cecile had something to do with her calm. The promise of safety. Cleangirl went up with her, then came down – obviously not required.

Cecile has now definitely begun to mix and match. Today, she wore her alligator shoes with the purple blouse and skirt (rather than the matching purple shoes) – and it worked! My god, she looked bizarre, but only in such a way that one, too, wanted to look bizarre. This is her *Vogue*-effect.

10.15 p.m. I should really write a description of watching Edith talking to 'the ghost' in her sleep – for this is what she does, it's clear. Lying on her side, semi-foetal, eyes closed, giving the odd kick with her legs – like a dog chasing dream-rabbits; she mutters, grunts, shakes and now and again sends out a long, high, thin wail.

X and I were lying in bed at about twelve o'clock when there came a thumping from one of the other bedrooms. At first, it alarmed us: ~~was it William, taking something out on Simona?~~ was it someone hitting someone? No. The thumping was too regular for that. It started slowly, and then sped up, and then started syncopating: boom boom boom became buh-boom boom-buh boom-boom buh-boom, etc. We realised then that there were actually two thumps, one nearer by, one further off. At moments they came entirely into sync; but then – like two alarm clocks on either side of a bed, their ticks slightly over and slightly under a second – they went out of phase. It was sex, and it was happening now, between people we knew, and could envisage – or rather, couldn't, in the circumstances, help *but* envisage. The louder thump was Cleangirl and Henry, and was coming through the wall at our heads; the quieter one, and for the moment slower, came from William and Simona's room, at our feet. 'What about Edith?' I said.

'What about her?' X replied.

'She can hear,' I said. 'She can hear her parents, doing it.'

'She's either asleep –'

'This would wake her up.'

'– or they must be fine about it. At home, too.'

'But William and Simona have joined in.'

'Unless it's Alan and Fleur,' he suggested.

'You don't think so?' I said.

'Not really.'

'I'll just go and check.'

X took gentle hold of my wrist. 'I don't think you should spy on them when you know they're having sex. You're not going to learn anything from it.'

'I am,' I said, 'I'm going to learn *who's* having sex.'

'You already know.'

'No, I don't; I'm not absolutely sure.'

'Yes, you are. It couldn't possibly be Fleur and Alan – they wouldn't dare make so much noise.'

'Fleur can't help it,' I said, 'she even prays loudly.'

'You just want to have a look at them, having sex. Don't pretend it's anything else.'

'Well, don't you?' I asked. 'This is the only opportunity you're ever going to get.'

'No,' he said. 'And I don't think you'll learn anything much from it, as a writer. People having sex just look like people having sex; if you want to see that buy a video.'

'You know that's an absolute lie,' I said, 'and I don't know why you're even bothering to tell it: I always write sex scenes in my other books; it's expected of me.'

The thumping had continued throughout all this – the louder

getting quieter and the quieter louder; then, abruptly, the thumps of Cleangirl and Henry took off again. It was exactly like listening to an old car engine starting up, on a frosty morning.

'I've got to see,' I said. I was out of bed, and using the pole to reach for the ladder-hook before X moved.

'They'll hear,' he said, quite loudly.

'Shh,' I said, 'they'll certainly hear even more if you shout.'

'Come back to bed,' he said.

'No,' I said, 'this is what I've paid all this money for.' I pulled the attic door open, and the ladder began to slide and scrape down. It was rather loud, but the thumping (thumpings) neither stopped or slowed – in fact, they were both going so rapidly that I thought I wouldn't be able to make it up to the screens before it was over.

'I disapprove,' hissed X.

'Disapprove, then,' I said, 'I'm having a look.' I scurried up the ladder, following my instincts, my vocation, my prurience. The screens were on; I left them like that the whole time – there was no reason not to. Cleangirl and Henry were doing it doggy-fashion; William and Simona were Missionary. ~~(Strange, I'd imagined the couples quite the other way round.) When he withdrew to change position, I saw William's penis: it looked remarkably like a rabbit, skinned and ready to be cooked – dark, muscly and so so ugly.~~ I looked at the other rooms. Fleur had gone foetal, the sheets and blankets whirling around her: she was trying to block her ears with her hands. Alan appeared to be sleeping through, as – at first – did Edith; but then I saw her turn over, side to side: it was hard to tell, with the resolution of the screen so rough, whether or not her eyes were open. One thing I did notice, she was sucking her thumb. I wondered what a child psychiatrist would make of that little detail, at eleven and a half years old. She seemed to have stopped talking to the 'ghost'. It was only as an afterthought that I took in what Cecile was doing: it was quieter than what the couples were doing, and it was solo, but I suppose it counted as the same activity. ~~Her~~

~~hands were beneath the bedclothes, her legs made a lifted triangle of them, and there was no mistaking – from her face – what was going on beneath.~~ I glanced back at Cleangirl and Henry, who juddered to a halt, then William and Simona, who were still going. ~~I felt far guiltier for seeing the smile upon Cecile's face than their barenaked humping.~~

Shamefacedly, I climbed down the ladder. X had turned his back to me. Quiet as I could, with only a slight metallic scrape, I pushed the ladder back up into the roof. Then I climbed in on the right side of the bed, and X turned his back on me again.

'I'm sorry,' I said. 'You were right; I shouldn't have done that.'

He did not reply. I tried to get close to him, move my lips in over his ear; he shrugged me off.

Simona and William's thumping came to an abrupt stop, and the house was newly silent.

I lay, lonely and ashamed, for at least an hour – failing to get to sleep, and failing to clear my mind of the image of Cecile's small private joy. Or perhaps it wasn't joy; perhaps, given the background noise, it was only practical.

Despite him not talking to me, I was glad to have X's male bulk beside me – as tidewall against the bitter seas: emptiness, loneliness, childlessness, ridiculousness. I wished, very much, that we too had had sex. Perhaps it would have made this feeling worse (sex often takes me from a perfectly good mood into deep existential crisis), but at least it would have given me something recent and contrasting to remember.

'I'm *sorry*,' I said to X.

He didn't even grunt.

Friday

Day Nine Week Two

This morning I woke to the harsh sound of nearby drilling, and assumed it was merely the dawn chorus up to their usual cacophony. But it turns out that for the next few days there will be workmen down on the road, mending potholes.

You say something very similar to this a few pages on. You can cut this or that, but one of them will have to go.

Oh no, it's doing something I really didn't want – turning into country-house gothic. ~~I'm entirely unequipped to deal with this and I have no inclination to *become* equipped.~~ Why did I end up with the damned B-Team? That's where all my troubles began. If I'd had a simple hutchful of bedhoppers, I could have coped: coupling and uncoupling, it's what I do – it's my stock-in-trade. I didn't want ghosts and children's bedrooms and toilet paper and stairs... I didn't want freaks: I wanted normal, healthy, nymphomaniac thirty-year-olds. That's what sells. But instead this huge house full of adults has come to be dominated by the hysteria of a schoolgirl. How? It's silly, for a start. It's ludicrous. It's absolutely ridiculous. Cecile referred this morning, in the kitchen, to 'the house behind the house' ~~– meaning, I suppose, the spectral one contained within this actual.~~ She had spent a good hour in Edith's bedroom, talking quietly with our star. I watched: Edith saw the ghost again, last night. Same thing: sheet, whoo-whoo. Cecile and Edith were astonishingly intimate, hugging and crying. There seems now to be a mystical bond between them. This, I couldn't help but think, has something to do with the map of Cornwall on Cecile's wall. Perhaps something ghostly happened to her, too. Edith is looking dangerously washed out. It's hysteria, plain and simple. Sleeplessness. If I were her mother, I'd be asking myself some serious

Necessary? Patronising?

questions. Where, for example, can I find some nice boys for her to meet? I think a decent pash would set Edith back on the right track. But there seems no chance of her developing a proper crush on X.

This morning, I went into Edith's former room, the Nursery, in order to check through the titles of the books. I wanted to be sure that there were no ghostie ones – nothing that might have knocked her onto this particular path of silliness. I was hoping, I suppose, for a copy of something gothic, *The Monk, The Castle of Otranto, Dracula* – or at the very least, *Northanger Abbey*. But it was like looking along the shelves of an antiquarian bookseller: the yellow spines of the Collins' Enid Blytons, and the blue and white striped spines of the Brock Books ones – with a Scottie dog on, as insignia of publisher. And so, I can find no literary cause for this outburst.

Oh, I know this is all a-scrambled up; irredeemably so. I shall have to spend months sorting it out into an acceptable order, and then fictionalising it. It's such a relief to know that no-one will ever read these particular words, and that they for ever will remain for myself only. And perhaps X. And Simona. And I might pick out the odd choice section and sell it to the *Guardian* Women's Page.

we got a far better offer from the News of the World.

I wonder about Edith's psychohistory, and I wonder whether it's really worth wondering about. It must be sex, surely. Hysteria. It can't be anything else. I can't believe that Cleangirl and Henry have caused her any trauma – other than by being so immaculate that she feels she'll never live up to them. That's the kind of thing that, one day soon, you'll be able to sue for.

11.15 a.m. Down to the beach. O these days of coatless weather, I wish England would always be like this – it's better as a slightly desiccated version of itself; as a flower, flattened and pressed between the pages of an anthology of Romantic poetry. ~~The only~~

~~water sufficient is the undrinkable sea, spreading itself around us like amniotic fluid – misshapen baby (and placenta) that England is. It's when one walks along the margin that one really appreciates all that is behind one, or to one's left or right; the rest of the time the middle is muddled by the too close upness of our vision~~. ~~Victoria, specifics: now.~~

Victoria, shut up: now!

Quick and nearly disastrous word with Marcia after lunch. 'Your eye seems to be on the mend,' I say. 'Oh, no problem *there*, any more,' replies Marcia. 'It must have been nasty...' 'What?' she asks, stopped. 'How you got it,' I say. 'What do you mean?' asks Marcia. 'You don't *know* how I got it.' I think: I could lie, and say Fleur told me about Mo and the fight; but Marcia is sure to check, and then I'll be discovered. Better far, I decide, to look a bit stupid. 'Well, I assumed you'd been mugged, or hit, or something.' '*Wrong*,' says Marcia, 'I was trying to get a book down from the top shelf, and the book next to it came too – blam, straight in the eye. Serves me right for wanting to read *The Jungle Book* when I was pissed.' 'Oh really,' I say, 'I thought it was something more violent than that.' I should have shut up – I should have just shut up. 'Why?' asks Marcia. 'Because I'm a victim?' 'I didn't mean that –' But in some ways luckily she wheels off in a mini-huff.

2.15 p.m. What with all this ghost-nonsense going on, knocking the entire project off kilter, I have found it very very difficult to keep my eye upon my many other plots.

Disappointingly, there seem to have been no further developments between Alan and Fleur. Since he took Domino to the kennels, there has been no need for them to come into conflict over petty issues. They don't avoid one another; neither, as far as I can see, do they seek one another out. (Audrey, though, has been a little more visible, skulking through the flowerbeds.)

Whence has the passion of that first scene upon the beach gone?

They can't *just* have hidden it away in their emotional sock drawers, taking it out to look at late at night.

Fleur writes her diary; I've seen her doing that all her life. She also prays. It's hilarious – I haven't described it yet, have I? – kneeling at the bottom of the bed, like a Victorian genre painting; except sometimes she lifts the palms of her hands up towards the imagined countenance of heaven. (The only time I have made a similar gesture is in German or American hotels, in worship of a particularly divine power-shower.) Fleur does her best at such moments to look as if God's Holy Grace were raining down upon her, torrentially. And perhaps it is: inside her head. I'm writing about her as if she knows I'm watching her. She is praying now; I can see her lips move. Like all higher souls, there is something deeply affected about her.

As I entered the drawing room, a full-scale discussion of recent events was taking place; for once, it didn't stop the moment I came in.

'We need to know,' said Cecile to the others, 'if anything went on in this house, in the past, however long ago, we need to know.'

Edith was sitting beside her, being half-cuddled even as Cecile leant forward in the earnestness of her argument.

'Victoria,' said Henry, his concern making him look particularly handsome. 'I'm glad you're here. This involves you as much as anyone.'

Cleangirl patted the space beside her on the sofa, but I decided to remain standing.

'All I'm saying is, what good would it do?' said X. 'Whatever Edith saw, it wasn't a ghost.'

'Still on the ghost?' I said.

'Very definitely,' said Cecile. 'We have a request – Edith and I.'

'You don't want to move rooms again, do you?' I asked.

'No,' said Edith, quietly, croakily. And I realised that I'd embarrassed her, by making her speak in front of everyone in the room. (Just about everyone was there – apart from Alan, who I guessed was taking the idea of Domino for a walk on the beach.)

'It's not that at all,' said Cecile. 'What we'd like is if you could just put us in touch with the owners of this house. We would like to ask them, directly, if there has ever been any paranormal activity here.'

I couldn't help slightly scoffing; Cecile is, now and again, a woman of hidden shallows.

'Do you think that's likely?' I asked, making sure that Edith knew I wasn't expecting her to reply.

'We do,' said Cecile.

I looked at everyone else. They were paying full attention to me for almost the first time since we arrived. (My *riposte* to Fleur's speech being the main exception.) I wasn't going to waste this.

'No-one wants to take this opportunity to confess to having walked up and down the upstairs corridor, draped in a sheet, moaning?' I said.

People laughed; it was a wonderful, warm sound. I remembered it well.

'Very well, then,' I said. 'I don't see any reason why I shouldn't give them a call.'

'We'd like to speak to them ourselves,' said Edith, bursting out.

'No,' I said. 'I'll be very tactful. I just don't want them thinking they've let the house to a –' I realised I had to be careful here '– an even bigger bunch of lunatics than they thought they had.'

Another laugh; a laugh warmer still.

'I shall go and call from upstairs. I'm sure you can manage to contain yourselves for a few moments.'

I turned to go, but – 'Can I come with you, at least?' tumble-mumbled Edith.

With this crowd, there was no saying no. 'Come on, then,' I said.

We went out of the room. Experimentally, I put my arm round Edith. She did not shrug it off. In fact, she seemed to appreciate it.

Once the door was closed behind us, I said to her, 'You realise I feel a little responsible for all this. I don't want to get everyone in a panic. If it appears that I'm not taking you as seriously as I might, that's only because I want to avoid – well, something horrible.'

'I understand,' said Edith, quite the good girl.

We went up the stairs. Edith was wrapped in a brown and orange blanket, with tassles, that had come from the wardrobe in her room. She was also, I noticed, wearing a long silk dress that had obviously belonged to the daughter of the house. Not the sort of thing that Edith should be wearing; now wasn't the moment to chastise her, though.

We went into the Master Bedroom. I tried to prevent myself from glancing up at the attic hatch.

'You sit on the bed,' I said to Edith. She humped herself up onto the counterpane.

The Owners' number in Tuscany was at the top of a laminated sheet labelled 'In Case of Emergencies' that they'd left tacked to the wall in the kitchen. I'd taken it down, on Day Zero, and placed it in the drawer of my bedside table. I picked up the phone, took a moment to breathe in, smiled at Edith, then dialled.

There was no reply. I waited about half a minute. 'No-one home,' I said. 'We'll try later.'

'There's a mobile number, too,' said Edith, who'd picked up the 'In Case of' sheet from the counterpane, where I'd let it fall.

'You really are determined, aren't you?' I said.

I dialled the mobile number. The husband answered after a couple of rings. We said hello; he asked whether everything was all right. 'Fine,' I said. 'So far we've only burnt down the garden shed.' He laughed, tightly. 'No, really,' I continued, 'we're having a fantastic time. It's really a perfect place. If I owned it, I don't think I could bear to be away from it – particularly at this time of the year. It's so lovely.'

Edith gave me a very teenage grimace of impatience. I wondered for a moment if she'd have done that before seeing 'the ghost'? Was she growing up? Fast?

'We have a question,' I said, before Edith started to make teenage impatience-noises, too. Having had no time at all in which to phrase the question, I decided I might as well blurt – but blurt comically, 'Is the house at all, you know, *haunted*? Because, you see, someone here has seen a figure draped in a white sheet walking up and down, on the upstairs landing – oh, and they were making a moaning noise.'

Edith nodded.

There was silence on the line.

'Hello?' I asked. 'Are you still there?'

'It is,' he said. 'It's haunted. Oh God.'

I'd expected a little more resistance than that.

'You don't seem too surprised at me asking the question,' I said.

'Who saw her?' the Owner asked.

'Her?' I said. 'The ghost's a she, is it?'

'Oh yes,' said the Owner. 'Who saw her?'

'Who saw her?' I repeated.

Edith made a lunge, grabbed the receiver from my hand. 'I did,' she said. 'I saw her.'

He asked her a question, to which she replied, 'I'm eleven and a half.'

She listened for a long while, then handed the phone back to me.

'Well, I'm glad –' I said, into the receiver.

'He hung up,' said Edith. I looked at her a little angrily. It was only then that I heard the noises from downstairs; they can only be described as a commotion.

We went out onto the upstairs corridor; me half expecting us to encounter the disruptive sheeted figure. The commotion continued, if anything getting louder, closer. Fleur swung towards us, up the stairs. 'We heard,' she said. 'We listened – in the kitchen, on the extension.'

'You...' I said, speechless. Others, too, were coming towards us.

'We know,' said Fleur. She ran to Edith and put her arms round her. 'I'm so sorry I ever doubted you,' Fleur gushed. 'Oh, you poor thing,' she added. Cecile was there, too. And Cleangirl.

X looked at me and shook his head, disapproving again. The scene continued, in an unbearable and irrelevant fashion.

Agh!!! I'm not equipped for this, as a writer or as a woman. Why? Two main reasons: first, I don't believe in ghosts; second, I'm absolutely bloody terrified of ghosts. These may seem mutually exclusive but they're not. I don't believe in ghosts because I don't *allow* myself to believe in ghosts; I don't allow myself to believe in ghosts because, if I did, it would seriously retard my ability to deal with the world. Ever since I was little I've had that feeling of the supernatural picking me up by the scruff of the neck; as if the Unknown were abusive old Sister Grimshaw, come back from the dead to drag me once again by my collar to the front of class. Cut? There's enough about you and your problems writing the book already.

One of my first thoughts was that I might have caught the ghost on camera. But I remembered almost straight away that the upstairs landing was one of the few places in the house that *weren't* covered by a spy-camera. Costs had been getting prohibitive; and I couldn't anticipate anything particularly interesting happening in the corridor. If bedhopping was going on, I would see which bedroom had been left, and which arrived in, and I'd thought that would be sufficient in and of itself. And anyway, I wouldn't be able to tell anyone about what I'd caught on tape until after the month was over, and even then... It was frustrating either way. I wondered if motion-sensitive cameras would have picked up the ectoplasmic nightwalker. Then reminded myself that I didn't believe at all at all in ectoplasmic nightwalkers.

An afternoon of shock. A lot of very quiet conversations.

X, when I got him alone, told me what the Owner had told Edith, after she grabbed the phone.

'We had a daughter,' he said. 'About your age. She died. She fell off her pony and died. Once, when she was about ten, she dressed up as a ghost in a sheet and ran up and down the landing, wailing. She still does it, sometimes.'

Then he started crying and hung up.

4.10 p.m. Confession. Simona and I discussed ghosts. Bizarrely, she thinks I've handled the situation very well. I did not confess the full extent of my panic.

The ghost-craze is in full whoop. Most of the others are going to stay up tonight to watch out for it, discreetly.

With great difficulty I have persuaded X not to join in; he will stay with me: hiding beneath the covers, chanting a couple of rousing choruses of *Oh my God, Oh my God.*

Cecile wore pedal-pushers today; with a Breton jumper, and Chinese shoes with no heels. Style personified. The jumper wasn't one of those cheap acrylic things one can buy in any number of Southwold shops. It was the dense, sailor-suited wool, warm in the cool, cool in the warm, that is only available in Brittany. The collar was cut square, revealing her marvellous-hideous neck in all its agèd glory.

I think it is a measure of how relaxed Cecile is feeling: how much neck she reveals. For, of all of her, it is the part that most discloses her age. Of course, there are the ridges upon the backs of her hands; and, of course, there are the liver spots. But the neck is a work of wonder, ~~a woodwork. It is Yggdraskil the world-tree.~~ When she turns her head to look over her shoulder, it is like the retwisting of a half-untwisted rope. Her supra-sternal notch is deep enough to hide an entire marshmallow, pre-toasting.

Pretentious, if not B.B.

All of which bespeaks a lifetime of successful dieting, and a determination to look magnificently slim even in one's grave-clothes.

(I'm sure, somewhere in her will, Cecile has left note of what she must be dressed in, for the great dinner party in the sky.)

To keep my spying discreet, I have avoided being absent for suspiciously long periods of time – during the day; and so, I have made most of my discoveries about my guests in the late evenings: it is their going-to-bed rituals with which I am most familiar.

Hence, I've learnt that Alan is unable to go to sleep without listening to his tape of Woody Allen's early stand-up comedy routines (about 40 minutes). He usually starts to nod during the bit about the Moose going to the fancy-dress party, muttering along with the punchlines in a semi-slumber. 'The moose *mingles*.' But it is only when the cassette finally clicks off, quite loudly, that he is truly gone – starting to snore almost immediately. Of course, now I want to ask Alan about why he does this, when did he start doing it?

I've also learnt that Cleangirl's boast (in the men's magazine) about her and Henry's once-a-day sex life was at best an exaggeration, at worst a lie. This despite their performance the other night, when every couple was at it, comically, apart from X and I.

Before she saw the ghost, Edith used to stand on the spot and turn around three times both ways before getting in to bed – as if she'd seen a magpie, and a magpie in a mirror. Since then, I'm not sure what she does. I shall have to take another look.

William lies in bed ~~farting~~ whilst Simona undresses. ~~When she complains, he farts; when she laughs, he farts. When *she* farts, they have a long conversation about degrees of hypocrisy.~~

Cecile combs her hair out for half an hour, on retiring. Then she sets out her next day's wardrobe. She sleeps, strange to say, foetal.

Whilst getting ready for bed, Marcia talks about the day's events

A touching vignette which adds much to the mood of the piece, but I'm afraid it'll have to go.

in the third person, saying, 'And then Marcia had an interesting talk with Edith, about boys and girls and what they do together, these days. And Marcia thought what an intelligent and well-balanced young woman Edith was. And Edith said it was one of the best conversations she'd ever had. Marcia felt flattered.' Sometimes I truly believe this woman has no interior life at all.

Despite terror, am curious; watch screens for half an hour. X already asleep. Edith sits on her bed, waiting and listening. Hard to tell if she's even awake. Others stalk corridor, giggle and shriek.

Nothing happening.

1.10 a.m. This house is so old, I hadn't realised how old it was before; I thought it was quite a new house – Georgian, I mean – but X, who knows a bit about these things, has just told me he's fairly certain parts of it are as old as pre-Elizabethan. It must have more ghosts than one. I'm babbling, I know; I know I'm babbling. I'm typing this because as long as I keep typing I know I won't have to think about whether or not a ghost is going to walk through the door and start telling me off because I haven't done my Maths homework.

For some reason, I can't get the Holy Sisters out of my mind. Probably because they used to try and persuade me out of believing in the supernatural by getting me to believe in the supernatural. Their yo-yo Jesus, dying, rising again, dying, rising – well, he didn't do much for me. He got through entirely to Fleur, which is why she'll be up all night. Although she said she believed Edith saw what she saw, she privately believes that there was nothing objectively *there* to see. If any of the rest of us had been there, we wouldn't have seen a sheeted figure. For her, the choice is either this or diabolic possession – and she doesn't want to see Edith as an instrument of Satan. Sometimes I wish so intensely that I could tell individual guests what I've seen through the cameras. I'd tell Fleur not to worry, Edith dreams it all.

It's so grotesque: a girl pretending to be a ghost becomes a ghost pretending to be a ghost. Perhaps Edith will go wraithlike over the next few days, completing the equation, becoming a ghost pretending to be a girl. (You can tell Sister Grimshaw didn't do very well with my Maths, despite the dragging.) Edith is already, in some ways, haunted. If I were her mother, I'd take her instantly away. What was that... It sounded like Marcia, whispering up the stairs. She has taken with gusto to all this voodoo and is running the ghostbusters. I'm not quite sure what the others want to do; and I'm not going down there to ask. Perhaps tomorrow. When it's light outside. I think they just want to talk to the ghost, to tell it not to fear them. As if they'd be able to speak. I think they've watched too much Shakespeare, that's what it is. Look what trouble talking to ghosts got Hamlet into...

Sleepless. 2 a.m.

Trying to think back as to whether I've had any feeling of haunting in this house. Any night-bumps. Then, suddenly... that stupidly drunkenly forgotten detail from the night we all got rolling – I've just remembered what it was: Alan told me that a few days before, while I was taking Simona's confession, he'd been sitting on the upstairs loo when he heard someone unlock and enter the Master Bedroom.

He could also see a sliver of them, through the crack in the door.

Thinking it was X, and wanting a word, Alan finished up, washed his hands (a detail he insisted upon) then came along and was just about to knock when he heard 'a strange noise'.

When I asked him to describe this, he said it was a bit like a barrow rolling along with a rusty wheel. I knew, of course, that it had been the attic ladder – at least, I thought I knew.

'What did you do?' I asked.

Alan said he knocked on the door. No reply came. Knocked again. Again, no reply.

When he tried turning the handle, he found the door was locked from the inside.

'X?' he said. 'Is it you in there?' No reply. 'Are you alright?' No reply.

With this, Alan gave up. 'I thought it um might be the bed-springs,' he said, cryptically.

He seemed for a moment to have finished, but then he said: 'The odd thing was, when I went out to the garden, X was there.'

'What did you think?' I asked. 'That he'd climbed down out of the window, to give you a fright?'

'I just thought it was a bit spooky,' said Alan.

We left it there. X is the only other person with a key to the Master Bedroom, so at the time – when Alan told me – I thought it must be him or nobody. Now I realise it might simply have been our own dear sweet ghost – the squeak was her wail, not the ladder.

Saturday

Day Ten Week Two

In the gaps between the drilling, the dawn chorus seems slightly subdued: outdone by machinery (the workmen on the road). It's a small compensation, the thought of their birdy disappointment at not being the loudest thing on earth.

Breakfast conversation in kitchen. Marcia, Cecile, Edith, Alan and Simona. Marcia says, 'I dreamed last night I was living in a big house, not this one, and we woke up one day to find a big hole in the *bed*room wall – like the kind of hole you get in an Edam cheese; another *big*ger one appeared in the wall in the kitchen; and then a *bigg*er one still, in the middle of the front door; then one in the ceiling, in the far corner of the room – the *bed*room. Some of the holes you could see through, from room to room to room. It was getting so there was more hole than house; and then a hole appeared in the floor right be*neath* my feet, and I fell down it, a long *long* way – and then I woke up with one of those *te*rrible bed-bumps; you know – like you've *fall*en off of a building. It was *ho*rrible.'

'I wonder what it can mean,' said Simona.

'Well...' said Alan.

'I don't think I want to know,' said Marcia.

'I do,' said Edith.

'Not if Marcia's afraid,' said Alan.

'Oh, go on,' Edith pleaded.

Marcia nodded.

'I think you feel there's something odd about this house – something permeable. Perhaps it's the idea of the ghost...'

'Elizabeth,' said Edith.

'...walking through walls.'

'Hmm,' said Marcia, unconvinced. 'Maybe it's best left alone.'

'Maybe,' said Simona.

'Fine,' said Alan.

He doesn't know about the cameras; he *can't* know.

10 a.m. From the bedroom window, I saw Henry go out into the garden. There was an empty deckchair under the apple tree; in fact, all the deckchairs under the tree were empty. He moved it out into the direct sunlight, sat down and started to read. Allowing him ten minutes to get bored of whatever was in his hands, I went out after him – hoping for conversation and flirtation. If I'm going to go ahead with dumping X, there has to be some sign of interest pronto. Of course, I hoped Henry's book was one of mine. When I got close I was disappointed to find out it wasn't. I asked him to turn the cover up. We were relaxed; words replaced by sun-baked grunts. It

was called *The Rings of Saturn* and is by W. G. Sebald. 'I didn't know you liked science fiction,' I said, involuntarily. 'It isn't that,' said Henry. 'It's more like, oh, I don't know, philosophy of one sort or another; or autobiography – poetic autobiography.' 'Sounds wonderful,' I said. 'Actually it is rather,' replied Henry, with the implication it was a deal wonderfuller than I. 'Can I borrow it after you finish it?' I asked, feeling, as I seem to do all the time these days, *extrêmement* schoolgirlish. 'We've started a sort of communal library in the drawing room,' said Henry. 'Everyone's putting the books they haven't started or have finished in there. It's a very good idea. The Sebald's Marcia's, actually. You don't have to ask her, exactly; but you do have to wait until it's back on the shelf.' 'Oh,' I said, 'I see.' It was rebuff; unmistakable. 'I should be finished by this evening, if you're all that keen.' 'I am,' I said. 'I haven't read anything good in ages.' Henry looked at me sorrowfully, as if expecting a writer to say something a little more incisive than that. 'It was Edith's idea,' he said, 'the library was. Apparently they did it on some holiday we sent her away on – encouraging the girls all to get to know, and trust, and speak to girls they wouldn't have otherwise. She had about ten penpals, I think, at one point, from all over the place. It's gone down a bit, since then. I'm very worried that any day now she's going to start stamp-collecting.' And with that, he hurled himself definitively back into the page. Penpals, I thought, as I walked towards the beach. I had a vaguish hope of finding a few more of the guests out there, in interesting and suggestive and unexpected combinations. But the entire strand, from long side to long side, was quite empty – apart from the black dots in front of their colourful regular-shaped splodges (beach huts) in Southwold. I closed my eyes, breathed in, trying truly to *be* in this moment of blessedness – as my non-existent guru would say. (I spend a lot of time, these days, consulting my non-existent guru. She is an amalgam of all I've read in the self-help line, smelted together with my mother, idealised, Cleangirl, Cecile, the Mahashi Mihesh Yogi?

(??check – the Beatles' mate) and God as he appears in Monty Python: cloud, lightbeams, trumpets, white-haired wisdom.) ~~Pen-pals... the thought came back to me. I'd had a penpal once. And~~ girls really still have them? Obviously they do. But do they take them with the great buffoonish solemnity I once did? It seems likely – girls don't change all that much in, what, two generations. I should expect by penpals Henry actually means e-pals or net-mates, or some such chop-suey barbarism. What do I remember of my penpal? She was blonde, and I thought her very stupid; but then, in one letter, she attacked me for talking down to her (she was Finnish), and although I began to respect her a lot more, I liked her a lot less. I think we thought we could make a small contribution to world peace. I got her through the telly, *Blue Peter*. It wasn't as good as winning one of their national 'Design a Postage Stamp' competitions, which were always won by some deprived child who'd made a splodge that they had the temerity to call a blue whale. (Nor did I ever make it onto the *Take Hart* gallery wall, either.) Together, in our letters, she and I did our best to end the Cold War, save the Panda, and swop stickers. Some of her letters about unilateral nuclear disarmament were quite pathetic. She was the kind of girl who also wrote to world leaders, and was excited by the formulaic replies she got. We did an exchange, during which all she wanted to do was visit sights of local historic significance. Once you've gone to a long-barrow, climbed up it, sat down upon it, and looked out over the surrounding landscape, there isn't much more you can do – apart from have a cigarette. She didn't smoke, which for an eleven-year-old continental is obscene. She was meant to bring me at least 200 duty free. Instead I got a picture book about Finlandisation and Hope. Her visit was a week. We stopped speaking after the third day. Luckily, she got on particularly well with my mother. I feigned a stomach bug, and they headed off to the Tower of London; I made myself vomit, they visited three National Trust properties in a day. My father knew what was happening, but he had that parental loyalty to the spirit of whatever's going on: everything must be a success. It was only the twitching of his eyebrow as my penpal spoke that gave him away: he hated her, too. For a week after she'd left, I loved my family, deeply, hugely. Most of all, I loved Fleur.

I'm bored. And so will your readers be, if I let you leave this in.

2 p.m. I needed more dialogue; and here's some, blistering. A: 'I can't take much more of this abuse, I really can't.' B: 'So?' A: 'I'm thinking really seriously about going out there, getting in that car and just driving away.' B: 'What are you waiting for? Do you think I'd care? Look, here are the keys. I'll send your stuff on afterwards. You can clear out of the flat, too, if you want. If this is the end, it may as well be final. Go and stay somewhere; find a nice little cosy B&B. You've got the rest of the summer to work out what you're going to do.' A: 'I will, you know – I will, if you're not careful.' (I can't keep this up for much longer.) And A is? My God, it's William; and B is Simona. Shall we replay that: William: 'I can't take much more of this abuse, Simona, I really can't.' She *hits* him; really belts him – with a big windup and a long follow-through. All that banging and slapping we heard, and assumed was male-on-female violence, no: *she* clouts *him* round the head like WWF fishwife. We heard 'Agh!' and Smack! at the same time; we thought that was him hitting, her flinching – the Agh!, though, is her war cry, the smack is her palm against the side of his head. When he came down looking red-faced, we thought it was from the exertions of battery; if we noticed the scratches on his neck, we saw them as the signs of self-defence. I'm shocked. She kicks him to pieces; and what does he do? Tells her he loves her; again and again and again and again. He hardly even defends himself. And then, and then, afterwards, they cuddle and make up. This is the silence we assumed was filled with inaudible-from-downstairs sobbing. I know this, I've seen it, but I can't mention it.

No, you can't. Not here.

Ever since my not-taking-Edith's-ghost-seriously, Cecile has shunned me. She has turned from Cecile into Icicle: freezing cold, hanging around, transparent... no, that doesn't work. She is far from transparent; she is opacity exemplified – Cornwall and all.

Just after lunch, I made the attempt to seek her out. It happened like this: I was up in the attic, and I saw her in her room – looking bored, staring out the window (N.B. fully dressed).

Quietly as I could, I came down the ladder, slid it away, locked the Master Bedroom and knocked upon her door.

'Who is it? asked Cecile.

'Hello,' I said. 'It's just me.'

'Oh, Victoria,' she said, 'well, I'm afraid I'm not dressed. Is it anything important?'

'No,' I said. 'I just felt like a bit of a chat.'

'Perhaps later,' Icicle said.

'Of course,' I replied.

3 p.m. Marcia has taken to her bed with an imaginary illness – brought on, she says, by the strain of thinking the house is haunted. I hope she's not litigious – or rather, I hope she is: I'd like a court to have to listen to the kind of nonsense I've put up with these past few days. Fleur has taken over nursing duties, which is one of the reasons I'm not taking it seriously. Having one of the world's seven greatest hypochondriacs looking after Marcia is hardly likely to speed her recovery. Fleur can get ill just by *thinking* about the instructions on a packet of paracetamol. It's one of the main reasons she turned to God in the first place. I should have known that any kind of invalid in the house would attract her as surely as sweets children. God makes Fleur ill, to punish her for wrongdoing; God makes Fleur better, in reward for snuffled prayers and groggy imprecations. God is a little bit of a torturer, as far as I can see; Fleur's God – Jehovah in Laura Ashley.

Marcia, as I learnt on about Day Two, comes from an extremely atheistic background. If religion is the opium of the masses, her adoptive parents were drug counsellors – selling copies of their own anti-bible, the *Socialist Worker*. It's a wonder they were allowed to adopt her in the first place. At least her incapacitation has meant that I've been able to keep her in one place for long enough to get to know her a bit. I have wanted to. Not because, after her attack upon me, I'm making any particular effort to find her interesting or likeable; there's something about her – a hidden humour that I think would tally with mine. I can hear a secret laugh within everything she says, even the angriest, most take-me-seriously outbursts. 'It's all a bit silly,' she seems to be saying, 'there's so much pain – it's funny, really.' And I'd love to know how I can get through to this, because it seems a marvellous place to be. ~~Somewhere similar to the place I'm in right now. (A lot of pain.) I think it's a stage upon which we could meet and genuinely befriend one another.~~ *Self-pity – not interesting.* Until now, we have failed to recognise our deeper kinship. We need a recognition scene. The best thing would be for me too to fall ill, and be placed in the bed beside her in the ward. But obviously I can't afford illness, not right at this moment. And she's not in a ward. Anyway, Fleur won't let me take over nursing duties. I think she'd think I was doing it not out of sympathy but from a deeper selfishness – a selfishness which she believes she's the only person in the world to have perceived. I think my selfishness is pretty much on the surface, beneath that I'm immensely beneficent.

One good thing is that, because Marcia and Alan are so close, Alan will under these circumstances be forced into company with Fleur. I have already watched one excruciating scene play itself out. Alan came in, to bring some flowers for Marcia – came in, that is, to Marcia's room. Of course, he handed them initially to the invalid. She took them, sniffed them, thanked him, then passed them to Fleur – who went off immediately to find a vase; which left Marcia and Alan alone. They talked about their health. What they didn't see, meanwhile, was Fleur, in the kitchen, inhaling the scent of the flowers – roses – so deeply that she might have been trying to take the whole bouquet up her nose and into her head; turning the flowers straight into memories. And so, indirectly, without him knowing it, Alan has given flowers to Fleur.

3.55 p.m. You'll never guess who just left, having arrived perfectly in time for confession: the local Vicar! He'd read about us and what we were doing in the local paper, he said (that piece by the mousy girl); and so he'd decided he had better come down and introduce himself. I think he thought he was going to catch us shooting a blue movie, or having unfilmed orgies. No doubt, being East Anglian, he also suspected diabolic practices in the dead of night. Hauntings, etc. He was therefore quite surprised by our gentility. I only narrowly avoided saying, 'More tea, Vicar.' But he did have several cups, and went away entirely converted to our cause. Of course, it helped that I pointed out that several of our number had already attended his church on Sunday. He gratifyingly said, 'I thought there was something unusual about them.' Then I remembered that I myself had been among the worshippers, and that he'd failed to recognise me – even though he'd said goodbye to us all as we filed out of the church.

Halfway through the conversation, I stuck my head out of the door and asked whomever happened to be passing – it was Edith – if she could go and find my sister, bring her in.

When Fleur came, I introduced her to the Vicar: Fleur is never more gaga than with a member of the clergy. I was hoping she would invite him back, and she did.

5.15 p.m. The Parlour. Without warning, Cleangirl turned up (caught me after I'd seen the Vicar off) – hasn't really spoken to me in three full days, and now it all came out in a flood: 'You know what you said the other afternoon. It's left me feeling so guilty, because I know what you must be thinking... You must be feeling I was entirely innocent of what you said. I mean – I'm not saying this very well; what I mean is that because I didn't say anything in reply, you went away thinking you were the only envious, hateful one – and probably you also think that you were the only one of the two of us to think that was the basis of our relationship: your envy of me. But I was, too – I was envious; only I envied *you.* I did – I really, really did.'

'You did?'

'Oh, I thought you were so interesting – you had so much inside you, and I felt so empty, so dull. I knew that men were going to find me attractive, but I never thought I'd keep one because they'd get bored with me so quickly. I wanted intellectuals. I wanted someone blind, who didn't even know what I looked like. It's a horrible *cliché*, I know, and one that no-one really wants to hear, but I felt my looks as a burden. I took them for granted and I despised them at the same time. But you –'

'I didn't have that problem. Thanks.'

'No. It's not that. You were wrestling with so many things. You were fizzing with twists and oh I can't really express this – but I got the feeling that I couldn't open my mouth without destroying whatever good impression I might have made. ~~So I felt like a frame, too – I felt like an introduction without a book. And that was why I started to work so hard, in competition with you. I needed to build myself a brain. It took me a while – it took me well into my twenties. Then I realised I'd had a brain all along. Not the same as you, though. I had a brain that connected things, not one that made them – or made them up. It helped, reading your novels. I could see from inside you, for a while; I could see that I hadn't been wrong about the twists. I could even recognise the ones that I'd put there myself.~~

'~~Don't be too sure.'~~

Did she really say this? I'm not convinced by it at all. And your character is strangely subdued.

'I'm only telling you this for me. It's not because I want to make you think worse of me. I just don't want to think worse of myself.

You see, I am as bad as I am. I accept that. Envy was the basis of our relationship, right from the start. But I still do love you, in a very strange way. Now it's over, in that form – now we have confessed – it's time to see whether we have anything left, or whether we can turn it into something else.' She was crying. I let her continue. 'So many of my friendships, so called, have the same basis; we never get round to saying what we really feel – the competitiveness, the shame. Maybe that's what I like most about you: you are madly honest. When you lie, it's so diametrically opposite to the truth that it becomes a form of inverse truth.'

'Thank you,' I said.

'So, I'm not going to leave; to leave would be hypocritical. I came because something in me wanted to take part in your world, on your terms. At first Henry said he didn't want to come, but I know he did. He admires you.'

'He isn't speaking to me.'

'He's scared I'll be jealous.'

'Will you be?'

'Or perhaps he's scared I won't be jealous. When you get to a certain stage with a marriage, it's hard to tell what's what any more.'

I asked again: 'Would you?'

'Why don't you try it? Then we'll both find out.' She stood up to go. 'Don't hurt Edith,' she said. 'Edith may not be pure but she is...' She took a handkerchief out of her sleeve and blew her nose. 'Oh, *you* know what she is – she's a chance of something better. Don't put that at risk.' I let her leave.

Strange. Even though I set this up to advance relationships, I didn't really expect...

When I walked, just now, into the drawing room, X and Henry were arguing; at least, I'm pretty sure that's what they were doing. The moment I came into sight, though, they put on a pretend-amicable conversation. Although on approach I'd heard if not raised then certainly intense voices, I hadn't dared stop to listen. Their falling out, if that is what it is, doesn't surprise me. I've been expecting there to be trouble among the men, all along.

Audrey update: Fleur's cat is now prepared to stand just outside the French windows, but cannot be persuaded inside. Various attempts have been made: bowls of cream, plates of sardines, etc. There must still be a whiff of Domino about. Whenever she hears the front door open, Audrey zips off back to her fence.

I go in to attempt to speak to Marcia; she sends me away. I need to do something about this – write her a letter or something. She clearly won't listen to my side of the War with Fleur.

Icicle wore a skirt-suit in outsize herringbone print, in chocolate, with a bright red beret: the daring, the chutzpah, and yet the sureness!

Cleangirl cooked dinner for all of us – making far less out of it than did Fleur and Marcia. We had fondue to start, Cleangirl having found a set deep in a kitchen cabinet. Then we had Swedish meatballs with mashed potatoes. For dessert, pink blancmange.

A domestic concert this evening; William played some of his spookiest Schubert for us, in the front parlour. (Now those are the kind of sentences I began this project wanting to write.) We were gathered together, against the gathering dark. William has a lovely touch, very light and liquid. Simona always said he could have been a concert pianist, if he'd wanted; or at the very least, an accompanist to singers. They did a Schubert song together. I didn't know she could sing so well. It wasn't a professional voice, it didn't have that distinctiveness or power, too husky; but somehow, because of that, it gained in emotion. It was more like hearing pop music being sung, or someone singing in the shower without expecting to be overheard; the music itself was undeniably great, but the interpretation was personal; to do with delighting those immediately in front of one. I've always wanted to be intimate friends with some musicians. Whenever I've been round to dinner at William and Simona's, accompanied by X or some other, they've always pooh-poohed their talents – despite the complex music on the piano stand. I was teary-eyed by the end. ~~mainly at the thought that their lovely musical partnership will soon be broken up, along with their unlovely non musical one~~.

Thank you.

Of course, after the recital has finished, Marcia (out of bed for the occasion, blanket-wrapped) suggests that we all find some way to entertain the others – and though everyone knows that, after the performances of Simona and William, it will be a shameful come-down, people feel forced to agree. 'Delightful idea,' says Cecile, whom I'm sure would hate nothing more than standing up in front of us and 'doing a little turn'. What is it about groups of people, that always, immediately they're formed, they start engaging in acts of mutual humiliation? This, I suppose, is how they form themselves. The concert tonight was a powerplay, by William; wanting his talent to dominate us. I could see, when he got to the passionate, thumpy bits, that he was trying to speak to the groins of all present: *Know me*, he seemed to be saying, *as a sexually dark being*. There was candlelight in the room, upon the mantelpiece and one – daringly risking the Liberace effect – on the piano itself. Candlelight is such a transformer of things; ~~I always feel, reading Victorian novels, that I have to remind myself of this, whenever there's a night scene – candles, candles, candles: the characters can't see anything, their shadows are richer and deeper and fuller of terrible things than are ours. But, this evening, in the parlour, we did our best to create some obscurities of our own. I am glad;~~ there is a richness here; one that, perhaps, I didn't expect. In an atmosphere so intense as this, someone is bound to fall in love with someone

This is your Victorian novel, Victoria.

they shouldn't. The whole project is like a seduction: I have created the backdrop, the music, the lighting, the alcohol – I should probably mention that the red wine, at dinner and afterwards, must have contributed to the feeling of an old, plangent depth; it was rich, and rolled around the tongue as solidly as an oyster. When swallowed, it made everyone feel stronger, and more philosophical – as if their thoughts were worth thinking, and utterances worth hearing. When I looked at the painting above the piano, which is a Bomberg of a hillside, I couldn't see the colour of the image, only the ridgy texture of the brushstrokes – like the sea outside, seen by moonlight. This was a precious moment, ruined by thinking that I'd have to remember it accurately; and then by thinking of a couple of phrases with which to describe it, and worrying that I'd forget them before I had a chance to escape up here and type them out. My memory for sequences of words is pretty good, by now, and I don't think any of the ones I came up with earlier on have escaped. Cleangirl looked so lovely, listening to the music with her eyes trustingly closed – as if the music itself had made us all promise not to look at one another too closely, whilst it was delighting us. ~~Her eyelids were orange with translucence from the light behind them, and looking at them was like being a child and trying to look through them – towards a torch or the sun.~~ Beside her, head on her lap, Edith glowed with a similar, though brighter, whiter light; she is so young as not to need an external light-source to bring out her glow. Others allowed themselves recess in the shadows: Alan, in the furthest, darkest corner – seeming very snug and Edwardian, happy to mull things over, and not act. Marcia, next to him, with a harder, more angular shine coming off her skin. I was wondering what she made of this – the civilised music, the evening without television. X was behind me; I could not see him – but I could feel his breath swooping down the back of my neck, like it does when we are all a-spoon in our big bed at home. Fleur was sitting cross-legged on the floor: ensuring that some stiffness of limb was allowed to come between her and her pleasure; and that, for the rest of us, more comfortably seated ones, there would be an un-get-ridable smear of guilt across the bottom of the face of the evening, across its chin. William had his back to us, but something about its surge and lurch suggested that his face couldn't be anything but a-flicker with fast-forward emotions. Simona stood, as if to announce the professional coaching she had at some time had: hands pursed, so as not to get in the way; feet triangulated. Her eyes were open, but she did not over-egg the whites: we were allowed to blaze with our own intensities, not those she forced upon us.

This was our second big moment of unity. I wonder if there will be another quite like it.

To bed, all believing in ghosts.

It's now 1 a.m.

X, the bastard, despite me waking him up several times, has gone to sleep. He is the biggest non-believer in the house – which in one way is a relief, because at least he's not taking part in the craze.

Bloody hell. I didn't know what that noise was. It was X, snoring – showing off, even in sleep. I don't think I'm going to be able to get any sleep tonight. And I need a pee really badly. And of course the place I'd normally go is the upstairs loo. Which is at the end of the corridor. The long ghost-haunted corridor. Separated from this room by two thin inches of easily-pass-throughable wooden door. If I were to go there, which I'm not, but if I were, I'd have to pass right over the spot where... Hang on.

Sunday

Day Eleven Week Two

I did it.

At four in the morning. X didn't even notice when I pulled the top sheet away from him. I managed to slip out into the corridor without him waking up, then I put the sheet on over my head.

I felt a lot safer, for some reason, running up and down going (in my head) whooo!

But then, all of a sudden, I felt as if I'd run through a waterfall of ice-cold water. And I knew that, dressed as a ghost, I'd blundered straight through a girl-ghost dressed as a ghost-girl. That was when I started screaming.

I don't remember all that much more of the half an hour that followed.

Embarrassingly, I'm told that Fleur looked after me – and that I clung to her, refusing all other comfort. I think I thought she was our mother.

How am I ever going to be able to face the guests again? I woke them all up, even Edith – but perhaps she wasn't asleep.

Dawn chorus a blessing. World seemed semi-normal again. No drilling.

It's now 7 a.m. Outside is a real thin, cold, sinewy East Anglian dawn. The light coming into the room is pallid but with every second revives me a little more. I'm getting dressed in warm clothes and going down for a stroll, alone, along the beach.

Restored, I think.

Had X bring me breakfast, and took the excuse offered by my ghost encounter to stay upstairs and do a full morning's spying.

Another discovery: Henry and Cleangirl are texting one another, constantly. I was able to observe this. Cleangirl, alone in their room, sitting on the counterpane – thumbs in her message; Henry, not alone but unwatched (except by me) in the drawing room, receives the message and replies. Cleangirl spends the interim combing her hair, a longtime displacement activity of hers when nervous. She then replies, he texts back, she thumbs in some more, etcetera, etcetera. This went on for about fifteen minutes. I think their messages even began overlapping. Hard as it is to tell, they seemed to be flirting – text-sex or whatever it's called. At one point, Cleangirl got quite agitated. This is why I've been so confused up until now: *something* seemed to be passing between them, but *nothing* seemed to be passing between them. Now I know: it's all been little abbreviations, glanced at then replied to. I think I may have to intervene, subtly. They are cheating. They could be feeling anything: I've been watching them very closely, right from the start. How can I write about them, though, if all their most important communication goes from phone to phone?

Don't know how to understand this: William alone in his and Simona's bedroom, bawling like a baby. He was fully clothed, in suit, shirt, shoes; sitting on the side of the bed, just as if about to go to a funeral, or just back from one. Simona hasn't mentioned any recent bereavement. His mother and father died at least ten years ago. I can't think of any incident with which to connect it. Of course, I haven't seen *everything* that's happened, this past few days; I'm fairly sure I would have heard if he and Simona had had another fight. It certainly didn't happen this morning: I haven't moved away from the screens, and William hasn't left the house. The cause of his tears must be some secret grief; probably I shouldn't worry about it any more than I have – not unless it starts to interfere. My instinct, watching, was to go and comfort him; it still is. But given the way we've related to each other so far, even an overemphasised, 'How are you?' would be noticed: I just *don't* ask William how he is. My character doesn't care about him. This problem seems insoluble.

When William appears downstairs later, he has changed out of his suit and gives no sign of previous distress.

X has again been arguing with Henry. For some reason, they have fallen out as never before.

When I try to get an explanation from X, I am met with the blunt grunt of injured maleness. 'But what was it about?' 'You know... grunt.' 'What? I can't hear what you're saying.' 'Something.' 'Something what?' 'Something grunt.' 'Are you being deliberately annoying.' 'Something not worth bothering about.' 'Then why are you both upset about it.' 'I'm not upset.' 'You're sulking.' 'I am not sulking.' 'You've been out all morning, fishing – fishing means sulking.' 'No it doesn't.' 'It may not to you, but it does to me.' 'Fishing means happiness.' 'Happiness and sulking are not mutually exclusive. Having a little wrong to brood upon, to keep one warm – I'm sure that can be very pleasant, whilst waiting for the fish to bite.' 'You don't understand – you never have.' 'And now you're talking like a stroppy teen.' 'We'll sort it out; I'll talk to him.' 'After you've gone fishing.' '...a few more times – I need some air, some being-away-from-here.' 'And from me.' 'Yes, Victoria, I'll say it if you want me to: "And from –"' 'No! No, I don't want you to say it. And I'd prefer it if you didn't even think it... Are you going now?' 'Yes,

I'm afraid I'm going now. We'll sort this out later.' 'When will you be back?' 'I don't know – half past grunt.'

With Fleur out at church, X fishing, and nothing much going on downstairs, I took the hour's opportunity to compose a long letter:

Dear Marcia,

I didn't want to have to write to you like this, but as you refuse to hear me out in person I shall have to. I won't pretend that I'm not furious at your prejudice against me – for prejudice is what it is; you haven't listened to me when I've tried to speak to you, to explain. What you've assumed is that the person who first screams, '*I'm* the victim,' or who screams it loudest, or longest, or most melodramatically – you've assumed that that person is, in fact, the victim. Fleur spends her life crying victim, and I spend most of mine refusing under any circumstances to do so. You of all people should know the ease with which one can slip into the safety of this *rôle*. I'm sure you've been tempted. But as we've all seen these past few days, you haven't succumbed: you're not a victim to your own life, you're the agent of it; for which I and everyone else respects you. All of which is only to say, ignore this if you want, but please please read what follows. It explains if not everything then as much as can be explained, by me alone.

It's time – it *is* time – I told you about 'Fleur and Her Tragic Past'.

When she was thirty, Fleur met a very nice young man, a Christian and quite handsome, called Clive Parsnip. (Not really; I made that up – he was called something equally silly, and vegetable-related.) She met him through her local church. He was either a barrister or a solicitor, I'm not sure which; and I'm certainly not going to ask her, to check. Anyway, they courted – actually *courted*; they had coffee, took long walks, went to the theatre, gave each other presents. They went to ask our parents if they could get married (this was before they'd had sex, mind); and I don't know who was the more embarrassed – the blushing couple or my outraged parents; outraged because they were being dragged into Fleur's warped Victorian throwback of a world, where grooms asked parents of brides for the honour of their daughter's hand in matrimony. They would, I know, have been more than happy with a phonecall and a *fait accompli*. But Clive (encouraged by Fleur) insisted on doing everything 'properly' – he was desperate to don his imaginary frock coat and doff his imaginary top hat. And because of this, it was, when it took place, one of the loveliest weddings I've ever been to. They got married in the Forest of Arden, near Birmingham. Clive's parents lived in Tamworth. The day was autumnal. Everybody was happy – yes, even me. I was hoping that the wedding day would put paid for ever to the mad spinster in my sister. She looked as beautiful as she is ever going to, processing down the aisle to the drone of Mendelson's Wedding Cliché; she walked past me, and I felt jealous. But I also felt elated. My elder sister was getting married before I did: I was conservative enough to feel that that still meant something. (I do not myself entirely lack the Victorian gene.) The wedding was a success, as was the honeymoon. They went to Venice, where they'd both always wanted to go. I saw the photos of them, canoodling in a gondola – I assumed the marriage had been consummated, satisfactorily. And it had. Four months later, Fleur announced that she was pregnant. They were living in Birmingham by this time, Clive having started in a law firm there. He was thirty-five, Fleur was thirty-one. Then... then she went and had some tests, one of them being for Down's Syndrome. This is the bit where I start crying, without really being able to stop. The baby almost certainly had Down's. (Of course, I only heard the full details later – but I did hear them, from both sides, as you'll see.) They took the news surprisingly well; Clive was there with her. They were calm. They drove home. Each, I think, assuming that the other was silently condoning what they themselves thought the right thing to do. They got home, made instant coffee, sat down at the kitchen table, and within half an hour the marriage was all but over. Clive, Christian to the core, believed that God had chosen to give them *this* particular baby – this particular baby with Down's – and that they should welcome the child into the world as best they could, and do whatever they could to give it a wonderful life. Fleur was, Victorian word, mortified. She knew in her soul that she couldn't have this baby; or rather, that she *could* have the baby, but that there was no way on earth that she was going to be able to bring it up. (Her words.) She was revolted, partly by the idea of what was growing inside her, but mostly by herself, by her revulsion. Consciously, in whatever part of her Christian mind that can be called 'rational', she knew that Clive was right. His theology might have been verging on the Catholic, but she was prepared to accept that. She blamed God, for giving her this particular unbearable burden. The instant coffee was drunk; Fleur became incoherent; Clive went quiet. A couple of days later, they went to another hospital, a private one, for further tests – just to be certain. The tests confirmed the previous tests. Fleur held firm, so did Clive. They were irreconcilable. The marriage was over. But for some mad reason I've never fully understood, they got in their car and drove all the long way to my house. I suppose, Victorianly, they thought that at times like this a sister should fulfil a sister's function. And do you know what? I did.

I was living alone; the fling I'd had with one of the guests I met at Fleur's wedding was over.

When I'd heard everything, from Fleur, and then from Clive, I backed my sister up completely. When they started to argue, I said she could stay with me if she didn't want to go back with him. He gave her an ultimatum; she looked at me, nodded; I chucked him out. That was it.

With a little help, I collected all Fleur's stuff from Clive's flat. She slept in my bed; I took the sofa.

A week or so later, Fleur had the abortion, at the same private hospital she'd had the second set of tests. Then she began to put her life back together. It was a different life, though. When she had the abortion, it was as if she had had all her blood transfused, and exchanged for white paint and turps – her hair went immediately grey and she began to corrode from the inside. As part of starting again, she moved to Herefordshire. She found the farmhouse. She bought the Saab. She moved out. The divorce came through – with him giving her half of everything. Their court battle was actually over the fact that he insisted upon this, and she wanted as little as possible to remind her of him. The *decree nisi* came through. Fleur continued to go to church. She now knew what her cross was: the guilt of having refused the cross that Christ intended her to bear. That's how she put it to me, in a letter. She's so perverse. Far more than I am. But, you see, ever since I helped her out, she's never forgiven me. When she gets angry, she will tell you that I forced her to have the abortion. I think what she means by this is, having wrecked her marriage, and been absolutely definite about why she was doing this, she began to have last-minute doubts. I didn't force her into anything: I asked her what she really wanted. I told her to phone Clive and talk about it, again. I even dialled half his number for her; she stopped me.

Fleur believes that, by giving her a way out, by being a loyal sister, I enabled her to avoid doing God's will. I am somehow, therefore, unholy. Whereas the truth is, Fleur did everything herself. And what she can't face is the responsibility for her own actions, and the admission of her own instincts. She hasn't forgiven herself; she is haunted by the idea of this child that she could have had. Her relationships, since then, have all crashed. And Fleur, in her worst moments, believes herself to be as unholy as I am.

Occasionally, she glimpses her way through to forgiveness, realising that that is, after all, the Christian ideal.

Often, I find her hideous; as if she is possessed by something I once had power to rid her of. Perhaps, when she was twenty, and not going out of the house, I should have invited her along to some of my sixteen-year-old's parties. Instead, something else happened: during one of those long evenings in with my parents, she created – out of boredom I'm sure – the God that later turned round and spoke to her. It can't be that facile; though Fleur frequently is.

And so you see, after all this, I don't think I'm the guiltiest party; I'm certainly not the one feeling the most guilt.

For myself, I don't have any doubt that I'd have had the abortion. Which isn't the point, I know.

The point is, if Fleur could just admit that once upon a time she felt a force within her (disgust) that was stronger than her rational belief in an irrational deity – if she could confront that, and then let it go, she would be giving the rest of her life to herself, as a gift – and getting her sister back, too, into the bargain.

I don't expect you to reply to this now. The whole episode is too involved to be summed up simply. But please consider the idea that I'm not a beast; and admit, in theory at least, that there could be another side to whatever story Fleur has told you.

More likely (given her usual *modus operandi*), she hasn't told you any of this at all, just – whenever I or babies or marriage are mentioned – ended sentences abruptly, and drifted away into long fugues of melancholia. This of course on top of her *pièce de resistance* outbreak at the dinner table; which sets everyone up to look out for signs of my evil wherever they can find them.

And me being as kind and gentle as I am, as solicitous of Fleur's feelings, even in the moments after she's mashed mine to a pulp, for the thousandth time – me, I let it go, take the stares, allow the whispers.

Love,

Victoria

p.s.

Her doctor at the time told her that it had been a fluke; she was still young; there was no medical reason why her next pregnancy needn't be perfectly normal. But Fleur wasn't satisfied with that: she was determined to figure herself as one of the accursed of the earth. Ever since then, this determination of hers has ruined every chance she's ever had of a good relationship. She tells them – men – that she can't have children. She lets them go away with the impression that she's messed up inside – and she is, but it's in her head, not in her womb. I'm not sure how many of 'them' there have been, since Fleur doesn't tell me very much and I don't ask her very much. I'm sure there are men who are attracted by the forlorn, just as much as women are.

Since it happened I've had only one proper conversation with Fleur about it; she told me she was terrified of having a daughter, because the daughter might have to go through the same thing she had – and so she wasn't going to risk having a child of any sort.

Clearly, Fleur isn't a very well person. It's not that she *lies* so much as she sees the universe in a very distorted way. Where we hear the silence of infinite space, she hears the silence of infinite disapproval. She's turned God into an angry, and a very bad, parent. Which is why she's going to church this morning – to try to placate him.

I reread the letter, printed it out, sealed it up in an envelope, and went and handed it to Marcia. She didn't look too pleased to receive it, but she couldn't refuse to take it.

Confession with Simona. And I finally told her about William's flash – the one that happened very early on, on the upstairs landing. She didn't seem at all surprised. 'Not much to write home about, really, is it?'

'Has he done this before?'

'He doesn't do it on the streets, if that's what you mean.'

'As if it's any better when you're a house guest.'

'Well...'

'He did it on the beach, too.'

'Oh, that was completely different. He just didn't want to be the scaredy-cat.'

'Does he get turned on by it?' I asked.

'No. Not in the way you're thinking.'

'Sexually – for power; it must be.'

'It's not about that. Take it as a compliment – a celebration of life. It means he likes you. For him it's about self-affirmation.'

'I felt degraded.'

'Did you? Did you really? I don't think for one second that that was that you felt. You were flattered and thrilled – you went straight off and wrote it up.'

'I did not.'

'Well, you probably thought that William had finally come alive as a character.'

I was flabbered. 'How did you know that?'

'I guessed. I'm your editor – I know you well enough. And I know you too well for you to try to play shocked and appalled. If it were most other women, I'd give William a real telling-off – one he wouldn't forget. If it had been Edith, I'd beat him to a pulp.'

'I'm sure you would,' I said. But she didn't respond. ~~It's very difficult: there's no way to bring up her beatings of William without mentioning the cameras.~~ 'Look, it might easily have been Edith –'

'Oh no. He's very careful, he's very devious. He plans.'

'He didn't know who was coming down the landing. He just barged out.'

'I'd bet you anything that he'd been down on his knees, staring out through the keyhole.'

'But Edith might have come along too, at just that moment.'

'He'd have made sure she was somewhere else. He wouldn't leave it to chance.'

I took a moment to think, then said, 'Could you please ask him not to do it again?'

'Oh, he only ever does it once.'

We talked of other things.

5 p.m. When I found her, Icicle was alone in the garden, in a deckchair, under the apple tree, reading Balzac, in the original. We small-talked for a while; and then, attempting transition without it being recognised as such, I said: 'What do you think of where I'm doing this? Not so much the house, I think I know what you think of that. But Southwold? Suffolk?'

'I think it's wonderful,' said Icicle. 'You've managed to find a place where none of us have ever been, or have any history. That's quite an achievement. It might have ruined things.'

I took this statement as a hint Icicle might be prepared to talk about her secrets in other parts of the country, so continued: 'I did think about trying to find a house elsewhere. In Scotland for example; or Devon, Cornwall...' I trailed off, without significance. Unable to *dare* even a glance at Icicle, I looked round the sloping dusty lawn for a while. Then, with my head feeling heavy as a medicine ball on my shoulders, I turned towards her. She looked blanched; I had never seen such suppressed emotion. Her face remained white beneath its foundation; but her neck had gone very dark; and at the point where the tendons took root, there was a splodge of purple. And did it pulse? I rejoiced: it was as if I could see her heart through her chest.

'No,' she said, recovering, 'this really was the right place.'

Anything might torture her now, and so I said, 'Have you ever been to –' and without pausing at all '– Devon?'

My daring was a mistake, I see now; it gave her an easy escape. 'I've been everywhere,' said Icicle.

'Except here,' I replied.

'Except here,' she confirmed, then glanced regretfully at her book. She was hinting that I'd interrupted her in a valued pursuit; to stay would be ill-mannered. I risked thirty more *gauche* seconds – not to harass her further, but to allow her to think my conversation had been merely random. 'Yes,' I said, 'I think you're probably right. The weather up here has been delightful. I don't think anybody could complain about the location.'

'No,' said Icicle. She looked up at the sky, as if deliberately to display the disappearance of the crimson splodge. It was almost a taunt, and I took it as such. I stood up.

'The weather in Cornwall's been awful,' I said. Then turned away before she had the chance of a chance to react.

Inside again, I went up to my room and through the hatch into the attic.

Sure enough, Icicle was back in her room within five minutes. She sat upon the counterpane, gazing at the map of Cornwall as if it were the clear round full moon. It was the past she was looking at; a past I am now more than ever determined to penetrate.

No reaction from Marcia to my letter. I have stayed downstairs more than usual, so as to make myself accessible to her. No joy; she wasn't ready.

I know she's read and re-read it: I've spy-watched her. She cried so much – I don't think anything I've ever written has made anyone cry quite so much.

We have only been alone together once since she received it; that was in the drawing room, and she wheeled herself away fairly smartish. I sense a suppressed fury.

It will be interesting to see which of us she goes to first, myself or Fleur. If she believes what I wrote, it's slightly more likely she will approach me. Her tears suggest she does believe.

8 p.m.

'I've always had a strange feeling about this house,' says Fleur.

'What?' says Marcia (who has made a full recovery, and is out of her sickbed – a twenty-four-hour bug, or hysteria?). 'You, too?'

'As if sometimes I were being watched,' Fleur continues, 'watched by something evil.'

'Yes,' says Cecile.

'It's uncanny,' says Cleangirl, 'I can feel it like a spider down my neck.'

The four of them were in the parlour, just now, as I eavesdropped from the attic; arrayed around the room, on wheelchair, sofa and piano stool.

'It doesn't feel like a *gho*stly watching,' says Marcia.

'No,' says Cecile.

'How does one know what that feels like?' asks Fleur, seriously.

'Oh, I know,' Marcia says. And tells them, at length, about Jamaican folk myths.

They then return to the topic.

'Of course, we are being spied on,' says Fleur.

'We are?' says Cleangirl.

'By Victoria?' Marcia says.

'By Victoria,' chimes Fleur.

(At this point, looking at the screens, I am almost dead of a heart attack.)

'Do you think she's sneaking around, listening to us?' says Cleangirl.

'Of course,' says Marcia. 'Haven't you seen her... *hovering*?'

'She's so unsubtle,' says Fleur.

They laugh; all of them.

'It's when I haven't seen her hovering that it makes me worry,' interjects Cecile.

'What are you saying?' asks Marcia.

‘Oh, nothing,’ Cecile says. ‘Just that sometimes Victoria seems to know things that you haven’t told her.’

(I am dead. She must mean this afternoon, the apple tree, Cornwall.)

‘She would call that her artistic sensibility,’ says Fleur.

‘Or lucky guesses,’ Marcia jokes. ‘Or *psy*chic *po*wers.’

‘No,’ says Cleangirl. ‘I think Cecile is right.’

‘Perhaps she’s spying on us now,’ says Marcia.

There is a moment’s *maybe* before they all again laugh. I am deader, still. Blessedly, the subject changes.

I am going to have to be so careful, from now on. They are a long way from knowing the full truth, but they seem to have the half truth already.

Must go down, appear ignorant.

8.25 p.m. After dinner, we gathered in the front parlour for Alan’s Woody Allen lecture. He had changed his topic. ‘To be quite honest,’ he said, ‘I’ve become a bit bored of Woody Allen’s unfunnies. So I’m not going to talk about them. Instead, I’m going to do some of his stand-up comedy routines.’ And off he went, word perfect, through ‘The Moose’ and other old favourites. Then, very cleverly, he stopped; and started to take apart what Allen was doing – looking into his seriousness, his Jewishness. It was all very impressive, and I think will give Alan’s reputation the boost it needs within the house. Fleur, I noticed, was quietly in attendance. (Marcia too, though she avoided my eye, my smile.) Fleur laughed, as at something with which she was familiar; very gently, with smiles in between. I didn’t see Alan look at her, not even once, but I got the feeling the performance was to a greater or lesser extent directed towards her. Why does she resist him so? He is a decent man, and would be very good for her. I only wish I myself were the kind of woman he’d be good for. (No, I don’t; but I can imagine it; that kind of tweedy, tea-drinking stability.) They would be very happy together, if only they could see it. Perhaps while Fleur is still speaking to me, I should try saying something. It wouldn't be welcome, but it might work.

Icicle wore – well, that's not so important any more; what is is that Edith has started to dress only in clothes from the wardrobe in her room – clothes once owned and worn by the Owners' daughter. And Icicle has helped her put her outfits together. There can be no other explanation for how Edith has so suddenly begun to acquire *chic*. My disappointment, my *chagrin*, is inestimable: they are playing dressing-up together, and I'm not included. It's my party, I've given them all the cake, and they won't even let me play Sardines with them. Needless to say, there is a deal of limitation on the outfits that even someone as ingenious as Cecile is able to put together from entirely pre-1979 pieces; blouses with flounces around the arms, tight pullovers, flared corduroy trousers. Yet I believe that, before she died, the Owners' daughter had, once or twice, been down to London for shopping trips – and had either gone, or been taken, to some fairly expensive *boutiques*. The dresses suit: Edith is tall enough and mature enough in the face not to look as if she's straining for adulthood. As all old clothes do, they make her look older: because we associate them with people whom we have seen age after wearing those outfits – people in photographs and the audience of *Top of the Pops*. Luckily for Edith, the daughter's taste seems to have been for a silky flamboyance that harked back to 1972 rather than anticipated the polka-dot horrors of 1982. The fabrics are, for the most part, entirely natural. There is even fur; fur without guilt – how fantastic: like grandmother's fur, but in a cut you'd have bought new; a cut you'd have throttled a mink for.

Cornwall update. No news. (And none likely, after my blab of earlier today.) But they're so intimate, so always together, Cecile and Edith; I can't *believe* Cecile hasn't told Edith some of her secrets, including Cornwall. Anyone curious, sitting in a room with a map on display all that time, would surely ask about it. Perhaps I can find out what I want to know from Edith – *sans* prying.

Tuesday

N.B. Day Thirteen Not Day Twelve Week Two

I can't believe it: I've lost an entire day's work, somehow or other. I think the laptop just couldn't be bothered to save. Some such. And I didn't save it to a floppy disk. The *one* day I forget; that's the day it happens. Which annoys me so much I can hardly type. Perhaps I turned the thing off without saving it. Or didn't make it a bloody cup of coffee. How do I know? I don't understand how this thing works. I just type into the bloody thing and it remembers what I type. That's what's meant to happen, anyway. If something goes wrong, I have to call X in to help. He is the one man, in all the world, who has read the manual. He understands what's going on inside the opaque box. (However, there is sensitive material on here – about me and my plots and plans – and I'm not going to let him get a chance to see that, now am I?) And so now I feel that everything I put in is falling into the void. From today, I will back up everything and e-mail it to myself, just to be 100% sure I'm not going to lose any more. And, of course, in retrospect, yesterday's work, now lost for ever, seems numinous – as if it had the halo of all greatness around it. There was a long passage about how the dinner table was the scene of cannibal feasts for the upper middle classes. How the victims were brought in, served up, ripped limb from limb, or slowly dissected. And I was thinking just how marvellous an insight this was – and now it's *gone*. And the only way I can bring it back is in feeble ghostly afterimage. Which I've just done, but I'm

Thank the Lord. I think we've had more than enough of your insights already.

not going to bother to do any more. I hate technology. If I'd written this down, I would have the pieces of paper in front of me still. Unless the house burnt down. (Pray the house doesn't burn down.) I'm sure those yesterday words are somewhere in this bloody black coffin of a thing. ~~The battery has started to go, it drops drastically whenever I'm away from a power source for more than ten minutes. It's meant to last up to six hours, but the clock starts to count down as soon as I unplug it to go mobile. No more working on the beach for me. At the most, I get an hour. I'm going to write a letter of complaint. No, that would be a waste of time. As it recording all this.~~ You said it, sister.

It really was a very good passage, about the cannibal feast. It would have been one of the things that people remembered about the book.

Actually, I don't know quite why I'm getting upset. It's not as if anyone is going to read *these actual words*. By the time the thing comes out, I shall have revised it so many times that it will be smooth as smooth. And while it is annoying, I suppose in the long run it doesn't matter. I probably wouldn't have used that passage about the cannibal feast, anyhow. It was meat too strong for my faint-hearted readers. They want romance, and they're not getting enough, *en ce moment*. (Henry has gone all distant again.)

It could have been worse: I could have lost everything. I don't know what I'd have done then; possibly gone up into the attic and barricaded myself in there, refused to come out until everyone had written a clear account of their acts, thoughts and emotions over the past two weeks.

I shall just have to carry on writing up today (Tuesday), & try to catch up with yesterday (see below) – at the same time.

In my last dream before I woke this morning I had a clear thought: I'm going to be in a daisy-chain for the rest of my life & I'm going to be in *this* daisy-chain for the rest of my life & I'm going to be in this *daisy-chain* for the rest of my life, & on and on.

I thought we might set these sections in italics, to show that they were originally hand-written. What do you think?

It might be too fussy. But then, should we take out the &s? Best left as is, probably.

After yesterday's losses, I don't know if I'm prepared to trust technology any more; so, for the moment, I've reverted to a pad of paper & my Montblanc pen. It seems more fitting to the spirit of Virginia. I've been looking through some of her journals & letters again. ('I am making up "To the Lighthouse" – the sea is to be heard all through it.') They were meant to be my summer reading, but there's so terribly much of them. Although *To the Lighthouse* is supposedly set in Scotland, Virginia's real childhood lighthouse was in St Ives – or off the coast near St Ives. She cheated on the quality of the weather in Scotland, & lied directly about the kind of plants you could grow in a garden up there. (Red-hot pokers, I don't think so.) I don't wonder she didn't fib about the cost of renting the place, too.

The Gulf Stream means that many unexpected plants grow on the west Coast of Scotland. But I'll leave this in, as it's your mistake

In dismay again (me, I mean): the spy-cameras, I find, are next to useless. ~~Since the revelation about Simona beating William up~~, I have learnt practically nothing about the guests that I didn't already know, or suspect. Because the weather has been so delightful, most of them spend most of their time outside; & the ones that do stay inside, stay in alone. I learn, therefore, that Marcia sometimes likes to take an afternoon nap – & that she sometimes uses traditional means to help her get to sleep. (She also says the Lord's Prayer quite often.) The daughter's wardrobe has a full-length mirror on the door, in which Edith now spends hours staring at her dressed-up self. (When they see Edith is occupied, Henry & Cleangirl have once or twice seized the moment. But these are hardly revelations: sex is the first thing one expects to find, behind closed doors.) Alan keeps a diary, which he writes every night before dinner. Edith writes, almost every day, to her penpal. Cleangirl, too, corresponds incessantly. Simona & William, total hypochondriacs both, have a whole black bag full of medicines... & so, I'm beginning to think it might have been better – I might have achieved an atmosphere more intense – had I chosen January or February as my month. Which of course is neglecting the fact that no-one, probably, in those circumstances, would have come; it's also ignoring the possibility of a midwinter sequel.

Henry has suddenly become more flirtatious, though I have no idea why. He seeks me out. He is careful to wait until Ingrid isn't around, which isn't often. This morning, for example, she took Edith into Southwold to buy a sketch pad & some pencils. Henry was upon me almost as soon as they'd driven off. It was quite embarrassing. 'What are you doing?' he asked, when anyone could have seen I was reading Virginia Woolf's diaries & smoking a borrowed cigarette (William's: I now owe him three packs) – this was out on the lawn. Henry squatted down on the grass; there was no other deck chair close by – I had taken mine & moved it into a triangle of clear morning sunlight. The sky above was a pale clouded white, grey towards the east, but soon – I was sure – to turn solid blue. 'I've never read very much of her, I have to admit,' Henry pursued. 'Well, I'm hoping to arrange a reading group,' I said, 'we'll do *To the Lighthouse*.' 'Now *that* I have read,' he said, 'a long time ago – at university. & that other one, with the boy not in it – based on her brother who died.' 'I think you mean *Jacob's Room*,' I said, though I was quite enjoying watching him flail. 'That's the one,' he said. 'I always thought they were rather –' 'Please don't say anything negative,' I said quickly, 'right this moment Virginia is very important to me.' 'I was only going to say, they seemed rather special.' 'They are,' I said, although I knew this *wasn't* at all what he'd been going to say. He'd intended to say that she was too woman-y, too domestic – something like that. Henry always did like to use argument as flirtation: at university, he cultivated an entirely bogus Tory persona, in order to get himself into blood-stirring situations. This is perhaps why he was so sexually unsuccessful. Like most affectations, it expressed a deeper truth & ended up becoming character – I'm fairly sure Henry's pencil slips a little further to the right every time he enters the voting booth. Ingrid calmed him down, though – Ingrid diverted that frustrated sex-energy into earning money, looking after Edith, creating the perfect home. Now he's on holiday, the energy is back – & he hasn't a clue what to do with it. Just like I said in the Synopsis – though I think I predicted it for the first week. 'Well,' I said, 'if you'd like to join the reading group you're more than welcome. I can lend you a copy of the book: I brought quite a few.' 'That would be great,' said Henry. 'Now,' I said, 'go away & leave me alone.'

Later, I left a copy of *To the Lighthouse* just outside his & Cleangirl's bedroom.

Next time I saw him after that, he was already I'd guess fifty pages in, head down, reading fast – & being sketched by Edith, who had no idea what she was drawing. I shall have to ask some other people to join the reading group now. I'm hoping to get – everyone.

Left further eight copies of *To the Lighthouse* on a side table in the drawing room. Put a note of explanation on the top. Will let the guests find their way to the book gradually, not make any grand, off-putting announcement.

There is a plan, today, for a trip; none of my doing, I promise. Several people (Cecile & Edith, Fleur, Alan, Marcia, William) want to drive down to Aldeburgh, take a look at the Benjamin Britten relics, eat some of the famous Aldeburgh fish & chips. Chips are becoming something of an issue: there is a yearning for them, generally; I've asked Chef *not* to do them – we aren't running a greasy spoon here. Edith, particularly, misses chips. It would be funny to feed her up, see a little pot-belly appearing on that model's frame – like a burial mound in a Norfolk field. (Alternatively: like a bee-sting two-thirds of the way along a string of spaghetti.) I'm placed in the awkward position of not knowing where the action is going to be, at home or on the trip. Hell. Clearly, I know the house, & the garden, & the beach – & so, by now, will my readers; a change of background might be good for the book. But I also have to wonder whether the most interesting situations occur in the half-empty Wherewithal. One further consideration is, in the place where I'm not, who would be the most reliable informant? This, I think, probably decides it. No-one going to Aldeburgh, were I not there, would be any use at all in telling me what went on; Simona can always let me know what happened whilst I was away from the house. I also get to see Alan & Fleur close-ish up, doing the avoidance dance of adult courtship. Watching them at the moment is like watching an executive toy, a line of dangling silver balls, bang on one end means bing on the other, & vice versa. (Note: Have to do some Benjamin Britten research when I get back; pretend I know all about him. He was gay, wasn't he? & liked boys with high voices.) After much faffing, we've decided to take three cars. Heaven knows why, apart from so that Alan & Fleur can travel separately. Alan & William will go together, in William's car; I'm driving Cecile & Edith; Marcia is taking Fleur. (Note: I don't think Marcia has mentioned my letter to Fleur, yet. When she spoke to me about it yesterday, I didn't dare ask whether she was going to.)

I thought for a while about saving you this embarrassment. For a couple of seconds, at least.

I haven't said anything about Marcia's car, have I? It's quite a marvel. She drives it without touching the pedals. X was very keen to tell me that it uses the same technology as Formula One racing cars, whereby the gear-change is done by pressing buttons on the steering wheel. He was deeply impressed &, I believe, sexually excited, by this idea. Marcia well nigh shrieked, 'It's not an automatic,' whilst showing everybody the car's various features. There has been quite a craze for getting her to give one lifts into & out of Southwold. I think it's the way people think they can demonstrate their *au fait*ness with her disability. She's pretty quick at either end; & can do the whole wheelchair in-out business herself. But it would still be quicker for the guests to get a lift from, say, me; & I'd be quite happy to give it. Because of the space taken up by the wheelchair, Marcia's car only carries three.

I hear calling; we're about to go.

I was very disappointed by the drive down to Aldeburgh. No revelations. Edith, as expected, sat silent: I have, for her, been in partial-Coventry ever since I forced her into the nursery, & total-Coventry since I doubted the Haunting. & this she keeps up despite my own spectral encounter on the landing. In confirmation of my impression yesterday, Icicle, too, has decided to relocate me in Coventry. (Perhaps because of my Cornwall reference – which I have regretted ever since: it was petty, it was dangerous.) She didn't blank me on the journey with thick, obvious silence, as did Edith; she maintained a conversation – but it was all given *from* myself *to* her, she offered nothing that wasn't, in some way, forced. I felt very hurt. My only consolation was the hope that Icicle was doing this to keep in with Edith, & that she knew (without her having to explain the situation) that I would understand. If she was too friendly with me, Edith would get jealous, *wouldn't* understand, would be unpersuadable. The drive therefore passed with nothing more by way of conversation than a few widely interspersed commonplaces. This, too, was how the landscape appeared – as seen from the speeding car: flatness, undulance, flatness, village, flatness, flatness, village, pond, flatness, military installation of some sort, gentle slope; I can't remember the exact order.

Aldeburgh itself was a gentle joy: a long seafront high street, with banks & charity shops upon either side – an aspiration towards Bath, a hint of Brighton, an unfortunate echo of Blackpool. We drove all the way along it, past the chip shop we'd visit later, until we came to a sort of raised jetty – from which we could look at the sea (the same sea as seen from the beach a hundred yards from Wherewithal). Of course, when I made a remark about this, Fleur reminded me that it wasn't as easy for Marcia to get a look at it as it was for *other* people. True, & bang went any chance of even daytrip *politesse*, between sissy & I. Alan, I noted, was steering well clear. Gradually, though, I became convinced that Marcia & Fleur had had *the* talk – in the car on the way down. Fleur looked post-tearful, I could see the signs; Marcia seemed more relaxed, & was happy to laugh as usual. After her funny reaction yesterday, I can't be sure how she will have dealt with Fleur. What have I done?

While we were walking along, eating our chips, a horrible incident. We were approaching the beach, & where we'd left the cars. For once, we were in something of a group, all together, & although the subject of our discussion was only the quality (very good) of the fish & chips, it felt like a proper moment of unity. Anyway, the seagulls were clearly interested in our food. They are large birds, here, with white bellies, wide grey wings (a beautiful grey) & yellow beaks slashed with black – nostrils, I think. Our numbers & our movement kept them off. But Cecile was walking a little ahead of us all. She seemed very energised by the surroundings, & our activity – which made me wonder about Cornwall. The whole thing couldn't have been more English summer seasidey. Perhaps she was remembering her fondest time. As she walked further & further ahead of us, she seemed to be attracting more & more seagulls. They became so thick in the air that she seemed to be walking along in a dome of wings. Her self-absorption – looking out to sea & tasting the hot oily fish – was such that I don't think she noticed them at all. Maybe she thought it was her joy, thrilling through the air around & about her. We saw her spot something out to sea – this was the odd thing, as I remember it: I'm in no doubt that all of us were watching her; I think, on some level, we knew what was going to happen. She saw this thing – I still don't know what it was – & she stretched her right arm out to point. The remainder of her fish & chips was held in front of her stomach. As one, we saw the largest & most aggressive of all the seagulls rise up from behind her. It had a plan; it wasn't acting randomly; it had done this before. For a moment it was right behind her head – wings outstretched to either side of her. They looked like the ears of a hare, long & pointed. With horror, we thought that it was going to land with its claws in her hair. But it didn't; its momentum lifted it in an arc over her head. I think we had stopped walking, terrified. None of us could say anything fast enough to prevent what was about to happen. The seagull dipped down over Cecile's head, still not having touched her. That was part of what made us so anxious – the attack was so controlled, & Cecile was so completely unaware of it. For a moment her face was covered by the diving body of the bird; we thought of its claws so close to her face, her forehead. But then it went those few inches further down, & did what it had planned. With its beak it dove for the last, large piece of fish in Cecile's left hand (her right was still pointing out to sea – though the darkening of the sky, brought by the seagull in front of her eyes, was already making her flinch). The bird took the chunk of white meat in its yellow beak, & now it needed a launchpad from which to make its getaway. It was right in front of Cecile's tummy, like a huge grey bouquet. It stretched its wings out to either side, kicked its feet in the chips, & in a jerky rush it was suddenly coming towards us. Cecile had finally become fully aware of what was happening; she shrieked. The escaping bird came directly towards us, & some of us shrieked, too. It was not rising in the air – it rammed straight through us, sending some into the road; luckily, with no cars coming. Cecile now had logic back with her; she knew it wasn't something inexplicable that had happened, just something horrible. Like a hurt child, she dropped the chips in their off-white paper to the floor. She put her hands up over her head. We thought of the seagull's claws, pushing down into the chips, & felt as if our own had also been dirtied – dirtied by the possibility of the idea of this. Cecile looked so small. But dropping the chips had been the wrong thing to do. A thick fighting carpet of seagulls formed at her feet. She panicked. Her hands flapped. Her mouth went into a tall O. At which point, Alan stepped forwards & with a few definite kicks rescued her. Throughout, he held his own fish & chips high & safe. He only dropped them when it became clear that Cecile was in desperate need of a hug. This isn't something he would ever have tried before, even on saying goodbye. But at this moment, he enfolded her so completely that it seemed, from behind, that she had disappeared. We rushed forwards to keep the seagulls away from the two lots of fish & chips that were now on the pavement. Not that we expected anyone to eat them; but to keep the gulls from eating them would be a victory for our side, for humans. Cecile sobbed. We could hear her, but her face was hidden. Alan must have whispered the right things, because she soon emerged – wet & radiant. 'How silly,' she said. But we had all seen her at her weakest, & she knew that we weren't going to forget. We drove back, breaking the speed limit, in a strange collective euphoria. The story will be retold & retold.

Audrey Cat was installed on the sofa when we came back, having finally overcome her cowardice. The Maid, I think, has been working on her: treats, strokes, praise. Fleur overjoyed.

Aldeburgh seagull unity soon gone.

Every time I walk into a room, everyone goes silent. Heading outside, to try to get away from all this, caught X behind the apple trees, talking intensely to Cecile. They, too, silenced by my approach. I need to find out what's happening.

It is striking to me how often – over the course of the past week & a half – I have ended up having one-on-one conversations, rather than with two or three others present. I feel as if we were playing a children's party game, where I am a leper of sorts, & the others avoid me as much as possible – sacrificing one of their number to the obscenity of intimacy, but, generally, keeping far back against & behind the walls. This may be wrong as an impression, but even so it's very hurtful as a delusion.

Fleur came & found me.

'Marcia told me,' she said, 'about the letter.'

'On the way to Aldeburgh?'

'Yes. I'm very upset and annoyed. Why did you do that?'

'Because it was the only way,' I said. 'Everyone was thinking I was the villainess.'

'Well, you are, aren't you?'

'I just wanted to explain my side of things to Marcia. I knew she'd be fair about it.'

'She *has* been – perfectly fair. She spoke to you, & then she spoke to me.'

'Has she shown you the letter?'

'No. Which again shows how fair she's been.'

'You can read it, if you want.'

'I don't. What I want is for you not to go behind my back any more.'

'You don't leave me much choice. If you won't tell people why you hate me so much, I'll have to.'

'Marcia is a good person.'

'I agree.'

'You haven't made her like me any the less.'

'That wasn't my intention.'

'Are you sure?'

Fleur turned & walked out. More mending to be done.

7 p.m. Simona insists upon a quick fifteen-minute Confession-session, before supper. I'm so glad she's here, looking after me. ~~I'm finding it increasingly difficult to talk to Simona in this way; now that I know her account of her relation-~~

ship with William, & her avowed intent to leave him, is, as they say, economical with the *verité*. She continues to hint that she will leave him tomorrow, & to find reasons why she can't leave him today. The whole situation is surely going to damage our professional relationship. I don't think I'm going to be able to trust her as my Editor, any more. If she lies to me so glibly about the evil of William, why should I expect the truth from her about my books? Plus, I'm of course going to have to put something of this in the finished text. If I don't have this, all I'll have for William & Simona is a bit of downstairs bickering, Simona's first marriage confessions, William's piano-playing. As characters, they'll be dead weight entirely. & I can't afford that. I could cut them completely. That might work. Their entanglements with the others haven't become so Gordian as to be unpickable. I could always put Fleur in for Simona, & Alan for William, whenever they interact with anyone else. That might solve the problem.

It's rather remorseless, really: this compulsion to get it down; I wish it would go away – no, that's a lie: I wish everyone else in the world would go away & leave me to get on with the job of getting it down.

Nothing satisfies me, when I'm in this mood; it's as if my head is full of fur, & in order to think I've always needed a head full of minimal steel & porcelain & tall lilies in a glass vase & quiet; but what I have is brown fur, in acrylic, not even real fur, not bison or bear, just fake fur like you'd see in an ironic fashion-shoot that no-one expects anyone to take seriously & buy or wear. I wonder if Virginia got like this; I bet she did; worse, I expect – it drove her batty in the end; ~~it drove her fishy in the end.~~

What else is happening?

Dinner. Minestrone. Monkfish, new potatoes & broccoli. Chef is doing a great job. His infatuation with Cleangirl continues... He's always finding some excuse to be around her. I thought, after the biscuits, he might give up – but he's obviously a determined sort. He's found out she likes mint tea, and has brought in a whole bushel from the garden, so that she can always have it fresh. She smiles and thanks him.

Spent most of the evening catching up with yesterday, & so missed whatever may have happened today. When I asked X if anything was going on, he said, 'Nothing.' A quick check of the spy-cameras seemed to back him up. Everybody is outside, apart from Cecile, sitting perfectly still in her room.

How I envy cats: when they're feeling randy, they just take themselves out onto the back fence & advertise, very lewdly, for a siring.

Monday

Day Twelve Week Two

What happened on Monday: I suppose I should make a note of it, in case I forget. Not likely to. I'll type it straight in, print it straight out; it's faster than pen. Began, as usual, by writing something about the dawn chorus. I think it was attempted-witty: 'This morning I wanted to find whichever yokel it is the Countryside employs to operate the Dawn Chorus Generating Contraption; "It's okay," I wanted to say to him, "we get the idea: Nature, far-away-from-the-city, every day God's newest blessing, so many little lives pulsing, etcetera... Now, bloody turn it off!" Drilling, however, has stopped. Praise be.' Breakfast with Alan, Simona and Henry. Odd combination. Henry shifty. Kept going off into the garden for five minutes. When I asked why (I thought he might have flatulence), he said he was getting text messages all the time from his collaborator on *Summerdream*. I asked him to show me; he showed me not the messages but the phone, very smart. I wonder if the texts were from his collaborator or from Cleangirl. What can they have to text about, at this time in the morning? Alan enjoys his cornflakes, loudly – truffling, snuffling. Upstairs again afterwards for a bit of catch-up writing and a quarter hour's spying. No great insights. Interrupted by Maid, wanting to dust. Out onto the lawn to appear public. Wandered around the house for a while before lunch, looking for events: none. Then ate. Brie sandwich. I'm bored of sandwiches. More writing; more spying. Down ladder again. Without preamble, Marcia began (we were in the kitchen, she having found me alone): 'You were wrong to write to me that way. What happened – the pregnancy – was a *pri*vate thing for Fleur, and I had no real right to know about it.' 'I had every right to tell you,' I said, 'if I felt it might explain my sister's attitude to me.' 'In a strange way, I *am* glad I know. But it *does*n't change how I feel about Fleur: I knew there was *some*thing. With you, I feel sorry – sorry that you were so *des*perate you would use your sister's pain as a way of making me like you more.' 'It's not to do with that – it's to do with Fleur being dishonest. She lies to herself about our relationship. That hurts me, a great deal. I don't know what to do; I've already tried and tried talking to her about it.' 'And what does she do?' 'Well... she just doesn't talk about it.' '*Ex*act*ly*. And why should she? It's not a part of my life I'd care to revisit every other day.' 'But she does, every single day – and she visits it upon everyone around her.' 'Wordplay isn't clever; it doesn't make something *true*.' 'You're at least talking to me now. Before I sent you the letter, that just wasn't happening.' 'No,' said Marcia, '*you're* talking to *me* – and that's what wasn't happening.' 'I don't know what you mean.' 'It's to do with your idea of me – that's who you were talking to before. Remember our last conversation about this?' 'You're wrong,' I said. 'The *pro*blem was your idea of me.' 'We disagree.' 'We do.' 'Good,' she said. 'It's a start.' She laughed, richly;

I'm finding it harder and harder to dislike her. 'This is a lovely house,' she said. We talked of other things, and it was as if we had never had a cross word. Amazing woman. Two o'clock. The Vicar came back for a second visit. Fleur obviously felt I wanted to display him to the others, make a spectacle and fun of him. So, although I answered the door, and asked him in, she wafted through almost immediately and took him off *to her room*. (How did she know he was around? Her clergy-radar, I suppose.) He must have thought this was rather odd, and rude; though I'm sure he's seen odder and ruder things in his time: Vicars, like anyone who gets to see people at their worst – doctors, publicans, tour guides, booksellers – can't be shocked. I followed them upstairs, going instead into the Master Bedroom and thence the attic. The Vicar sat in the armchair in the far corner of the room, Fleur on the bed! They talked for a while or two about how each of them was. Then Fleur offered him some tea, the Vicar accepted, Fleur went off to make it. ~~And – joy joy – the moment he'd heard her footsteps going down the stairs, the Vicar got out of the armchair and started exploring the room.~~ He seemed most interested in the contents of the wardrobe and then the chest-of-drawers. Assuming a cup of tea to take a minimum of five minutes to make, and assuming no-one else had the right to come into Fleur's room, the Vicar felt quite secure in getting it out. I could see Fleur, down in the kitchen, fetching the teapot from a shelf: there was a delicious moment when I saw her pick up the sugar container – was she going to come back up, and find the Vicar rubbing himself against the slinkiest of her dresses? (She has a special occasion one, in blue shot silk.) No, she decided to decant some sugar into a smaller bowl and give him the choice upstairs. The Vicar moved on to the top drawer, the knicker drawer. He didn't appear to sniff them. Instead, he dried his mouth out with his handkerchief then, one by one, put the knickers wholly inside, shut his lips, turned around three times then spat them out, examining them afterwards for any sign of wetness. Then he replaced them at the very bottom of the drawer, putting a similarly coloured pair in their former's place at the top. I couldn't believe it: I had here my Vicars & Knickers farce. Fleur is used to making cups of tea, her routine is very apt. As she left the kitchen, a loaded tray between her hands, the Vicar was daring one final triple-spin; as she began to mount the stairs, he was replacing the knickers at the back of the drawer; as she came to the top, he was deciding whether or not to risk another chomp or not. But then he must have heard something, a creak. He shut the drawer, and – as Fleur outside put the tray down in order the better and safer to open the door to the room – he rezipped his fly. When Fleur came in, he did his best to look unflustered. However, there was one final moment of farce when the wardrobe door, which he hadn't properly shut (by giving the lock a turn), slowly began to seep open. It was behind Fleur's back, she was on the bed again. But the Vicar clearly saw. He almost spat his tea out. The whole incident, while being delightful (and something I'm not sure I can put into the book) was also quite hard to believe. ~~How can a man like that face himself, knowing he is such a *cliché*? I suppose it's no different to any other kind of sexual kink – they're all an expression of a vivid lack of imagination. Much better to have straight, normal sex and an absolute orgy of weirdness going on in one's head.~~ Over tea, they talked about the church, its difficult financial situation, its successful missions in Africa. Then Fleur brought her real subject up: the ghost. She wanted to know if it would be possible for the Vicar to perform an exorcism; Edith, she said, showed classic symptoms of diabolic possession. At first, she hadn't worried – she thought it was just an over-vivid imagination; but when Edith started wearing the daughter's clothes... It was terrifying. 'I've had to pray about it a great deal, before coming to the conclusion that I should tell you.' The Vicar asked her lots of questions about the 'manifestations'. She asked him again, could he do it? He confessed that, yes, he did sometimes perform blessings – to help the spirits of the restless dead

All liked, I'm afraid.

move on, toward their final resting place. Fleur asked, could he exorcise Edith? And here, thank God, the man began to make difficulties. There was no way he could do anything of that nature, he said, without the permission of the owners of the house. If the church caught him engaging in such renegade activities, he'd practically be defrocked. ~~(And sticking women's underwear in his mouth was what? A perk?)~~ Fleur pressed him. Surely, when there was no assurance the owners would agree, an exception could be made? Sometimes, the Vicar said, we have to allow the devil his small, local triumphs, to ensure his final destruction. Fleur looked very upset, but in control. She said that she would write to the Owners, in September. If necessary, she would come and visit them – implore them to do something about the evil that was present in their house. She was just asking his advice as to how she should behave towards Edith when X came and called me gently down from the attic. I told him off for not relocking the bedroom door behind him. There was a crisis, he said, with the Maid. She and Edith had fallen out: Edith didn't want the sheets changed on her bed. The Maid had taken them off, and Edith had retrieved them from the wash-basket. They are unlovely, orangey brown. She had remade the bed with them herself. Leaving Fleur and the Vicar, I went down into the kitchen to intervene (the two of them were sitting in different rooms, refusing to speak – which is why I hadn't noticed their bust-up on one of my other screens). 'It's very simple,' I said to the Maid, 'if she doesn't want the sheets changed then don't change the sheets.' 'Thank you,' said Edith, from behind me. 'But they're –' 'Whatever they are,' I said, 'they stay where they are. Is that clear?' 'Yes,' said the Maid. 'Now don't be upset,' I said when Edith had delightedly gone. 'She's almost an adolescent – you know how they like smelly, sordid things.' The Maid, though still annoyed, sniggered. 'I should know,' she said, 'I've got two of my own.' 'Exactly,' I said. 'Boys,' she replied. 'And that's far worse, isn't it?' I said. She then proceeded to tell me a couple of anecdotes

I felt dirtied to have heard, and which I'm certainly not recording. By the time I got back upstairs, Fleur had taken the Vicar out for a stroll around the garden. I saw them from my window, closely examining the flowerbeds. Drat. I don't know what they agreed upon, ref. Edith. Will he take action?

3.30 p.m. Vicar gone. Out again onto the lawn. The next section I think I can reconstruct almost *verbatim*; I'd made some notes in my notebook, in advance. It's a useful scene, I think:

Isn't it funny how the people whose confidences one least wishes to hear – gutrot tramps, stagestruck girls – are always the people who are keenest to confide? This afternoon William sought me out in the garden. I wasn't taking confession, it was at least another couple of hours before that was due to begin; I was reclining in a deckchair, preparing myself ~~for the disappointment of Simona turning up, and no-one else.~~ William sat down beside me – on the grass, for there was no other chair. (Where have they gone?) He was all rolled-up shirtsleeves, mufti entirely. He so emphasised the fact that he was relaxed, on holiday, he put so much work into it, that one couldn't help but feel exhausted. 'Do you mind if I tell you something?' he said. 'Of course not,' I replied. 'After all – that's what I'm here for; that's what *we're* here for.' 'Well,' he hesitated, 'Simona accepted your invitation on my behalf. I didn't want to come. You're probably thinking that I'm going to say, "But now I'm glad I did." But I'm not. I'm not going to say it because I'm not glad. Not yet, anyway. That's the first thing I want to say: that I can now imagine some point in the future when I shall be glad for having come. The second thing I want to say is this: I'm not yet glad for having come because there are so many things going on in my heart and in my head that I just don't want to confront myself – and so the last thing I really want is for those things to be publicised. By you.' Really, I thought, it was like some pop star pleading with a Tabloid

Editor not to out them. 'William,' I said, 'so far as I know, neither your head nor your heart are in much danger of exposure.' 'Good,' he said, 'I don't think I could cope.' ~~It was remarkable: I could already see what he would be like if Simona really were to go ahead and dump him: a pile of guts spilled out into everybody's lap. He would need a motivation for unseaming himself, but once he had it we'd get everything. I realised that if I wanted any joy (misery) from him, I'd have to work on her. He stood up to go. I felt as if I had been cornered by a sweaty man at the office party, and asked not to look while he photocopied his big fat bottom.~~ Went back inside to write up William, and start thinking about getting ready for confession. Quick spy in the attic, but – DANGER. I'm good at remembering dialogue, but it's hardly likely I would have forgotten this: Edith in the drawing room with Marcia and Cecile. Edith slouched across a sofa, Marcia upright in her chair, Cecile leaning back against the chimneybreast. Edith said: 'I'm sure there's a lot more I could find out about the daughter.'

'What?' said Marcia. 'Ringing up her parents?'

'No,' she said, 'there must be other things in the house.'

'Such as,' said Cecile.

'I don't know. Maybe they've put them in the attic.'

'You get into the attic through Victoria's room,' said Marcia. 'There's a hole in the *cei*ling, where a ladder comes down. I've seen it.'

'Do you think she'd mind?' asked Edith.

'Of course not,' said Cecile. 'Why should she?'

'I might find a diary,' said an excited Edith, 'or letters.'

'You won't know less when you come down than you did when you went up,' said Marcia.

'Will you ask for me?' said Edith, to Cecile.

'We can ask together.' Oh God, I thought. What the hell can I do? In a panic, I hurried down out of the attic – just in case a deputation was that very moment setting off up the stairs. I lay on the bed, pulled a pillow over my head. If they come now, I thought, I'll sham illness. I can keep that up for a day or so; I doubt if they'll find it suspicious. They didn't come. Which made me feel worse – I was sure they'd ask me the moment I got downstairs. What was I going to say? I was in a terrible bind. Couldn't I just explain that I wasn't allowed to let anyone into the attic? That would be the easiest option: blame it all on the Owners. I could say that I wasn't really even meant to allow Edith to sleep in the daughter's bedroom (which is true) and certainly not to wear her clothes (also true). I groaned, and pretended to suffocate myself with the pillow – always a comfort. After that, I could say that if she created any more fuss, she'd have to move back into the nursery. I wasn't really convinced this line would work, though. It took me half an hour to regain composure. Then I went downstairs, ostensibly to take confession. As anticipated, the scene took place almost immediately. Icicle asked, could Edith just have a quick look round the attic; I said no. They asked why? I said because I didn't have a key – the Owners had taken the key. They expressed their disappointment. I asked them to try and imagine if it were *their* daughter that had died; would *they* want strangers rootling around in her business?

'But I'm not a stranger,' said Edith. 'I know her already. I just want to know her better.'

I said that was nonsense.

'We can at least phone them,' said Icicle, 'and ask their permission.'

No, I said. I refuse to bother them again. If we cause any more trouble, they may very well just ask us to leave.

This was when Cleangirl came in from the garden. When it was explained to her what was going on, she – bless her – straight away took my side. How could Edith think of going through another person's private things? How would Edith feel if someone did that to her?

'If I was dead, I wouldn't care.'

'And if you were a ghost?' I said.

'I'll ask Elizabeth tonight, for her permission,' said Edith.

'No, you will not,' said Cleangirl, 'and you'll go and get changed out of those clothes right this minute.'

'No,' squealed Edith. 'Let me wear the clothes.'

Cleangirl looked at me for guidance. Ordinarily, I would have wanted to capitalise on having Cleangirl's support: get Edith out of the daughter's wardrobe, too. But, for the moment, defending the attic was the most important thing.

'What harm does wearing her clothes do?' asked Edith.

'It may not harm the clothes,' said Cleangirl, 'but I'm not at all sure it's good for you. If I hear any more nonsense about you going through other people's private property, we will leave. Do you hear that? I will take you away.'

Icicle did not interfere. She knew better than to come between mother and daughter. Edith tucked herself away, under Icicle's arm. They went gloomily up to Icicle's room. I could imagine what Edith would say: 'I hate them. I hate them all. They don't understand.'

'Thank you,' I said to Cleangirl.

'I didn't do it for you,' she replied.

'Well, thank you, anyway.' I was angry enough at this point to make a convincing exit – back upstairs. No confession today. I would have liked to go up to the spy-room and watch their reaction: that already has become something of an instinct with me. But for safety's sake, I decided I had better leave well alone – at least for the next couple of days.

A quiet evening in. We sat in the drawing room. Alan and William read their books, seated to the right and left of the fireplace; mostly they limit their comments to grunts of appreciation. Fleur sat *beside* Alan, and seemed content to do nothing more – she didn't read, she merely stared into where the fire would be, were we to have a fire.

Beside her was Marcia, to her left, also on the sofa: she likes a break from the wheelchair. Marcia talked much of the time, but we are now so used to the sound of her voice that we hardly ever hear. I think for the past few days she has been reliving her childhood visits to Jamaica. There have been comic stories involving fruit that wasn't fruit, mad barbers, rum, mad goats and a lecherous uncle who probably wanted to commit an indecency upon her. Simona sat beside William – sometimes reading a paragraph or two over his shoulder. Cecile sat to Simona's right, occupied by thought. Henry and Ingrid sat at opposite ends of the sofa facing the fireplace. It is a four-seater, and I was beside Ingrid. (X dozing beside me.) She was reading an interior decoration magazine which someone bought for her in Southwold. Henry was working on the text of his play. I was trying to concentrate on Virginia Woolf's diaries, but kept finding myself distracted into observation of the others. Edith was absent; upstairs, talking with the dead. Before, she used to sit on the carpet, her head on Ingrid's knee. Chef was in the kitchen, making yummy smells.

Dinner went past in a sulk. Juicy, tender steak on a bed of *roquette*, roast potatoes and parsnips. *Tarte aux pommes*.

Casually, I ask Fleur if she had a nice chat with the Vicar.

'Yes,' she replies.

'What did you talk about?' I ask.

Fleur turns away, talks to someone else.

After the plates and everything had been cleared away, Icicle and the men sat down for *another* game of poker. They have made quite a pet of her. Her lucky streak continues, or so I'm told.

I'm bored with all my clothes. I've worn them all, again and again. I want new ones. I want to go shopping. Buy shoes. Have my hair cut.

Given your biographical note, I think a few more mentions of shoes might not have gone amiss.

Wednesday

Day Fourteen Week Two

All a-spoon in the arms of X, post-sex, awaiting full waking, null and happy beyond happiness: that was *not* me at seven o'clock this morning.

Given up on the Montblanc: it takes too much time; typing is time-efficient. Also, the laptop seems to be behaving itself a bit better today. Spent an hour typing up my handwritten notes for Monday – left it exactly as it was, ampersands & all.

Why is everyone – apart from me – so screwy, so cranky, so lost? Edith wafts around in long flouncy dresses; being treated by the rest of the household for all the world as if she were a female magus, or the head of some particularly unconvincing (to outsiders) cult. I'm hoping it's just a craze: the ghost-craze.

I could, of course, make a great deal more of my own encounter with the ghost – but I have chosen not to. This takes a deal of self-control: several of the guests have pestered me about it, wanting choicer details. However, I am doing my best to downplay what happened; pooh-poohing is the order of the day. I have, I tell them, an over-vivid imagination.

Scene just now in the drawing room, with Cleangirl and Henry.

I was sitting there, on my own, with a thrice-read teen magazine (Edith's) and a going-cold cup of coffee.

Cleangirl was first to come in. I expected her to go, but she stayed, and we began to chat. I sensed that she very much wanted to talk, but only in an attempted-frothy way; this was not to be about confidences, just time-passing. It was her way of restoring our friendship, after the betrayal, etc.

Then Henry came in, and all hope of froth was blown away. He wanted purpose, action, plans. 'Tomorrow,' he said, 'shall we do anything?'

I didn't know which of us he was asking, and neither, clearly, did Cleangirl.

'I think we'll do something,' she said. 'But nothing major.'

'Go out, you mean?' he said, still not explicitly directing the question at her.

'Well, we might. In the car.'

I could see that it was turning into one of those desultory, mid-marriage conversations – full of aggressive love and coded insult.

'We've been almost everywhere nearby.'

'We've only been to Aldeburgh.'

'And all around Southwold.'

'I'm sure there's still more to do,' I said.

'Why don't we ask Edie?' said Cleangirl, turning to look at Henry for the first time.

'I already have.'

'And she said?'

'Oh, the usual: that she just wanted to stay in her room. I was hoping we could come up with something to get her enthused.'

Cleangirl glanced towards me, very aware of my recording presence. And then it happened: she abandoned herself to argument.

'If she's enthused about staying in her room, what's wrong with that? She's doing lots of reading, isn't she? Why do we have to force her out? It means we get a bit more time...'

Henry, too, was aware of me. 'It's not urgent,' he said. 'I just thought you might want to get out of this place.'

'I *do*,' said Cleangirl, 'but not to go and eat ice-creams in the car, again.'

Henry left. Cleangirl gave me a sphinxy-minxy look. I was hoping now that our chat would turn serious, but no such luck.

Cecile seems quickly to have recovered from the seagull attack. (Having seen her looking so vulnerable, I don't think I can any longer call her Icicle.) She and Alan have become a lot more intimate (caught them breakfasting together); they now speak French to each other. He is something like a Daddy to her – large, lumbering, protective, warm. She is therefore prepared to flirt with him. It's good to see; it is distracting her somewhat from Edith, who has been threatening monopoly.

X came back from 'fishing' (that's where he told me he was going, anyway) with scratches on his left cheek, grazes on his hands and ankles and, as I privately observed, bruising on his abdomen.

Henry also came back with injuries, although so far I have yet to see them, have only heard about them indirectly, from Marcia. I'm told he had a split lip, a puffy eye and was holding his right wrist awkwardly.

Neither man will admit to having been in a fight with the other; when I ask X, he smiles in a *faux*-tough manner, as if to say, 'Call that a fight?' Infuriating.

It seems, from what I can tell, that they arranged between themselves to slip off, find a quiet spot, have it out. I don't know where it was – down on the beach or perhaps in the corner of a field. I'd like to know; somehow, it makes a difference.

12.22 p.m. Strange scene with Simona just now. She sought me out, in the garden. 'Listen,' she said, 'I just want you to know that whatever happens, I'm on your side. Remember that.'

'What do you mean?' I said.

'I can't say any more,' she said. 'I shouldn't even be seen talking to you.'

'What's going on?' I asked. 'I know something's going on.'

Just then Alan came out of the house.

'Lunch is ready,' he shouted.

'Wonderful,' shouted Simona, and trotted, ~~ungainly,~~ gracefully back through the French doors.

Awkward politenesses of plate filling and emptying.

Sat in the brilliant sibilance of the beach, wind-ripped, feeling the skin upon my face go dangerously dry. I tried to think what I should do about X and Henry, but all I could think of was, 'Moisturise! Now!' Then, suddenly, all anxiety goes. I am deeply, instantly, calm. I am feeling the kind of absolute beatific serenity that I know from experience is caused by the imminent arrival of a thought, the thought being: *Oh my God, I left my purse on the train* or *Bloody hell, he was the love of my life, and I dumped him*. Suddenly, then, all anxiety returns – redoubled.

Strange. I just saw Simona and X down at the bottom of the garden. They appeared to be arguing. X had his hands on his hips and was bending forwards. His fingers were straight, and though he didn't point with them I could tell he wanted to. Simona more calm, but arms tied in a knot under her bosom. I was in the Master Bedroom, having gone up there to look for X. I only glanced out the window in frustration at not finding him. A pair of binoculars there, used by the Owners for birdwatching, came in handy. The argument went on for several minutes, becoming, as far as I could make out, less and less bitter. Simona untied her arms and X hooked his thumbs into his pockets. When they parted, Simona came back into the house; X remained walking up and down by the far wall, pensive.

Immediately, I went downstairs. Simona was already in a conversation with Ingrid about Edith. I didn't interrupt. The only sign of Simona's having just been in an argument was her speaking slightly louder than usual.

Out into the garden to talk to X, but he was already halfway back to the house – moving fast. I stood in the doorway, hoping to halt him. His eyes did the telling: Get out of my way. I did. He was rude, and didn't care about being rude.

X ran upstairs; I followed him – not saying his name. I didn't want to attract attention. He was inside our bedroom and had locked the door before I could reach the handle.

I left him alone.

Next half hour.

Like a child, I had gone back three or four times and tried the handle to the bedroom door, to see if it turned. The fourth time, it did.

I found X lying on the bed, gazing up into the ceiling.

'What's wrong,' I asked, tenderly. 'I suppose I'm just,' X replied, 'feeling the pressure.' There didn't seem any point in pretending ignorance – if I did, it would mean we couldn't move on to the real subject. 'I saw you and Simona, on the lawn. What were you arguing about?' 'We were just talking.' 'Don't lie,' I said. 'You were arguing. And when you finished arguing, you came in here to sulk.' 'We're not getting along very well, that's all – her and me.' 'Anything in particular causing difficulties?' 'Yes,' he said, 'your book.' 'And what about my book?' 'The *fact* of your book. How would you feel, if you were me? I'm very vulnerable.' 'I'm not going to put in anything that would hurt you. Why are you worried – you're the hero of my book.' He was about to say something, but stopped himself. 'Yes?' I said. 'I can't tell you,' he said. 'Why?' 'I can't tell you that, either.' 'Well, what can you tell me?' 'You want to know what happened, don't you – with me and Henry?' 'Of course.' 'Well, I'll tell you that.' 'Why didn't you tell me earlier? Everyone else probably knows by now.' 'No they don't. Ingrid might know by now. I expect Henry and her have had this same conversation.' 'Tell me,' I said. 'We haven't been getting along,' he said. 'Don't be so bloody evasive. Why haven't you been getting along?' 'I don't know, exactly. He just started to annoy me, and obviously I started to annoy him, too.' 'Over what?' 'How should I know? Over being in the same room together, occupying the same space.' 'It all sounds very gay to me.' 'We *are* both quite competitive men.' I was sitting cross-legged on the counterpane, doing my damnedest to be calm; my posture was good, my spine was straight, my weight was centred, my breathing was regular. 'And you wanted to find out who was top?' I said, sarcastically, 'Was that it?' 'I think we both wanted some release. We've been cooped up in this house so long.' 'That *isn't* the real reason,' I said. 'And if you won't tell me, then I'll have to winkle it out of Henry.' 'I'm sure he'll say roughly the same thing.' 'Why? Have you agreed a story between you?' 'We talked about it afterwards.' 'After what?' He sat down on the bed, quite close to me. He smiled a smile that in a better mood I'd have taken for roguish. 'Tell me *now*.' 'Actually,' he said, 'it was quite funny. We left the house separately and met up where we'd prearranged, a little down the lane – round the corner, out of sight. Then we went to try and find somewhere quiet –' 'Did you talk?' 'No. Look, would you mind not interrupting?' I gave him my best flint-face. 'We walked down a long track. The problem was finding somewhere hidden from plain view. There were lots of large fields, but very few secluded places. Eventually, we found some tall hedges with a gap in them. We weren't that far away from the path, but we were out of sight. We hadn't seen anyone as we walked along; we were fairly sure we wouldn't be interrupted. And then we started...' He laughed. 'I haven't been in a fight like that since... it wasn't as long ago as school; I got into some fights at university; I think it was outside a bar, in Toulouse. That must be eight years ago, at least.' He caught sight of me, still flinty. 'We stayed apart, threw a few punches; none of them hitting anything solid. It feels stupid, that Marquis of

Queensberry stuff. You can try to come over all Mike Tyson street fighter, but you know you look like some formal Victorian gentleman putting up his dukes. So, pretty soon we ended up on the floor, trying to grab one another's hands, putting in little close-range jabs when we could. He got me pretty well.' X lifted his shirt; the bruises had darkened since the last time I saw them. 'I think I got him back. And then...' X snorted at the memory. He looked at me with glistening eyes. '...this ostrich jumped on top of us. That's how we got most of our injuries – this bloody great bird and its horrible feet. Of course, we tumbled away. Henry got the worst of it – the bird was pecking at his face, quite nastily. It wouldn't leave him alone. So, I had to get in there and shoo it away. I threw a few clods of earth at it; it backed off pretty quickly. Henry went a bit mad, started throwing rocks at it. I stopped him. The bird lost interest in us. It must only have attacked us because it felt we were a danger to it; this great tussle on the ground, fists flying. Henry and I looked at each other, and we just pissed ourselves laughing. And that was that. We started back to the house. Henry called the police on his mobile. It sounded as if we'd seen the most wanted ostrich in Suffolk. It had escaped from a farm about five miles away. Henry gave them a good description of where it was. They didn't ask us what we'd been doing there. And... have I answered your question?'

The weather has to be mentioned, at least once a day, or readers don't really know where they are. I don't think I've included enough references, this past week. Here, then, are some descriptive sentences, to insert wherever necessary. 1. 'It's a high clear bright day, only a little too windy for comfort.' 2. 'Another fine morning, the sky silting up later with high white clouds.' 3. 'The most purely summery of all our days so far; we really could be on a Greek island, what with the clean-cut shadows and the pure colours.' 4. 'The day started murkily; the sea took back its vapours mid-morning; ever since then, we've been blessed with cloudless blue and not-too-breezyness.' 5. 'This is the kind of day I brought everyone here for: warm, English, bright, but fragile: like a woman of fifty, when she smiles one notices the smile more than the lines.' 6. 'What can one say? Blessed again: shadows as small as edges.' 7. 'Today was marred by a gauzy haze, which gave the air a candy-flossy tang; ozone, I suppose, of some variety.'

No-one apart from X is talking to me.

The story of The Ostrich has reached the rest of the guests. Marcia laughed and laughed and laughed when she heard. (I knew what it was, even from upstairs; nothing else could have had that effect.) 'Have you heard?' said Edith, coming towards me full of playground excitement. 'My father and your boyfriend had a fight, and then they were both beaten-up by a big bird.' I suppose it *is* too good a yarn to go untold; Henry and X must have agreed to let the cat out. In a strange and unexpected way, it has brought people closer together again. In strange ways. Even as X was describing the whole silly episode to me, I couldn't help but think that he and Henry were practically the same person – in their desires, their dislikes. Their difficulty wasn't that they had some great disagreement which took them off to opposite ends of the universe; it was that they both wanted to occupy *the same exact space*. If it weren't too vain, I'd say that this space was me (although I'm not sure I like the idea of being occupied; it sounds a bit too like pregnancy).

Spying. Cleangirl to Edith, sitting in the daughter's room. After scene of two days ago, they are making up.

Cleangirl says, 'I feel I haven't spent enough time with you.'

And Edith replies, 'Don't worry about me.'

Awkward silence follows.

'Do you want to talk about it?'

'Only in the way you want to talk about a holiday or a new present – not the way you think.'

'It's been a good experience so far, hasn't it?'

'The best of my life.'

'That doesn't make me feel very good. What about all those holidays we took you on, the presents we gave you?'

'Oh, those were wonderful, Mummy. Don't worry. But this was something that came to me because I was *me* – me on my own, I mean. Not because it was the summer holidays, or my tenth birthday; not because someone needed to give me something, or I'd feel bad.'

'We give you those things because we love you.'

'I know. And this happened because someone else loves me. Elizabeth. Or at least she *likes* me – likes me enough to want to make friends.'

'Be careful, Edith.'

'I don't need to be careful. I'm being looked after.'

Cleangirl stood up. 'Well,' she said, 'this isn't a conversation I ever imagined myself having with you; not until boys came along, and then in a slightly different form.'

'Boys don't just come along,' said Edith.

'What?'

'We invite them, don't we?'

Cleangirl shook her head. 'Oh no,' she said, 'they'll come for you – just you wait and see.'

'They already have.'

'No,' said Cleangirl, 'believe me, they haven't.'

Today is a lovely day, but I sense a heaviness in the air. I detect a change in atmosphere... Who am I trying to kid: I think they may have found out about the cameras. Marcia this afternoon was quite different to Marcia this morning. I said hello, in passing; she didn't reply. Gave me a very black look. Going down to test my theory.

Didn't get very far. Still no-one will talk to me.

I'm marginalised; I'm edgy, I'm ledgy. I've gone from the most important space in the house (the Master Bedroom) to the most insignificant (the downstairs lav). As I write this, I hear the beasts outside: plotting; plotting in beastly grunts; plotting to make me look like a fool. There's no way I can cope with this, unless I have an ally; and I don't have even the hope of an ally. I have lost all allies. I feel remorse; I know it's remorse because it has that sorbet texture in the mouth, as if one's tongue had turned to ice and were about to dissolve without one first being able to say the words, the word, one wanted. 'I'm sorry, everyone, I'm sorry to each and every one of you, individually, and for absolutely individual reasons. If I could make amends, I would; as I can't, I can only ask your forgiveness.'

Tricked!

I went up here into the attic only because I wanted to do some innocent spying and to find out what was going on downstairs, really, what the beasts were plotting, and before I knew it blam! X had pushed the ladder up behind me and slammed shut the hatch and shut me in. I thought it was a joke, but a loud dangerous one. And by the time I'd jumped down and grabbed it to give it a tug, he'd put the padlock on and locked it and I'm scared, I don't like it up here. I'm starting to calm down but right at the start I really panicked, when I realised it wasn't a joke, and typing this is quite calming because I can look at the light of the screen and think, 'At least I've got this to see by.' I don't have to be in the dark, which is off to the edges of everywhere around me. No, I don't have to go into the far corners, either – corners which are dark and may contain things. I can stay here. Safe-ish. After X locked me in, I shouted and screamed and banged, but he didn't reply. I couldn't hear anything – I listened, and was soon sure he'd gone downstairs and wasn't just down there ignoring me. But then I went back over to the screens to see where he was, and saw that he really *had* stayed in the Master Bedroom and was just bloody standing there, quite still, looking calmly up at the hatch. I banged and screamed and shouted, again. Maybe one of the others would hear and come and get me out. Alan or Fleur. The Maid. But no-one came, although I was very loud, and when I next checked on the screen, he had gone. Oh, I can't write anything more now. I'm too upset again. Crying and betrayed and can't see too well.

I need a pee. Where am I going to pee?

Have slightly recovered. They can't keep me here for too long. Probably just until this evening. Although inconsolable, I watched the screens as I sobbed: X went ruthlessly through the house, with some gaffer tape he'd found somewhere, covering up the lenses of the spy-cameras. I've gone technologically blind: I feel deprived. Those screen-spaces that I got to know so well, in their clear deep flickering greyness – all winked out; all apart from one. X remembered where each of the cameras in the house was, except one – the Nursery. It's not much use, but at least it gives me something to look at; and a little light to see by, more than the screen of my laptop. Things aren't quite as bad as they first seemed. I do have something to drink here, five left of a six-pack of decaf Diet Coke; and a small secret stash of chocolate that no-one was meant to know about. There is an overhead light up here, but the bulb went and I never bothered to have X replace it. I quite liked the hugger-muggerness of sitting in the dark, illuminated only by screenlight.

Now I feel a fool. But I suppose my imprisonment at least looks and feels like imprisonment.

What X failed to do, in going round the house, was cover over the microphones, too. I haven't given up on him entirely; perhaps this was deliberate. Perhaps the covering over all but one of the lenses was a diversion tactic – to keep the guests from lynching me.

Oh no, I'm crying again. I started just now to think about the possibility of the ghost-girl being up here. But she's not; she only haunts the upstairs landing, doesn't she?

Had fifteen minutes ghostly-yet-afraid-of-ghosts wailing, but no-one – supernatural or not – paid any attention.

As I was saying, X forgot to, or deliberately didn't, cover up or detach the microphones. He knows that the house is wired for sound as well as sight.

They can't pull the power on the attic, because it covers two of the upstairs rooms, too. There was much negotiation about power sources, with the man installing the cameras.

Couldn't wait any longer, and couldn't find anything more suitable, so peed into the upturned wooden top of an old Singer sewing machine – which started leaking almost immediately. Had to put it on top of an old blanket to stop it going through the floor. Shoved it as far away as I could bear to go. Now I'm worrying what I'll do if...

After they had shut me in, and X had blacked me out, the house went completely silent; I listened in to every room on maximum volume, but got only the ticking of clocks and the creaking of timbers. They must all have gone out; out into the garden or down to the beach. Probably to decide together what to do with me – how long I am to be kept here. I suppose the Maid and the Chef are in on all this, too. Enjoying it.

If it's deliberate, leaving the microphones on, X is being very clever. In some ways, me not having any sight makes the whole experience more novelistic – like listening to the voices of the characters, speaking in my head, and then writing down what they say, amazed at their declarations, confessions. The pictures were a distraction, and I rarely learnt anything from them: perhaps only that Alan shoots looks at Fleur whenever she's not looking at him, and that she sometimes does the same back. Inscrutable looks, though. That's about it, I think. Oh, and Cornwall. And the Vicar. Quite a lot, I suppose.

Huge kerfuffle. Marcia has left.

There were attempts to persuade her to stay, mainly from Alan and Fleur. She was implacable: 'I *can't* – I have to go,' she said, in her room – followed by several heavy-footstepped others. She was crying.

'Where will you go?' asked Fleur.

'Well, I'll go home to London, of course. I need a lot of time to think.'

'You will come back, won't you?' said Alan. 'We need you in the house.'

'I'm leaving my clothes and everything. But I'm feeling very hurt and exposed.'

'We all are,' said Fleur.

'If I stay here tonight, I won't sleep. I want to be far away...'

They helped her pack, load up. All the guests (I think) gathered in the hall for goodbyes, then went outside to wave her off.

By putting my ear against the slope of the roof, I could hear the little car driving away.

I am very worried. Marcia's departure makes it more likely others will follow. What if the whole thing falls apart?

I can't believe that Henry and Cleangirl aren't thinking about leaving, too.

The house is once again making something like its usual range of noises. Mostly conversation.

I sit and look at the dolls on the shelves in the Nursery, spineless, slumped, dead loves of a dead girl. I could, I suppose, make some attempt to escape, bash my way through the roof – but I don't really want to damage the fabric of the house; not if I don't have to, anyway. (I pay for anything that happens, down to coffee-cup rings.) There is a sense in which *this* is what has happened: this, me being found out. So, if I'm being true to my project, I need only to follow the developments, suffer the consequences. The guests certainly seem to have been quite energised by the discovery of my naughtiness. All of them, including X, are in the drawing room. There are so many of them talking at once that it's very hard to make anything out. The snatches and snippets of conversation that I *can* catch seem mostly to be concerned with what I may or may not have seen them doing. In the way of these things, my name jumps whenever I hear it: in Edith's high voice, in Cleangirl's low. They know by now that there was no camera on the upstairs landing, but they are still speculating as to whether I have any footage of the ghost. Mostly, though, they are obsessed by the cameras in their bedrooms. I can hear a lot of laughter; louder and harsher than I remember it being before. Like any collection of people, they are delighted with the discovery of a scapegoat. I'm trying to detect outrage, but I can't hear any; they're *enjoying* themselves – without me, they're more relaxed than ever before. Of all realisations, this is the most sobering: they're happy.

I still have hopes that someone will plead for me.

I am in disgrace. It feels quite good, quite homey. I've been in disgrace so many times in my life that I know my way around the place pretty well. ~~(I'm familiar with Coventry, too.~~) Disgrace has many benefits; it's like rehab – one has peace and quiet and space and time, but one knows, eventually, that one will have to confess all and put a great deal of effort into being forgiven. In the early periods of being in disgrace, the first fifth, one doesn't want to bother with this. 'I can deal with the peace/quiet/space/time,' one thinks. There is defiance. Then, remorse fills the second fifth; desperation the third. The fourth is calm reassessment; the fifth, readiness. I'm just about to head into remorse.

The dinner gong reminds me how hungry I am, despite the four chocolate bars. I think about leaving the last one until tomorrow – or the day after – who knows how long they'll keep me here – but then I eat it anyway. The sounds of mastication that come from the dining room are quite disgusting. Alan is a particularly loud eater. One never realises, when sitting round eating with people; society has trained one out of listening to their chomping. Unless they are old, in which case it's polite to notice, and to make jokes afterwards about what a juicy racket they made.

There is a thin gap around the edges of the attic door. This gave me an idea. I had plenty of pads and pens, for taking notes on my spyings. An hour ago, I sat down to write X a plea. With some difficulty, I restrained myself from making any direct threats to parts of his anatomy. After I'd finished, I dropped it through the slit. As it fell, it flew to one side – landing I didn't know where. On the chance that it might have gone under the edge of the bed, or the dressing table, and might fail to be discovered, I wrote a second. Then, just to be sure, a third. This just said, 'I've dropped two notes through already. If you can see this one, and not them, then look around, you'll find them.'

Later in the evening, the guests are tired; they speak more slowly and are more respectful of one another: they interrupt less, listen harder. Sitting up here in the dark, I can imagine them sprawled out across the drawing room sofas. They are talking about me.

'I think she did it for power,' says Cleangirl, 'so that she would know everything about us.'

'Well, obviously...' says William.

'As I said before,' Simona says, 'I didn't know anything about this. It was a complete surprise to us.'

'It's alright – we believe you,' Henry says. 'But if you protest your innocence much longer...'

'Why is it obvious she did it for power?' Edith asks.

'She's a writer,' says Simona, 'they don't have very much of it – when they *do* get some, they go terribly silly with it.'

'Unlike editors,' says Alan.

'My point exactly,' replies Simona, ~~surfing the~~ and everyone laughs.

'It is such a cruel thing,' says Cecile, 'the spying – it makes me feel...'

'What?' asks Edith.

'Not nice,' says Cecile, remembering that Edith is a child.

'She's suffering for it now,' Fleur says. 'She should suffer a bit.'

'Victoria hates the dark,' says X.

'Oh, yes,' says Fleur.

'She was like that at school,' Cleangirl replies. This is a lie; it was Cleangirl who was afraid. She told me she only overcame her fear when she had Edith.

One can't help being fascinated by how distorted one finds oneself, in the conversation of others.

'I think it's hypocritical for us to be too shocked,' says William. 'After all, we knew we weren't here just for a simple holiday. We're none of us paying for food or accommodation. Victoria just wanted something in return.'

'She wanted too much,' says Fleur. 'She wanted our souls.'

'I agree,' says Edith.

'I really don't know,' Alan says, 'aren't we underestimating the amount of um spying that goes on in every house? We've all listened at doors...' Some people protest, but only as a joke. 'When we get to read the finished book, we'll see what she's learnt.'

~~‘Don’t worry,’ says Simona, ‘I won’t let anything upsetting get through.’~~

~~‘Can you cut me out altogether?’ asks Fleu~~r.

~~‘I’m afraid not,’ Simona says. ‘You’re an important character.’~~

‘What do you think?’ Cecile asks. It takes a moment before I realise the person addressed must be X.

‘I just feel guilty,’ he says, eventually, ‘for letting it go on as long as it did without telling you.’

‘We’ve already been through that,’ says Simona, getting him out of trouble.

‘It wasn’t *that* long, anyway,’ says William.

‘Too long,’ says Fleur.

They talk on for quite a while, but that is the last they say of me.

During the course of the conversation I realise something: Marcia really has left – she might not come back – her voice might never more be heard – her opinions – her laughter. Sad. I was just getting to like her. → Don’t know why you’re only realising this now. You knew it had happened.

It’s the end of week two. I’d say ‘already’ but it seems to have lasted six months.

Couldn’t sleep. ~~Wrote this to pass time.~~

As they strode out into the clearing the sun lanced down through them like a Zulu spear, piercing to the core of the body, where the heart pulses like an upturned turtle on a sunny beach.

‘Are you quite sure about this?’ hissed Major Snow through his tall white teeth, which glinted in the sun.

‘Quite, quite sure, old boy,’ replied Secret Agent X. ‘Your insult to Lady Victoria was quite quite unforgivable. Unless you apologise forthwith, I shall be forced to take it out upon you, physically.’

‘I think not,’ sneered Major Snow, his voice oozing through his teeth like a snake through the grasslands.

They walked on for a short while, neither man venturing to

speak, but both taking the opportunity of a sideways glance or two. Where was their opponent's weakness? How best to attack? Secret Agent X had seen Major Snow play Bridge, and knew that he had a tendency to come in too strong. Once upon a time he'd seen him bid three no trumps with a handful of trash. If Secret Agent X was to win this fight, and defend the honour of Lady Victoria, he would have to use every ounce of nous in his estimable noddle. Major Snow was a military man, trained inveterately in the arts of war, especially one-on-one hand-to-hand combat. But Secret Agent X, striding along with his limbs feeling especially limber that hot August day, felt confident of victory.

Suddenly, without warning, Major Snow leapt upon him.

'I say –' was all that Secret Agent X had time to say, before Major Snow was throwing unfair, ungentlemanly punches into his hard tight belly.

'Of course,' thought Secret Agent X, even in the midst of the unseemly scuffle, 'I knew he'd come in hard and fast, I didn't reckon on him cheating, though. How could he possibly expect to get away with this? He knows that, when we get back to the club, I'll tell all and sundry about the *dénouement* of our *débâcle*. He can never expect to live this down. Unless...' And for the first time in his life, Secret Agent X faced true terror face to face. 'Unless he means to kill me, dispose of the body, say that we were attacked by a vicious panther whilst out taking a stroll, and marry the Lady Victoria in a small chapel on a Welsh hillside on a beautiful May morning in June.'

The dazzling sunlight combined with the extreme physical exertion had brought both men out in a heavy sweat. There were dark blue rings of perspiration beneath their armpits, in the material of their khaki shirts. Their bodies rippled against one another, flesh meeting flesh in a beautiful ballet of violence.

The two men grappled on the floor, first one seizing the initiative, then the other, then the first one seized it back again, and then the second one managed to wrestle it off the first, and so on, very excitingly, for quite a while. Until, from somewhere secreted about his person, probably hanging from a leather pouch within his shirt, Major Snow managed to produce a Bowie knife.

'Ha-ha,' he said, 'I'll bet you weren't expecting *this*!'

'On the contrary,' said Secret Agent X, who took the opportunity of Major Snow's brandishing the glinting weapon above his head to grab ahold of Snow's crotch and squeeze like billy-o.

It was just at this point, when Secret Agent X had definitively won the fight, defended Lady Victoria's honour, and practically ordered the banns for that small Welsh Chapel in May, that there was a rustle in the sun-drenched undergrowth and a dark shadow moved out into the light of the clearing.

Both men sensed it at once, with an animal alertness of the twitching nostrils. This was something more powerful than either of them, more powerful, perhaps, than the two of them combined together working efficiently as a team using all the human rationality at their command. It was a vicious panther, and it roared at them with a mouth that seemed, white-teethed and wet glistening red fleshed, to open before them a gate that seemed to lead them down, in imagination at least, to the very pit of hell itself.

~~Etcetera, etcetera~~. Lovely parody. No use whatsoever.

Time passes.

Thursday

Day Fifteen Week Three

It's twelve hours since they locked me in the attic. I'm starting to suffocate – no, I started to suffocate yesterday, what with all the dust; today, though, I'm seriously worried I might die.

Whenever I hear, or think I hear, someone walking along the upstairs corridor, going into their room, I bang on the floor.

It makes no difference. They've decided to murder me... by starvation.

Typed up my notes, *and* read through the catch-up version of the lost day. Rewrote a passage or two from even earlier – that scene with Cleangirl, with my speech about the paintings.

Used the sewing-machine lid again – well, what else was there to do? It was spoiled already.

Discovered about an hour ago that my laptop has a computer game on it: Tetris. Wonderful. I am one of the Top Ten Comrades. My hi-score so far is 2,452. Time passes much faster, rearranging the little blocks as they fall.

Hi-score now up to 7,792.

Gorgons, as far as I can find out, live in the 'far West'. However, medusa (the beautiful one) lived in a cavern. I'm going to leave this in – and forward any letters from pedantic Classicists.

...and now I have a caffeine-deprivation headache, to top it all.

I woke up this morning feeling and I'm sure looking like a gorgon risen from the depths of some unholy pool – do gorgons rise from pools? Check.

My period better not bloody start – not while I'm stuck up here; that would be too much. It's not due for a few days.

Last night, I waited until twelve, before sorting myself out with somewhere to sleep. (Luckily an old mattress is among the items discarded up here.) Before then I still believed that I would be released – either by the collective decision of the house or, secretly, by X. Neither happened, and I was forced to explore the attic by the faint light of the screen of the laptop. I hate dust, particularly the kind of dust that you get in attic rooms, dust that is gritty and seems semi-alive, capable of getting everywhere you don't want it;

and I hate cobwebs, except literary gothic ones, and these up here, because they have been for so long undisturbed, are festooned with nuggets of fallen plaster. Whenever my head hits one, it is instantly as if I were wearing a beaded head-dress – made of cobweb, plaster, mice-poo and whatever else disgusting lives high-up in attics. I really did start to think I might go mad; and I screamed a couple of times for good measure. Downstairs they must really have thought I was accommodating myself to my *rôle* as well as to my room. I did some stomping and creaking, too – just to keep them awake. The mattress was over in a far corner, tied up with string; I wonder why they kept it. I dragged it across to where I was going to sleep, in the biggest expanse of spider-free-looking piece of floor. (How glamorous am I?) Then I pulled the string off either end, and it flopped out. I had expected to see stains of various sorts, but it was quite clean – newish, even. Which is probably why they kept it. There were no blankets, but I'm not sure I'd have dared use them anyway – they would have been so full of creepy-crawlies. I began to get scared, and obsessed with the idea of insects which bite. Once, staying in a very old house belonging to a friend of mine, I woke up and the vision in my left eye seemed to have gone all black and fuzzy. Then it cleared, by itself, and I felt, simultaneously, a light prickling moving over my forehead – and I realised... a huge house spider had been climbing my face! The attic wasn't too cold, right then; but I knew that the chilly coastal dawn would in a few hours have me shivering. I looked around for something with which to cover myself. There were suitcases full of clothes, some of which obviously had belonged to the dead daughter. (They were kiddy clothes: romper suits and bibs.) But it was not until I undid the tie on a black plastic bin-liner that I came across what I required: curtains. They were large, long, green or brown (it was almost impossible to tell in the laptop light) velvet; very heavy. I pulled them out completely; mothballs bombled onto the floorboards. (Perhaps I should say more about the floorboards, they are dust-grey and have a half-inch of carpet-dust laid on top of them. If one moves too fast, the dust is awoken. It licks up, like flames, and chokes, like smoke. I walk round the attic as if it were the surface of the moon – an unknown moon, where aliens might be lurking behind every rock, sewing machine or cardboard box.) I rolled up some of the softer cotton clothes from one of the suitcases, to make a pillow. After all this botherment, I thought, X was almost bound to come and liberate me. The menu bar clock on my laptop told me that it was a quarter past one. Below me, the house was still not quiet; conversations continued in the drawing room. I wanted to be interested in them; I wanted to force myself to be interested in them. I couldn't. I was sick with choking. I tried to get to sleep instead of choking. Sleeping through this was the only way. It took me a long time to get off, however – I didn't turn down the microphones; the human voices comforted me; I wasn't completely alone. Though I knew that if I screamed, no-one would take it seriously. I didn't know how I could get people's attention. Morse? I knew nothing of it, and neither did anyone else. And I'd already dropped those notes for X.

At about two the talking stopped. I got myself up, draped in velvet, and went over to look at the single screen. X was undressing in the Nursery. I looked towards that end of the attic. I wanted to go and jump up and down above his head; but that would reveal I could still see into the Nursery. If I did that, they would blind my final eye – and I would have even less light than before. I watched him getting into bed in the Nursery; I did not reach out to stroke the screen tenderly. Well, I did... He looked so cute – with all the dolls on the shelf above him, and him having to go half-foetal in order to fit onto the child's bed. Was it my imagination, or did he glance just once towards the camera with a glint in his eye before he turned the light off and went to sleep? Even with the light off in the Nursery, the moonlight streaked in from the left. I could see the edges of X, the side of his face, his long arm. At about two thirty, after watching him go completely to sleep, I went back to my mattress and tried to forget about spiders and eyes, eyes and spiders.

10 a.m. Everyone out of the house again this morning, after breakfast. Heard them arranging it. Psst psst, meeting under the apple trees, have you heard? More discussion of me, no doubt.

It cheats! Tetris. I'm sure it cheats. It never sends me the block-shape I'm in need of – the one I'm working towards: usually one of those four-squares-in-a-row ones. There's a long thin slot downwards, created especially for it to fall into and fill, and I have to block it up with some annoying zigzaggy one – just to survive. I've decided I don't like this game. Also, it sends me ones that are entirely bloody awkward – that I can't do anything useful with. Alexey Pazhitnov, 30-year-old Soviet researcher, I hate you for inventing this diabolic game; Vadim Gerasimov, I detest you for programming it. You are evil geniuses who ruin lives – mine included. Let me go. If I don't break 10,000 today I shall go batty.

Lay on mattress.

Dirt. Anxiety. Most of all Hunger.

Dropped another note for X. 'Could you at least *feed* me?'

This afternoon, Cecile came back to her room; it was extraordinary – she started talking, as if to me: confidentially. 'Oh, Victoria, what a state things are in. You've done such a very good job of setting everyone in this house against you.' I leapt for the keyboard and started typing what she was saying. 'When I came here, I thought we were going to get on so well. And somehow, you alienated me. But we were meant to be such great friends.' It was as if she were praying; I could imagine her, kneeling beside the counterpane. Her voice was motherly, liquid with compassion. 'You seem to me to be everywhere in this house. I find it strange to think you're just above my head, but can't see or hear me.' I almost stamped my feet, to let her know. 'Where's this all going to go? We still have ten days left. And I *so* wanted to spend some time really getting to know you. You're such a fascinating person – so full of delightful life, so wicked. But the rest of them seem all for breaking the house up, going home. That wouldn't be much of a story for you.' I was nodding my head. 'I can't imagine you, up there. X tells me it's very big and dusty and full of old broken things. My heart is like that – my heart becomes more and more like an attic the older I get. Because it's not a downstairs room, you see – no-one is living in it.' So sad, she was. 'Someone did, once, live there. I'm sure you guessed, being so sensitive, that I am a woman stricken in the past by tragedy. That must have been what drew us together in the first place. I remember our meeting so clearly. You, with your hundreds of bags; me, helping you into that taxi which took so long to come.' I smiled at the glistening, twinkling screen in front of me. 'I fell in love with him a long long time ago. His name –' She broke off. 'Oh dear – this feels so silly; sitting here pretending to talk to you, when you're not even in the room. Perhaps I should pray instead, like Fleur does...' She went silent; I couldn't bear it. After turning the volume up on the speakers, I got up and walked over until I guessed I was directly above her room, then bashed three times with my heel. 'Oh,' I think I heard her exclaim. I bashed again, slower. Then three more quick times. (•••–––•••) She gave a yelp, as of sudden pain – a needle-stick, a stubbed toe. I repeated the beat. 'Who is that?' Cecile asked. Of course – I'd forgotten she might think it was the ghost, also. I beat out duh-der-pause-duh-der: Vic-tooo-ree-yah. 'One tap for yes, two for no,' Cecile said, sensibly. 'Are you dead?' Two taps. 'Are you in this house?' Two taps. 'Are you Victoria?' One tap. I heard, even coming through the distant microphone, a long ragged sigh from Cecile. 'How are you? Are you all right?' I hesitated. One tap. Now was not the time to go into my complaints. 'I'm glad to hear that. Have you got enough food and other things?' Two taps. Silence. I thought she might even have gone, having ascertained I was still alive – perhaps the others had made her make a promise not to come and talk to me. (She could, of course, have come into the Master Bedroom and just shouted up. I don't think X is locking the door any more.) 'Can you hear what I'm saying, clearly?' One tap. 'Are you listening through the floor-boards?' I couldn't really explain the high-techness of my set-up, so: One tap. 'You do realise that a lot of the people here are very angry at you?' I gave the most penitent tap I could, slightly feeble, slightly tremulous. 'Are you feeling sorry for what you've done?' One tap. 'Truly sorry?' One tap. 'We're very fond of you, Victoria – very fond. But you are such an impossible child, sometimes. I really wish that I could properly talk to you. There are so many things that we might have to say to one another.' One tap. 'I feel as if whatever I said to you would be published – would be given to other people, people I hadn't chosen to talk to.' Two taps. No! 'You're a writer; I know what writers are like – your loyalties are elsewhere: you don't have friends, you have... source materials.' Two loud taps. How could she think that of me? When – apart from now – have I ever exploited my friends in that way? (Oh dear. Maybe she'd heard from Fleur about Chapter Twelve of *Spaciousness...*) 'It's not good, Victoria.' I heard a zip being done up or undone. Cecile was getting dressed, undressed. 'Were you listening to what I said a while ago?' One tap. Another pause. I wondered, was she feeling violated? Her prayer had been intended private. 'Is that the time?' she said. 'I have to go – I'm meeting someone.' I wished there was a tap for *Who?* 'I will see you when you come down.' One tap. 'Well, goodbye, for the moment, Victoria. It will be good to see your face, the next time we talk. Now, have I got everything?' She made a small hum. 'I think so.' And the door to her room shut behind her. I wondered who Cecile might possibly be meeting. The way she referred to it made me fairly certain it wasn't another one of the guests.

Perhaps she had a friend who lived nearby. When people get to be Cecile's age, they accumulate acquaintances in the remotest of corners; friends swill around the world so much, and one has so many of them, that soon it seems like every town and village hosts someone one might call upon.

I came back to the screens, sat down and typed this out. The present tense becomes a little tiresome for dialogue, after a while, so I chose the past for this.

I'm not sure if I should even say this, but in Marcia's absence the house seems calmer. I have no idea why. Perhaps I don't mean calmer, perhaps I mean duller – less colourful – verbally colourful, as much as anything. When Marcia is in a room, there is speech, and flirtation, and laughter. With her gone, there is less of all three. Which, I suppose, is only to say that – despite being stuck up here – I quite miss her.

I wonder if she will come back. My guess is that she'll turn up again in a few days, clear out her stuff, and drive off again without speaking to me – always assuming I'm out of the attic by then.

Henry and Ingrid are in their room right this very moment, talking about their relationship. Blah blah blah, until...

'You've been flirting with Victoria.'

'We always flirt,' says Henry. 'We always have.'

'You're attracted to her, aren't you?'

'She's a very attractive woman.'

'You know what I mean. Don't pretend you don't.'

'I'm not going to do anything about it.'

'What were you thinking of doing about it?'

'Oh, I don't know. Of finding her alone on the beach, taking her behind a sand dune and ravishing her.'

'You've never ravished me.'

'I have. I ravished you only a couple of days ago.'

'You call that ravishing?' Ingrid says.

There is a pause.

'You really *are* attracted to her, aren't you?'

'Like I said, she's a very –'

'I'm not joking any more. You're in love with her.'

'I am not.'

'You'd like to be with her, and not me.'

'Ingrid, you know that isn't true.'

'I've seen the way you look at her, sometimes.'

Then Henry whispers something.

'I *am* serious,' says Ingrid. 'I'm not joking. This is the truth.' And I can hear she's crying.

'Let's go outside,' says Henry. 'We don't want to have this conversation in here, do we?'

'Don't be such a smooth bastard.'

'I'm far from smooth. Come on. It's much more *convenient* outside.'

'Let go of me.'

They don't say anything else until they are in the drawing room.

Ingrid says, 'And our marriage – what about that?'

Henry shhhes her, and I hear no more.

I didn't manage to get the start of their conversation, but it wasn't that interesting. They talked a bit about Marcia. I didn't get really interested until they got onto the flirting.

I am *so* hungry. Hearing them eat dinner was just terrible. The only consolation is to think of the weight I'm losing.

I have hopes that, tonight, when everyone else has gone to bed, X will secretly let me out. Or come up and visit.

Another night; they kept me here another night. Inconsolable.

9,112

Did it! Broke 10,000 for the first time!

Friday

Day Sixteen Week Three

Morning of the second attic day.

I miss being clean more than I miss X or sex or London or my friends. When they let me out, *if* they let me out, I'll look *such* a hag – such a terrible warty old hag of a bag of a hag. The skin on my face feels as if a thousand mice with miniature brillopads on their feet had stampeded across it. I have cried over this, a little. When I next get to a mirror, I will find lines that for the rest of my life I shall be able to trace back to this past couple of days, this attic sojourn. Will this have been worth it? Will I get a prize? At least now they're feeding me. When I woke up this morning I found that someone (I think it was X) had managed to sneak a cardboard box of supplies up without waking me. It's quite a considerate package, taken all in all: toilet paper, a potty, two large bottles of still mineral water, apples, bananas, nuts, and, most revealing of all, that Sebald book Henry was reading. (I won't be able to read it, in this light – but it's a thought.) This is the first sign of sympathy I've had for over twenty-four hours; being so used to cruelty, the hint of a relenting almost broke my heart. He has thought of me, I thought. He has slipped this in, knowing I wanted to read it – thinking I might be bored. I drank about half of one of the bottles, then made immediate use of the potty. The Singer thing will have to be disposed of – taken to the tip, burned in the garden. I'd be surprised if they can't smell it downstairs. Hence the potty.

I am thinking of the morning, outside. Seven a.m. I only slept for four and a half, five hours. I'm surprised I slept at all. My dreams were tranquil, of inland waters with birds above them. Perhaps my subconscious was rewarding me for the nightmare that surrounded me. I expected to be haunted by the ghost-girl, at some stage; she did not appear. Always, I felt, she was off to one side, a centre of coldness oscillating to one side of my vision. I searched through the box for a note. There wasn't one. I sat down to look at the single screen, the broken-backed dolls upon the shelf. (X had already vacated the Nursery, disarranging the composition still further: the sheets rucked up, without me to smooth them; one of the pillows dumped on the floor.) From the clarity and brightness of the morning light coming in through the window upon the screen, I guess it is a beautiful day outside. The cold of the night is still hanging on up here, in drapes; walking around, one sometimes passes through a sheet of it – like a ghost through a wall.

It was not until eleven thirty that I found the note.

I had been listening in to breakfast and its aftermath. Another outing was being planned. Half the group, for reasons I couldn't begin to fathom, had decided to head along the coast south of Southwold – first to Dunwich and then to the nuclear power reactor at Sizewell B; the others, also in cars, wanted to go back to Aldeburgh for more fish and chips.

After the house had passed into what passes, in this house, for silence – a very quiet racket – I picked up Henry's book.

The note fell out from between its middle pages, gothically. It was in an envelope of thick, laid paper.

I treasured the opening of it, expecting the written voice of Cecile. (Could she have packed writing equipment in her suitcase, too? Or did she buy it on a Southwold shopping trip?) Disappointment followed: the chosen scribe was Fleur.

We decided, after discussing it for a while, that you are to be let out at six o'clock this evening. Hence, we have provided you with the necessaries until then. Do not try to escape. We are all still very angry with you, and will want to talk to you about it when we can. A few of us are on the point of leaving. This is not what we expected. But we wish to forgive you. It's a terrible terrible thing you have done. But we will wait to see what you say, about this violation.

The note was a pretty mess of voices; I spent a half hour in trying to disentangle them. I could detect my sister, *But we wish to forgive you*. And Simona, *we will wait to see what you say*. (Simona, as my editor, is always waiting to see what I say.) I suspected William to be the author of the line, *A few of us are on the point of leaving*. This would give him an excuse for departure, without having to explain why. ~~the split from Simona.~~ The *Hence*, too, had a touch of William's legalese about it. Edith seemed to speak loudly in, *It's a terrible terrible thing you have done*. I couldn't detect Cecile, perhaps she'd been decorously elsewhere during the dictation. *Hence, we have provided you the necessaries until then*. Alan? The gangly awkwardness of *necessaries* seems characteristic of him. X, perhaps, added, *Do not try to escape*. Thinking of the practical; looking out for my safety; reassuring me, codedly, everything will be all right. The first sentence, twisted back-to-front, is committee-drafted.

I can hear the Chef, doing the washing up; the Maid, going from room to room with her hoover.

10,936

I've been thinking about what I'm going to do when I get out – God, I sound like an inmate in Broadmoor. First, a long hot bath to get the attic out of my hair and bones. Second, some hot food that includes meat. Third, a walk on the beach (or just in the garden, if I haven't time). Fourth, a House Meeting and a general apology. Fifth, allow them to attack me for however long it takes. Sixth, bed with X – at either a decent or an indecent hour – for semi-silent sex. Seven, start afresh tomorrow.

11,005

3.47 p.m. One of the two outings comes back.

4.03 p.m. In the kitchen, just now: 'I'm sorry,' Fleur says, 'if I've been at all impossible.'

'Oh no,' says Alan, 'it's not you.'

'I don't bear you any ill will – I just find this very difficult – difficult to go through. And particularly now.'

'I know,' says Alan, then amplifies, clarifies, 'about the difficulty – it makes one reassess what one has done, how one's been.'

'As if one weren't self-conscious enough about it anyway,' Fleur says.

'It makes me want to go and hide in a corner and not speak to anyone,' says Alan, 'It makes me –'

'Oh, don't do that,' Fleur says, 'Victoria's doing very well in filling that *rôle* herself.'

I hear metal clattering against metal, and guess that Fleur is doing the washing-up. Tea-things. Naughty girl.

'Hearing about it, well, it's made living in this house very difficult – especially since we've been going to bed with her over our heads.'

'I agree,' says Fleur, 'it feels as if the house is doubly haunted now – by the dead and by the living.' (Quite good that – as an observation: I'm proud of her. Help. Get me out of here.)

'Would you like to get out for a while?' Alan says, 'Go for um a walk, I mean. I was planning to go into town, Southwold, this afternoon. But it doesn't matter if you don't; I'm um going anyway.'

Oh, just ask her out, why don't you?

'That...' Fleur says, flirting – is she flirting? it's hard to tell – 'would be very nice.'

They haven't spoken to each other for days, and now that I'm well and truly stuck in the attic they practically start having sex on the kitchen floor!

'Meet you out the front in, what? half an hour?' says Alan.

'It's a shame Domino isn't still here,' Fleur says, 'It would be nice to have him with us – I think he and Audrey would have found some way to get on, eventually.'

A concession? An apology? How dare she? Probably because she knows that I'll be let out eventually. Wait a minute... No, Alan's left. There's no more of that scene.

Fleur knows I'll come down and resume my spying, so if she does something interesting in the meantime it will really annoy me.

Have I been exaggerating the extent to which the guests have plotted against me? No, I don't think so – my being locked up here suggests I have underestimated, consistently.

I should be happy: Alan and Fleur are back on the course I predicted for them in my Synopsis. That I won't get to see it, and that if it comes off and they're happy I won't get any other than a negative credit for it – these things shouldn't really matter. But they do. I feel hurt. The callousness of hiding me away. Given time, I shall come to resent X. At the moment, I just want him to come and rescue me. But what's this? The door is opening into the Nursery. Downstairs, the hubbub continues in the drawing room. It's William and Simona. Why haven't they gone to their own room?

'I agree,' says William, 'we've needed to do this for a long time now.'

It's so good to *see* people – to see them move.

'Oh, Brompton,' says Simona, 'how did we end up in such a terrible state?' She is sitting on the bed; he teeters upon the child-size I don't know what to call it. It is one of those desk-and-chair outfits that, when you move the desk, the chair moves, because it's joined to it with metal rods.

'In a way, you know, I don't think it's really our fault – yours or mine.'

'What do you mean by that?'

He grimaces. Pauses. Giving me time to – no: 'We just came to the end of each other a lot sooner than we expected. And that's not because we're neither of us for the long-term, *for someone*. It's just, we both work through people very quickly. We work through them, and we end up thinking we've worked them out.'

'And that's it.'

'And that is it.'

'So,' says Simona, 'this is it, is it?'

'It is... I think it is. What do you think?'

'Oh, I don't know, Brompton.' Why does she call him that?

'If by it you mean us, the whole of us, not just us in public, when other people can see us – then I agree, completely.'

'But for the same reasons?' he asks.

'Oh, I have some other reasons, all of my own – but I'm sure they're fairly similar to yours. That's the frustrating thing; one of the frustrating things: if we have similar or identical reasons for putting an end to it, then maybe that proves there's a level of similarity we're too stupid to recognise. Maybe we're doomed to miss each other because we miss the signs of how well we're suited.'

'I'm so unhappy, at the moment,' he says.

'I am too, believe me – and this isn't helping.' She gestures round the room, includes the house.

He chuckles, as if acting a chuckle for somebody other than Simona's benefit. 'My Monkey-Girl,' he says. Will she hit him? No. It's a nickname. They are embracing. Brompton and Monkey-Girl. An enigma wrapped in a mystery wrapped in a cypher wrapped in one another's arms. She has started to cry. I've seen her cry before, a few times. This seems forced; as if she won't believe the relationship's over unless she cries at the end of it. He comforts her. Strokes her hair. Puts her head on his shoulder. I can't see his rage; the rage Simona told me about. Where are the threats? They pull apart.

'I'm very fond of you,' says Simona, 'It's just – I hate you.'

He laughs. 'I know... I know... I'm worth hating, you know. I am.' They embrace again.

'I don't like... the idea of being alone,' Simona says. 'Not now... At this time.'

'Monkey-Girl's a spring chicken compared to me...'

'You ruined my life, Brompton,' says Simona.

William pauses. 'You did a pretty good job on mine, too,' he says, 'turned it into a monkey's tea-party.' What is this? Pet-names should end where love ends.

'I don't have much more to say.'

'Write me a letter,' says William. 'Like you used to.'

'I did, didn't I? Do you still have them?'

'Oh yes, every last piece of paper.'

'Burn them, will you?' They are exiting.

'Of course,' he says. And it's over. I cry; I smile. I shall have to go back and put a few more descriptive passages in. The bit I liked most was when Simona started talking about him ruining her life – she picked the doll off the shelf, the big one, the one I've been wanting to move ever since I was stuck here, and she held it to her breast. It was such a kitschy detail; I wouldn't dare make a character of mine do that in a book. It was almost Victorian in its aspiration to pure schlock: like a child-with-big-teary-eyes-and-broken-doll poster. But people *do* these things; that's what I'm learning. The obvious – it's where they live. Oh, this is a Vindication of the Rights of Women Writers. Wait... William and Simona are just arriving in the drawing room. And... they're not saying anything at all. No... Nothing. Absorbed into the happy burble of the hubbub. One of them will be sleeping in the Nursery tonight, no doubt; then leaving tomorrow. William, I guess. I'll find out – but not soon enough. The doll which Simona held, one of those long rag dolls with arms that aren't quite as bendy as you'd expect – it is lying all perfectly upon the bed. It is laid out, long-limbed, on the bed with, yes, its arms folded across its chest – quite as if dead. Simona left me a symbol. I hope it's her in the Nursery. It would be a cute reversal: Edith out, her in. And she does sometimes talk to herself. She told me she even talks in her sleep. (She was worried William might hear something of her plans to leave him.)

Oh, this is so good and so bad at the same time. Here I am, triumphant in prediction – Fleur and Alan coming together, Henry and Ingrid under pressure, Simona and William falling apart – and stuck in the attic. But maybe my predictions are only coming true *because* I'm stuck in the attic. There's no way to tell. Because people no longer feel they're performing for me, they're behaving as they would have done had I not been there. (That's not quite true: were it not for me they wouldn't be in this house. If there are issues, I've forced them – physically present in the room or not.)

Really, though, I'm sick of meddling. I just want X's arms around me. What Cecile said to me in our little *séance* of yesterday was right – I shouldn't have used (abused?) my friends in this way.

I'm a bad person. I'm bad partly because I should be feeling worse than I do, having done the things I've done.

If only I could work up a real tempest of remorse; then I could put on a proper performance when I'm released.

It's true: I'm beginning to believe that they will actually release me – cobweb-woman that I am. Moth of the ceiling. Dusty.

5.10 p.m. Oh, I'd like a cigarette, too – even though, as I keep telling myself, I no longer smoke.

5.13 p.m. And I want to brush my teeth; the chocolate of the day before yesterday must have done some damage. I've made it this far without fillings; I'm not starting now.

5.20 p.m. It would be a nice gesture, don't you think, and boding well for the future, if they were to let me out a little earlier than promised?

5.22 p.m. The Hubbub is gathered in the drawing room. I hear it like a distant thunderstorm that, now and again, mutters an intelligible word: *Victoria, sternly, leave, stay.*

5.30 p.m. Torturers. They've now all left the house. I hear only Chef's clattering – which is partly what has kept me sane up here; though his periodic whistling of current chart hits has had quite the opposite effect.

5.33 p.m. I'm not going to write any more; I'm just going to be sensible and save everything I've done to disk, and then hide the disk.

5.40 p.m. Have to record this: Marcia has returned. Car-engine outside. Great cries of greeting from the hall. It can't be accidental she's arrived just this moment.

5.55 p.m. Come on, come on. What if they were being cruel before, and never really intended to let me out? What if they've just decided to leave me up here? Or leave themselves? But they haven't taken any of their clothes – I'd have heard them packing. Maybe they've gone to look at another house down the road, and will come back for their stuff. Oh, it's unbearable. I wish I had a comb, some lipstick, a mirror. Hang on. Noises downstairs. Noises coming upstairs. The thunderstorm approaches. It's time. The hag is about to descend. Until later, faithful oblong of light.

Saturday

Day Seventeen Week Three

I was too shattered to write anything once I'd been let out. So, this is what happened between then and the end of yesterday:

I was seriously traumatised – which is, I think, exactly what they meant me to be.

I wasn't allowed to go and make myself look decent; I was dragged – some of them did pluck at me – dragged down into the drawing room and forced to sit in an armchair; the Hag, not me – the Hag they didn't allow to work her magic to become a princess again. Simona was spokesperson for the whole group, though the whole group cannot really have stood unanimously behind her.

'We've decided...' Stay or go, stay or go? 'to stay – but only under certain conditions.'

I nodded.

'You must clear out of the attic entirely, said Simona, sternly. 'You will lock it, then give us the key. There will be no more of this spying. The attic is completely off-limits.'

'Don't worry,' I said, 'you won't get me up there again in a hurry.'

'Listen to us, Victoria: the attic is to be locked, and you are not to be allowed a key until after the end of the month. Apart from this, things will carry on as before. No-one here denies that they knew they were going to be spied upon, in one way or another; everybody here knew you would write them up, as you saw fit. We're not innocents. But we didn't think you'd be watching us sleep and undress – all those precious private things. We feel, like our note said, violated. I'm not sure if two weeks is long enough to build that trust back up from the ground – which is where it is right now.' I looked around at the faces; faces – it was good to see faces, even such surly ones.

'I'm very sorry for doing what I did,' I said.

'We have *more* to say,' ~~Simona~~ said. 'All of us have a lot more to say, but I won't be saying all of it now. You will have to talk to each of us individually. You will tell us exactly when you spied upon us, and what you saw us doing. Then we shall tell you whether or not you can use that information when writing your book. Agreed?'

'Agreed,' I said. 'If this is going to go on for a while, could I at least have a drink?'

X, bless him, went off into the kitchen. The gesture almost made me weep. After seeing him sleep alone in the Nursery the last two nights, my feelings towards him have become terrifically maternal.

'You're not paying attention,' said Marcia.

'I am.'

'You were looking at the kitchen door.'

'I'm hoping it's going to be a gin and tonic. Perhaps I should have said.' There was some scoffing at this – they were all trying to maintain the united front of being hugely annoyed. Some of them, I could tell, really didn't care at all. What they didn't want, however, was to risk expulsion into the Land of the Pariahs – where I lived. Currently alone. (The Pariahs didn't have a land, did they? I shall have to ask Fleur.) They stood in a semicircle and looked down at me. I didn't feel intimidated; I refused to feel intimidated by something so obvious. I felt like the poor fool hussy brought out on some chatshow to confess they've been cheating on their man; the hypocritical boos, the melodramatic accusations. Even Audrey the cat was there, feline witness to my humiliation. Then I looked at Edith, and saw how sad her face was. And I had a realisation: *they really meant it*. I had lost my popularity. This wasn't a game; or if it was a game, it was no longer the same game I'd been playing. Cecile had had enough of standing, and sat down on the far end of one of the sofas. Most of the others were on their feet. This was a big scene, for them; some of them had been working up to it ever since my iniquity had been discovered. But I couldn't quite manage any rise myself: my biggest moment of the previous forty-eight hours had been descending the ladder. Once they'd let me out, I knew there was nothing worse they could do. Unless they really had gone pagan. Human sacrifices in the offing, etc.

X re-entered with a bucket-size tumbler full of G&T. I reached out and he held it towards me.

'No,' said Fleur. 'She's not having that until we've finished with her.'

'But it'll go all unfizzy,' I said.

Ingrid laughed – her only contribution.

'I'll make you another,' said X, but was wary of getting involved any further.

'I'm sorry,' I said. There were tears, somewhere in my head – there was always a huge ocean of them, sloshing around there; it was just a question of locating them, tapping them, relaxing. 'What else do you want me to say?'

They didn't give me any hints – cross-armed like fishwives greeting late-coming, pub-haunting husbands, Fleur and Marcia were quite prepared to let me flounder awhile longer. Alan, though, hung back; did I sense sympathy?

'*Are* you sorry?' asked Edith. This was a surprise; she was a very brave girl.

'I am,' I said. 'It was a mistake. Everything I seem to do...' and I found the tears, at last, 'turns into a mistake. I wanted to find out about you, show you something about yourselves that you didn't know already. It's what I do. You know that.' The room was quiet; I remembered the hubbub, the thunder. 'Could I at least have a cigarette?' The smokers among them couldn't resist this plea. William produced one, handed it to me, leant over and lit it. 'Thanks,' I said. He gave me a smile which, at one and the same time seemed ~~simultaneously~~ to say, *This too shall pass*, and, *Why the hell did you do it, bitch?* I was saved by the dinner gong. Simona said, 'There's more to say; and you'd better believe we're going to say it.' Like crystals dissolving, the structure of their anger began to weaken, go wispy, wash away. Court dismissed. They went through into the dining room.

X came over and gave me a big hug, the gin and tonic glass making a tantalising crescent upon my neck. 'You silly girl,' he whispered. I wasn't in the mood to be patronised, but neither was I in the mood to argue.

'You left the microphones on,' I whispered back.

'Of course I did,' he quietly replied. And suddenly I realised all over again why I loved and wanted to marry and have children with X. He had remained loyal, during my exile. He had helped me stay sane.

I was still furious with him, though. There were things we needed to talk about.

'I'm going upstairs now,' I said. 'Do you think you could save me some of whatever they're having for dinner?' He said he would. I twisted around in his arms, liberated the gin and tonic, slunk away on hips to make me seasick and him lovesick.

And I went upstairs and turned both taps on, full.

Sometimes a bath isn't just for getting clean; sometimes it's a necessity of the soul. This one, I have to say, was semi-mystical – nirvana with bubbles.

Ate. Alone.

Mmm. Food. Meat.

Told X about the sewing-machine lid and the blanket. He dealt with them both; small bonfire in the garden. Only Edith noticed.

I miss the cameras. I want to be able to go up into the attic and find out, very straightforwardly, what is being said and done downstairs. From now on, I shall have to be a lot more ingenious in making my discoveries.

I've been thinking about this ever since I saw Edith's sad little face: how to find some way to demonstrate my character's remorse? how to construct some scene in which that is the value? I *am* sincerely remorseful. But it's no good me writing that. I know that if I just write that, my readers won't believe me. *Show don't tell*, as professors of creative-writing courses always say. I could just forget about the book, bin it; maybe I already have. (I'm scared – I don't want to lose my old life entirely.) I want X.

'I know what you're going to say,' said X at bedtime.

'Okay,' I said, 'what am I going to say?'

We were in the Master Bedroom, on either side of the bed. I couldn't help but be aware of the hatch in the ceiling.

'You're going to say that I could have done more to protect you –'

'Yes.'

'– and that somehow, if I'd been clever enough, I could have prevented you getting locked in the attic.'

'*You* locked me in the attic, remember.'

'You're going to say that I should have defended you more – that you heard what was said, some of what was said, when you were in the attic, and that I let everyone attack you.'

'That's true.'

'You're going to say that I was saving myself. I knew about the spying, right from the beginning, and yet I managed to avoid the anger of the guests. It was only you that got locked in the attic.'

'You were sneaky.'

'You'll say something like, "You'll never know what it was like, stuck up there for two days."'

'Which is true.'

Surely the first thing you asked him was how the guests had found out about the spy-cameras? Or were you deliberately avoiding mention of that, to keep the one ally you had left, or felt *you had left?*

'And finally you'll threaten me with... I don't know, with throwing me out of the house.'

'No. You're wrong about that. I want you to stay. You're going to have to make up for what you did.'

'Oh, I'd forgotten that one. You'll say I'm going to have to atone.'

'Yes, and you're going to have to apologise.'

'Why?' he said. 'If it weren't for me and Simona, all you'd have left is an empty house. We kept everyone here. But letting them take their anger out on you, in a minor way, we kept the whole project going.'

'Well, thank you both so very much.'

'I'm sure when you've calmed down, you'll realise that I did the only thing I could. Right from the beginning, I was in an impossible position. If people thought I was your spy, they wouldn't talk to me. I needed to distance myself from you.'

'You didn't need to do that when we were alone, as well.'

'It carried over. I'm sorry.'

'I am not going to forgive you,' I said, 'not in the course of this conversation.'

'I might as well give up then.'

'Was there anything else I was going to say?'

'You might have said that you still loved me, despite what I'd done.'

'I might have done,' I said.

Slept.

This morning (Saturday), I got up, breakfasted, then wrote about yesterday.

I feel like a convalescent, happy at the mere fact of being allowed outside into the air after months beneath brown blankets. It is pure

If you're going to lie about your age, at least be consistent.

joy to look at the Saturday sea; and I appreciate the Saturday landscape so much more than when I treated it as flats – as the dull background to the grubby goings-on I planned to orchestrate within this beautiful house. Very rarely in life does one find oneself in the perfect place for the moment one is in~~; very rarely does one stumble across a fallacy sufficiently pathetic~~. Perhaps ten times in ~~thirty one~~ *twenty-nine* years has merely being where I am been enough to make me ecstatic. The garden here looks so delightfully fresh and alive, compared with the dust and deadness of the attic. To walk forwards through the seaside air is a great refreshment; I'm not sure if I've ever felt quite so grateful to live upon a sungraced planet. I may have got that all a bit backwards (no light, no life), but most religious-type feelings are essentially absurd.

They – the guests – were so kind and generous to let me out, after only two days. I find it incredible to think that all that time I was up in the attic, I didn't realise that what people really wanted from me was an apology. They weren't going to let me out earlier, but when they did release me I think they expected a little more contrition. I am trying to make up for that now.

I've been so mad, so isolated; crouching hidden behind my project, I haven't been able to recognise that them being here is an act of generosity; a gesture of trust. All that really remains for me to do, in order to have a wonderful book written, is watch their individual uniquenesses – through the day-to-day experiences we share: just as Virginia herself did, or attempted to do.

Her project was so much nobler than mine (nobler: not a word I use often). She wished to explore people, not to expose them; to comprehend, not exploit. Throughout this whole misguided enterprise, I have thought almost entirely of the benefit I myself would derive from it. *From the Lighthouse* was a book which rather than wanting *to write* I wanted *to be known as having written*, and that's bad faith if anything is.

In proving that I wasn't in control of my guests I have proven, in fact, nothing. It (my lack of control) is the conclusion any sane person would come to, given half a minute's thought.

I must stick to specifics from now on, examining this nuanced planet of ours with wonder and gratitude, and the people who inhabit it with greater humility and a purer forgiveness. I have learnt my lesson. I have had my vision. Indeed, I have had several people's vision.

Edith came up to me, as I was strolling, and asked if I'd watched her undressing. I promised her that I hadn't; that I'd never do such a thing. (I did, several times, watch her *dressing*, though – just to see how she did it: whether there was any hint of supernatural possession in the way she opened the wardrobe and picked out the dead daughter's clothes. However, the experience was entirely domestic, unspooky.)

I am surprised it's nudity that worries people. I've already had to give several assurances that it was impossible for me to make videos, or to take still images.

'I think Marcia was the most hurt,' said Edith. 'I think she felt you had crossed a real line. I'm surprised she came back, actually.'

'So am I,' I said. 'Have you seen the ghost again?'

'Oh yes,' said Edith, 'every night. We're quite good friends now. But I don't like to make a fuss about it – it scares the others.'

'The other ghosts?'

'No, the other people in the house.'

Whilst we were talking, Simona came to join us. 'How are you liking life in the outside world?' she asked.

'Very much,' I said. 'The contrast makes everything special. My cup of coffee this morning was marvellous. You can see why medieval saints had visions of ecstasy, after depriving themselves of everything for a year.'

'You weren't deprived because you were a saint,' said Simona. 'You were very naughty.'

'She was worse than naughty,' said Edith, 'she was vulgar.'

It did not seem possible that she had come up with this formula herself: Cecile was behind it. I was hurt. I was more hurt, in fact, than if Cecile had said the words to me herself. That she had whispered them to Edith, without an injunction never to pass them on to me, even unattributed, suggested to me that she thought me beyond the pale.

'I'll forgive you for that,' I said.

'Because you must think it's a little true,' said Edith.

'I probably do,' I said, 'but that's mainly because I find novel-writing vulgar.'

'You get vulgarly well-paid for doing it, though,' Simona put in.

'Which is part of its vulgarity,' I said. 'I wouldn't work if I didn't have to.'

'Nonsense,' said Simona. 'You haven't *had* to work since that film company optioned *The Sweet Spot*.'

'It could all go away very easily,' I said, 'all the money, everything.'

'I think I'm going to find Cecile,' said Edith. 'We're cooking this evening, you know.'

'Something unvulgar, I hope,' was what I said.

'*Bien sûr*,' she replied, besting me. Simona and I watched as she walked into the house.

'When she grows up...' Simona began, but left the sentence to complete itself.

Had the first of my official post-camera one-on-one meetings: Marcia.

It was bad. She was very angry.

I told her, with complete honesty, that I hardly spied upon her at all. She told me again, at length, of her feelings of 'violation'. The rape analogy was used, several times.

'I liked this house. I felt relaxed here. I was *en*joying my*self*. And you ruined that.'

'I'm sorry,' I said, at length.

Timidly, I asked her where she went during the day she was away from the house. 'Home,' is all she is prepared to say.

Tetris is ruining my life; I'm still addicted. Every time I sit down to work on the laptop, I have to have a game or five. Can't get much beyond 11,000; can't tell anyone. It takes up more than an hour a day – time I know should be spent working.

Lunch. I love food.

Chat afterwards with Maid. She is very amused by the whole thing. I am, I think, her most entertaining employer, ever – which is quite an achievement.

Her two sons did something quite atrocious with a cow and a motorbike, two weeks ago.

Afternoon.

Some of the guests have made efforts to rehabilitate me, if only for themselves. I have done my best to make myself publicly visible; as if to assure them of my *bona fides vis-à-vis* the spyroom.

'Where did I mess it all up?'

'I think the idea itself was bad from the start.'

Alan and I, in the front parlour: he answering without hesitation, as if he'd given the subject a lot of thought –

'And why?' I ask.

'Because it presumes too much – that your friends will accept what you're doing to them. They won't. Not spying.'

'It *wasn't* spying. I intended –'

'It felt like spying, and we're the ones to judge what it was or wasn't.'

'Yes. I suppose you're right.'

'I think you overestimated the value most people in this house put on your work.'

'I'm sorry for that.'

'You turned listening to your friends, being interested in their lives – you turned that into an aggressive act.'

'But what can I do about it now?'

'You've already apologised. That's made a lot of difference. You may not see it, but I do. Several of the others were on the point of leaving, even yesterday. If you hadn't said something like the right thing, they'd have gone.'

'Who?'

'Cecile.'

'Really?'

'She cried.'

I almost said, *I didn't hear her cry*. I stopped myself. 'You saw her *cry*?'

'Very gently – when we were out in the garden discussing what to do. She said she felt what you'd done was... vulgar.'

This came as confirmation of Edith's earlier slip. The two of them were now in the kitchen, creating buttery, oniony, French cookingy smells.

'It's good for me to hear this. And what about now? Is everyone happy to stay? Who else thought of leaving?'

'~~Simona was very angry. She claimed she knew nothing about the cameras. You'd never mentioned them to her, she said.'~~

~~'That's true. But did she say she might leave?'~~

~~'Well, William said he was prepared to go, if she wanted to.~~'

~~'Really? You surprise me.'~~

~~'They felt your readers might disapprove of what you'd done.~~'

~~'My readers aren't going to know. I am not going to use anything at all that I've seen through the cameras. It was just research.'~~

'If you're not careful, Henry will take his whole family away. I think secretly he admired you, for being so ruthless – that's with his producer's hat on. Ingrid is very unhappy. Edith doesn't want to leave, of course. She's enjoying it here more than anybody.'

'Thank you for telling me all this.'

'Well, I won't say *No one else would*, but you'd be hard pushed to find someone who'll tell you so directly. And that's because I'm still trying to be your friend, Victoria. I don't know why: I felt hurt, too. Mainly because you didn't trust me enough to tell me in advance. I'm one of the weird ones – the ones that might have agreed to come along anyway, even if I'd known about the cameras beforehand. It doesn't seem to make all that much difference, as far as I can see it: better to be spied on in the cause of literature than of viewing figures or High Street Shopping.'

I leaned over and kissed him on the cheek. 'Bless you,' I said.

(Throughout the conversation, I had to prevent myself asking him how his walk with Fleur went: I'm not meant to know anything about what happened whilst I was in the attic.)

4 p.m. Simona came to confession this afternoon~~; she continues to be my most unremittingly constant attendee.~~ Not that she ever has anything to confess – she takes the opportunity to talk to me about 'how the book is going'. It's as if she's ~~pretending to be~~ half-author of it, ~~and that annoys me. All she's going to do is insist that bits of it are cut out. She would destroy it entirely, given the chance.~~ Today, she wants to talk about the attic incident. 'Are you going to include that?' 'Of course,' I said, 'it happened, so I'm going to have to include it.' 'I'm worried, darling; I'm worried that it doesn't show anyone in a particularly good light.' 'Novels,' I said, 'generally don't.' 'This isn't a novel,' she said. I replied, 'I meant to say works on the cutting edge of non-fiction.' She sat back and sighed~~; I got the feeling I was being chided, childed. O Simona, how patient you have been with me, o thank you.~~ 'Anyway,' I said, 'at the moment I'm just trying to get as much of it down as possible; afterwards, I'll sift.' 'And of course, I'll help you,' Simona said. 'By the time I hand it in, it'll be quite finished,' I said, 'as usual; and, as usual, there'll be hardly anything for you to do.' 'Like the "hardly anything" in

I don't need to insist, I just cut — see.

wrong. I would have you write the midwinter sequel.

It was a pleasure.

Spaciousness.' 'That,' I said, 'was an exception.' 'It certainly was,' said Simona, and shook her head. ~~Her *Woe is me* act was narking in the extreme.~~ I was giving out readings so high I was in danger of breaking the Feist-o-meter. Change subject. 'When is William leaving?' I asked. Simona, taken aback: 'But he's not.' 'But you agreed with him that he would, in the Nursery: I *heard* you.' Simona smiled. I couldn't believe it, or understand it. She wasn't meant to *smile*, she was meant to be outraged. 'Well, of course I heard it,' I said, 'all the microphones in the house were on. I heard everything.' Simona chuckled~~, the chuckle of an old French crone looking at a *fillette très très belle* and thinking of the follies of her youth~~. 'We thought you wouldn't say anything about that,' said Simona. ~~'We thought you'd have the decency to keep quiet about it.'~~ This was... this was something; I didn't know exactly what. This was bizarre. 'You mean,' I said, 'you *knew*.' 'Of course we *knew*. Do you think Cecile usually talks to herself out loud?' I said nothing, shocked. 'Do you think,' Simona~~'s fun onslaught~~ continued, 'Alan and Fleur talk like characters out of some bad Victorian novel?' 'So,' I said, 'what I heard wasn't real.' ~~This brought the biggest cackle yet~~. 'Real? All of this, and you're still insisting on *real*? Oh, Victoria – I don't think you understand yourself very well.' 'Tell me then,' I insisted, 'tell me *exactly* what I don't understand about myself.' Simona reached out to pat me on the knee~~; I flinched away – she made a couple of hundred grams of pathos out of this~~. A gentle-faced smile, a lopsided shrug. 'I feel like saying, "How long have you got?"' she cooed. 'But that would be wrong. If the problem is with the real, then you've never been all that interested in the real. Which is fine. Your readers aren't all that interested in it either. That's why they like you so much – apart from *Spaciousness*.' 'Yes,' I said, 'you don't have to keep mentioning that; I'm quite aware of how badly it ~~did~~, thank you very much.' 'I don't think you are,' said Simona~~, really risking a complete break with me~~. 'And there was a reason for that: it went too far. What your readers want is something they can still bring themselves to believe is real, even while they're revelling in it as pure wish-fulfilment.' 'I don't understand.' 'You're not meant to. I probably shouldn't be telling you this – it might damage what you do~~ – though I think you're pretty impregnable.~~' I was in full sulk-mode. ~~I remembered to glance at her, to see what she looked like at this moment. The only word I can think of was sanctified. This moment was her moment; one she'd been sculpting, verbally, for quite some time: shaving each sentence down until its edges were just as smooth or sharp as she required.~~ A great deal of my brain was still occupied by the thought that they'd staged those scenes for me, like some sort of radio drama: Henry and Ingrid, too; *Cecile*. Simona continued, 'I think what your readers want from you is exactly what you give them, most of the time. They want to believe that life, occasionally, is like the life that people live in novels. Which means, before you ask, that things happen a lot more easily. People go to bed with one another, people fall in love, people gently suffer. When you turn the first page of a novel, you know *something's* going to happen. For most people, in their real lives, the last thing they want is for something to happen.' 'But some of my novels have unhappy endings.' 'They don't,' Simona ~~almost scoffed it out~~ said, 'they have richly melancholic endings. If one of your characters is going to be miserable, they make sure they check into a very nice hotel and order up some room-service, before they start.' 'But that's just –' ~~She interrupted me, her script unfinished~~. 'People, women, like to think that there is something artful about their emotions; and the fact that someone like you can come along and make them seem so – make them seem *worth* having, because they can be turned into something that looks permanent – well, your readers are very grateful for that.' She gestured around her, like some Hindu statue~~, doing I'm-a-little-teapot with both hands~~, to mean the nice room we were both in. 'It's something they're prepared to reward you for very well. You should be grateful to them.' 'I am,' I said, 'of course I am.' 'And you should do your best to keep providing them with exactly the kind of thing they want: which, as I'm trying very badly to say, is almost nothing at all to do with "reality". Write them some more novelly novels – it's what they're waiting for.' I began to cry; quite proud of myself for having resisted for so long. 'Oh, Victoria,' she said, 'I thought you might know a bit more about what you're doing; you do it so well, you know. You really are one of the best, but what you're best at isn't... well, it isn't really real. That's why the idea of *this*...' A swoon of her hand indicated the house, the people in it, everything. '...is *so* wonderful.' Me, through a throat curtained with choke: 'It is?' 'Yes, because, don't you see, it *proves* to your readers that life can be like a novel.' 'But nobody's slept with anybody!' I moaned. Simona smiled, and her eye glinted ~~with naughty memories.~~ 'Not with anybody *interesting*, anyway,' I said. 'It's brilliant,' said Simona. 'What you've done: behaving badly. Making everyone your enemy. You've got a house seething full of conflicts, including yours with me. They're just not *real* conflicts.' 'And what I saw with you and William in the Nursery wasn't real?' 'We're not bad actors, are we?' 'No,' I said, 'you're just very bad human beings.' ~~As she didn't know how to take this, she deflected it.~~ 'I think that's generally what the guests are thinking about *you*, right now.' 'I don't know if they're thinking anything of the sort,' I said. 'We'll see,' said Simona. 'I didn't know your opinion of me was quite so low. It's a bit of a shock, that's all.' 'It isn't low; it's higher than you can possibly realise – because you know what people want without even knowing that you know. And I think that's a gift; and I hope I haven't destroyed it by telling you about it. But you'd have realised for yourself, one day, sooner or later: I've just sped up the process, slightly. ~~And I feel I can rely on your vanity to bring you back soon enough to your steady state of extreme self-regard; just as soon, that is, as you've dismissed me as a dull nonentity who never really understood you – because that, after all, is my function in life, isn't it?' 'Well,' I said, 'if you were~~

~~trying to make a speech that goes straight into the book, you've *failed*. I'm not going to include anything that madly navel-gazing. This isn't about me, it's about you – you and the others.' Simona smiled at me, patronising in the way that only a dull nonentity such as herself can be. 'I'm glad you think that; I really am~~. Now go and do some writing.'

She walked out, leaving the door open. It was four twenty. Still ten minutes of availability to go~~; I needed a lion-size tongue to lick my kittenish wounds~~. Where was X when I needed him? Two minutes passed. No-one was going to come now. I went out into the downstairs hallway. The house seemed disturbingly quiet. I went to the drawing room. Perhaps, if X wasn't there, I could get a little sympathy from Cleangirl. The drawing room was empty; I went to the kitchen. I thought, in her way, that Simona had probably been trying to console me. But it felt more like an attack – a mugging. The kitchen, empty. I put my hand on the kettle, it was scorching. Out into the garden, and there they *all* were. 'Is it true that Simona told you?' said Cecile, stepping forward into the spokesperson spot. 'What?' I said, 'that I'm a writer who doesn't know what she's doing?' 'No,' Cecile said, annoyed, 'that we put on a little radio-show for you, while you were up in the attic.' 'Yes,' I said, 'she did mention something about that.' And then... I felt the bang of a migraine, arriving in my head; I felt the swoosh of nausea drain down through me; I felt the seeping of tears from my eyes. It was as if I had a fireman inside of me, with a big fire-hose, and he'd just turned it on and pointed it at the top of my skull. 'And did you believe us,' she asked, 'while we were doing it?' I reached for one of the handles of the French doors. 'Yes,' I said, quietly into their silence. They cheered and applauded and one of them whooped and then they started hugging. The principal actors – William and Simona, Alan and Fleur, Henry and Ingrid, and most of all Cecile – were performing a quadrille of mutual congratulation. 'I can't believe she believed you,' said Edith to Alan. 'You must be a really good actor.' 'Well...' said Alan, and mentioned the school play. Cecile herself, the greatest and falsest of the fakers, was having her lower half hugged by Marcia. Henry stood to one side, frowning with delight. X was sharing a joke with Ingrid – who did, I have to say, look towards me with concern. I broke the gaze, hoping she would come over to offer me some comfort. When I looked again, she was back whispering into X's ear. I had seen quite enough. I turned and sloped off into the house, hoping at every moment to be stopped, brought back, forgiven, assuaged – like a child dragging its snuggy-comfort-blanket behind it. (My only snuggy-comfort-blanket being that I would write them up, get them down, show them up, bring them down.) In the bedroom my collapse was complete. ~~I went into that vortex of self-absence that, apart from sleep and sex, only happens in the whirl of extreme grief~~. I was mortified. The house was united – against me. I had completely failed in everything I wanted to achieve. Or had I? Didn't I, when I was planning all this, want to make myself the arch-villainess? And isn't that now *exactly* what I've become. But I gave up on that plan before I'd even written the synopsis; I thought people wouldn't confide in me if they didn't trust me. And now, this. It's almost too much to take.

I have recovered myself, almost – and I have been thinking, thinking hard.

These little scenes they played out for my benefit, for my humiliation, they are telling me something: *Simona has read my Synopsis.*

How otherwise did she and William know so exactly what to say in the Nursery?

Then I remember all her confessions with me. Of *course* she knows what I want to happen between William and her. I've told her directly.

But then what about Alan and Fleur? Is it so obvious to them that I've been trying to force them together?

How could she not know? You hardly left the poor woman alone all month.

And Ingrid and Henry? My flirting with him?

And Cecile? How does she know that what I want most of all is intimacy with her?

It is too wild a chance that all four scenes were so accurate in parodying my Synopsis.

Simona publicised my Synopsis; she directed these performances, just as Henry directs Shakespeare.

And what's worse is, she doesn't mind me knowing this – she wants me to know this.

By opening the Synopsis early (when? the moment it arrived?), she has completely betrayed my trust.

This, too, she wants me to know. Not only that, she wants to flaunt the fact – share it with the other guests – risk the total failure of the whole month.

Why? ~~Does she hate me so much?~~

~~Another thing I've just realised: I mentioned the cameras in the Synopsis. So, she and William must have known all along that they were being watched. Were all their scenes fake, too?~~ Bingo!

Oh my God. I'm in such trouble.

Henry appeared to me just now, erupted in front of me as if from the very ground; I had been walking in a trance along the evening beach, not too far from the house. Henry stood before me, holding in his hands some papers which I at first only vaguely recognised. 'I've read it,' he said. 'I've read it, and you can't do this to people. You'll have to decide one way or the other.'

'You've read what?' I said.

'X or me – that's your choice.'

'Is that the Synopsis?' I said, horrified.

'I love you,' Henry said. 'God, it's a relief, telling you that. I *love* you.'

'How did you get it?' I asked, then said, 'You love me.'

'I do. These last few days have been terrible. Ingrid and I had that big scene, which was meant to be for your benefit – but then it turned real. We said things that we really meant. And ever since then, I've known there was a possibility.'

'Did Simona give you the Synopsis?' I asked.

'No,' Henry said, taking a moment to drag himself off his declarations. 'I stole it. I knew she had a copy – she read a little of it out to us on the lawn. But I could tell she was giving us only edited highlights. Hardly anything happened in it at all. She mentioned that you'd predicted Ingrid and I would go through a torrid time. But I knew there was more – and I was right. You want me. You're attracted to me. You even say that you think you might be in love with me. Well, you can be, now. It's safe.'

'Henry.'

'It's far easier for you to get out of your relationship with X than for me to break up my marriage, and leave Edith. But I'm prepared to do that, if it means I have a chance with you. You don't really know X – you don't know what he's really like. He isn't the man you think he –'

'Henry, stop.'

'I know this is too fast,' he said, stomping around on the sand. 'It's probably the wrong way – but it's romantic, isn't it? It's impetuous. You like romantic things.'

'It isn't going to happen.'

For the first time, I felt like I had his full attention.

'Why not?'

'Because I love X.'

'But you say here.' He waved the Synopsis.

'If you read it through –'

'There's some hope, at least. You want to have an affair with me, to see how it is when we're together. Well, that's what I'm offering. And it doesn't have to be thwarted. I know it seems fairly desperate, but I think my marriage to Ingrid was over a while ago. You've seen us –'

'I don't need to know this.'

'You do. This is what you wanted. You said I was magnificent. It's happening – a chance with me.'

He stepped in close. His arms reached out to take me.

I stepped back.

'Henry, calm down.' This was awful. I needed more than a moment to think, but a moment was better than nothing.

'Sit down,' I said.

'I can't,' he replied. 'I'm too full of energy, too full of love.'

I looked into his face and sadly saw that it was so; his eyes were completely radiant with it.

'I'll admit that I wrote in the Synopsis that I was attracted to you, and I was considering the possibility you might be attracted to me –' (I was trying hard to remember exactly *what* I'd written.)

'I *am*.'

'Please, let me finish.'

'Sorry.'

'But didn't you read the rest of it? That was only to make X jealous, and to bring you and Ingrid back together again. I've realised since then that it really is X I want to be with, exclusively.'

'That's cowardice,' he said. 'Why did you think differently before?'

'Because I hadn't realised what an idiot I am, and I hadn't realised how lucky I've been to find someone like X who is prepared to put up with someone as idiotic as me.'

'I am, too.'

'You're not,' I said. 'You think you are but you're not.'

'I'd like a chance to try.'

He was trying now, to get close again.

'Think about it for a few days,' I said. 'You'll see I'm right.'

'How will I see? I won't believe I'm wrong until I'm proven wrong – and that will only happen if we give it a go.'

'No,' I said. 'Really, *no*.'

He looked distraught. I wanted to comfort him, but didn't feel I could risk anything like an approach.

'Have you told Ingrid?' I asked.

'About what?'

'The Synopsis. You wanting to leave her.'

'She knows in her heart that it's over. We haven't spoken about it, though. We've been having arguments.'

'Texting each other?'

'Yes. You noticed?'

'Leave it a few days. Don't do anything now.'

'That's going to be so hard.'

'Think of Edith, the effect it would have on her.'

'I'm sure she knows we're not happy, too. I mean, look at her – how she's behaving. Is that balanced?'

'If you break up your marriage, you're not doing it because of me. I'm asking you not to. I'm telling you not to.'

'I can't go on like this,' he said, and gave a sob.

'Henry,' I said, and feeling fairly sure he wouldn't any longer take it the wrong way, I put my arms around him.

'I'm so miserable,' he said. 'I didn't know I could be this miserable.'

I held him for a while, worried that another of the guests would come along. He calmed down, apologised.

'Not very attractive, is it?' he said.

I smiled as sympathetically as I could.

'I'll go back to the house.'

'Can I have that?' I asked.

For a moment he didn't realise what I meant, then he handed me the Synopsis: Simona's copy, with annotations.

Evening.

Cecile and Edith's meal: pungent, surprise-filled *bouillabaisse*;

medallions of pork in a sweet sauce, with potatoes and *haricots verts*; then *crème brûlée*.

Couldn't really concentrate on it. I sat quietly at the table, and tried to listen to the conversation. My guests were very polite to me.

Hid myself away after dinner.

There are so many things I need to work out. I think I can trust Henry not to speak to Ingrid. But perhaps now he's got this idea into his head of himself as a passionate, romantic hero he'll do something really stupid – like passionate, romantic heroes are meant to.

The thought of Edith should stop him, but what if it doesn't? Perhaps now I've put him off, he'll calm down. Forlorn hope, I fear.

I wonder how X will react, when he finds out. Another fight? And what *was* that fight with Henry all about? Jealousy, like I thought? Them fighting over me?

And then there's the play-acting. I know now that I can't trust any of the guests. They all willingly took part in making a fool of me.

I suppose it was just their revenge for me spying on them, and it is quite funny; I have some funny scenes out of it.

~~But Simona and William must have been putting on an act right from the start.~~ They knew about the cameras, so they decided to have some fun. The arguments? The play-fighting? Her beating him up? William's sobbing? William's flash? I don't know what to think of any of it.

Simona wants to make sure something happens during the month (she can't be worried about that any longer), and William will help her in any way he can. Perhaps that's the best explanation I'll get.

I'm sure she has thought about leaving him. She mentioned that to me long before I had the idea for this.

~~I don't think I can ask her directly~~.

Pick up the phone.

Sunday

Day Eighteen Week Three

Rain, first for days, coming like an order of muslin, to drape a stage-set.

You're overdoing the pathetic fallacy just a little too much there, O Lord. Be careful, or people will start believing we really *do* live in a Romantic universe, where trees stoop under the weight of our cares and clouds are the biggest crybabies of all.

Speaking of God: Fleur intends to go to church, as per. I bet she tells the Vicar about my iniquitous behaviour, attic, spying, etc.

I'm worry about what Henry's up to. Has he told Ingrid about our little scene on the beach yesterday?

I think, if he did, she'd come and see me straight away; that's if she didn't just get in the car and drive off.

I have so many things to think about. Whether, for example, the break-up of their marriage has anything to do with Edith's mental state.

I don't doubt the existence of Elizabeth, really; not after my own encounter with her. But I think something must have caused Edith to become so hypersensitive. Inventing an invisible friend isn't such an odd thing to do; disovering one is slightly freakier, but not all that much.

I wish X were around a bit more. I'd feel safer from Henry; that he wasn't going to have another easy opportunity to jump me. I feel certain...

Interrupted by Simona. She had come straight from her room.

'Victoria,' she said, 'we have a situation. The Synopsis has been stolen from my room.'

'Has it?' I said, playing for the moment dumb.

'This could be disastrous.'

'Why?' I asked. 'They all know what's in it, anyway.'

'They don't. I only read out a very few bits. If some of them hear what you thought they'd be doing...'

'Then what?'

'They'd leave.'

'They're going to read it in manuscript.'

'But you don't want it generally known, in the house.'

'It already is.'

'Who do you think stole it?'

'I have no idea,' deciding right then not to tell her it was Henry, or that I had the Synopsis, or that I'd read her annotations.

'What can we do?'

'Wait and see?'

'You don't seem very worried.'

'Everything has gone so wrong already. What does this really matter?'

She went away, peeved. I wonder which of the guests she'll think is the thief.

2 p.m. A rainbow, and no-one told me about it.

It was there for about five minutes, about half an hour ago. Only visible from the front of the house. Most of the others gathered there; nobody came to fetch me.

This, since I came down out of the attic, is the most hurtful thing to have happened.

Am I to be excluded from everything? It seems I am. Have I forfeited the right to be part of the house? It seems I have.

Apologising to Fleur; or trying to.

I've been thinking what I should have done differently with *Spaciousness*. Perhaps I shouldn't have written it at all. I did base

Araminta too closely on Fleur. That was an artistic failing of the first order; I allowed a petty motive of revenge to get in the way of creating a fully rounded character. I'm worrying now that I'm going to do the same thing in this book. But does it matter? Don't I truly think – with her God and her hang-ups – that Fleur *isn't* really a fully rounded character? And if that's what I think, then shouldn't I make her come across that way? Shouldn't I strive to keep her one-dimensional? Or two? She's a big doughnut: round, but with a big hole of sugary air in her middle.

I decided to seek her out, after church. She wasn't anywhere to be found downstairs, so I went and knocked her up in her room. 'Come in,' Fleur said. As I opened the door, she was getting up from her knees. 'Oh,' she said, when she saw it was me. 'I've come,' I said, answering her unvoiced question (*What do you want?*), 'to have a talk.' This time she voiced it: 'About?' 'About you and me – our relationship; about me putting you in *Spaciousness*,' I said. 'Oh, Victoria,' she said, 'does it have to be right now?' And I suddenly felt, having broached it, that I did truly desire to talk about it, in detail, at length, honestly. 'It doesn't *have* to be now,' I said, 'there's no absolute reason.' (Apart from that I've just decided that I want it.) 'I think about it quite a lot,' said Fleur, 'and it exhausts me – but I'd prefer if you gave me... if you let me get my thoughts in order.' 'Can't you just say the first thing that comes into your head?' 'No, Victoria,' she said, 'you got that gene; I missed it entirely.' We both sensed the argument between us; it was on the floor, like a bonfire, and we were both carrying lidless petrol cans. 'Another time, then,' I said. 'Victoria,' Fleur said, 'let me come to you; and when I do, don't – for once – put me off.' This was my sister; she could make me feel terrible faster than anyone else in the world ~~(with two exceptions: one, that I didn't see, the other, that was unseeable)~~. 'I'll try,' I said, 'just don't interrupt me when I'm having sex.' She sniggered. She knew what I was alluding to – the camping holiday in the Black Mountains, she aged 15 and me, aged 13; me in the tent

I don't get this. The only thing I think you can possibly mean by it is your parents, one of whom is alive, and you don't see, and the other is dead, and you can't see. But it's too obscure to be any use.

with Rhys, a local gypsy, her getting rained on outside, our parents having argued themselves off into opposite directions, different pubs. 'Let me in,' Fleur kept saying – to no reply. When Rhys and I finally emerged, and he had gone back to the caravan park where he lived, I had said to my sodden sister, 'Don't ever interrupt me when I'm having sex.' Now, in the bedroom, Fleur snorted. 'You weren't having sex,' she said; which was her next line. 'I wasn't, but he *definitely* was,' I said; which was mine. My sister, who could also make me feel joy faster than anyone else.

I retreated; Fleur returned to her knees and her holy holy holy.

I ate a late lunch, alone.

12,092

Simona tried to insist upon a Confession, but I put her off. I'm really not in the mood for it.

Gong followed by dinner.

Chef has cooked Ingrid's favourite ever foods: lobster and summer pudding.

Simona very tense. I could see her, looking round the faces of the guests – she wants to know who the Synopsis-thief is. I am careful not to let her catch me watching her.

At the same time, I am anxious that Henry will give her some sign. I'm not sure what this would be. This comes on top of the anxiety that he will burst out with a public declaration of love. He seems subdued, though – hardly says a word. Perhaps he's going to skulk back into his marriage, and I'll never hear anything from him again.

At the end of the meal, Chef comes out to ask if Ingrid liked the meal. Ingrid says she loved it, and gives him the brightest smile of the whole month. Henry doesn't seem to notice.

The house's toilet fascination seems to have ended. As far as I can tell, this coincided with my attic days. I don't see how these two things can be in any way linked.

X has been avoiding me, again.

He got up early this morning, and was out of the house most of the day. Sea-fishing, I think. The first chance I got to talk to him was after we'd turned in.

'You know, I am grateful you left the microphones on. I think it stopped me going mad.'

'Everyone else went mad instead.'

'Were they very angry?'

'Marcia decided to go almost as soon as she found out. She only came back because Ingrid called her up.'

'Why didn't I hear that? Why didn't she use the phone in the house?'

'I don't know. Maybe she did.'

'She didn't.'

'Then I suppose she used her mobile. I only know because Henry told me she was going to try.'

'I shall have to thank her.'

He was taking his trousers off, sitting on the edge of the bed. Without turning to look at me, he said: 'You got me into real trouble, you know. I was very close to being shoved up in the attic along with you. They were... You only saw them when they'd calmed down. From now on, I'm not going to be able to defend you.'

'You won't have to. Because from now on, I'm going to behave.'

'I hope so.'

'Now, come here,' I said.

X got in. I put my arms around him, kissed him. His lips stayed tense.

'No,' he said.

'Why not?' I asked.

'Just no,' he said.

Monday

Day Nineteen Week Three

Morning.

In my room just now, scribbling a face on top of my face, when behind me, quite slowly, the door, which had been an inch ajar, creaked open. Really, *creaked* – as in a haunted house it should. I, on the far side of the bed, twisted round expecting to see our girl-ghost. And there was nothing there! My heart was sucked up into my throat through a bendy straw. Then, bravely, just to check, I started round the bed to close the door – and I felt a thrill up the inside of my left leg, a cool electric furry thrill. Hardly did I dare look down! It was Audrey the cat.

12,092. I'm going to have to give this up, really I am.

I should do something useful with my time, like go to the Lighthouse. At one point, I thought I might gather all the guests together, and we could go as a group; at another, I thought I might just go with X; now, I think I'll go alone. Soon.

Arranged for this evening, the *To the Lighthouse* reading group. I had given up on this; thought my personal unpopularity would do for it, too. But it has picked up a momentum all its own – as guests picked up the copies left in the drawing room. Marcia, in particular, is very keen; Edith almost as much.

Late morning.

I was out on the lawn, sunbathing, when suddenly – a camera crew from the local news programme. The Maid had let them in;

she was very impressed because she'd seen the reporter on television from the age of about fifteen. (He was so washed up he'd become leathery with it). A cameraman in a baggy leather jacket stood beside him, looking bored. I was in a bikini, and said I couldn't talk for at least half an hour. They asked if they could get some shots of the house. I said, 'No.' (I'm sure the Owners would be upset by this.)

'What about the garden?' they asked.

I was already thinking about what I was going to wear.

'Fine,' I said.

I went upstairs and put together an outfit: chinos, a pale-blue shirt, pumps, sunglasses – The Princess Diana Minefield look. Glancing out the window, halfway through changing, only a bra on, I saw the camera pointed directly up at me. I don't think it got anything below the neck. More alarmingly still, Marcia was on the verandah, the reporter standing over her, and they were – help! – chatting away. As I watched, the camera turned round and focused on her face; the chat had just turned into an interview. Aaaaaagh! I rushed to pull my top over my head, slip some pumps on, and get my hair into some kind of shape. Then out into the garden where: 'I thought I told you not to film the house,' I said.

'We were filming the flowerbed,' chipped in the cameraman, as the lower orders usually do, 'and I just followed the ivy up the wall.'

'To my bedroom window,' I said. He was pointing the camera at me. 'Turn that thing off, now,' I said. 'I only gave permission for a formal interview.' The cameraman looked at the leathery journalist, who nodded back. The lens remained pointing at my face, recording.

'Is it true,' the journalist asked, 'that you installed spy-cameras in every room of this house, even the showers and the toilets?' The camera was going for a close-up reaction shot.

'No,' I said, 'it is not. I would like you to leave. Now.'

'They weren't in the showers and toilets,' interjected Marcia, 'but they were everywhere else – corridors, bedrooms.'

I was not going to lose control; they'd have liked nothing better than for me to attack the camera.

'You were locked in the attic without food or water for three days, is that right?' the journalist asked me.

'Please go,' I said, before he could say anything else. 'And you,' I said to Marcia, 'keep quiet.'

I turned to lead them back through the house, camera off. I walked in the French doors; they didn't follow me. When I turned to look back, the cameraman was still filming me: my shouting, my storming off. To see the three of them there, coolly watching me, was infuriating. 'Would you just *go*!' I shouted.

I ran upstairs; from the Master Bedroom, I looked out the window. Marcia was still there with them on the verandah, continuing her interview to camera. I listened; she answered every single question, in great and damaging detail.

Ten minutes later, she led them through the house and waved them off down the drive. I decided, after careful consideration, to kick her out.

Ingrid *knows*. I don't think Henry's told her; she knows.

I went into the kitchen, and found her openly flirting with the Chef. Canoodling, almost. He was feeding her some kind of goo on the end of a piece of celery.

'Oh, hi,' he said, when he saw me.

'Victoria,' said Ingrid. I expected a blush of guilt, but none came.

Just then, Henry came in behind me. (This is the kind of scene I just love writing, but being in it was horribly embarrassing.)

Still there was no sign of shame. Ingrid took a step away from the Chef, but only to come semi-aggressively towards me and Henry.

She aimed a *yes?* over my shoulder.

'Nothing,' said Henry. 'I was just wondering where you were.'

'Well, I'm here,' replied Ingrid. 'Now you know.'

'I'd like a word,' he said. 'About –'

'Edith,' said Ingrid. 'Yes, you always do, don't you?'

He turned and went out. She followed him, without exchanging glances with me.

'I'll come back,' she said, over her shoulder.

'I look forward to it,' said the Chef.

I thought about saying something to him. *You're fired* was one possibility. But I couldn't stand to stay in there with him. So cocky.

Lunch. Where is Marcia? Ill again, I'm told. Hiding, more like. I have all the same changed my mind about kicking her out.

William also absent. He's gone to the pub. The drinking makes him look unwell; he seems generally more subdued.

Early afternoon. Preoccupied: Henry, me, X, Ingrid, Chef.

Fleur appeared in the drawing room. 'Let's go for a walk,' she said to me. I didn't hesitate – not even to put on something slightly warmer. I had been sitting on the sofa with Alan, not talking about very much: life. When Fleur entered, I tried to detect a *frisson* between them; couldn't. We strolled out over the lawn. I waited, didn't start speaking. What had she said, yesterday? 'Let me come to you; and when I do, don't put me off.' I clasped my hands behind my back, to keep my body language as open as possible. Fleur started in the moment her feet moved from grass to sand. 'I can only think,' she said, 'that you want to bring this up now, specifically *now*, because it's useful for you – which is one of the many reasons I'm reluctant to talk. But I've thought and prayed about it, and I realise that it's as well to take any opportunity that comes along. We might not have another.' I nodded, thinking I must look like a junior nun escorting the visiting Mother Superior. 'You hurt me very much, writing what you did. I think – yesterday – you were coming to apologise, weren't you?'

'I was.'

'Thank you, is the first thing I should say – though it rather sticks. I assume that means you think you did wrong.'

'What I did didn't help the novel.'

'But it hurt me.'

'And I'm sorry for that.'

'I don't know if you understand exactly how it hurt me.' As we walked away from Southwold, Fleur explained *exactly how*. I'm not likely to forget what she said. It took quite a while, and there's no point writing it here – I'm never going to use it. Overall, what she said was this: I had spent my life trying to be seen, she had spent hers trying to disappear. By putting her in *Spaciousness* I had ruined her attempt. And whereas I had the power to drag her, unwilling, into my world, she felt unable to do anything back. She wanted to; she couldn't. But then she realised that revenge wasn't possible. The best thing she found to do, to make her world have an effect upon me, was forgive me. 'I pray for you, Victoria,' she said, 'I pray for you all the time. I know you hate to hear me say that.'

'I don't, actually,' I said, 'I've changed. I'm coming to like it more and more.'

Then she said something else. She had realised that trying to disappear was vanity, was, in a way, blasphemy. 'God doesn't want us not to exist – He created us to exist. Perhaps you're right, and we *should* try to make our existences as large and permanent as we can.' This is the first time in years my sister has admitted I might be right. 'Which is one of the reasons I decided to come here – as a concession to you, as an experiment for me.'

We then moved on to talk about our parents. I did this on the strict understanding that I would never, in speech or print, reproduce what was said.

Just back from Lowestoft hospital (A&E department) to which I had to take Alan, after he lost a toenail. The accident happened like this: Alan – unlucky boy – had just finished in the upstairs loo; Fleur, desperate to go after another long walk on the beach, was rushing along the landing (downstairs was occupied, by Marcia, now no longer ill; but I still haven't spoken to her about the journalist incident); Alan unlocked the door and was turning the handle when Fleur, not having heard the small slide and click, came smashing through; Alan, I should add, was barefoot. The impact popped his left toenail clean off; all that remained behind was a cherry red hole. Fleur was distraught. Alan, without tears or complaint, hobbled downstairs and asked if anyone could take him to hospital. (A few of us had been in the drawing room, discussing the difference between my spy-cameras and the cameras of local newsmen – although I was the only person who seemed to think the difference important.) There was much concern, everyone offered lifts. Alan, however, said *yes* to me; and *that would be great*, and *thanks*, and *are you sure?* I was surprised – Marcia would have been the obvious person: returning the favour for all those intimate lifts (into and out of baths, toilets) Alan had given her. Still, I was ready to go in about five minutes. The drive took about half an hour, and was far from uneventful; by the end, I was wondering whether Alan hadn't deliberately sacrificed his toenail, just for an excuse to talk to me at length. And about what? Well... He started in as soon as we'd got beyond the drive and were motoring down the lane. 'About Fleur.' 'Mmm-hmm.' 'You know what happened, don't you?' I tried to think. Of course I knew about Domino and Audrey, but that was too long ago for him to refer to it as merely *what happened.* I also knew about their faked-up love scene in the kitchen. Perhaps he meant the walk they arranged then, assuming they'd gone on one. 'What exactly?' 'After you introduced us, we started seeing each other, without telling you. It lasted about two months.' I took my eyes off the road for a moment, glancing down at Alan's bejewelled foot. 'Really?' I said. In the past week, I've become so used to guests telling me lies and otherwise deceiving me; this time,

I wasn't rising to it. 'We did,' he said. 'I'd drive down to see her one weekend, and she'd come up to London the next. We'd go out, but only to places we were sure we wouldn't meet you.' I was curious to see whether Alan had any details – invented or otherwise. 'Such as?' 'Oh, places in South London: Italian restaurants, dodgy pubs. And if we went out in the centre of town, we'd go to the theatre. To musicals. To *matinées*.' This touch, surely, was too comic to be false. 'You mean it?' 'Of course. Hadn't you guessed?' 'Guessed how?' 'From how much we've been avoiding one another?' I remembered my Synopsis: it's amazing how distant those predictions sometimes seem. Since it became clear that Simona had made at least parts of it public, I've hardly bothered about them at all – as predictions that may be right or wrong. The guests are now too concerned with thwarting me to behave in the ways that I had foreseen; and of course, I hadn't foreseen my predictions becoming known to them. 'I thought you'd been getting on quite well.' 'Oh, and from us pretending to get on – I thought you'd see.' 'How could I guess it from that?' 'I don't know – in some novelistic way that isn't revealed to the rest of us mere mortals.' I hated it when Alan talked in *clichés*, it was beneath him. 'To answer your question directly, I had no idea.' We were now heading out into country lanes, and I needed a little map-reading to get us there without wrong turnings. Alan obliged. I began to ask him questions.

The affair started immediately after my dinner party. Alan, unprepared and improvising, managed to write his phone number down – in eye-liner, on one of the tear-out subscription forms from the women's magazines beside the loo in my bathroom! This he slipped into the inside pocket of Fleur's coat. When I recovered from the shock, and told him this seemed out of character, he merely agreed, in a slightly pleased but also rueful way. It was as if he were saying, 'Yes, and look where it's got me.' On setting out in a homebound taxi, he was expecting hours if not days of agonising uncertainty. He hadn't had an opportunity to whisper, as he'd intended, 'Look in your pockets,' or some such, into Fleur's desirable ear. I had been too watchful – searching their faces for signs of mutual attraction. Fleur might overlook the note entirely, not finding it for weeks, months. But when he arrived back at his flat he found awaiting him a message on his answerphone – left only five minutes before. It was Fleur, phoning from the house of the friend she always stays with when up in London. Alan wouldn't tell me exactly what she'd said. I detected a doted-over memory, and did not press. Before Alan had a chance to phone back, Fleur called again. Within half an hour, she had taxied over to his flat and... Alan left me to imagine the rest. He also left me to imagine a version of my sister capable of such romance. After her marriage to Clive ended, I'd given up entirely on my sister as an impulsive being.

In the languorous morning, they knew they wanted to keep seeing each other. And so began the trips to Italian restaurants in South London and *matinées* of musicals neither of them wanted to see. (I wondered why they hadn't chosen art-films, which I hardly ever attend. But 'hardly ever' is entirely different to 'only at gunpoint' – which is how it is with me and musical theatre.) 'And why are you telling me this now?' I said. 'You could quite easily have gone through the next whatever, twelve days, without me ever guessing.' 'Please don't force me to say it; it's too embarrassing.' My delight was mixed with exasperation: why had it taken him almost three wasted weeks to get going on this? 'You're a pair of sly things, aren't you?' I said. 'You always *did* have that in common.' 'I want her back,' he said, 'and I think she wants me.' 'Oh, Alan,' I said, and took my hand off the gear-stick to touch his, 'poor you.' 'Has she said anything to you? You went out for a long walk today, didn't you?' 'She's said nothing, and I certainly haven't asked.' He turned away from me and stared ahead, glum. 'This is something quite passionate,' he said. 'I don't think I really know how to deal with passion.' 'You don't deal with passion,' I said, feeling far more comfortable now, 'you *suffer* it: passion is passive.' 'Then you'll have to do something to help.' I left the silence to ask *Why?* for me. 'I'd almost managed to get over her, before I came here. And now it's as bad as it's ever been. It's a terrible helplessness, a paralysis. We're so close, and yet it could all go so wrong. I feel now like there's only about four words I can say to her – yes, no, please, and really. If I actually construct a sentence with a verb in it, it's a declaration of undying...' Now it was him who was letting the silence speak the word he wanted. 'I'll help,' I said. 'In fact, I already have, by bringing you together again; four words are better than none. If you want it to happen, I'm sure it will.' 'I can't wait for term to start,' Alan said, 'then at least I can have a few hours of respite.' He bit a crescent off his fingernail, combining this with a mournful dipping of his head away from me. 'How's your toe?' I asked. 'It's stopped bleeding,' he said. 'Unlike my heart.' Alan was an amateur at emotion, and therefore very embarrassing; his dialogue will have to be improved.

We drove the rest of the way without speaking, but a pact had been made.

Whilst we sat in the waiting room, I read the problem pages of the magazines, for amusement, and – perhaps – tips. In a way, I *was* Agony Aunt for the whole house: I caused the agony, and then I removed it. With Alan and Fleur, I couldn't allow myself to fail. There needs to be a happily ever after somewhere, and theirs is the only one in the offing. I seem to remember thinking something similar earlier in the month.

Alan's name was called and I helped him hobble towards the two light-grey swingdoors. They turned him around in just under fifteen minutes. During which time I didn't even look at the magazines; I plotted, just as I always used to.

When Alan emerged, it was on crutches. His toe was dressed in clean white gauze, through which the blood had already started to weep. 'I'm fine from here,' he said to the nurse. He was, in fact, fine all the way to the car. But once he'd sat down and put the seatbelt on, he started soundlessly to sob. 'Alan?' I said, gently. He wailed words I couldn't understand. Despite the awkwardness of the gear-stick, and the people walking past looking at us and wondering what terminal illness he'd just been told he'd got, I pulled him into a tight hug. 'Tell me,' I said. 'I hate hospitals,' he self-scoffed in a phlegmy voice. 'That can't be it,' I said. 'I feel like a child again,' he said. These complex people and their simple emotions: Christians at the mercy of lions. I began to cry, unable not to remember the helplessness of two-years-old and the wrath of three and the hurt pride of four and a half. When we'd wept ourselves to a standstill, Alan said, 'Do you think um it gets better or worse, over time?' And I said, 'I never could tell – worse probably.' 'I meant passion,' he said. 'Oh,' I said, 'that? – that definitely gets worse before it gets better.' I hadn't meant to be cruel, but he cried again. My comment, however, had peeled me off away from him – like a scab: I was insensate, he newly sore. 'I almost cried in front of the nurse,' he said, blowing his nose. 'I'm sure she's used to that,' I said, and the thought of all that commonplace pain made me want to get away from the hospital as fast as I could. Reversing out of the parking space, I almost pranged a car coming through my blind-spot. As we drove home, we talked about how fantastic Fleur can be, sometimes.

I'm told we – the house, me, Marcia – were prominent on the local evening news. I missed it; was in the shower, washing away hospital thoughts. The third story, after one recent murder and one anniversary of a schoolgirl abduction. They made a big thing of the spy-cameras, and of me being held captive in the attic. No mention of ghosts. When I asked (it was Edith who gleefully told me) if the shot of me getting changed had been used, she smirked; I conclude it has. I tried to find Marcia, but she had already gone to bed – not feeling too well, again, I was told. Fibs.

12,705. Silently I record it – as a dedicated addict records her methadone dosage.

Supper. A strange mood round the dining table; excited, almost celebratory. Some hypocritical disapproval of our local fame (guess who). Simona, overjoyed; William, amused. Overall, the guests feel justified in having shoved me up in the attic. 'And then they said...' said Edith, again and again. Although she hadn't been on screen herself, she was excited by the mere idea of being close to a centre of public interest. Henry and Ingrid did not make any attempt to calm her: both of them were long-faced and silent the whole meal. They may be thinking of leaving, I fear. I wish I'd heard their conversation, after the scene in the kitchen. Simona seems to have relaxed considerably about the stolen Synopsis; perhaps, because nothing bad has happened yet, she feels it's with someone safe. I think she may even suspect me – I am the most obvious candidate. Some anticipation of the Reading Group. *You were, indeed.*

I feel fairly sure there will be a bit more press coverage; mousy local news journalist might come back, chasing the story she missed first time. Can't see it going any further than the East Anglia region, though – despite this being the Silly Season. Simona disagrees~~, and spends some of the evening in her room making calls to London.~~

Fleur has been all over Alan with apologies, ever since he got back from the hospital. Before dinner, she fetched him a beer; during dinner, she talked to him; afterwards, they went out into the garden – she helping him to hobble. Alan, despite his self-consciousness at my now knowing how he felt, was surprisingly relaxed. From what I heard of the comments they exchanged over the dining table, they were talking only about the trip to hospital. On a couple of occasions, he made her laugh. It was at my expense (a reference to my love of browsing in hospital waiting rooms? my erratic driving?), but I don't mind that at all; whatever I can contribute, directly or indirectly. They were out in the garden together at least a quarter of an hour. Some of the other guests noticed; glances were exchanged, and smiles. What do *they* know?

The *To the Lighthouse* readers' group. Participants: me, Fleur, Marcia, Alan, William (although he admitted he'd only read half of it, and was going on memories of a film he'd once seen), Simona, Henry (very keen – keener than me) and Edith. Of course, it would be easier just to say 'X, Ingrid and Cecile sat in the garden', and I bet they were far more Bloomsbury than the rest of us. It was a superb evening – long ribbons of cloud in the sky, outrageous oranges and firebrand reds. Remembering my failures with house meetings, I took the risk of delegating leadership of the group to Henry (he offered over dinner, I accepted); I didn't want the thing to fail because everyone thought I was trying to boss it into shape. Henry, I grant, had done his homework: he had more information on the book than was printed in the introduction. I believe he'd found his way down to Southwold library. After a beautifully brief biographical sketch of Virginia Woolf (I didn't know she'd once sneaked aboard the *Dreadnought*, dressed as a sheikh), Henry said, 'I thought we'd begin by discussing the end of the book – and work our way back to the beginning.'

'Well, it's called *To the Lighthouse*,' said William, 'but they never get there, do they? It's famous for that.'

'Exactly,' said Henry.

'They're *al*most there,' said Marcia.

'But his foot doesn't touch the ground,' said Edith. 'The book ends before he's actually on the lighthouse island.'

'Yes,' said Henry, encouraging his daughter, 'and why do you think that is?'

Edith could tell she was being patronised, but really did want to answer. Everyone, to give them their due, waited her out – but when it was clear nothing was coming, Marcia said: 'Woolf likes things which aren't *fin*ished. If you look at the middle section, Time Passes, that's all about what's left out.'

'And *Jacob's Room*,' added Henry, 'that's about a character who never appears.'

'Did she write that before or after *To the Lighthouse*?' asked Fleur.

'Before, I'm pretty sure,' said Henry.

'Before,' confirmed Alan. 'But I'd like to go back to what Marcia said: I'm afraid unfinished things and things left out are quite different.'

'Well, they're the same sort of thing,' said Marcia.

In other circumstances, Alan would never have let this woolliness pass without giving it a good categorical comb. Fleur had to do his stepping in and sorting out for him.

'You can see why a novelist like Woolf does both – they're very modernist tricks,' said Fleur, 'but they are quite different.'

'I wouldn't exactly call them tricks,' I said. 'They are the truth of the novel. I think that's what Henry's trying –'

'Do you mean like the moral of the novel?' said Marcia. 'I didn't think modernist novels had morals.'

A few people laughed; Edith looked puzzled, and couldn't stop herself asking, 'What's modernist?'

Henry gave her a quick explanation, which was very impressive. Alan nodded along to it, all except the part about modernism being a reaction against Victorianism.

The talkflow had temporarily been stemmed.

'So...' said Henry, hoping to unplug the barrel.

'I think what she's trying to say with the ending,' said Fleur, 'is that that's what life's like.'

'What do you think?' Henry said, turning to me. 'Being our resident novelist.'

I looked around, just to check that no-one objected to me taking a little while to answer. Surprisingly, I seemed to have the whole group's enthusiastic attention. This, I'm afraid, rather put me off.

'Well...' I said, 'I think her decision was more to do with the design of the book.'

'By which you mean...' Henry prompted, with a flash of his eyes towards Edith.

'I mean that there are, all the way through, moments when time stops – for instance, when they are throwing the ball.'

'Oh, that's wonderful,' said Marcia. 'I think that's my favourite part of the book. I cried.'

'So did I,' said Edith, 'though I wasn't sure why.'

'And why do you think that is?' Henry asked, bringing the talk again back to me.

'Why the pauses?' I said. 'Well, Virginia – I mean, Woolf – called them "moments of being".' I looked at Edith. 'I think, by that, she meant moments when things are most themselves – when people are as alive as they're ever going to be. The end is the most living end she could think of.'

'Ex*act*ly what I said,' shouted Marcia.

'If you were to describe the book, in one sentence,' said Henry, addressing everybody, and trying a different approach, 'what would it be?'

'I'd say,' started Edith, encouraged by the directness of the question (and definitely thinking in schoolgirlish terms of tick and cross), 'it's about what happens inside people, sometimes.'

'That's lovely,' said Alan.

'Mmm,' agreed Fleur.

'William,' said Henry, trying to draw in the glum silent figure, 'what would you say?'

Without hesitation, William began: 'It's about women, isn't it? It's about a purely female view of the world – hazy and emotional and full of smells and how things feel. It's about –'

'One sentence,' said Henry, anticipating a rant.

They looked at one another, hard. Fleur intervened with, 'I think it's about having children and not having children – the difference between the two. Being a parent or being, like Lily Briscoe... not a parent.'

'I love Lily,' said Marcia. 'I think she's my favourite character.'

'And in one sentence?' said Henry, the guide. 'How would you describe the book?'

'As a lovely, rich, fantastic exploration of everything that's beautiful and painful about life,' said Marcia.

'Surely,' I said, a little annoyed, 'you could say that about most novels, most good novels. If you wanted to describe it so that people would know specifically what you were talking about –'

'That wouldn't really do,' said Henry.

'Well, if that's what you're asking,' said William, 'it's about a boy who wants to go to a lighthouse.'

'You've already had your go,' said Edith, chidingly.

William laughed, delighted to be told off by someone so young. 'Sorry,' he said, holding up his hands.

Simona, who I'd noticed had been very quiet, said, 'I would say it's a novel about a house during the summer, containing a family and their odd assortment of guests – and about their relationships with one another, and with whatever it is that concerns them most; for Lily, it's art, for the boy, it's the lighthouse.'

'Bravo!' said William, applauding his wife. 'Top that, if you can.'

'This really isn't a competition,' said Henry. 'If we start getting like that, the whole thing will degenerate into –'

'Something fun,' said William.

'*William*,' said Simona, sternly.

'Alright, alright,' he said. 'I think I'll go and join the others in the garden. I need a fag.'

Making as much as he could of standing up, gathering himself together and walking out, William went – and until he was outside, no-one spoke.

'I'm sorry about that,' said Simona. 'He went to a public school; he can't do anything in a group without feeling he has to win.'

We laughed; tension diffused.

'I'd like to talk about the triangle in the painting,' said Edith. 'I think that's the most important bit of the book.'

'From the artistic point of view,' I said, 'I think you're probably right. Lily is like Woolf, but in the book.'

But Henry said, 'Let's not be reductive. Lily is also the Artist, as Mrs Ramsay is the Mother, Mr Ramsay the –'

'Who's being reductive now?' I said.

'I don't think saying someone is a mother or an artist is re*duc*ing them,' said Marcia.

'I mean autobiographically,' I said. 'Lily thinks like Woolf writes, in her diaries.'

'I'm afraid we haven't all read those,' said Henry.

'It's a lovely book,' said Marcia. 'I think it's very wise about families, and about how people interrelate in different ways.'

'She's always describing the light, isn't she?' said Edith. 'Why do you think that is?'

'To make the book beautiful,' I said. 'If you put in that sort of thing, it helps.'

'No!' said Fleur. 'She can't help it. The light is part of her vision of something transcendent – something she can't express through all the social trivia.'

'In other words, God,' I said.

'I don't think she'd call him that,' said Fleur. 'I think she sees God as too paternalistic.'

'Well,' I said, 'I don't think Woolf *sees* the social as trivial. That's what's so marvellous about the Bloomsbury people: they see people as values – it may in one way just be Strachey or Carrington, but they also stand for something as important as something in Plato, something ultimate.'

'Ladies,' said Henry. 'Order.'

'I don't really understand what you're saying,' said Edith. 'But I think I agree with Victoria.'

'This book is against order,' said Marcia. 'It's an anarchist book, I think.'

'That's very interesting,' said Henry, desperate to reinstate some sort of civility. 'Would you care to expand?'

Nothing further of any great sense was said by anyone except me, Henry and Edith – who, I think, was probably the person most in sympathy with the book. Even I had too much to prove, in my relations to it; I feel so close to it at the moment, it's almost as if I and not Virginia wrote it.

Aftermath of the readers' group. Henry – in the drawing-room – takes the opportunity to tell me, privately, that he agreed with almost everything I said, but that during the discussion he couldn't be seen to be biased. I get away as fast as I can, before he changes the subject.

Alan and Fleur again together, this time with whiskies on the sofa.

Bedtime. Confronted X.

'We haven't had sex since that first night we got here,' I said.

'I know,' he replied. 'I could probably tell you the exact number of hours, if you gave me a moment to think about it.'

'But why haven't we?'

'I didn't think you wanted to,' he said. 'I thought you'd want to concentrate all your energies upon the house.'

'I do,' I said, 'but I thought you'd still miss it.'

'I do,' he said. He was attempting the gear-shift into Romance, but it wasn't going to work. The gearbox sounded as if it had ten bags of nails inside it. He moved closer; I shrugged him off. Gently, he touched my neck; I shrugged, as if his fingers were a wasp. 'I've wanted you *so* much,' he said. 'I've been denying myself because I thought that's what you wanted.'

'We should have talked about this,' I said.

Tuesday

Day Twenty Week Three

6 a.m. A loud knock on the front door. Marcia, being nearest, and awake already, answers; then shouts up the stairs to wake me. It's a journalist, and a photographer, and Marcia's invited them both in! Gorgon that I am, in dressing gown with bare legs, I go down, covering my face. 'No photos,' I say. The photographer slowly lowers his camera. 'Hello,' says the journalist, a middle-aged woman with brittle blonde hair, 'I'm Sheila Burrows from the *Mirror*. I wondered if you'd seen this.' She put a tabloid in my hands: the *Mirror*. It wasn't the front page, it was page 4; it wasn't me, it was BIG SISTER. 'No comment,' I said. 'Now get out.' 'If you'll give me half a minute,' said Sheila Burrows, 'I'll tell you the best thing to do.' I shouted X's name; he didn't have far to come, he'd been standing at the top of the stairs, eavesdropping. 'If you sign up with us, we can protect you from the other papers. They're on their way now. I only got here first because I ride a motorbike.' 'Out,' I said. 'You're making a mistake,' said Sheila Burrows. The photographer tried to get a shot of me, but I put my hand over the lens. This, I have to admit, felt quite glamorous. X went round us and opened the front door. Sheila Burrows dropped her card on the consul table. 'Give me a call if you change your mind.' I picked it up and ripped it to strips as X closed the door upon their not-particularly-disappointed faces. Immediately, I turned on Marcia. 'Why did you let them in?' 'Because I thought you'd want to see

them.' 'You didn't think to ask which paper they were from?' 'I did ask; I still thought you'd want to see them.' The copy of the *Mirror* was still in my hand. X was trying to read it, even as I used it to point at Marcia. He snorted. I held it up in front of my eyes, and read – it was as bad as it could be, worse than I could have imagined. The juiciest allegations were all attributed to 'a source inside the house'. 'We have a spy in our midst,' I said. 'What, you mean another one?' said Marcia, who had been watching as I read the first article (there were three sidebar articles). Before I could answer, she wheeled back into her room. She didn't do this particularly fast, but still I couldn't think of anything decently acerbic to say. I must be slipping. I read the rest of the pieces, with X looking over my shoulder. The slightly bad morning smell of him, like something gone off in the fridge, a yoghurt, was comforting to me – it was so familiar. I longed to climb into the smell and disappear, vaporised. I'd woken up to a different world, a harsher world – where people wouldn't believe anything I said. I was being passed back and forth across a million breakfast tables, with grease stains penetrating deeper and deeper. I knew that I would sell more books than ever before, but I hated to think what my newly acquired readers would be like – what their expectations of me would be. I think X wanted to say something along the lines of, 'It's not *so* bad,' but having read every word of the paper's coverage he decided that he probably couldn't get the words out sincerely enough.

'What do you think?' I asked.

'Well, you're famous now,' he said.

'Infamous, you mean.'

'I thought there wasn't a difference any more.'

Who is it?

Who is the 'source within the house'? I must find out – and get rid of them. Who is my enemy, and why are they doing this?

Ever since I saw the paper, I have been going through the candidates; the Definitely Nots, the Maybes and the Very Possibles.

Definitely Not:

X, just because; Henry, for similar reasons; Alan, he wouldn't, he couldn't; Edith, she's too young; Cecile, she wouldn't do something so vulgar as sell her story to a tabloid.

Maybe:

Simona? Can just, at a push, see this. But I can't see her wanting to risk the novel never coming out at all. She's put too much money into it. ~~She knows that if she betrayed me like this, I could never forgive her~~. Would she risk that? Surely not.

This remains to be seen.

William? He would never do anything contrary to Simona's wishes, so the arguments hold for him as for her.

Ingrid? To get back at me for Henry? I can't see her being this vindictive. She writes all those letters, though – what if they have been daily bulletins to Sheila Burrows?

Very Possibly:

The Maid. The fact she hasn't turned up for work today is very suspicious. She is the main suspect. But some of the details quoted in the report are about incidents the Maid wasn't present for – unless one of the guests has been telling her everything; which is what comes of trusting servants.

The Chef. Because he smirks so much. And because he hasn't turned up yet, either.

Fleur. Who may also have been the one telling everything to the Maid. Fleur has all the motives for revenge, but all the motives for forgiveness. And would she go about revenge in quite this way?

Marcia. I don't know her well enough to know what she's capable of. But she talks so much. The way she talked to the leathery local journalist.

The Country House Murder Plot has returned. Someone is trying to murder my career, by murdering my book.

9.30 a.m.

As soon as everyone is up (which given the banging and ringing is pretty early), I call a post-breakfast House Meeting.

We all of us sit down at the dining table, myself at the head. The guests settle without my having to bring them to order; they are very keen to hear what I have to say. (The Maid and Chef I shall have to speak to later – if they ever reappear.) I begin with: 'I suppose by now you've all seen today's *Mirror* newspaper?' It lay, soft as cloth, on the table in front of me. Everyone responds: Cecile looks grave, Edith giggles, Alan winces, most of the rest just nod neutrally. 'And you've heard the phone ringing, until we unplugged it. And you heard the doorbell ringing, before we disabled it.' My eyes pass over Marcia as I say the word *disabled* – damn! 'Well, then you'll know that everything has changed.'

'Again,' says William, aside.

'We are in the middle of a tabloid frenzy.' Edith grins at Alan, who frowns back. 'We can't go outside without being photographed. Do if you want to, I'm not keeping you in – but be aware that you'll probably end up like I did this morning.' Some smile, some smirk. 'Which, I can tell you, wasn't all that amusing to me. Anyway, I'd just like to say to the "source within the house", whoever they are, that I'm very disappointed. Perhaps some of you think this controversy is only what I –'

'Vic*tor*ia,' says Marcia, 'I think I speak for everyone in saying, "Shut up." You are no *longer* in sole charge of this house.'

I look around at the faces. 'Does she?' I ask. 'Does she speak for everyone?' Suddenly, it is as if they are sitting around a roulette wheel: all eyes watch it spin.

'I mean that in a nice way,' says Marcia.

'I think what Marcia is trying to say,' intervenes Simona, 'is that perhaps from now on House Meetings should be a little more democratic.'

'But they've always been democratic,' I say.

'What you want to know,' says William, 'is whether anyone is going to confess to ratting you out. Now, it's clear that they're not going to – or they would have already.'

'Is that true?' I say. I look particularly at my chief suspects: Marcia and Fleur; neither of them flinches.

'Victoria,' says Alan, 'why don't you just sit down and let other people talk, as they seem to want to?'

I don't take much notice of the rest of the meeting. I am head-buried in X's chest, sobbing as quietly as I can.

All morning the phone has been ringing; journalists, mainly Sheila Burrows. She asks whether I want to put 'my side of the story'.

What is this? Lesson One, Chapter One of 'Teach Yourself Journalism'?

I tell her quite firmly that my side of the story is going to be *my* hundred thousand word novel, not *her* piddly thousand word article.

She then begins asking about the book. What will it be called? When will it come out?

And I feel obliged to answer – which is exactly what she wants; but there's nothing one can do in these situations. One has been brought up to be polite, and journalists know and exploit this. They know that we've never – since adolescence – just put the phone down on somebody. They keep asking leading questions, always another and another. Eventually, I find a way to get off: 'Talk to my Agent,' I say. Then immediately I phone my Agent and say, 'Whatever you do, don't talk to Sheila Burrows of the *Mirror*.' ~~Maggie~~ My agent says fine, and asks how it is all going. Either she hasn't heard or she *has*, and is waiting to see what I think of it by how I bring it up. An old tactic of hers.

'Well,' I say, 'you know I was worrying that things weren't going to happen?'

Yes, says my Agent.

'Well,' I say, 'I needn't have worried.'

I explain; though she pretends dismay, she is delighted; and I still can't tell if she already knew or not.

Lunch. We picnic in the kitchen. Bread and cheese. Oranges.

The tabloid frenzy has affected the atmosphere in the house; which, after my coming down from the attic, had actually returned to something approximating if not to normal then at least to holiday.

The deckchairs in the garden were lined up, and people were always coming in and out to make drinks, hot or cold. There was gossip and littletalk of other sorts. The guests were feeling especially private – having ejected my eyes from their bedrooms. A new intimacy was being forged, from everybody having come through something together.

And now, disarray, imprisonment, mistrust.

Afternoon.

Henry, despite my precautions, manages to catch me alone in the drawing room. He seems dangerously excited. His hair is untidy.

'Don't worry,' he says. 'I'm not going to jump on you.'

'I'm glad about that.'

He loses some impetus, has to start again: 'Ingrid and I have decided to have another go.'

'Good,' I said. 'That's the right decision.'

'It's not that I don't have feelings for you.'

I looked around at the doors, sure someone was bound to come in. Where were they all?

'We've already talked about that,' I say.

'But Ingrid is still my wife.'

'I know that.'

'And that means something.'

'Yes,' I said. 'It does.'

'I still love her,' he said. I felt sorry for him. 'It's just not the same –'

'There isn't any hope, Henry. Don't expect anything from me.'

'I don't,' he said. 'That's why.'

Before I could extricate myself, he'd got me in a tight, misty hug. At which point, William strolls through from the hall.

'Interesting,' he says.

I've made a decision: from now on, I need to be informed about what's going on outside.

There's no point any longer in me pretending this is a pure Bloomsburyan paradise, unsullied by contemporary values. (Was there ever?) And so, I've phoned ~~Maggie~~ my agent up again and told her to arrange to have every paper delivered to us, every morning. Then I phoned ~~Sally~~ the publicist at the publishers, and asked her the same thing, just to make sure.

I am going to ask X to bring the television down from the daughter's room; then at least we can monitor what's happening in the world outside.

Since this morning, we have had all the curtains drawn at the front of the house; the slightest twitch of them gets cameras raised. I think there are now about ten film crews out there, and twenty *paparazzi*. I have no idea what they think they're going to get.

We are still able to sit in the back garden, on the verandah, I think; the gate is closed and locked; the walls are so high, no-one has yet managed to find a vantage point from which to spy upon us there. It's too far from the beach for them to set up on the dunes; they wouldn't get any decent shots. So at least everyone in the house is still getting some sun.

Rebellion is simmering, however. I know what they're thinking:

if it hadn't been for the cameras, and me watching a couple of them having sex, none of this would have happened. They know what's likely to happen from now on, and I don't think one of them is looking forward to it. We are about to enter a parallel universe, that of minor, summer celebrity.

Say it simply: I was in the kitchen, William was there, too.

I thought of mentioning, explaining the Henry-hug, but decided that might make it seem even more *interesting*.

William had some cigarettes and I asked to borrow one. 'I'll send you a whole carton when I get home,' I said.

'You do that,' he said.

The warning on the pack SMOKING CAUSES CANCER halted my reaching fingers. I took one anyway. But after I had thanked William for lighting me up, I said, for want of anything better, 'Doesn't it ever worry you?'

He looked baffled.

'The warnings,' I said. 'Cancer.'

'Oh,' he replied, 'it's a bit too late for that.'

'You think you're too old to give up, now?'

He turned towards me and said, straight as you like, 'No, I have cancer already.'

'What? Where?' I said. 'I mean, what kind of cancer?'

'Well,' he said, turning to the window as if to check, 'I think by now it's cancer of the just about everywhere. But it started, they say, in my lungs.'

'I'm so sorry. Why didn't you tell me?'

At last you see it.

'Because I didn't want to.' He smiled, friendlier and more father-like than ever before. ~~His dyingness gave him, in his view, a maturity above my own. True.~~ Don't overdo it, though.

'And so why tell me now?'

'It came up, didn't it? Naturally. In conversation.' He took a long drag.

I swore, hesitated, went to bite a nail, took a long drag. 'Do you mind talking about it?'

'It isn't my *favourite* subject. I try to avoid it if I can.'

(Don't think I didn't think he might be lying. I was suspicious of another performance, for my benefit, for my humiliation.)

'Have they given you any idea...'

'You mean doctors?'

I nodded, smoked.

'Doctors,' he said, and let his cigarette doodle greyly the air. 'Doctors...' His hesitation conveyed a thousand wry and pointless obscenities.

'I shouldn't have asked,' I said.

'"Months rather than years."'

We spent a good half-minute in silence.

'Then why did you agree to come along to this?'

'I thought it might be interesting – a more intense bit of life than just sitting at home. I was right. It has been.'

'Don't you want to travel?'

'I've travelled. No, I just want to live longer, that's all. Travelling wouldn't do any good.' Without bitterness, he stubbed out his butt. 'I'd hate to think I made you give up,' he said, nodding at my cigarette. 'Being an object-lesson to nonsmokers is probably one of the reasons I don't tell people. I wish I'd lived to ninety and smoked ninety a day. But I'm not going to manage that.'

With a smile, he left the kitchen. And for the first time, I *liked* him: I liked him to his departing back. I don't know if he felt it. I don't know if people *do* feel things like that; that the people you're leaving behind will miss you when you're gone.

Then I remembered him flashing at me. Perhaps, in a perverted way, he was trying to tell me then – expose himself completely; or perhaps it was just an added freedom that he now felt able to take. He wasn't going to be punished.

It surprises me that more crimes aren't committed by the termi-

~~nally ill: bank raids by AIDS cases; suicide bombers with MS. Death makes one value life, perhaps – something as Sunday School banal as that.~~ Very profound. Very cut.

I hadn't seen Alan and Fleur all afternoon. Rumour has it they spent a long while in her room, talking. (In this case, Rumour was Marcia – once again speaking to me.) They continued their conversation over dinner. Quite a few of the other guests are delighted by this sly little romance; even if it does confirm my Synopsis.

Chef had bought tuna steaks, which Ingrid was happy to griddle. Salad. Fruit salad.

At the table both William and Henry were as they usually are, the one surly, the other mild. Ingrid seemed more vivacious, but that may be false. Edith is enjoying the siege – spying on the journalists through a slit in the curtains. Marcia, too, has been teasing them with glimpses into her bedroom.

Late evening.

Told X about the Tetris addiction, and he told me the obvious thing to do: delete the programme entirely. I said I didn't think I could go through with it; too much pain, loss.

He said, 'Give it here,' and it was all over very swiftly. 'Are you sure it's gone?' I said, when he handed the laptop back. 'Yes,' he said. I wept, mostly out of relief. I have a little more of my life back.

Sex with X.

I hadn't exactly forgotten how good it was, but my memories weren't anywhere near as satisfying as the real thing.

Why have we not been having sex? What a waste.

We love each other: I told him that, he told me it back.

Wednesday

Day Twenty-one Week Three

10 a.m. Can hardly bear to get up and face the day, the papers. The articles in the *Mirror* continue to quote 'a source inside the house'. I'm convinced it's Fleur or Marcia, or Fleur and Marcia together. My other suspect, The Maid, again didn't turn up to work; and neither did Chef – we shall have to continue fending. A quick check reveals cupboard's bare – no bread, milk almost gone. Bugger.

A publicity girl from the publishers.

~~Sally~~ called Simona. She wanted to let Simona (and via her, me) know how *delighted* they are with the coverage we are getting for the book. She has been on to some of the broadsheets, to see if they are interested in doing profiles, interviews, etc. The response has been fantastic, she said. We could sell my story six times over. And there is already huge interest in serialisation.

Notes on being doorstepped. TV cameras like black-painted tanks, turned sideways, on stilts – with shiny lenses stuck on the front (war tanks, not water tanks); or maybe not stilts: on Victorian box-camera old-fashioned tripods. Three legs or four? Count them next time I get a look. Lights – when on – like bright lights always are: like permanently burning distress flares, going woozy as your eyes start to water in them.

The journalists – dull clothes; brown, blue and gray; warm for night. They all smoke; they all listen to the BBC news, on the hour; they all, now and again, stop talking on their mobiles; they are very few of them slim. Occasionally they laugh harder at a joke than it really merits; laugh sadistically against the unfunniness of most of what they've seen – which is terror, distress and the outside of not-particularly-interesting buildings.

Now and again I get to feeling almost sorry for them – want to take them out tea & biscuits; be a good sport – make them love me. *Then* I remember a choice quote or two from today's papers, and make the effort to connect that with them – 'Big Sister Victoria, 32, author of raunchy sex-comedy *Incredibly Well-Hung...*' That done, my heart cools faster than imaginary tea.

The reaction in the house to all this media attention has been mixed: some swear they saw it coming, others are dismayed. For myself, I don't know quite what to think. Obviously, it will be good for the book – but that's a long way off; and I shall have to write it differently, as a result. The public will already know *what* happened, and so they'll want to know *how* it happened. I think I can handle that, as an adjustment; it is a bit bloody annoying, though. And do I really want to do it?

Quiet morning.

We need to organise to entertain ourselves, as if this were the Blitz and we were sheltering in the underground. We can't just sleep, chat, ~~fart~~ and sing; we must struggle against the darkness and the rats. But if I call a House Meeting, they'll say I'm trying to play dictator again. I don't think I can face that.

A strange moment with Ingrid.

We meet one another on the staircase; she on the way down, me on the way up. And for just the merest hint of a second, she stands in the middle and won't let me pass.

When I try to look in her eyes, read her meaning, she has already stepped to the side, and is pretending nothing happened.

Ever since the cat-ghost incident, Audrey has been quietly following me around. She likes to be with me whenever she can, all day long. I'm sure if Fleur and I were at opposite ends of a room together, and both called Audrey to us – I'm sure, in her present mood of devotion, she would come to me. Cats are such hurtful creatures, so fickle; which is why the melt of their disdain is so thrilling. Audrey really does have awful restraint: she brings Fleur over the course of days to the glassy point of tears (by ignoring her, by being absent) and *then* she devastates her with a lap-leap, a cheek-lick. All cats are expert sadists; Fleur has found her perfect 'top' in Audrey. And now, because I right from the start disdained her, Audrey is trying to bring me round, charm me – so that one day I too shall be in her awesome, sharp-clawed thrall. (This is very amusing. X is starting to joke that Audrey is a lesbian-cat, and is besotted with me. Audrey has nothing to do with him, and never will: she thinks him common, which makes me at moments think him so, too.) Trouble is, I'm falling for it, falling for her. In fact, I have caught myself once or twice coveting her. Shooing is becoming a pain of a different sort than before; it has changed from an annoyance to a stab. When I look in her eyes, I see my feline dominatrix looking back – coming to power, ready to scratch.

11.55 a.m. Just when it seemed too late, Cecile and I finally start to get on in the way I hoped we would. She caught me in the upstairs corridor. Exquisitely, she made it clear she'd like a talk in private; even now, I don't know quite how she conveyed this to me: a dip of the head, almost a nod? I turned back into the Master Bedroom, from whence I'd a moment before emerged. Cecile couldn't possibly have been waiting for me, could she? As if in apology, she was wearing an outfit I remembered from Day Three or Four – artist's smock and plain blue trousers. We sat side by side on the counterpane.

'Victoria, I want to apologise,' she said. 'I don't think I should have agreed to come.'

'Oh, Cecile, no –'

'Please,' she said, 'I have something...' But she faltered, started again. 'This is a beautiful house, but I can't see that it's beautiful. To me, it seems ugly and...' I knew the word she was going to use next, 'vulgar. This house makes people do ugly, vulgar things.' I wondered which people in particular she was referring to, and which things; there aren't exactly a shortage. 'What you wanted from me, Victoria, I couldn't give it – not under these circumstances.' A glance to the attic, a smile. 'I feel changed, upset. You have affected my life deeply. It is not a simple matter of... betrayal. I want you to see that. I want you to *know* that.'

'I'm sorry,' I said, and for a moment Cecile seemed to misunderstand me.

'Yes, I think you *should* be sorry. People cannot be forced together – or perhaps they can, but it will alter what happens to them afterwards. Even if they stay together, they will be weaker. Grafted. Hothouse.' Her fingers were in her lap, interlaced and pointing upwards – twitching like hungry fledglings in a nest. 'I hope that, when we come to the conclusion of this, we can try to be unforced friends. Please, whatever happens, remember that I said this.'

I decided to try asking the question – *one* of the questions: 'I know about Cornwall.'

On the instant, Cecile hardened. 'What do you know about Cornwall?'

'Through the camera,' I said, 'I saw the map on your wall.'

She seemed relieved but did not speak.

'Was it something very terrible?' I asked.

Cecile smiled at me, fondly. 'If we are still friends at Christmas, I will tell you. But you must not ask again. You should not have asked at all.' She stood gracefully up.

'Thank you,' I said.

'Oh no,' she said. 'That is for later, if ever.'

Lunch. Tinned tomato soup, cheese and biscuits. A few apples, halved, shared. Food is already running out. We have about enough for the rest of today.

Simona and I have a talk, in the parlour.

'William told me,' I say.

'He must like you, then.'

'I'm very sorry to hear –'

'You don't like him very much though, do you?'

'I got him wrong.'

'You did,' she says.

We wait for another subject to occur to us. One does, to me: 'Henry stole the Synopsis. He confessed, almost immediately.'

'Oh,' says Simona, 'and why are you telling me now?'

'To put your mind at rest.'

'~~It was at rest~~,' she says. 'I'd guessed it was him.'

'How?' I say.

'He had the best reason.'

'Which was?'

'You.'

'Oh dear. I thought he'd been quite self-controlled.'

'I could see it. He loves you, doesn't he?'

'He's trying again with Ingrid.'

'I'll take that as a yes.'

'Why did you read out the Synopsis? Why did you let the guests even know it existed?'

'I thought it would be more fun, that way. It gave them something to think about – rather than leaving.'

~~'But it meant things stood no chance of happening the way I'd predicted.'~~

'~~I don't think they ever did~~.'

~~'Perhaps not,' I say.~~

~~'That was the point, wasn't it?'~~

~~'You and William,' I say, 'you were never going to split up, were you?~~'

'~~No, no~~.'

~~'You were putting on an act, right from the start.'~~

~~'Not entirely.'~~

~~'But I suppose it's up to me to pick out the bits which were honest.'~~

~~'It was all honest. But it's up to you to pick out the bits which weren't acted.'~~

~~'Any hints~~?'

~~'No.'~~

I enjoyed this scene.

Early afternoon.

The committed smokers (William, Simona and Alan, but also X, Marcia and Fleur) came to a decision: they hadn't yet run out of cigarettes, but they were getting close. A raid on Southwold was planned. They will get food, too. I came in about halfway, Marcia having found me in the parlour and asked whether I wanted anything myself. They were in the drawing room, all hugger-mugger on the sofas – a defiant fug surrounding them. It had been decided, before I arrived, that Henry and Ingrid's was the car to use: faster and more manoeuvrable than the others. Henry had been nominated as driver. At the point I joined the discussion, William was making it plain how keen he was to be involved. 'I don't mind having my picture in the papers.'

'You can wear a hat,' said Fleur.

'Why bother?' said William. 'I want everyone to see it's me, don't I?'

'Do you?' asked Alan.

'Oh he definitely does,' said Simona, and I think I understood why.

They debated whether anyone else needed to go, too; they decided nothing would be gained by it.

'How about if I create a distraction, while you're sneaking out?' I asked, keen to be part of this.

'What exactly?' said Simona. She was looking at me as if I'd suggested I might do a streak for the paparazzi.

'I don't know,' I said. 'I could give a press conference.'

'Doesn't that defeat the object?' asked Alan. 'We're meant to be doing this as inconspicuously as possible.'

'Victoria, that's a brilliant idea,' said Simona. 'But it's a little elaborate for now, I think. We need some time to decide how you're going to present yourself, what you're going to say.'

'I just want to make a dash for it,' said William. 'That's half the fun.'

'Let's go,' said Henry.

We all went excitedly through into the hall.

'I'll unlock the door,' said Simona. 'You hide out of sight.'

William and Henry stood, ready to go, while the rest of us shuffled into the front parlour.

William nodded. 'Now!' said Henry, and out they went. Through the parlour curtains, we watched them stride towards the car. Surprised by this sudden eruption, the photographers took a moment to start clicking. The reporters were faster – shouting out questions, which William and Henry ignored as they got into the front seats. Henry started the engine, revved it aggressively a couple of times and then shot the car forwards. The photographers were leaning in towards the windscreen, to get close-ups. Henry drove straight through them, clipping one with his right wing-mirror. We, the watchers, gave a small cheer. The car roared down the drive, spewing gravel to either side. Several of the photographers got onto motorbikes and took off after them; enough remained behind to keep us trapped in the house.

We went back into the drawing room, to await William and Henry's triumphant return.

4 p.m. Still waiting for them to come back.

Did Henry do this to impress me or Ingrid or both of us?

Simona didn't appear for Confession; nobody else did, either.

Oh dear, the irony.

The spy-cameras have been off for a week, and yet I've just done my most glorious piece of eavesdropping. It was so simple – I was sitting in the Master Bedroom, looking through the open window towards the sea; Alan and Fleur came out onto the verandah, sat down on the steps, and started having an intimate conversation. This time, I'm almost certain, it wasn't faked up for my benefit. Ever since the days of Attic, I've been wary of spending too much time out of sight. But I needed a quiet while alone, so sought it upstairs.

'We weren't too young,' said Alan, continuing what they'd been saying inside.

'I think it was more that we were too old,' said Fleur, 'or liked to think so.'

'You mean bachelor and spinster, both a bit disgruntled to have been disturbed in our misery.'

'Yes, and damn you if I'm going to upset my lovely cat just for a bit of hanky-panky.'

'Did you really feel that?'

'Audrey is a very aristocratic animal – you and your visits, with Domino at your side, were quite putting her off her food.'

'I'm sorry.'

'Not at all. She shouldn't have been so precious, and I especially shouldn't have let her get so precious. I knew, in the end, they'd get used to each other. It was us I wasn't so sure about.'

'They're a funny pair,' said Alan.

'Not half so funny as us,' said Fleur.

'I'm glad we're a pair.'

'Oh, so am I.'

They kissed, I think. I didn't look – couldn't bear to.

'I do so hope it works this time,' said Fleur.

'What can we do to help make it?'

'Do you know,' said Fleur, 'I've got absolutely no idea whatsoever – except, I shall have to try and stop being so mad...'

'And I shall have to stop sulking.'

'I'm sorry for telling you off about that –'

'No, it's quite alright. It's true. That's not the way to go about things. From now on, I'm going to argue right back. If you're not careful, I might even start slapping you around.'

And my sister laughed.

(They're so relaxed together. They *must* have had sex. But when?)

5 p.m. No sign of Henry and William. Ingrid tries to call Henry on his mobile, but it's turned off; Simona does the same with William, ditto. Perhaps they've fled back to London; or, more likely, they are in the pub. With journalists?

Small chat with Edith, in the hall.

I ask her how things are with Elizabeth; she is very unsupernatural in her reply. It's a holiday friendship between girls.

I try to tell her about my encounter on the landing, but she isn't interested. 'You're worried about your father, aren't you?' I say.

'He'll be okay. He's always okay.'

I think that's it, and am turning away, when Edith says, 'Your sister's very intense, isn't she?'

'Oh, yes,' I say. 'Why?'

'She looks at me in a strange way. Like she thinks I'm ill.'

'She thinks most people are... lacking.'

'It's just, I wish she wouldn't.'

'I'm sorry. That's just how she is.'

6 p.m. Edith was right: Henry was okay. He came back, but on his own. William has been arrested for assault on one of the photographers. He is in a police cell. Henry looked dangerously pale, surrounded by plastic shopping bags. We gave him a drink. The story came out. Getting to the shop was easy. Parking wasn't a problem. But the photographers caught up. Followed them into the shop. William went through the shopping list, filling a dozen or so shopping bags with food, alcohol, cigarettes and tobacco. When they got outside, they found the car parked in – two motorbikes, one at the front, one the back. William asked them to move; they didn't; kept taking photographs. William got annoyed; Henry tried to calm him down. 'It was a set-up,' said Henry, distraught. Ingrid had her arm round him. 'One of the photographers got him riled up, another called the police.' William, he said, dropped the bags, the contents spilled. The photographer stepped on a packet of Simona's brand of cigarettes. William started to push the photographer. He wanted him to go back into the shop, buy some replacements. Other photographers were getting all this on film. 'Then,' Henry said, 'he just said, "Bollocks to this," and punched the photographer in the guts. The guy dropped to the floor. There were lots of witnesses. Cameras flashed. The police arrived a couple of seconds later. They arrested William straight away. I've been at the station, trying to persuade them to let him out.'

Simona very weepy. Wanted to go and rescue William. Henry said there wasn't anything more to be done. The police were set on keeping William in overnight; show him what's what. Simona got more details from him. He had a card with the station's number on. She called, and spoke to them; then spoke to her solicitor in London; then to another local solicitor. They went to the police station, on her behalf. Called back about an hour later. William was to be kept in all night. Simona inconsolable. 'He's ill,' she said. 'Don't they understand? He's ill.'

We have a sombre meal: mushroom risotto, followed by cake.

Lots of defiant smoking afterwards. Henry had brought all the shopping bags back; they weren't needed by the police as evidence.

End of the third week. Thank God.

Thursday

Day Twenty-two Week Four

Woke up very very early. Fell back to sleep. Slept through the dawn chorus. Got up. Looked through the narrowest curtain slit: odd to see the lawn, glassy wet with dew; odd to see the sky so colourless. Put on a jumper, feeling everything in the house drawing to a close; feeling my period about to start – insides very sorry for themselves. When Virginia's period comes, she always writes in her diary: 'Owing to the usual circumstances, I had to spend the day recumbent.' God, how I wish I could spend the day recumbent. Took painkiller, had shower. I miss Tetris. In last night's dream I was a skeleton, upright and underwater, suddenly let go, all my interconnections failing, bones falling, drifting apart, spreading out into the black blue, picked at by fast and brightly coloured fish.

Morning. Oh, I have decided to change the title of the book. *From the Lighthouse* now seems too pretentious – as if I could compete with Virginia. I'm settling with *Finding Myself*; which has probably been used 100 times before, by self-help gurus, but originality isn't any longer the issue, honesty is – if that isn't too too pretentious.

P.B.B., my darling.

9.30 a.m. William returns. Great relief. Messy hair and crumpled clothes, grey stubble on his chin – seems perfectly well: the Hero of the House. (Thinking back, so many have occupied this position: Marcia, Fleur, Edith... even me, for a moment.)

His violent exploits of yesterday have brought us more tabloid coverage; some in the broadsheets, too. Today we find in-depth profiles of every single person in the house (although, as one might have predicted, they seem to have less on Cecile than any of the other adults – no dirt there); we are being introduced to the general public, our characters delineated – all unflattering, apart from Edith, who is a child therefore a victim. Out of everyone, I come off worst: I am the archmanipulator; the spy in the house of love. When one reads this kind of gutter journalism, one can't help but say, in one's head, *No, you've got me entirely wrong, let me explain who I am and what I really did and said and thought and felt.* I expect this is what stars feel all the time; and they learn to cope with it, somehow or other – probably by going down into the dungeon and counting their gold for a couple of hours; those of us with no gold, and an attic instead of a dungeon, shall have to find another way. Soon enough, the papers will tire of us.

Mid-morning.

I decided, in consultation with Simona and Sally, that it was time to issue a statement. (Personally, I'd thought a press conference in the front garden just the thing, but Simona dissuaded me: too unpredictable.)

I spent fifteen minutes drafting one, then let the two professionals tweak it into a final shape. It reads:

> Following the controversy over the 'Big Sister' house, Victoria About would like to issue the following statement. 'I did not force anyone to take part in this project. All the guests knew the basis on which they had been invited to the house; all the guests were given a contract to sign. In the contract it was made plain that they were in the House for one reason only: to be watched. It was also made clear to them that their actions would be very closely scrutinized. The fact that some technological means were used in order to pursue this end is, really,

> beside the point. It should be pointed out, in the face of much criticism, that since the "revelations" in the press *none* of the guests has expressed any desire to leave the house. In other words, everyone here is here of their own free will. Publication of *From the Lighthouse*, Victoria About's novel inspired by the project, will take place, as planned, in the Summer of next year. Thank you.

I decided not to complicate matters by telling Simona the title had changed to *Finding Myself*. It's easier to do that if and when I deliver it.

Lunch.

Alan and Fleur are now the happy couple all over the house; she is changed entirely – they both are: Alan is no longer to be found standing, staring; Fleur has decided to forgive me every bad thing I've ever done (for bringing the two of them back together). At dinner last night they shamefacedly asked if they could sit beside one another, and Marcia gladly swapped places with Alan. This was greeted with warmly sarcastic applause. 'At last,' sighed Edith, with all the world-weariness of eleven-and-a-half. Alan and Fleur publicly kissed – just a quick lip-peck. It's nice to see that at least one part of my Synopsis was accurate.

At two o'clock this afternoon there began a persistent thumping on the front door. Marcia was in her room, painting her toenails purple. She would have ignored the noise, as we've all ignored the various doorstepping techniques of the journalists, had it not been for the shouting. At first she paid little attention; then she caught a few words: 'in' – 'house' – 'ours' – 'can't' – 'come on!' – 'police'. She squinted out though a small gap in the curtains, and saw two people there who didn't look like journalists; for one thing, they were too old, for another, they were semi-circled by suitcases.

Without waiting for her nails to dry (she had only one foot

done), Marcia swung herself into her wheelchair and came to find me. This wasn't hard; I was in the drawing room, washing the French windows. 'Victoria,' she said.

I hardly looked up. 'Hmm,' I said.

'Victoria, I think you should answer the door.'

'Why?' I said.

Marcia explained.

'But it can't be,' I said. 'They're not due back until the end of next week.' I ran through into Marcia's room. She had been right to call me: it *was* the Owners.

I checked myself in the hall mirror, then opened the door. 'How delightful,' I said. 'Did you –'

'Don't come the soft soap with me,' Mr ~~Johnson~~ said. 'We want you out of here, *now*.'

we shall have to give him, them, another name. Any ideas? Jones, or is that too similar? I'll ask the lawyers.

The journalists were listening; the photographers, taking pictures. Some of the guests had assembled behind me – the opening of the front door forming somewhat of an event these days.

'Please come in,' I said. 'We can talk about this inside.'

'I don't need you to invite me into my own house,' Mr ~~Johnson~~ said.

'Please,' I said. He picked a couple of the larger suitcases up, lugged them into the hall. His wife barged in, without carrying a thing.

X, bless him, went out and grabbed two more cases; Alan helped with the beach bag and a cardboard box.

Once everything was in the hall, I closed the door upon the furore of questions; without a pause, Mr ~~Johnson~~ began: 'It's this simple – we've heard what you've been doing in this house, and frankly we're disgusted by it. We feel that, because of this, you are in breach of the contract we signed – in breach over several clauses, and we would therefore like you to move out forthwith.'

'That's impossible,' I said. 'We're staying here until next Wednesday. We're far from finished.'

'Oh yes you are,' he said. 'You have caused material damage to the fabric of the house.'

'I have not.'

'You've put cameras up in the bedrooms, for Christ's sake!' He was shouting. His wife, beside him, showed her anger and agreement by alternately blanching and flushing.

'Come and see,' I said, pointing the way into Marcia's room. 'If you squashed a fly against the wall, it would leave a bigger splat.'

All the guests had by now come to the end of the hall.

'You've used this house for illegal and immoral activities,' Mr ~~Johnson~~ said.

'Such as?'

'Spying.'

'All these people,' I said, 'signed contracts saying I could observe them. They weren't too happy about the cameras, so I turned them off.'

'They kept you in the attic.'

'Oh,' I said, 'so you've read the papers.'

'Of course we've read the ~~fucking~~ papers – that's what brought us back here. All our friends have been calling us up, ever since Tuesday. We didn't need to *read* the papers: they were only too eager to read them *to* us, down the phone. But, yes, we know exactly what you've been up to.'

'No, you don't,' I said.

'Are you Elizabeth's mother?' asked Edith, walking up to Mrs ~~Johnson~~. This came so suddenly, and so out of context, that she simply answered before thinking, 'Yes, I am.'

'I'm Edith,' Edith said. 'And you're Elizabeth's father. I spoke to you on the phone. You do remember, don't you?'

'Ingrid,' I said, 'could you please take Edith away?'

Ingrid stepped forward, about to comply.

'Please don't throw us out,' said Edith, 'we all love it here so much – and we haven't hurt the house; and if we have, we'll mend it or pay for it.'

'Would you like to go into the front parlour?' I asked. 'We can talk privately there.'

'I'm not going to be persuaded,' Mr ~~Johnson~~ said.

'Hello,' said Simona. 'I'm not sure you remember me: Victoria's editor, Simona Princip.'

'Oh, hello,' said Mr ~~Johnson~~, for the first time slowing down. Simona scared him, or at least impressed him – I'd seen this before, when we were negotiating the lease.

'Victoria,' Simona said, 'why don't you let me and Mr and Mrs ~~Johnson~~ discuss this quietly by ourselves.' She turned to the Owner: 'I promise, Victoria will abide by whatever I recommend.'

'Will I?' I said.

'You will,' Simona said, steely, 'because it's either that or we all start packing our bags – right now.'

Mr ~~Johnson~~ liked seeing me spoken to with this disrespect; Simona was already getting a response out of him.

'We can't leave yet,' I said. 'I haven't got an ending.'

'I'm no author,' said Mr ~~Johnson~~, 'but this seems a pretty damn good ending to me.'

'You look just like her,' said Edith to Mrs ~~Johnson~~.

'Ingrid!' I said.

'Shall we?' said Simona, and went into the parlour. Mr ~~Johnson~~ followed her, then looked back for his wife. For the second time, she spoke: 'Darling, I'm going to have a word with Edith. If you're going to chuck them out, this may be our only chance.'

'Please,' he said.

'No,' she replied.

'Come on,' said Edith, and led Mrs ~~Johnson~~ off by the hand to the daughter's bedroom.

As I moved towards it, reluctant to cede all power to Simona, the parlour door shut, firmly.

I turned to X. 'What do I do?' I said.

'Let Simona deal with it,' he said. 'I'm sure she doesn't want us turfed out early.'

'But what if this is the ending?' I said.

'You'll make something out of it, I'm sure.'

Half an hour later, Simona and Mr ~~Johnson~~ came together into the drawing room. Apart from Edith and Mrs ~~Johnson~~, who were still upstairs, they had the whole house as audience.

'The agreement is this,' said Mr ~~Johnson~~, he paused, partly for effect, I think, and partly because he hated what he was about to say. 'You can stay – but only until Sunday; you're all out of here by Sunday evening, and that includes the cameras, microphones and whatever other equipment you've had installed.'

'Agreed,' said Simona, looking at me, and without even the hint of a question mark.

'I need a moment to think,' I said.

'No, you don't,' said the Owner, 'You either accept or you leave now.'

'X, come with me,' I said. I took his hand and led him out through the half-finished French doors. A few steps onto the lawn, I asked him: 'What do you think?'

'I think you don't have very much choice. What else do you think's going to happen in those extra couple of days? We're all stuck inside as it is.'

'Anything could happen,' I said. 'Anything's already happened several times over.'

'Then why can't you be content with that?' he said. 'Simona has just done a very good deal for you. He came in here intending to chuck you straight out. I'm sure he was really looking forward to calling the police.'

We weren't really discussing the agreement: I wanted X to know that he was with me again, that his was the only opinion of which I took note.

'Give me a kiss,' I said. He obliged, though it was hardly passionate.

Holding hands, we went back into the drawing room.

'Agreed,' I said, without bothering to insert a dramatic pause.

Simona made Mr ~~Johnson~~ and I shake hands. She then explained that the Owners were being put up at the Swan, the best hotel in Southwold, over the weekend, at *my* expense. I couldn't believe I'd been tricked like that. 'No,' I said.

'Don't worry,' said Simona, 'you won't actually have to *pay*, we'll just set it against royalties. But the deal is this: they stay at the Swan, eat at the Crown.'

Mr ~~Johnson~~ smiled at me, evilly. I could tell he was already thinking of the devastation he could inflict on the mini-bar, the sumptuous towels he would be bringing home.

In the silence of my outrage, X offered to phone for a taxi.

'I'd better just go and see how ~~Shirley's~~ getting on,' Mr ~~Johnson~~ said. 'I think she went upstairs, didn't she?'

It was another half an hour before the Owners, and Edith, walked into the drawing room.

What she had said to them, I have no idea – if there is a single scene I most regret having missed with the cameras, it's this one – but they looked completely exhausted, bewildered, devastated. 'You can call a taxi for us now,' said Mr ~~Johnson~~.

They went and sat at the kitchen table, holding hands, not speaking.

The taxi arrived ten minutes later. William and Alan carried the luggage out again. Edith saw the Owners off, quite as if she and not they were in possession of the house. They answered her, quietly.

The guests returned to the drawing room, and I fell into

uncontrollable hysterics: I laughed until I cried until I laughed until laughing started to hurt and I cried so as to make myself stop.

'What did you say to him?' X asked Simona.

'Ah...' she said, but said nothing more.

Just now came upon Ingrid and Fleur in the parlour. Their faces as they talked, from the glimpse I caught as I entered, were serious and closed; lemon-lipped. The only words I heard was 'Edie must', from Ingrid. It was clear they didn't want to be interrupted. They waited out my departure, although I delayed it as long as I comically could. What can they be up to?

5 p.m. Someone, I think, has been hacking my laptop. How can I tell? Well, because each document has a time and date for when it last was changed; and the document for Day Twenty-two Week Four (Today) was changed at 4.37 p.m. this afternoon – just when I was sitting down with Simona for another of our confessions. (We had little to say. I complained about the deal she struck with Mr ~~Johnson~~. She said I should be glad we didn't have to move out immediately. *Impasse.*) The laptop was in the Master Bedroom; the door was locked; there are only two keys; that leaves only one possible suspect: X. Of course, now I'm remembering a few details from the past weeks. He must have been hacking before; that was how I came to lose Day Twelve – he deleted it by mistake. I'm also remembering again what Alan told me that time we were very drunk, on one of those early nights: about the locked door, and the squeak of the attic ladder. During the ghost-craze, I thought it was the ghost, but of course it couldn't have been, could it? No, it was someone up in the attic. It was X. Otherwise, if it had been someone else, they would have told the others about the spy-cameras; they were all so shocked to find out, later. He was the only person, apart from Simona, and I suppose William, to know there was something interesting going on up there. But although Simona knew, she had

no way of getting in there – no key. It must be X. I am shocked, bemused, almost unable to write coherently. My final trustful one has betrayed me. First thing he did, X probably wordsearching his way through the text – finding himself again and again. What did he find? Of course, I'm thinking of the very worst things he might have discovered about me: that I wanted to get him to ask me to marry him, and that I intended to do this by making him jealous about Henry, and that I was prepared to go quite a long way – all the way – to make him jealous. He'd hate to be thought of as a stooge. Hopefully, he'll also have read about the wondrous sex, and the way he makes me feel when we're together. As far as I can see, he hasn't made any alterations: the text still finishes on the same page it did when I left it just before confession. ~~Only if he's inserted an exact amount of different text, which I'm unable to waste time now trying to find. I don't think that's the kind of thing he'd do~~: ~~because that would definitely alter the date on the document. Bu~~t ~~maybe after he knew for certain he'd done that by mistake anywa~~y, he~~'d have made some changes just to take advantage of his cock-up~~. Confrontation is one response; sly spying is another; forget it, the impossible third. I shall have to calm myself down a good deal before I see him...

not necessary.

Interrupted Fleur, talking on a mobile at the bottom of the garden. (Whose mobile? She doesn't have one.) As soon as she sees me, she says, 'I'll call you back later.'

Who? A journalist?

She rushes off towards the house before I can ask. Very suspicious.

Despite William and Henry's supermarket run yesterday, there isn't that much food in the house (who let *them* make the shopping list?); no-one feels like cooking, so we decide instead that we shall order a half-dozen thin-crust pizzas.

I myself am particularly looking forward to a pepperoni and chilli combo. But after discovering that the nearest pizzeria is Lowestoft, we have to reassess. Under the circumstances, curry is the best we can do.

Simona helps me gather people's orders. Alan is the only one to require a vindaloo, everyone else goes for mild flavours.

I phone, and tell the delivery boy to ring three times – to show it is them and not journalists. Simona smiles; it is a bit mad.

X goes and reconnects the doorbell.

The curry arrives; we eat it – what more is there to say?

8.30 p.m. exactly, and there came a honk-honk-honk outside on the drive from a car that must very quietly have arrived. Around the table, we all looked at one another, mildly puzzled, half-expecting it to be another journalistic trick.

'Is anybody expecting?' I asked. Most were shaking their heads, but two were drawing back their chairs: Cecile and Alan. I missed it but X said later that he'd definitely seen a nod pass back and forth between them; Marcia was able to confirm, on my asking, that it originated from Cecile. The two of them stood up. 'Excuse me a moment,' said Alan, and went out the door.

'Well, everybody,' said Cecile, 'it has been delightful to meet you, those I haven't met before, and spend time with you, those I have. These three weeks have been so rich and lovely in so many different and unexpected ways.' She looked at Edith, whose eyes had gone sparkly with tears. 'Yes, my dear,' Cecile said, touching her small friend's cheek, 'I *am* saying goodbye.' I wanted to interrupt, in shock, but I also wanted to see what else she was going to say. 'I don't think I can stay any longer. There's something else I need to go and do. Victoria,' she said, and I was aware of not only her gaze but the whole table's, 'if you hadn't spied upon us, I wouldn't even have considered this.' The honk-honk-honk came again. 'But that was reason enough, even had they not offered me other reasons; quite a few thousand other reasons.'

'What?' I said, not yet realising she meant money.

'That's a car from the newspaper,' said Cecile, 'or at least I very much hope it is – if not we're going to have to spend a very embarrassing few minutes waiting for them to arrive.' I stood up.

'How could you?' I asked, pleaded.

'Very easily,' said Cecile, 'as it turned out. I had something they needed, information; they had something I needed, money.'

I was bewildered; I didn't know which argument I might try to make her stay: I was appalled by the possibility *none* of my arguments would work. 'Is it just that they're paying you?' I said, in my hardest voice.

'No,' said Cecile, 'in itself, that wasn't enough. But you intruded, unforgivably, into my privacy. And that's why this is...' Alan reappeared in the doorway, Cecile's suitcases, none of their mystery explained, in his hands – his shoulders apparently unstooped by their weight. It must all be in there, somehow, I thought: the clothes, the map. 'Goodbye,' said Cecile, her eyes circling the table, 'I hope to see you again. But Victoria,' she said, her eyes coming to rest upon mine, 'I think it will be a very long time before we are able to meet.' She turned to Alan. 'Thank you,' she said. As she moved towards him, he backed through the doorway.

I went to follow them; they were out the front door; the others followed me. 'Cecile,' I said. She did turn round, I'll give her that. I cried out in desperation: 'What does Cornwall mean?'

I could see Sheila, in the driver's seat, her face made ghastly (ghastlier) by the red and yellow light of the dashboard: like a stage devil in the Damnation of Faust.

Alan opened the boot and hefted the suitcase inside – the suitcase that still contained all the mysteries of Cecile's femininity; a suitcase that I would now never see packed or unpacked.

Cecile came towards me; kissed me on one cheek; the other; whispered in my ear, 'Cornwall means goodbye, Victoria.'

And with that, she turned and got into the passenger seat of the car – the door to which had already been opened by Alan. Now he closed it; now, the engine started; now, X was at my side; now, we watched them turn from bright headlight white to rich red, then specks of red, then thoughts of specks. 'What did I do?' I asked.

'Let's talk about it later,' he said.

'What good will that do?' I said. 'She's gone, now – talking won't bring her back.'

It was a scene. The others were watching, as if lined up along the touchline at a local football match.

'I'm going for a walk,' I said. I pushed my way out of X's arms, then through the crowd.

I ran into the house, down the garden and out the garden door – which needed unlocking. I was expecting a crowd of journalists, but only one was there: young, female, pretty, plump – sitting on a shooting stick, holding a flask of tea, reading the paper. 'Please let me pass,' I said.

She moved aside. 'Can I just ask you a few questions?'

'No,' I said, 'I'll talk to you when I come back.'

She didn't follow me.

It was a different beach I went down to, this time, than I'd walked upon before: lonely as if at first creation of the world – threatening, ominous even though within sight of the lighthouse and the lights of the other, non-rotating houses.

There is no other way to say it: I felt betrayed. Where were my values now, the ones based around Cecile's imagined civility? I wasn't thinking in big words, however – I was thinking of how far out to sea I could swim before drowning (not seriously); of how long I could stay out before the guests would come to search for me. Or might they let me sleep here, till it got dewy and light, to teach me yet another lesson? What galled me most was that the

Cecile who had done the vulgarity had not been unrecognisable to me – the poise remained, the gentleness was retained. She was the same woman as before, only with her sharp back turned towards me. And I felt thoroughly thwarted, as a storyteller – I don't like hanging ends, inconclusiveness: I'm a wrapper-upper. How can I introduce my readers to the idea of Cornwall, and all it suggests, of romance and the flitting past, of Cecile and a mysterious whom-ever – how can I give them that and then offer no true resolution? *Spaciousness* was moving towards a more inconclusive poetry of atmosphere, a kind of ambience through which the characters moved without very much happening to them at all. My readers didn't like that. Cecile's departure would form a natural low-point within the structure. But it would only have its full impact if I could catch some of the dismay of the other guests.

I had been on the beach about half an hour, and the moon had come out to bring some mildness to the scene. It poured long thin stripes of mercury across the waves approaching the beach; it strapped brightly shining swords to the verticals of the railings; it made my hands, when I held them up in front of my face, look as though they were made of living lead. Turning back towards the house, I almost immediately walked round a hillock of dune and into the arms of X. 'I'm all right,' I said, 'I've stopped crying now.'

'My love,' he said.

'How is everyone else?' I asked.

'They're pretty shocked, I should say. None of them expected something like this of her. The only person she'd told in advance was Alan, and that was mainly so he could help her downstairs with her bags.'

'Can we walk back to the house?' I asked. We pivoted, me beneath the arch of his arm, turning on the spot, he walking round me.

'I'd say,' X said, 'that people are worried what she's going to say, about you but also about us. Some of them think we went too far.'

'By what? By locking me in the attic?'

'Yes, and by faking-up those scenes.'

'But that's going to make the most amusing part of the book, isn't it?'

'It should do,' said X.

'And Cecile going is at least *drama*, isn't it?' I asked. He stopped me, brought me round to face him.

'When this is over,' he said, 'can we avoid drama for a while? Can we go somewhere and put blindfolds on our eyes, and headphones on our ears, and just lie back in the sun and not take anything in?'

I laughed, tinkly. 'That sounds like absolute hell,' I said.

The female journalist was there, waiting. I let her ask me a question, then said, 'I have nothing to say about that.' She asked another, which I didn't answer.

'Bitch,' I heard her say.

We strolled up the lawn and into the house. I'd felt a tidal change take place, whilst out on the beach. The high point was past, the danger over – now came the long ritardando of melancholy.

Friday

Day Twenty-three Week Four

My period is definitely about to start: this morning in bed I told X off for breathing too loudly.

Cecile's piece appears in today's *Mirror*. They've made her out to be a flirty Frenchwoman with an interesting past; posh, innocent. 'My three weeks of Hell in the Big Sister House'. I couldn't bear to read beyond the headline. It wouldn't be Cecile Dupont, it would be pure Sheila Burrows.

The house is sticky.

Since the Maid left, the guests have done a little local cleaning – mostly in their own rooms, and the kitchen.

But there is among them – so I believe – a general desire to take revenge upon me, revenge for so many things, revenge through dirt.

The downstairs toilet has become quite barbaric.

Immediately after breakfast Edith comes up to my room. Quietly she closes the door and starts whispering 'they' want to murder Elizabeth 'they' want to send her away from here from the only home she's ever known please please don't let them!

'Who?' I ask.

'They *are*. I heard them. She's evil, your sister is; and my mother, too, is against me. They want to send Elizabeth out there – into the wide world.'

'They're not going to –'

'Lizzie told me what it would be like for her if they succeed. It's hell and worse than horrible. It's like being a leaf whirled around and around in the wind, with no control ever of where you are or where you stop. This house is her tree, you see: if you take her away from it, she'll wither but she won't ever die because you can only ever die once. She'll be like a skeleton of a leaf; at the moment she's green and singing. This is where she really belongs, upstairs. Why do they want to get rid of her? She's never hurt or harmed anyone. She's a nice ghost – a little sad, but so would you be if you'd missed out on so much of life. She's been telling me what I should do.'

'I think that's what your mother is worried about.'

'Will you help me defend her?'

I thought about this for a short while, as Edith impatiently waited. I had known, during my days in the attic, what it was like to live on the ghostly margin. It was this, I think, which decided me.

'I will,' I said, 'if I can.'

Edith kissed me on the forehead, which was quite bizarre and BBC Edwardian.

'Thank you,' she said.

Went to look for Fleur and Ingrid. Couldn't find either of them anywhere. They have somehow managed to sneak out of the house, past the journalists – through the garden, I think. What are they up to?

The Chef was on daytime telly: as a guest, cooking one of the meals that he cooked for us. I didn't stop to watch it. I just said, 'Ha! there he is, the little bastard,' and carried on upstairs – where I was taking a cup of tea to accompany me on a journey into sulk. I'm told, though, by those who did watch, that he cooked a fairly jazzed-up version of the gumbo and beans he did us a couple of weeks ago. They asked him, of course, whether he'd been videoed having sex. 'No,' he said, 'but there was a camera on me in the kitchen.' (Which I hardly ever bothered looking at – certainly not to see what he was doing; just to see that he was doing *something*, and not idling his entire time away.) 'He was very good,' said Simona, thoughtfully. The presenters mentioned having him back, the following week. But he won't be so current – won't know what we've eaten during the final few days. Perhaps he's going to turn this minor break into a career in TV-cheffery; he has that irritating-for-anything-over-25-minutes charm. He'll probably do very well. I'm certainly not paying him his last week's wages.

Did it.

I dropped all pretence of glamour and went and gave it (the downstairs loo) a good all-over scouring.

This set me off on a spree: I immediately did the upstairs loo, too.

I had just started sweeping the front hall when Marcia came out of her room. 'Ah,' she said, 'cleaning – at last!'

'Yes,' I replied, 'it was all becoming too...'

'I know *exactly* what you mean,' she said, and offered to help.

'Thank you,' I said. She saw my awkwardness: I wasn't exactly sure what she could and couldn't do.

'Why don't you let me take over with the broom?' she said.

I handed it to her, and went and gave the downstairs bathroom a good going over – that took until –.

Lunch, for which Ingrid and Fleur were *still* not around.

Afternoon, I hoovered the upstairs landing whilst Marcia swept the rest of the downstairs rooms, including the kitchen.

Between us we seem to have started a mini-craze. Edith has been dusting all the knick-knacks on all the shelves; William took charge of the brass; Simona has a go at the mirrors.

The cleaning craze continues: there is now a queue of piles of sheets waiting to go into the washing machine; all the dusters and other cloths have disappeared from the kitchen cupboard; throughout the house I can hear quiet brushings, knockings; everyone, I think, wants desperately to go home.

5 p.m.

Coming into the house, through the front door, unexpectedly, using a spare set of keys to unlock it: the Owners and with them Ingrid, Fleur and the Vicar. The Vicar carries a tan suitcase. I look at their serious-set faces, and it takes me less than a second to work out what's going on.

'No,' I say. 'You can't.'

'Oh yes, we can,' says Fleur. She turned to the Vicar. 'Let's do upstairs first.'

'Fine,' he said, looking as calm as if he were about to judge the shortbread and the decorated coathangers at the County Fair.

There was a pause, however, whilst the Vicar went into the parlour – indicated to him by Fleur – and prepared himself. He put his suitcase down on the piano stool, put his thumbs to the locks and clicked it open. Inside, I could see white robes, plastic bottles labelled 'Holy Water', a Holy Bible and a Polaroid camera. He put on the robes and tied a girdle around his middle. It was all very businesslike – kissing everything, muttering prayers. Then he closed the suitcase and came out into the hall.

It was only now that I remembered my promise to Edith. 'You absolutely can't do this.'

'Don't interfere, Victoria,' said Ingrid, 'this has nothing to do with you – the people involved are all agreed that it's the best thing.'

'They've been persuaded,' I said. I looked at Fleur. 'By *you*.'

'No,' said Ingrid. 'By *us*. And before you say anything, Fleur didn't persuade me – I went to her.'

'Shall we?' said the Vicar.

Fleur led the posse upstairs and straight into Edith's room, where the poor child was innocently writing her diary. I followed them. It took Edith even less time to discern their purpose.

'Please,' she said, 'it's wrong.'

'Now, Edith,' Ingrid said, in a voice with the full force of eleven and a half years of motherhood behind it, 'please don't make a fuss. If you do, we shall have to hold you down.'

'I hate you,' said Edith, 'I'll hate you for as long as I live – I don't care if I live to a thousand, I'll still hate you.'

Fleur looked at the Vicar as if to say, *There speaketh Satan.*

'What's happening?' I heard Marcia shout, from the bottom of the stairs. She had, I later learnt, been napping in her room, and had only just been woken up. I wanted to go and tell her, but this was something I couldn't miss.

'Be calm,' said the Vicar, more to the room in general – the wallpaper, the curtains – than to Edith.

Henry pushed his way into the room, went and stood between me and his daughter.

'I've told her where we live,' said Edith. 'If she can find it, she's going to come and stay with us.'

'I think,' said Fleur, 'we'd better start straight away.'

The Vicar said, 'Could everyone join me in saying the Lord's prayer?'

'What's happening!' squealed Marcia.

Edith was distraught to the point of collapse. Her face was pink, pinched and her eyes were bulbous with tears. Crying too hard to speak, she appealed with her eyes. *Help me.*

'Stop,' I said to the Vicar. 'You can't do this.'

'We have invited him in,' said Mrs ~~Johnson~~. 'This is *our* house. Elizabeth was *our* daughter. It has been of some comfort to us, to know that she was still around – even if only to haunt us. But we realise that now is the time for her to be finally laid to rest. Fleur and Ingrid have helped us realise that. All of which is quite apart from the effect that staying in this house has had on this young –'

'Oh, shut up,' said Edith. 'You don't know what you're talking about.'

'Edith!' said Henry.

'Listen to her,' I said.

'I will begin now,' said the Vicar.

~~'No, you won't,' I pointed at him, 'because if you do, I will tell everyone here about the day you came to visit Fleur. I think you know what I mean. The cameras were still on, that day. And I was watching. And I saw what you did. In her room. When she went downstairs.'~~

~~The Vicar looked ashamed, but not mortified; I was annoyed to see that discovery was part of his pleasure.~~

~~'We are none of us perfect,' he said. 'I do not claim to be without sin.'~~

'Victoria,' said Ingrid, 'please get out.'

Edith looked at me desperately. My intervention had brought her some hope, all alone in the forest of adults – mine was the only friendly voice.

'Tell me something!' squealed Marcia. She, too, might have intervened on Edith's side – and Cecile certainly would; but with her gone, and Marcia downstairs, I was on my own.

'Come here,' I said to Edith. Without hesitation, she began to stand up – but her mother's hand fell on her shoulder, pushed her down.

'Stay,' she said, then to stop it sounding like a dog-command she added, 'right there.'

Henry touched my arm. 'Come along, Victoria,' he whispered. 'You can't stop this.'

'But it's wrong,' I said, ranted rather, having given up all hope of saving Edith, 'there isn't anything wrong with her. She's a perfectly healthy girl with a good imagination. I've seen her when she's talking to Elizabeth: she's asleep. She dreams those conversations. She's not possessed.'

'Shut up,' said Mrs ~~Johnson~~.

'This is going to happen,' Mr ~~Johnson~~ said. 'You can't stop it. Please go away.'

~~'He,' I said, pointing at the Vicar, 'played about with your underwear.'~~

~~'I don't care,' said Fleur. 'Don't you see? This is far more important.'~~

~~'He put it in his mouth,' I said.~~

~~The Vicar's eyes were closed, as if he expected the barracking to begin upon all sides.~~

~~Fleur was unable to stop herself taking a glance at him. But she said, 'It doesn't matter what he did.'~~

I looked one final time at Edith, but she did not reply. It looked as if she had gone catatonic – she was staring through the floor as if off the edge of Beachy Head.

Henry pulled me backwards, out onto the landing. Mrs ~~Johnson~~ pushed the door closed. I expect to hear a wail from Edith – something dramatic and horror-filmic. But I didn't hear anything – perhaps my breathing was loud – I was also beginning to cry – tears of anger and frustration. With a shrug of both shoulders I broke away from Henry – walked down the hall – went downstairs and told Marcia what was going on. She shook her head, gazed up through the ceiling in the direction of Fleur's room and said, 'It's a bad thing.'

The exorcism only lasted a couple of minutes, then the Vicar and the others came out and started to visit and bless the other upstairs rooms – including the toilet. He went alone into the attic, let in by Fleur, who'd somehow persuaded X to give her the key. He was able to see for himself the screens; I don't know if he blessed them, or if he thought them beyond redemption. Everywhere he went, he uttered clearly voiced prayers and drew little crosses in holy water upon the walls.

Downstairs took hardly any time at all, and then he started on the people. Marcia and I were the only two to refuse. We went and sat in her room, in protest. But the Owner came and opened the door, without knocking. The Vicar must, he said, at least be allowed to bless the room. Marcia reluctantly agreed. He said the prayer a couple of times, did a good few water crosses.

'Are you sure?' he said to both of us.

'Go away,' I said, ~~'pant-eater.'~~

~~His head went down. He could not meet my eye.~~ I heard Ingrid and Edith, upstairs, shouting at one another.

Fleur and the Owners and the Vicar said goodbye in the hall. Fleur was effusive in her thanks. The Vicar told the Owners that he would be back in a day or two to check everything was alright.

About half an hour after the Vicar had gone, I knocked on Edith's door. 'Leave me *alone*,' she wailed.

'It's me,' I said, 'Victoria.'

There was a pause.

'Come in,' Edith said.

She was a pink-nosed mess.

'Oh my dear,' I said. 'I'm sorry.'

I sat down beside her.

She lunged for my tummy, bear-hugged me, started to cry. I put my arms around her and rocked her, a little. Abandoning herself to tears, she started seriously to cry. It was terrifying – her sobs seemed bigger than she was; something about them affected me directly, physically, and I too began to wail.

She said something. I think it was, 'Why are people so cruel?'

We had a good cry, together. Then I left her alone.

Aftermath of the exorcism.

I am not speaking to Fleur or to Ingrid. A brief conversation with Alan tells me that he had his doubts but basically he supported them in what they did – which was, I gather, contact the Vicar and the Owners yesterday evening (a number of phone calls, one of which I interrupted), and then take the Vicar to see the Owners at the hotel this morning. The Vicar was reluctant, he said, to act so rapidly. (Though I remembered Fleur asking him about exorcism when he came to visit before.) But eventually he was convinced. The problem wasn't just the ghost, it was Edith *together with* the ghost – and if he waited, she would be gone.

'It's medieval,' I said.

'But it might um help Edith,' he replied.

'You can't believe that.'

'Her mother thinks so.'

'And do you think her mother's alright?'

'She seems perfectly alright to me.'

'Well, she isn't.'

I go and tell Marcia what Alan said, and she agrees that it's quite ludicrous.

Later. I go up to have another look at Edith. She has been refusing to speak to anyone but me. 'See if you can persuade her to eat something,' says her father.

She is very calm as I enter, after knocking as gently as I can. Her eyes are wet but clear. Her back is straight and she seems to have grown older by at least a year since last I spoke to her.

'I forgive them,' she says. 'But I think they've failed. I can't hear Elizabeth, but I still think she's here.'

'In the house?'

'I'm not sure. I think she found somewhere to hide while they were trying to get rid of her.'

'I'm sorry I couldn't stop them,' I say. 'I did try.'

'I know. Thank you.' This could be the end of the conversation, but Edith wants to say something more: 'I'm sure they wouldn't have dared even try if Cecile had still been here.'

'I don't know.'

'She would have stopped them.'

'Perhaps she would,' I say, though I can't see exactly what more than me she could have done.'

'Cecile knows all about ghosts.'

'I think we all know a little more, after this month.'

'Because of Cornwall.'

For a moment I am unable to speak. Edith, sitting on the bed, doesn't look as if she is about to torture me; the word has been spoken if not in innocence then without malice. Had she heard me begging Cecile to tell me the secret, the evening before, as Cecile got into the car of the journalist?

'Oh, you know about that, do you?' By pretending to be indifferent, I don't expect Edith to take me for indifferent; I think she might, though, give me some credit for not puppying all over her.

'She told me all about it – Cecile, she told me. Do you want to know?'

Such a splash of adrenalin hits the back of my neck that I nod in reflex; my mouth and throat gone entirely dry – as if liquid were never known there.

'You'll have to stay quiet, though, while I'm telling you; I don't want any interruptions.'

I nod my *promise*.

'Cecile grew up in France, you know that already, but when she was about fifteen-and-a-half she went to work in a country house, in Cornwall. She was a lady's maid, and helped her with all her clothes and perfumes. Her mistress wasn't a bad woman, but she didn't like anyone to work for her for too long; I think because they got to know all her secrets, and she had lots and lots of secrets. This woman had a dozen admirers; she had affairs. One of her children, she had three children, was really the son of someone who wasn't her husband. Her husband was a rich banker who spent most of his time in London, which was why she was bored and was able to have so many affairs. It was a big country house, with a long straight drive; there wasn't a view of the sea, but you could hear it. Cecile was unhappy all the time she was in Cornwall. Ever since she was six and had started attending school, she had been in love with a boy from the village next to hers, in France. She didn't tell me his name; that was too precious. But she said he was charming and handsome and never mocked her, like the other boys did, for being so small and fragile. Cecile dreamt that one day he would come over the sea and rescue her. She was lonely in the big country house, and sent him letters. At first he replied to every single one, in a day or two, but then gaps started to appear, and he only replied to every other one. Cecile was worried that he had been distracted by some other girl. It was two years since Cecile had come to England and in all that time she hadn't once seen her love. She wasn't allowed holidays. She did travel, and once she even went to the Riviera with her mistress and the family; but she was needed most of all when they were on holiday – to organise the clothes and the affairs. And then, one evening, when the husband was in London at a banquet for bankers, the mistress didn't come home. It was twelve o'clock, one o'clock, and she still was out. She didn't come home the next morning. Cecile didn't know what to do; she thought she should probably tell the master. The other servants found out: the cook found out when the coffee came back, not drunk; the chauffeur because the car wasn't back; other maids because the bed hadn't been slept in. Cecile told the Butler what she thought she could: that the mistress had decided to go for a drive, but hadn't come back. The Butler was about to telephone to the master's club in London, but there was a knock upon the door. It was the police. Cecile said she could remember them standing there in their blue uniforms, looking so old-fashioned. They had found the mistress's car, a small sports car, down a lane about five miles from the house, with the engine still running. But there was no sign at all of the mistress. The police were told that the mistress had been out since the previous night. They were embarrassed, Cecile could tell, but they wanted to know who had been the last person to see her. That was Cecile. She was terrified; she didn't know what she could tell them, without her mistress getting furious when she got back. She tried to say as little as possible.'

There is a gentle knock on the door. Both Edith and I jump so high we practically bang our heads on the ceiling.

'Go away,' says Edith.

'Edith,' coos her mother.

'Go *away*.'

We hear the creak of departing footsteps. Edith closes her eyes, takes a big PATIENCE breath and, luckily for me, is able to resume.

'They – the police – asked her where her mistress had gone. Cecile answered quite honestly that she didn't know. Of course, she knew who the mistress had been going to see. Even if the mistress hadn't told her, she would have known from the type of clothes the mistress wanted prepared, and from the perfume she wore: the mistress had a different perfume for each lover – she said it helped her remember their names; if she forgot, she could just close her eyes and breathe in and the name would come to her. Anyway, the police next asked Cecile if the mistress had been meeting anyone. Cecile said she didn't know. The police said she must know. Cecile was loyal, and said she didn't. The police gave her a stern look, but stopped asking questions. By the time Cecile came out of the bedroom, where they had held the interrogation, a rumour had gone round the house: the mistress had been murdered. And you might say that this was all that anyone ever knew. The mistress never returned. Her body was never found, but the house was quite close to the sea, and it could easily have been dumped there. All the servants suspected the master; they thought that he had finally had enough of the affairs and decided to do away with his wife. He had arranged an alibi in London, had travelled in disguise back to Cornwall, had found out where to wait so as to catch his wife; he had strangled her, got rid of the body, and driven back to London in time to take a late breakfast in his club. But there was no evidence. Cecile was fired almost immediately. The master didn't need a lady's maid, although it seemed likely that there would be a new mistress pretty soon. Most of the other servants, apart from the Butler, were also sacked – which meant that they all thought the Butler had told the master about where his wife would be, that night. Cecile went back to France, and found what she'd been afraid of: her childhood love had fallen for another girl, was engaged to be married to her. Cecile was angry at herself for having been away; she knew that, if she'd been around, she would have kept him. As soon as she came back, he was back in love with her and forgot the other girl completely. But that wasn't enough for Cecile. She was too hurt by his betrayal. She didn't know what to do. There wasn't anything for her in France. Her parents were both dead, which was why she had ended up as a Maid. They had been quite rich, but had spent it all on nice things. And so, Cecile borrowed a little money from an Aunt, and went back to Cornwall. She wanted to find out what had happened to her mistress. Because she knew so much about it, she thought she would do a better job than the police. And so she started doing what she called 'playing Sherlock Holmes'. She managed to track down all of her mistress's lovers. One of them, who was very upset by her death, offered to fund her investigations – for as long as they kept going. He was very rich, and Cecile had no other way of making her living – apart from being a maid, which she definitely didn't want to do again. She ended up investigating for five years. She went all over Cornwall, she talked to everyone her mistress had ever known. And in the end, she concluded that the master probably hadn't killed her: the Butler did it. He retired early, three years after the murder, and was able to buy his own large house in the country, and employ his own Butler. Cecile believed there was no way he could have afforded this if he hadn't been handsomely paid by the master. But there was no *evidence*. It was terribly frustrating. She moved into Oxfordshire, in the village next to where the Butler had settled down; she watched him madly, through binoculars, looking for some sign of guilt. She bribed the postman to show her his letters, but he never received one from the master. Meanwhile, the master had married someone else – the wife of one of his business partners. They had sold the house in Cornwall and moved to the South of France. Finally, the old lover of Cecile's mistress died, and the money for the investigation stopped. She went and told the police at Scotland Yard everything that she'd found out, but they weren't interested – or, anyway, they didn't do much about it. Cecile stayed in London. She didn't tell me what she did next.'

'Thank you, Edith,' I say, 'I'm glad to know.'

Fleur comes to talk to me.

'I know you don't condone what's been done...'

'I think it was despicable,' I say.

'We gave it a lot of thought.'

'Well, I hope you're happy now.'

'There are things you don't understand yet,' she says, sombre.

'Why don't you tell me about them?'

'I can't,' she says. 'It's not my place.'

'Then you're not much use to me,' I say.

And she goes.

Audrey continues to romance me, in a fashion which if it weren't so ludicrous I'd find quite disconcerting; I didn't begin this project with the intention of becoming the seductee of a Sapphic pussy. She demands my lap, so much so that I have begun, in anticipation, to wear grey non-Audrey-hair-showing clothes. When I deny her, she makes glancing passes at my toes; if I lock her out of the room, she commences singing the feline blues.

And after all that cleaning, guess what? –

The Maid. Just past 5 p.m., and she comes back to ask if I still want her to clean for us; she has let herself in with the key she'd kept – come straightaway to find me and explain.

Her absence due to a 'family crisis'. Nothing at all to do with the newspapers and the television.

I ask her directly whether she was the 'source within the house'. She says she wasn't, and I am almost convinced.

Do I let her back? Do we trust her?

I take her key, tell her I'll call her, send her away again. She, very apologetic.

6 p.m. We have a House Meeting.

We decide to give the Maid another chance, and to entrust her again with a key. (I speak in her favour.) I telephone her, and she says she'll come straight over. I say it's not necessary. She insists, and is here within quarter of an hour; sees the Chef isn't around, says she can cook, cooks.

Dinner.

We talk about Cecile, and why she felt it necessary to go. It is the safest subject. Everyone joins in, apart from Ingrid, who Henry says wasn't feeling too well, is having a lie-down – she is upstairs in their room, but she isn't having a lie-down: we can hear her moving restlessly about as we talk.

Maid finally goes about 8.30 p.m.

After she finished the washing up, she came to see me, very apologetic, again. I got the sense – perhaps unfairly – she was pumping me.

'How did you feel?' she asked. 'Being locked up in the attic all that time? You must've felt awful.'

I flim-flammed awhile, then tell her I have to get on. She stays longer than she has to.

After she's left, I ask a couple of people (Alan and William) whether they think she was more chatty than usual with them. They both say they didn't really notice, either way.

Men, they're so ~~shed.~~ rubbish

I know by 'shed' you mean 'about as useful as something you dump in a shed'. But your readers won't understand your private slang.

Late evening.

...and then we heard the screaming. It wasn't hard to tell who it was (very high-pitched): Edith. We ran towards where we thought it was coming from, which was upstairs. As we went past the hall, we saw suitcases – packed, lined and ready to go. Edith started squealing, 'No, no, no!' I'd never heard her make so much noise. I ran upstairs to see what was going on. She was in her room, clinging on to the bedpost; her mother had her arm round her, but was furiously being shrugged off. There were a couple more bags on the floor, packed. 'Oh no,' I said, joining in with Edith on the chorus. I tried to sit down on the bed beside the two of them, but there was too much flailing going on; it was dangerous; I could have been accidentally punched – black-eyed; I stood back. 'Why?' Edith was wailing. '*Why?*' Henry came in, businesslike, and picked up his daughter's suitcases.

'Why are you going?' I asked. He didn't reply. With a case in either hand, he turned and went off down the landing. Edith was crying so hard she couldn't speak; Ingrid was stroking her hair and murmuring into her ear. I took a moment to think: how could I possibly prevent this from happening? I'd already failed with Cecile. I looked out the window, and saw Henry stowing suitcases in the boot of their car; its headlights were on. In the dark of the drive, it looked like a lighted-up ship far out at sea.

Ingrid spoke mother-gently to her daughter. 'We have to go. You know we have to go. It hasn't been very good for any of us here.'

'You don't have to go,' I said.

'Look!' wailed Edith. 'She says we don't have to go.'

'Can't you see,' said Ingrid to her daughter, '*she's* one of the main reasons we have to.'

'No,' said Edith. There was a garland of snot beneath her nose. 'I don't want to.'

'We're your parents,' said Henry, re-entering the room. 'We've decided.' There was only one more bag to be taken; he picked it up.

'No!' Edith screamed, as if she were a mother and they were removing her child from her sight.

Henry scanned the room a final time to see if there was anything he'd missed. I caught a moment's eye-contact between Ingrid and him: it was efficient, mind-made-up. He turned and took the last bag downstairs.

'What can I say to make you stay?' I asked.

'Don't say anything,' replied Ingrid.

I heard the car engine start up. Ingrid was now working to pull Edith's fingers off the bedpost – one by one they came, with each trying to fight its way back to a position of grip.

'I can't go without seeing Elizabeth,' wailed Edith. 'We need to say goodbye! Let's stay tonight, just tonight. I'll go tomorrow and I won't make a fuss.'

'No,' said Ingrid. 'The decision is made.'

Henry strode back into the room. He seemed to have gained confidence, with the last of the luggage going into the car. 'Right,' he said. He glanced at me, and I felt what I thought was hatred; I reeled slightly, inside. What had happened to him? Why was he being like this?

Henry was more brutal than Ingrid in releasing his daughter's grip from the bed: he took her by the wrists, so that it hurt. She went limp almost immediately; the force of her father too much to resist. 'You're coming with us,' he said.

'If she doesn't want to, she doesn't have to,' I said. 'She can stay until the end.'

'Do you think –' began Ingrid.

'It's not going to happen,' said Henry.

'It's your fault she's like this,' Ingrid said.

'I'm not the one making her cry,' I said.

'Don't interfere any more than you have,' Ingrid said.

Henry had Edith half over his shoulder, like a soldier carrying a kitbag; she had given up on language, and was animal-weepwailing. 'Ready?' said Henry to Ingrid. She turned to me. 'If we've left anything behind, please send it on to us. Don't be so petty as to –'

'Alright,' I said.

Henry turned, almost banging Edith's head against the open door – then he was walking down the landing, down the stairs; there was nothing left of his daughter – she was all sorrow, snot and sound.

With a final glance around the room, avoiding eye-contact with me, Ingrid stood up. Then I saw her decide she was strong enough to take me on. At her full height, she came over to where I stood. 'I'll write to you,' she said, 'it will explain.' She leaned in to kiss me. I put my arms up to embrace her, but she batted them away – gently. 'This is awful,' she said.

'You can still change your mind,' I said.

'We can't,' she replied. Then she was out the door. I followed her into the drive. The other guests were there already.

Henry leaned over the back seat, fastening Edith's seatbelt; there was no longer any resistance from the daughter. Ingrid got in the passenger seat, after a quick check on Edith. Henry stood up out of the back. 'Please,' I said to him. He looked shamefaced; after the initial glance, he couldn't keep his eyes on mine. 'Goodbye,' he said, and got in.

We backed away from the car. It started up, drove off. I could see outlines and profiles in the wispy reddish light of the dashboard: Ingrid had the map on her lap, ready to start issuing directions. They were on their way home.

I'm exhausted.

If I could only be on an island, no journalists; me and X. Like in June. Iraklia.

Prose style gone completely, here. Oh, I really can't be bothered any more. What a mess!

Those left in the house now: me, X, Fleur and Alan, William and Simona, plus Marcia.

Last of evening spent in self-recrimination; Marcia fantastically forgiving, in a way I don't deserve.

Saturday (Penultimate Day)

Day Twenty-four Week Four

My Nights of Lust with Two-Timing X:
I Was Bedded by Big Sister's Boyfriend.

No, not a nightmare – the headline in one of this morning's skankiest tabloids. Although some attempt was made to keep me away from it, I eventually heard hints, asked and was shown (Simona, the bitch). The man in the photograph (yes, *man*), stripped to the waist, looked as if he should have been modelling briefs in a catalogue; he was wearing tight jeans and had no shoes on; he had very hairy toes.

I didn't at first feel what I suppose I was meant to: calmly, I went back upstairs to the bedroom; calmly, I got in under the covers; calmly, I swore to chop X's balls off.

After leaving me ten minutes during which to rave, X crept in. 'Victoria,' he said. He waited half a minute for me to say *What?* then continued 'I don't expect you to listen to me now. But, when you do, I'll explain everything.'

'No,' I said, sitting up. My face, I knew, had gone runny like an underdone egg. 'I can listen now,' I said. 'Tell me. Explain. Say it isn't true.'

'It is,' said X, 'in its completely distorted way, it's true.'

'You had sex with him.'

'Yes,' X said.

'When?'

'Around Christmas. He lives near my parents.'

'I don't want to know where he lives.' This was becoming more humiliating than I'd thought it could possibly be. I looked at X, who seemed defiant in a wholly heterosexual way. 'Why?' I asked.

His answer was immediate: 'Because we both wanted to.'

'I know our relationship was meant to be open...' I started, but I didn't need to go on.

'I'm sorry I didn't tell you,' X said.

'Do you often sleep with men?' I asked.

'No,' he said, 'I never sleep with men. But I sometimes like to go to bed with them.'

'How often is sometimes?'

'A couple of times a year.'

'Birthdays and Christmas,' I sneered.

'Strangely enough,' said X, 'it is often around Christmas, yes.'

'I suppose it started with Santa coming into your bedroom,' I said. I hadn't wanted to say this, it was comic relief when I didn't need it.

'No,' said X. 'For some reason I find men more attractive in winter, and women in summer.'

'That's the most stupid thing I've ever heard anyone say.'

'I know,' he said, 'but it's still true.'

'Go,' I said.

'I'm sorry,' he said, 'I should have told you before: I knew you'd find out eventually.'

'And that everyone else would find out, too?'

He went foot-shuffly. 'No, not that, particularly – or not in this way. How could I know about this?'

'Go,' I said, 'I'm not going to tell you a third time. If I have to say it a third time, then you can forget coming back.' Almost soundlessly, he left.

Once alone again, I had my little collapse. I tried to picture X having sex with the man in the newspaper, but gave up as the effort was too much; then I tried not to picture X having sex with him, but gave up as the effort was again too much. I was left in a halfway state – the image was there, was horrible, but wouldn't come to the surface. X had changed, in the way I saw him – utterly: I wanted to be held by him, but didn't want him anywhere near me. I wanted him to apologise and despite that be punished very severely. I felt ashamed, and ashamed of being ashamed. Logically, I knew that X had done nothing wrong: we had agreed we could both sleep with other people; we had not explicitly stated these other people would be of the opposite sex to our own. X, in fact, would probably have encouraged me to sleep with a woman: his sexuality, I'd thought, was that uncomplicatedly heterosexual; dykery was a turn-on to him rather than a serious emotional threat. Was I overreacting? I wasn't sure. I wished the old, imaginary Cecile had been there to ask; talking to her (in my idealised version) would have been like walking down some long, bush-lined avenue on a French country estate – there would have been lots of perspectives, all of them long, regular and leading to some issue. Besides all of which, my period was now in full flow: I was feeling pangy, weepy, defiant and obscurely insulted. I remembered what Henry had said to me: 'You don't really know X – you don't know what he's really like.' He'd been trying to tell me. And their fight? Had it really been a fight? Oh, X was so beautiful. Why hadn't I been able to see?

I *so* want to be grand and glorious and forgiving about this, fashionable even, setting a trend that will be reported in the magazines:

> When Victoria About found out about her boyfriend's infidelity, *with another man*, she actively encouraged them. 'Why shouldn't I want him to explore and express his sexuality to the full?' she said, reclining upon a *chaise longue* in her stylish Borough apartment. 'I'm not some sort of Victorian Governess, am I?' Victoria was wearing...

I am, though, aren't I? At heart, I'm a Victorian Governess: I want him bound up in smutty anti-smut regulations. Why aren't I less bourgeois, less wifey, more adult, more truly civilised? Here is an opportunity for me to be enhanced, and all I can manage to do is shrink, shrink away from it.

For half an hour the house left me well enough alone – to weep, moan, snarl, type.

Then there came a quiet knock upon the door. I had finished with the laptop, its screen foggy with my putting my fingers on top of the words.

'Oh come in, I suppose,' I said.

It was Fleur.

We exchanged a glance, from which I tried very hard to extract some triumph; she showed none, I displayed little.

'I don't know what you're expecting to find,' I said, 'but you won't –'

'You've been hurt,' said Fleur. And – oh God – that was all she needed to say.

The words, *I have*, came out in liquid form; and I didn't say anything solid for another half-hour, at least. Fleur became big sister; I became little sister; I was inconsolable; she consoled me.

Maid is here; I refuse to see her.

X comes into the room, asks if I want him to go. 'Of course I want you to go,' I say.

He looks at me, pained, so pained that I almost relent: I don't want to lose him; not over something as relatively trivial as this.

'I'll go then,' he says, just as I'm thinking of saying *Don't*. That moment passes, though.

He pulls down a suitcase and begins hurriedly to clear his T-shirts out of the dressing table.

'I'm going into the garden,' I say. 'I'm not coming back until you're gone.'

'Fine,' he says.

I get up and am almost out the door when he says, 'Victoria.'

Even in my anger, I hope that he will find some incredibly clever way to reconcile us: I love him; I am helpless. He looks at me, looks through me.

'If this is the way it's going to be, I don't want you using my name in the book. Not my real name – take that out,' he says. 'It doesn't matter that everyone already knows – I just don't want you to write about me in bitterness.'

And now everyone knows who he is, anyway — even though he's going to be 'X', forever.

'Fine,' I say, although I feel something like sheets being torn inside my chest. 'Your name won't appear.'

'Thank you,' he says.

'You've read it already, haven't you?' I say. 'You've been sneaking into the room when I'm not around, and reading my notes.'

He looks surprised, but he must be expecting me to bring this up.

'I don't know what you're talking about.'

'You do,' I say.

'I really don't,' he says.

For a moment I make the effort of trying to believe him; it doesn't work.

'Why lie?' I say.

'I'm not,' he says.

I stand in the doorway. 'I still love you,' I say. 'It's just – oh, get out, get out.'

'I understand,' he says, tenderly.

'No, you don't,' I say, and I go – thinking *You don't understand; I don't understand so how could you understand?*

I wasn't much use until late afternoon.

After I'd heard X being driven off, I went back up to the bedroom, got the laptop and *Find/Changed* his name to X. I did, even in my distress, think about calling him Y (why oh why did I fall for him in the first place?) or Z (for the endingness it implies). But maybe X marks the spot: in the future, there may be buried treasure, or he may really and truly be my ex-. I can't bear it.

Fleur had arranged to go with Alan to the kennels, to collect Domino; they went at about two. I went into Marcia's room. I was in need of sympathy, and she was marvellously sweet and understanding. By the time she'd finished with me, I was almost ready to talk to X again – call him on his mobile. She had to persuade me that wasn't a good idea, yet. Fleur and Alan came back, with Domino bounding on a lead. They had stocked up with dog and cat food on the way back. Only a couple of journalists had followed them, and they hadn't been particularly interested in the pet rescue. Before they left, they'd made sure Audrey was inside the house, and had left instructions she shouldn't be allowed out; a confrontation was being stagemanaged. Marcia persuaded me through into the drawing room, where everyone had gathered to watch. Audrey was hiding under one of the sofas; Domino was allowed off the lead. He went to sniff for Audrey. A paw flashed out from under the sofa, so fast it could hardly be seen, and Domino jumped back, nose bleeding from a nasty little slash. He trotted back to Alan, whimpering. Alan seemed upset but also slightly pleased. We stayed in the room as Fleur called Audrey. A few minutes later, she came out. Domino wanted to go in for another look. Alan let him, but this time he was warier; he held back out of slashing distance. Audrey stepped towards him, he retreated. This wasn't exactly reconciliation, but it was a mutual stand-off. There was a round of applause from all the remaining guests. They had been so interested in the animal drama that they hadn't bothered to look much at me, but now they did. 'I haven't got anything to say,' I said. 'I'm not very happy.' I was deluged with hugs; after which I went upstairs to be on my own for a little while, not crying.

On my own, I go into Cecile's old room. I hadn't considered the possibility of this, until today; which is silly: there was no reason why I shouldn't. But some sense of the still forbidden kept me away – the memory of that time, just after she arrived, when she wouldn't open the door for me; I'd been anticipating an intimate talk, and all I got was the sporting of the oak. The small bedroom still smells distantly of Cecile's perfume; the wardrobe, particularly, and the pillow even more so. I wanted to find some relic of her, be it only a hairgrip. She had left nothing, though, that I could see: a knotting of hairs in the wastepaper basket. I refused to allow myself to pick those out; that would have rendered me abject. Instead, I took the basket down to the kitchen and emptied its almost-emptiness into the bin under the sink. As a gesture, it wasn't particularly satisfying, but to have left the hair where it was would have been even less so. After replacing the wastepaper basket, I sat down on the bed and looked up towards the lens of the spy camera. Even knowing where it should be, I couldn't see it. I've arranged for the men from the security firm to come on Sunday and dismantle the equipment; eight hours, they say it will take – but I shall have to pay them extra.

First opportunity she got, Audrey was off and down the bottom of the garden again – revisiting the edge-fence-haunting days of earlier in the month; so, there was no miraculous development of love between her and Domino. Fleur doesn't seem *that* disappointed: 'They've made a start': that was all she said. Alan, too, is philosophical: 'Stupid mutt.'

3.17 p.m. Screaming, again. This time from Fleur, in Fleur's room. I happened to be passing, on the upstairs landing. Went straight into her room: there were two men I'd never seen before; one of them climbing out of the wardrobe, the other out from under the bed. The beneath-bed one had a big black camera around his neck and one in his hands. He is hardly to his feet before he starts trying to take pictures of me. Fleur, though distressed, puts herself in his way. More guests – Alan, William – have by this time arrived, and then the Maid.

'I don't need to ask what you're doing here,' I say, as Alan deprives the photographer of his cameras, gently. (He's so tall when he's angry.)

'Tell me how you got in.'

'I let them in,' said the Maid.

'Why?' I asked.

'I told you not to trust her,' said Marcia.

'They offered me money,' said the Maid. 'It was as simple as that.'

'What about the promises you made to us, just yesterday.'

'Oh, they told me I'd have to lie. But that doesn't matter – everybody wants to know what's going on in here.'

'That does not justify –'

'How does it feel to be one of the most notorious women in England?' asked the journalist, who was wearing a bad leather jacket.

'Can I have my cameras back?' said the photographer.

'Of course,' said Alan, and proceeded to take the film out of both.

'Are you a pervert?' asked the journalist.

'Come on,' I said.

'Do you enjoy spying on people?' he asked. 'Is that how you get your kicks?'

We processed down the stairs, the press like prisoners-of-war in our midst. Alan and William stood closest to them, large and menacing. They – the journos – recognised William, and had already seen him attack one of them. I could tell he wanted seconds.

We put them outside; Alan handing over the cameras last thing – minus film. Then we took the Maid through into the drawing room, and tried to get her to show some remorse. It was pointless; she had all the self-justifications of someone entirely in the wrong.

'But we trusted you a second time,' said Marcia. 'We had no reason to, but we did.'

'Well, you're just a bit stupid then, aren't you?' she replied, then said, 'Can I go now?'

Of course, I took her key away, and told her never to come back.

'Fine,' she said, 'I don't know why I'd ever want to.'

We showed her out.

'Good riddance to bad rubbish,' said Marcia.

Sunlight through the window onto the bedspread, diagonally, like the fishing lines of the anglers on the beach.

I can't work out Fleur's current mood. She seems to be two people: one of them bounces around weaving flowers into the fabric of the air (metaphorically); the other squats beneath a steel-gray thundercloud, wincing as if it were raining ballbearings down upon her.

I was ~~quite~~ glad of confession today~~; or, at least, I was to begin with.~~

Simona came and knocked on the door of the Master Bedroom at four o'clock exactly. She wanted to go downstairs, into the parlour where we usually meet. 'Can't we do it here?' I asked.

She hesitated. 'Of course.' She was about to sit down when she said, 'Would you like a cup of tea?'

Once upon a time, I had the Maid make me up a full tray; for quite a while, I've let that slip; and now she's gone, and it will never happen again. 'That would be lovely.' (It would also shorten confession.)

Simona went downstairs to the kitchen, and came back fifteen minutes later with a laden tea-tray; from somewhere, a packet of chocolate biscuits had appeared. ~~Almost as soon as she put it down, Simona's manner became more formal~~. She poured out the tea, distributed plates and biscuits, folded her hands and said, 'I've given it quite a lot of thought, recently, and I've decided that – when this book is finished – we'll have gone as far as we can, as writer and editor. It's only fair to let you know in advance.'

'What do you mean?'

'I mean that I think you'd be better working with someone else. After, this the next book, however brilliant it may be, is bound to be a disappointment. This month has been such fun. Why don't we admit that we're never going to better it?'

'No!'

'Don't worry about my commitment to this book; it is absolute – I am one hundred per cent determined that it's going to be your best book. I'm also one hundred per cent sure that it's going to be your most successful.'

'What if I don't want you to quit?'

'Then we shall have to talk about it some more. Eventually, you'll understand.'

'Why are you telling me this now – I mean, today... it's not exactly been a fantastic day, and here you are telling me this.'

'It's better to hear on a day that's already been ruined, than for me to ruin a perfectly good other day.'

'Is it working with me?'

'What do you mean? Of course, in a way, it's working with you. But that's not to say that I don't love the whole –'

'What if I say no?'

'I'm afraid you don't have any say. The publishers might put some pressure on me, particularly if you're as successful as I think you're going to be; in the end, though, it's my decision.' She drank the last of her tea. 'I'm going to leave you to think about it. We can talk some more tomorrow.'

'You can't do this to me,' I said. 'I need you.'

'That's very flattering,' said Simona, standing up, 'but you know perfectly well it's not true.'

I was trying very hard not to shout at her.

'Please reconsider,' I said.

With a slow smile she replied, 'Of course, I'll think about it some more – if you want me to.'

'I'm not going to let you leave me; not like everyone else.'

~~Simona didn't take this up. 'Tomorrow,' she said.~~

Of course, I changed my mind about this almost immediately.

William in the parlour, playing something half-joyful, half-melancholic on the piano; it keeps jigging from one thing to another, as if it can't make up its mind. I wonder what it is – I don't like it: it unnerves me. *This little description made me cry and cry – it is so William. I know that piece, though! can't name it.*

I am terribly sorry for William; I know he doesn't want pity, but he's 57 for God's sake – 57 and dying! I now realise just how young that is; five years ago I didn't.

I really can't see how he manages to go on, pretending to be chipper, but *knowing*... And Simona, too. I suppose they found out a while ago, and have found a way of accommodating their lives to the knowledge.

Imagine if it were X: I know that it would decide everything for us. I wouldn't even pretend to be interested in anyone else; I would be devoted to him for the rest of his life. I'm sure in the final stages of his illness we'd discuss me being with another person; X would insist, I would say I couldn't even bear to think about it. He would die, and I would dress very simply for a long time. I would wear sombre perfumes, discreet (undangly) Whitby jet and travel to a country I've never been – Tunisia or New Zealand. I would find a long beach, walk down it, cry out across the sea like a seagull and finally feel the grief break within me. Collapse, release. Then I would begin the long journey back; always imagining that X was about to appear, amused by the cruel success of his joke. Perhaps they would let me see the body in the hospital; perhaps I'd *have* to identify him – but that wouldn't happen... He would have died in my arms, so thin and so helpless. His breath would at the last have come out like paper tearing, then a long groan and a leak of liquid, then nothing more. I could cope, at that moment I know I could definitely cope. But all this makes me want to go to X, to find him, hold him for a long time without explanation. And I want to hold William, too – faithheal him with love; or at least, let him know that he is not alone. That is Simona's job, though; he must know that he isn't alone.

Evening.

I cooked the farewell dinner; not *boeuf en daube* – without Chef to assist me, I couldn't manage that. No, it was a simple roast beef with potatoes, parsnips, peas, carrots, gravy. A lot less demanding, the whole thing, with only five plus me to cater for.

Sofa-scene. Talking about the dearly departed. We shall all miss them all terribly, of course.

'The house seems empty,' says Marcia.

'Do you think there really was a ghost?' asks Alan.

'I have a sense of peace that I didn't have before,' says Fleur, to whom the question was directed.

'But surely that's just because there are less people here,' William says. 'And there's just that much less noise.'

'No,' says Fleur, quite definitely, 'the house is a different place. It feels fresher – I can't explain. I'm sure the blessing did its work.'

Alan does his best to look like he agrees, although he's finding it difficult; the rationalism within him is reviving.

'I don't think the ghost has gone,' Marcia declares. 'I think it's just cleverly hiding somewhere, until we go away.'

'I would like to think that,' I say.

'Victoria!' says Fleur. 'Would you wish those people to be haunted by their daughter?'

‘They clearly *are* haunted by her,’ I say. ‘How could they not be? Anyway, I think it’s Cecile going that has made the most difference. When she went the whole atmosphere changed.’

‘Do you think so?’ says William. ‘I really can’t say I felt it all that much. She was so reserved.’

‘But she held everything together,’ I say.

No-one feels like replying; they look shifty. Finally, Alan says, ‘Well, um someone had to – otherwise...’

‘Otherwise,’ says Marcia, ‘what?’

‘Otherwise it would have been even worse than it was,’ says Fleur, rescuing her awkward love.

‘In her way,’ William starts, ‘I feel that *Ingrid* was the hub of the house.’

‘Why?’ I ask, annoyed. ‘She didn’t do very much.’

‘Exactly,’ he says, ‘the still centre, and all that.’

I don’t feel like arguing with him, partly because he’s dying and partly because this scene will go much better without an argument.

‘When she looks back,’ I say, ‘I don’t think she’ll see this as a time of stillness.’

‘Stillness for others is quite different to stillness for oneself,’ says Fleur.

‘You’re right there,’ says William, and chuckles roughly. He glances towards Simona, and she takes it as a comment on their marriage.

‘You can’t talk,’ she replies, but it is flirtatious.

I did intend to go to the Lighthouse, didn’t I? That was part of the point. Perhaps I’ll find time tomorrow. Doubt it.

Suitcases in the hall; goodbyes in the kitchen; promises in the air; me in floods – I can see it already. However awful it’s been, I don’t want it to end.

Sunday (The Final Day)

Day Twenty-five Week Four

2.33 a.m. Woke up in thick black with my right arm dead in the bed beside me. Terrified. Back to sleep.

I've got pig-eyes this morning, from crying. My hair looks as if I slept with it in a bowl of egg whites; but I didn't, sleep I mean.

No journalists out back.

Snuck down on my own to the beach, saw the sun come up.

Gentle the waves onto the sand, in the half-half-light; quiet the whole world, apart from the dogwalkers – who detected and respected my wish for solitude.

'Look,' I thought, 'the sky's gone silvery.'

The light of dawn is even more special than the light of twilight, here; it suits the place – is pale yet warm, delicate yet incessant.

I've been more touched by the beauty of the sea during this month than ever before. I have found it a constant comfort: the sea always accepts and never disappoints.

I haven't done enough descriptive writing recently. Readers will know what happened, but they won't know what it looked like. Virginia is always very good on this, always very granite and rainbow. The beach, I feel, has been becoming more wintery; its tones are lighter, paler, more gentle in reflection upon the skin. When at sundown the sea goes milky, it is really as if it could be no other colour. The bay turns into a great bowl of mother-of-pearl.

Only now do I realise how much I love X, and how much he means to me; not just in the big ways, the giving love back, the physical dimension, but even when he's not there – the fact that objects in our room have moved around, slightly; the floor of the shower, at home in London, is wet by the time I get to it; us seeing the same item in the news, and having the same thought about it, and both trying to tell the other at the end of the day; the pride I feel in *him* being with *me*.

I wonder what today will be like?

Oh yes, the dawn chorus – heard it here for the last time. Tinkly.

As usual, I have finished packing far too early. Everyone else still busy, so I have time – too much time – time to... I don't know; there's nothing left that needs doing.

Had a big bubbly bath.

Lay there wondering if X was missing me as much as I was missing him. Where was he? In his flat, yes – but in the bed? in the kitchen?

I miss his being here in the same room as me, changing the weight of things, making the air denser; I miss the prickle of his chest hair against my nipple, as I lean over to kiss him; I miss how good I could have been for him; I miss the good I could have done him; I miss the opportunity, now lost, to do him good; I miss specifics, and miss things I'm not happy to admit – the idea of the children we might have had, of their burden upon us; I miss the long-term damage that any relationship sustains, the chunks gone, the areas too tender to press upon; I miss, like women in books, his smell – and would bury my face in his pillow, smelling the burnt-match smell of his hair, if I weren't so aware that I could never admit to it in print – turn myself into cliché-woman – which, let's face it, is really what right now I am: a woman spurned, a woman dumped. I wonder if he's in his car. I wonder if I'm ever going to see him again. I'm wittering.

When I got out of the water, and was sprinkling powder where one does, I thought I could suddenly hear the sea, amplified – but it was the talc popping the bath-bubbles, one by one, by the thousand.

The security men are here. They have taken over the Master Bedroom. We can, sitting as we are in the drawing room, hear them going up and down the attic ladder. I find it hard to believe I was able to do so for – what? – almost a week without being heard. There are creakings and bangings, and of course I'm certain that they'll break something valuable enough to have the Owners suing for compensation. One of the security men is removing the spy cameras from each room. (However, I made a sly request – that they could leave the one in the Nursery. It's a small rebellion, I know, but feels strangely satisfying.) I'm assured they will be finished by five this evening.

Marcia was the first other person to finish packing. She wheeled through into the drawing room, to see if there was anyone around to talk to. What she found, instead, was me. For once, I wasn't crying – but I was so enraptured by my own misery, staring out through the French windows and down the garden, that I didn't even hear her come in. (She moves when she wants to on silent wheels, Marcia.) 'Victoria?' she said – and that was all she needed to say. I had to tell someone, to let it out, or else... I wouldn't exactly go *mad*, but the things I was trying not to tell would have started spurting out of me uncontrollably wherever I happened to find myself: emotional Tourette's. 'I want him back,' I said, 'X, I want him back so much...' Marcia was so good. Gently, she lifted herself onto one of the sofas; then she said, 'Come *he*re.' I went, and she took me completely in her arms and said, 'You'll *get* him back – I'm *su*re you'll get him back.' I sobbed so violently that I felt like a door some drunken man was trying to kick down. 'There there,' said Marcia. How soft her skin was, her forearms touching my forehead – almost as if it weren't skin but body-temperature air – like those blo-hockey tables, with little holes to puff out wind; the ones on Southwold Pier. Hover-hockey. What's it called? Almost wrote *Have to ask X*. Oops, no... I refuse to start crying again. When Marcia had succeeded in calming me down, I told her everything. How badly I'd treated X. How completely I regretted it. How I'd already forgiven him for sleeping with a man – or more than one man. How much I wanted him back. She repeated, with total certainty, 'You'll get him.' 'Why?' I asked, 'Why do you say that?' 'Because you're *ma*de for each other,' she said. 'You *des*erve one another. And to pro*tect* the rest of us from both of you – think what it would be like if you were both on the loose.' She laughed at herself. I thanked her; she hugged me hard; I told her I hoped it would all work out with Mo; she grimaced and said, 'I can cope with *Mo*, I just don't know if Mo can cope with *me*.' After a final kiss, I went upstairs to reassemble myself – can't be in fragments on a day like this: a sweetly, sadly sunny day, outside. It's a September sun, this morning – August is only here in name.

Fleur insists she is going to church this morning, and Alan insists upon accompanying her there. 'I haven't missed Sunday service for five years,' she says, 'and I'm not going to miss it now, just because there are a load of cameras in the way.'

'I understand that,' I said, joking, 'but couldn't you just call the Vicar up, and get him to do a take-out – come round here and privately bless you, or something?'

'It's not about that,' Fleur said.

'Why don't we all go,' interrupted Marcia, 'like we did the first Sunday?'

'It's about being part of a community,' Fleur said, 'and that community showing its love for God by worshipping Him, together.'

'But you'd never even met the people at that church before a couple of weeks ago.'

'That's the wonderful thing about it,' Fleur said. 'I can walk into any Christian church, and be as much a part of that congregation as if I'd been attending there for years.'

'Yes,' I said, 'apart from the ones where they'd shoot you on sight.'

'And where exactly are those?' she said.

'I don't know,' I said, 'hot places run by men in uniforms.'

'I'm um sorry if it upsets you,' Alan said.

'It doesn't upset me,' I said. 'You just have to be aware that you'll be all over tomorrow's papers.'

They turned to go and get ready.

Fleur came down quarter of an hour later, dressed up in smart churchgoing clothes.

I looked at her, and couldn't help but smile – she was so perfectly ridiculous.

'We're both so stubborn,' she said. 'Aren't we?'

I said, 'I suppose we do at least have *that* in common.'

'Oh, there's a lot more than that,' said Fleur, 'if you'd just let yourself see it.'

This was now tending away from the touching and towards the sermonising. 'Give my love to God,' I said.

'I always do; and He always...'

'I know,' I said, 'sends His back to me.'

'Something like that,' said Fleur.

Alan, who – like a well-trained husband – had allowed the two sisters a moment or two on their own, entered the kitchen. He seemed exceptionally tall today.

'Well,' I said, giving his lapel a tug and a smooth, 'go and be famous.'

'Victoria,' he said, wincing, 'you know that's not why we're doing this.'

'Come on,' said Fleur, hooking her arm through his, 'or we'll be late.'

They made their way to the front door, and stopped for a moment to think and breathe. 'Oh dear,' I heard Alan say. I went to see what was going on. Alan undid the lock and they stepped out; hurriedly, I shut the door behind them.

I expected, of course, to hear the quiet clicking of camera shutters – it didn't come.

'They've gone,' I heard Alan say.

'Really?' I asked, through the door.

'Really,' said Fleur.

I didn't think they would try to trick me, not in this way, not on a Sunday, so I reopened the door and stepped out.

It was true: not a single journalist or photographer remained behind; after that final attempt this morning, their editors must have decided we were no longer newsworthy enough (or too much effort), and had called them away to bother someone else – a few chocolate-bar wrappers and lots of cigarette butts were the only proof they had ever been there.

'How wonderful,' said Fleur. 'I wasn't looking forward to that at all.'

I can't deny that I was a little annoyed: who *was* suddenly more interesting than us?

'Then let's um go,' said Alan, and took my sister by the arm.

When they walked off, it might as well have been to the drone of Mendelssohn's March in some draughty chapel; they were as good as married now – and I couldn't help but feel satisfaction at having been the adversity that had brought them together.

William dolloped a whopping glop of porridge into my bowl. 'Salt,' he said to Marcia, 'not sugar.'

'I can't,' she sensibly said, 'not for breakfast.'

'And you put the milk around the outside, then it doesn't all go cool at once.'

'But I want to put the milk in the middle, and eat to the outside.'

‘I’m just trying to tell you how we do it in Scotland,’ William said.

‘Why do there have to be rules about eating *po*rridge?’ Marcia said, needled. ‘There aren’t any about cornflakes.’

‘Thank you very much,’ I said, having constructed my bowl half in accordance to both of them – a smidgen of salt, but also some demerara; milk round the edges, cream in a divot on the top.

I went through into the drawing room; no-one had yet pulled the curtains open – when I did, I saw the most heartbreakingly beautiful day outside.

I sat down on the right-hand sofa. The light came through the doorway shape in the curtains, stretching out hot fingers of white. I looked at it for a long time, letting it do strange things to my vision; I did feel vaguely religious, at that moment.

I had almost forgotten my porridge, and it had had time to cool. When I dipped in my spoon, I felt nauseous: the substance in the bowl had that slightly gluteny-gelatiny sheen about it; it would, I was sure, taste slightly slimy. I scooped a wodge of it onto the tip of my spoon, and pressed it into the top of my mouth, behind my teeth. If the light was religious, this was mystical, transcendental: not at all slimy; comfortingly solid yet strangely light; poised between sweet and salty. I took another wobbly wedge upon my spoon. The effect was less overpowering, but more satisfying; this mouthful tasted saltier, but I was more accustomed to the saltiness – it felt right, not disgusting. The contents of the rest of the bowl, combined with the light and the emptiness of the room, gave me my happiest moments in days: I sat upon the sofa, looking into the brightness, eating the heavenly porridge, weeping absurdly. It was like a long-desired declaration of love; it was like a hug in a dream from a much-missed dead person. It made me feel very weak and very strong, all at the same time; and very ridiculous, too.

When I went back into the kitchen, William and Marcia were still there. He had managed to persuade her to have some salt in hers, and now he was trying to dissuade her from adding any more. 'How was it?' he asked.

'Heavenly,' I said.

'Really?' he said.

'Oh, yes,' I said, 'divine.'

'I thought you'd like it.'

Marcia the first to leave. I cry. What a good person she is, and how badly I misrepresented her, early on. I'm hoping we shall stay friends; the way I've treated her, and the way she's forgiven me – it gives me hope. It's possible I'll be going to stay with her this weekend.

All the remaining guests took advantage of our liberation: Alan took Fleur and Domino off in the car, with no explanation; Simona went shopping for presents and souvenirs (she bought a reproduction Southwold lighthouse); William played the minor celebrity in a couple of local pubs.

For myself, I took a final walk alone up the beach; and as I did so, I began to feel nostalgic for our earliest days in the house – when everyone was here: the early patterns we fell into: couples being couply, and single people avoiding and interrupting them; men vs. women; all the guests (apart, maybe, from Marcia) finding time to be quiet and settle in. I began to think of everyone, individually: Alan, padding round the kitchen in dressing gown and bare feet, with terrible tiger-breath, making himself a crappy coffee, then taking it, still barefoot, out onto the dewy lawn; Marcia always being tripped over, having rammed herself into one corner or another so that she could do her knitting; Edith's little songs and girlish jollity, before she met Elizabeth and started to waft naughtily around in her clothes – how haunting her haunting was; William practising Bach on the piano, whilst smoking; Simona pestering me for yet another confession (though it only slowly came clear how persistent in this she was to be); Cecile's *presence*, which I can't remember without the memory being tainted with bitterness – but the bitterness somehow, in its astringency, only serves to sweeten the rest: like salt in porridge; Henry's laid-out, relaxed, passionate reading of things – cereal packets included; Ingrid's withdrawals; the Chef's cooking and the Maid's ironing; Fleur's Fleurness, her Fleurisms, her Fleuraciousness; X's comfort, and what I did once take to be his love for me. (I think I probably still hope I do.)

Walking back up through the garden, I looked at the house itself, remembering its different lights and moods on different days and at different times. How morning through the seaward windows made everyone's skin look blue and photogenic; how the drawing room at night, curtains shut and candles ablaze, warmed us to a mush of contented flesh. Sounds, too: music in the house: Alan's Louis Armstrong and Duke Ellington tapes; Edith's boybands; Marcia's torchsongs, Dusty Springfield, Charles Aznavour; William's Bach and Schubert concert, his scales and his arpeggios; Cecile's little songs-to-herself, whilst dressing.

I realise, over the past couple of days, even before he left, that whenever I could I've been semi-consciously leaving X out of this diary. I'm not quite sure why; probably from a sense of loyalty – not mine to him but his to me. When the rest of the house turned against me, they could quite easily have turned against him, too; and if that had happened, the entire project would have been lost. By preserving himself, he kept open the possibility of my eventual rehabilitation. On my own, I would have lost my temper, lost my friends, and most likely lost everything. X was very clever and subtle. I put him into an impossible situation, and he converted it into an essential situation. And now I feel guilty for having failed him – failed in my belief in him. He forgave me for betraying him (placing him as brunt against the anger of the house) – he saw me as sacrificing him, along with myself... No, this isn't coming out right. When I betrayed him, he forgave me; when he betrayed me, I dumped him. It's as simple as that, if that's simple. And now he's gone, my regret of him seems far greater than my trust of him ever did. I know now that I could and should have trusted him up to and beyond the point of marriage. He would have been good for me, good in ways I am only now coming to see. I am not, in my negotiations with the world, anything like diplomatic enough: it is necessary for me to have an intermediary. X offered himself, and I used him – but I did not recognise what I was doing. How could I have been so stupid? (I must have written the previous sentence about a thousand times.) And yet, what I do now is analyse; I could be off and in the car, chasing him down. But in my stubbornness, even though I realise that I am the one in the wrong, I want *him* to return to *me*. It is a stupid gamble. To gratify my stubbornness, I am prepared to risk for ever my happiness. Even in the acknowledgement of what I need, I will not make a move towards securing it. I am so stupid. The ways, the ways, the ways and means. Perhaps I should try a phone call. His mobile will be off, I know.

His mobile was off. I knew.

Now it's over, some things that happened seem inevitable: how could I ever have thought I wouldn't be discovered, scuttling up to the the attic on that loud-scrapey ladder? Me being found out, becoming a pariah, that was part of the story: it was what I wanted, underneath my bravado. Because my heroines for good or ill are and have always been myself, usually with a different hair colour – just so people don't notice. I wanted to make Cecile my heroine here, but she refused: heroically, it would seem. If I were a different kind of writer, I could make that refusal into something exceptional, something truly poignant; but I can't, because I keep getting in the way of myself – I trip myself up, and jump out on myself when I'm turning a corner. And I'm doing it now, and I know it, and I can't stop, I really can't. But I shall, I shall take myself far away, where my words won't do anything other than buy me cups of coffee, pass commonplaces with soon-to-depart strangers, inform the hotel manager I'll be needing the room another week.

I shall do some desolate shopping – always a delight.

Alan has locked Domino in the front parlour, to give Fleur a chance to fetch Audrey in from the garden. It took about half an hour. Fleur's method involved uttering at regular intervals a high, flutey singing call, on two notes, descending. Audrey is now back in her cat basket, her travelling lawn beside her – the whole lot, on the rear seat of Fleur's car. She is going to drive Alan back to London (or so they say: I think they may be heading straight for her home). Audrey and Domino will have a four to five hour car journey in which to get to know one another.

3.50 p.m. This will be my final confession with Simona.

~~I will tell her I am not going to publish *From the Lighthouse*, in any form.~~

Afterwards, I will go to Southwold lighthouse.

I probably won't be able to get in, but I think I at least need to make the attempt.

EDITOR'S NOTE

As you have just read, Victoria had by the end of August decided for her own particular reasons not to write a novel version of *From the Lighthouse*. We, by which I mean her publishers, did not consider non-publication a viable option. The project had already generated so much public interest, we felt there was a real demand for the 'inside story'. It was therefore resolved that we go ahead with what we already had: Victoria's day-to-day account of the month and all the other material on the file from her laptop. In preparing this book, we have made one or two very slight cuts to the text – mainly from a desire to avoid unnecessary repetition. Apart from that, what you have just read (and, I hope, enjoyed reading) is exactly what Victoria herself wrote.

Since there has been some pre-publication controversy about the publication of a book in direct opposition to the author's wishes, I would like to set matters straight by quoting the following paragraphs from Victoria's contract for a book entitled *From the Lighthouse*. (NB. It was the second of a two-book deal, and hence is referred to throughout as 'Book 2'.):

2(e)

If the Author dies before the delivery of Book 2 to the Publishers or is prevented by causes beyond her control from fulfilling this Agreement with respect to Book 2, the Publishers shall be entitled to demand immediate delivery of all typescripts or other material relevant to the Work. Subject to sub-clause (g) that part of the advance payable under this Agreement already received shall remain with the Author and her Estate who shall also be paid such proportion of the royalties and other sums payable hereunder as will be fair and reasonable having regard to the state of the Work at the time of the Author's death or prevention from fulfilling this Agreement, subject to consultation with the Author or her Estate.

*

A further note should perhaps be added:

On the afternoon of the final day, Victoria *did* try to go to the Lighthouse in Southwold. When she came back afterwards, she was in a very bad mood and refused to talk about it. Which led everyone (all the remaining guests) to suspect that they hadn't let her in.

There were goodbyes and hugs and promises to keep in touch. Victoria, despite what you would expect, didn't cry all that much.

Victoria was the last to leave.

RESPONSES

In Alphabetical Order:

Alan
Cecile
Edith
Fleur
Henry
Ingrid
Marcia
Simona
William
X

Alan Sopwith-Wood

Fleur will have her own say, elsewhere. But I should like to tell you that we are very happy together.

Cecile Dupont

Was contacted by phone, after repeatedly failing to deliver her promised response. She dictated the following:

Perhaps I should make clear what I did and didn't do.

As you have probably guessed, I was going off to meet a journalist, Sheila Burrows of the *Mirror*, on the afternoon of Thursday 15th. I had contacted her, with a view to selling the story *not* of the house but of the ghost.

When it became clear that she was far more interested in the spying and the 'Big Sister' aspect of things, I withdrew. I knew that she would write the story, now she had it (although I did not mention that you were, that very moment, locked in the attic). And so, to gain some time, I told Sheila Burrows I was thinking of giving her an exclusive. She was as good as her word.

But somehow or other, the journalists from the television, the ones you were angry at Marcia for speaking to, they learnt about what had been going on.

From what happened afterwards, I guess that this was from the Vicar. He knew it all: Fleur told him. He disapproved. This was his reason.

Once the story was in the newspapers, I decided I had only a short time to sell my story. I needed to sell it. I am an old woman, and it is only very rarely I have something in which people are interested – interested enough to pay. I thought it better to do one very vulgar thing, and live decently on the proceeds for a long while, than live every day in vulgar poverty, and regret not having had the sense to profit from one lapse of decency.

If you had been in my position I know you would have done exactly the same.

I called Sheila and we agreed I would be collected from the house at 6pm the following evening.

I was sorry to add to your troubles, but I felt entirely innocent of having caused them. You did that, as everyone agrees, entirely by yourself.

So, please, feel free to blame me for what I did, but only, if you please, for what I did.

Otherwise, I don't know what everybody is getting so excited about; I had a marvellous time, and made a couple of delightful new friends, whom I hope to cherish in the time that is left to me.

And that is all I have to say on this matter. Thank you.

Edith Snow

Dear Victoria,
thank you very much for a lovely 'month in the country'. It is making me cry now, just to think about it. It was the most wonderful time of my life – meeting Cecile Dupont and then meeting Elizabeth. I never thought that my life would ever be as interesting as you made it. Mum and Dad are also writing letters to you, but I do not think theres will say the same thing. You made me feel more grown up. I'm even glad for you putting me in the Nursery at first!!! It made me and Cecile Dupont get so close so quickly. When I close my eyes I can think my way back into the house. I can feel it all around me, and smell it. If I reached out I almost feel like I could stroke it. I wish I could live in that house, or if not that *exact* house one very like it, with a friend and everything to be there with me. You must be very proud of yourself and what you have achieved, in such a short space of time. It was funny when we put you in the attic. Everyone was talking very intensely for hours and hours in the garden. And because I couldn't be left alone in the house, they let me join in. Alan Wood and your sister Fleur About were suddenly talking all over the place, like lovebirds. I knew they were going to kiss long before they did. It was so obvious to anyone with eyes. You predicted it in your Sinopsis. Well done. But you hardly got anything else right. Hard luck. I was very upset for a long time after they ripped me out of the house. It was a bad thing they did then. I wasn't in danger and I wasn't going mad, and it had nothing to do with the devil. But I understand they were worried about me. We have made friends again. Plus, I know that Elizabeth is still around because Marcia wrote and told me so. I

feel much better being sure that Elizabeth isn't being blown all around the world by winds that we can't see. She is a very lovely person and I will be grateful to you for ever and ever for making us meet. I am now back at school which seems very boring compared with the holidays. I don't think any of all the other girls had such an interesting and exciting time as I did.

Love,

Edith

p.s.

I knew my Mum and Dad didn't love each other a long time ago. Mum seems to think it is because of you that they are getting divorced, but I know it isn't true. Dad is being very silly, isn't he? I am sad at the moment but I think it will be better in the long run.

Fleur Sopwith-Wood

I considered a point-by-point rebuttal, but leave that to others. Instead, I want to ask you to forgive my sister for, in the old words, she knew not what she did. Victoria always means to do well. From her synopsis one can see what she hoped to achieve: bringing people together (as she did with Alan and myself) and giving those who have been together a long time a chance to reconsider (as with Simona and William, Ingrid and Henry). This may be misguided, but it wasn't evil. She hopes to make people happier, that's all. Victoria has always believed she could remake the world, better, if only she were given the power. I think this is why she ended up as a writer. Clearly, her powers of imagination are better employed when dealing with entirely fictional characters. The kind of mess she has achieved is, in its way, triumphant – it's *such* a mess. And from this, Alan and I have found one another (found one another a second time), and have laid the foundations of what we believe to be a lasting happiness. For that, we shall always be grateful to Victoria. We were one of the few things which came off as she had intended. (Though I'm sure you can see for yourselves exactly where she triumphed and where she failed.) I admire her bravery, her willingness to risk everything. It's a quality I've never had. Of course, this can lead to a semi-permanent state of infuriation for those around her – if they don't realize that Victoria is far more interested in the speculations of her own head than the real events in the real world. She is an innocent playing at being a sophisticate. As long as one remembers that, she seems a comic character. (But again, I'm sure you've discovered that yourselves.)

Henry Snow

Dear Victoria,

I still love you, and I still want to be with you.

My marriage to Ingrid was effectively over long before we agreed to take part in your infamous month. I think you were right, it *was* partly because we were too perfect for each other. It was a terrible pressure, being seen to have the best marriage of all our friends. (I wouldn't disagree that we certainly have the loveliest child.)

By the final year, Ingrid and I knew each other far too well. As you know, I wasn't exactly promiscuous at university. You were the only person I slept with there. And that was only a couple of times. After that, apart from Ingrid, I only ever slept with two other women: one before I got married, one a short while after. You don't know her. I hardly knew her.

Having a child with someone forces you to know them in ways you really don't want to – and it makes you feel guilty you don't want to know them in every possible way.

That's why I no longer want to be married, or to pretend that I'm in some infinite relationship. What I want is to be with you for as long as we want to be together.

Right now, I can't imagine not wanting to be with you. Since we left the house I have missed you every minute of every day. (I used to believe that was a figure of speech, now I know it can be literally true.)

I think you thought I was avoiding you, from day one onwards; I think you thought I was stand-offish, elusive, rude. And, yes, you were *right*, I was.

But only because I had convinced myself that what I felt for you glowed out of me so brightly that I wouldn't be able to suppress it.

I never thought I was much of an actor, but I seem to have succeeded horribly well in deceiving you. Couldn't you see? The more you pursued me, the more I hid myself away inside myself.

Almost as soon as we arrived, Ingrid became jealous of us. Whenever she saw us together, she would send me a text message giving me some stupid task to do.

I was under scrutiny, and I couldn't cope.

The longer this went on, the worse the situation became. I was mad with desire for you, but could only direct this passion into seeming indifferent. If I didn't do that, the whole thing would blow up spectacularly – harming Edith, harming everyone.

In the end, it felt as if I'd put myself into a box inside myself. I began to worry I would never again be able to act according to my own natural desires.

Which is why, when I heard about the Synopsis, I had to read it. I needed to know what you thought of me.

And when I did read it, it gave me hope. I know you told me that there wasn't any, but I think you were just trying to save the situation in the house. You were right. It would have been too complicated then. But it isn't any longer.

It's such a relief to be able to write to you now, in this way – open-heartedly.

My marriage is over, because of you, because of this bloody book, and most of all because of me. I am aware that Edith is likely to read this, if not immediately then eventually.

Edith, I am sorry. Your mother and I tried for as long as we could, then we just couldn't try any longer.

I suppose, knowing my feelings towards you, I should have insisted that we turn down your invitation.

Something good must surely come of this, and I think that something should be us being together.

Love,

Henry

ps

You may be wondering about what happened between X and I – I mean when we came back bruised. It was nothing, I swear: a very untidy scrap. He wanted to kiss me, half-way through, when we were rolling around on the ground, but I didn't let him. I fought him off. The kiss would have been aggressive, not tender. X has a side to him I don't think you've seen – beware.

Ingrid Snow

When I read this awful book, I can't recognise myself.

Cleangirl? I don't feel clean, I feel dirty; I don't feel like a girl, I feel like a hag.

You say I constantly excluded you but I feel myself excluded throughout.

Is this really what you were thinking? It seems so bitter. We talked more than you say – we laughed, were silly.

Most of all, I am glad of the two honest talks we had – on Day 7, Wednesday, and Day 10, Saturday.

I can't forgive you for what you did to Edith nor can I forgive you for what you did to my marriage.

You watched us having sex! How could you?

It wasn't a perfect marriage – I never believed in such an oxymoron. The 'perfect marriage' was your delusion. Ours was a good marriage, a decent marriage.

When you thought Henry and I were texting passionately, sexually, you were absolutely right and utterly wrong. It wasn't sexual, it was a passionate attempt not to start hating each other. We were in negotiation; face-to-face talk was too painful. You saw a little of that on Day 14.

You seduced Henry. But that wasn't exactly difficult. All you had to do to succeed was be present for him as a possibility.

Don't flatter yourself. It wasn't *you* – he didn't see *you*. You were completely transparent like a sheet of glass. It was the different life he saw *through* you, a different place he could be, that was what enticed him.

We can never be friends again.

Marcia Holmes

Where to begin? Mostly, I feel sorry for Victoria. She was a meddler, wasn't she? and meddlers always come to grief. That's what I think my birth mother would have said, if she'd hung around long enough to be my real mother. I find it very strange to think that what I write for the end of this oh so silly book will be read by more people than anything else I will ever write, probably. Perhaps I should copy out some of my poetry. It's not too bad. But no. Under the circumstances, I'm not really sure what to say: *Love one another*. Something like big pop stars end up saying when they feel they have to come up with a "message for the planet". There is a real temptation deep inside of me not to use this small platform to send out negative emotions. I think that if I were a better person than I am, I would hold myself back. But I can't. I'm not the better person. Whatever happened to Victoria, I'm sorry but she deserved it. Like they say, she had it coming. I don't really care what she said about me, and how stupid it was. Wasn't she intelligent enough to know how it would seem to the people reading it, out there? To you. Not all of you are as comfortable, materially or with themselves, as Victoria seems to think. Someone will have to call her a 'Racist' eventually, and I expect you're expecting it to be me. But I'm not going to. What Victoria was was very English and very (too much, for some people) honest: all she was doing was saying the things that most people think but never say. Spazz-ramps! It's a terrible thing for somebody to be punished for being honest. After all, it's what our elders always tell us to be. And Socrates, too. So I can't hate Victoria, because she was just being all over what she was in one part of her. I wish that part had been different. But do I wish I had never gone along with her? Was I dumb going? No, I don't think so. It was a learning experience, for all of us. I learnt something about belonging and about not belonging. I also learnt a lot about not wanting to belong. There are places in this country where people will let you pretend you belong and there are other places where they will pretend that you don't. But nobody belongs anywhere and everybody belongs everywhere, that's what I think. If this is all about feeling at home, then I don't want that. I want to feel that I am me, wherever I am. And I do. If people looking at me see something they don't like then let them look away. What I want to be is very solidly there wherever I am. Like a protester, like a Gandhi, sitting down in the middle of some dirty road, saying We Shall Not Be Moved. You can step round me, step across me but you can't step through me! I think Victoria tried to step through me. And when she couldn't do that, she tried to do the next best thing. She tried to *see* through me. But I'm not that easy to see through. I may be just black to some people on the outside but I'm not going to tell them what colour – or colours – I am on the inside. And I may look a bit twisted out of shape, and unable to move with grace, but on the inside I dance in my own way. And that may be the way I dance with my body. (I do dance. You should see me. I'm good.) But when I am in the mood for celebration, I don't want anybody telling me how or where. So for now I'm going to celebrate! One, I'm going to celebrate being in this book, which is the biggest thing that's ever happened to me. Two, I'm going to celebrate being Me in this book. Victoria said some true things about me, some ugly, but some true. Three, I'm going to celebrate the good friends I made and that Victoria didn't know how lucky she was to have. Hello Simona, you bad girl, and William, oh you should have said something, William, I'm so angry with you, hello sad Ingrid, hello foolish Henry, hello sweet Edith, say hello to Elizabeth for me, when you see her, hello naughty Cecile, hello my kind, lovely Alan, hello Fleur who I talk to all the time anyway, hello the man Victoria calls X, and hello to Elsie and Darren. Hello to all of you! Four, I'm going to celebrate YOU out there reading this scribble. I don't know why I should, but I'm going to do it anyway. It's your job to give me a good reason for doing it. So you better.

Simona Princip

Quite apart from my position of Editor, I have quite a few things of my own to say. Unless I do, I fear quite a large percentage of this book may seem non-sensical.

Of course, as soon as I received it, I steamed opened and read, with great amusement, Victoria's Synopsis. As anyone would, I was particularly interested to see what she had to say about what was going to happen to me. My relationship with William had, I am ready to admit, reached a sort of plateau: I knew about his illness, knew what it meant, and I wasn't going to leave him out of spite. Unlike most modern marriages, this one really was going to be 'till death do us part'. And, as you may or may not know, that is what has turned out to be the case: William died a week ago, a day after dictating his Response to me. He is mourned by all who knew him, including, I am sure, Victoria.

Reading that she had had cameras installed in the house came as a bit of a shock to me, but I had depended on Victoria's ingenuity to come up with some way of ensuring that things happened. I can't claim to have foreseen exactly what she was intending. William was very worried, at this point, before we started; he thought Victoria would spot what we were doing (copying her work); also he thought we wouldn't be able to be 'natural' in the house, knowing Victoria might be watching our every action. He needn't have worried. As I assured him right from before the beginning, Victoria clearly had no idea whatsoever what 'natural' looked like. We also did put on a bit of an act.

In attending Victoria's 'confessions' so frequently I had two main motives. Firstly, I genuinely wanted to encourage her on a day-by-day basis; secondly, I needed to give William the opportunity to sneak into her room, or sometimes into the attic, and copy her latest work to disk.

It was in the course of his amateur hacking that William inadvertently deleted Day 12. Silly sausage. I do have Victoria's original draft in my possession, including the wonderful cannibal dinner party passage, but it would disrupt the flow of the book too much if I were to reinsert it.

Right from the very beginning it was clear to me that Victoria might not have the stomach to see the project through to the end. I wasn't going to have my publishers part with the sum of money that we did, nor invest so much of my own reputation in the eventual outcome, without guaranteeing these investments. Victoria could, at any time, have decided to give up on the whole thing – particularly when her original plan of making the guests hate her started to work. I thought this was one of her most brilliant ideas.

As the month went on it was delightful to watch Victoria's struggles developing; I'm sure you, dear readers, have enjoyed watching them, too.

It was during the second week that X felt himself coming to the point of a decision. Apart from Victoria, and William and myself, he was the only person in the house who knew about the cameras right from the start. The whole ghost business turned the attic into such an issue that he was forced to take sides. Edith and Cecile had started plotting about how to get into the master bedroom, and then up through the forbidden hatch. It was quite possible, X knew, that with a little ingenuity they would succeed. They had already asked him for the key to the door of the master bedroom, and he was having difficulty coming up with a good solid reason for saying no. If they found out he'd been in on the secret, but had been helping Victoria keep it that way, X knew he would be in deep trouble. Then, of course, Victoria blabbed about Cornwall to Cecile, and the guests started to suspect that she really was spying on them. Fleur checked her room for microphones, found a tiny camera lens. After that, it didn't take long for them to realise that the attic was the obvious place for her to be spying from. In the end, for X, it came down to a simple case of Whose Side Are You On? And he wisely chose to side with the guests, and told them about the set-up in the attic.

With a little help from me, thanking him for his honesty, defending him from Marcia, etc. etc., I was able to prevent the guests from throwing him out.

We then decided collectively that he could show his loyalty to us by shutting Victoria in the attic; and this he did.

He also mentioned how we could block out the cameras so they couldn't see but leave the microphones working, and how Victoria would either believe he'd forgotten the microphones or had left them deliberately.

During those first long discussions in the garden when she was safely stowed away, we came to a resolution: Victoria should be kept in the attic for two days, the first, without food, etc., the second, slightly better provided for. There were voices for and against, but two days was the consensus. We were very democratic, hands were raised and votes counted.

It was at this point that I decided it would be more fun for the guests to know some of what Victoria had said about them in the Synopsis. I gave a public reading, and we had a part-hilarious part-horrendous hour in the garden.

Of course, I didn't read the whole thing – if, for instance, Ingrid had heard about Victoria's plans to half-seduce Henry, or, even worse, to have Edith fall in love with X, she would have been in the car and off. No, I took half-an-hour to make a carefully edited version, and improvised a few extra bits to fill in the gaps.

After that, it was impossible to stop momentum building for us to play a series of jokes on Victoria. Fleur and Alan, the prophecy of whose romance had caused a great deal of laughter and several sly sideways glances, were first to volunteer. Between the two of them, they were playing a huge number of double games, pretending to be indifferent when they weren't. William wanted to join in, too; and who was I to deny him one of his final pleasures? Henry and Ingrid were also keen, though it's very hard now to see why. Cecile was the great surprise. She felt patronised by what Victoria had written about her in the Synopsis, and wanted an amusing little revenge. Edith wanted to do a scene with Elizabeth the ghost, but Ingrid forbade it. Of course, I knew Victoria had already seen quite a lot of that already.

Everyone agreed that part of the fun would be waiting to see how long it would be, afterwards, when she had been let out of the attic, before Victoria cracked, and started asking about what she'd learnt during her eavesdropping. When that happened, the person she told was under strict instructions to tell everyone else immediately.

We started to get ready to play our jokes. Cecile went off for a while, to prepare herself; myself and William, Henry and Ingrid, Fleur and Alan had a few private rehearsals, outside.

And then the play began... We couldn't have wished for a more perfect outcome. I had personally thought that Cecile's performance, as the least naturalistic of all, would be the one to make Victoria suspect, and so shouldn't go first. But she insisted, and was proven right by the issue. These are some of the most wonderfully comic passages of the book, I think. They are by themselves enough of a justification for me doing what I did.

I had already thought ahead, to when Victoria found out that I'd let the guests in on what happened to them in the Synopsis. I would brazen it out. She couldn't have me evicted. I knew, when it came down to it, I would be supported by everyone else in the house, including X. The power balance shifted during this time, away from Victoria and towards the rest of us (and secretly, towards me). I was the one who knew the greatest amount of what was going on; I won't say everything, because one lesson of this month is that mere human narrators shouldn't pretend they are omniscient.

When the Synopsis was stolen from my room, I had a few real hours of anxiety. But I was able to have a look myself at Victoria's diary the following day, while she was at the hospital with Alan. Once I knew the thief was Henry, and that she had begged him to keep silent, and that she now had the Synopsis herself, I relaxed.

I realize that I'm quite seriously overrunning my wordcount, but no one's going to cut me, and I do have a few more important things to say.

One of these is that William wasn't a dirty flasher. He just didn't care, towards the end of his life, all that much about hiding his body away. It had been invaded by so many doctors already, half the staff of St Bartholomew's had had a grope of his prostate. Being seen naked was something he'd become very comfortable with. But he got no 'kick' out of it, and certainly not out of flashing Edith.

William was a lovely and difficult man, and I was very lucky to have been married to him. I miss him terribly, every day. For him to have joined in with me doing this was a great gift. But I think the way he saw it was this: he wanted to spend as much of the time he had left, his remission, with as many people as possible, and he didn't want them to be his closest friends. He preferred it when people weren't aware that he was ill, because it meant there was no atmosphere of false solemnity. People get terribly maudlin about terminal illness. They pretend they can be blithe and bonny in the face of death, but they can't. He wanted to have some fun. He was very well, right up until the last weeks. From the outside, you could hardly tell. Going to Southwold was a perfect opportunity for him to live every moment to the full. He really loved all the other guests. He particularly doted on Edith. She almost made him wish that we'd had children.

The question I get asked most of all, on chatshows and the like, is 'Don't you feel sorry for Victoria?' The answer is a resounding, 'No.' She got exactly what she wanted out of this, and anyone who thinks differently is completely naïve. She is now famous. Her next book, hopefully not with another publisher, and hopefully *with* the same editor, will bring her an advance of three or four times more money than *From the Lighthouse*. She has joined that very rare group of authors who have actually managed to enter the public consciousness. It is also completely naïve to think that one can make this leap without being distorted in the process. Becoming a bit of a cartoon villainess was the price Victoria had to pay, and I think, if you'd sat her down beforehand and given her the choice, she would have accepted the Faustian pact. I quite fancy myself as her Mephistopheles. This, after all, is the woman who, as a young girl, went to see *Snow White and the Seven Dwarfs* at the cinema, and came out begging her mother to make her an Evil Queen costume. She's enjoying her new role; you can just sense she is. It's a great new experience for her, being the subject of tea-break discussions the length and breadth of the country. All writers dream of causing such a stir. I'm just proud of the small part I played in bringing her to notice. She deserves every single bit of what's coming to her.

William Princip

I am not very well. I will not dictate much.

I enjoyed my time in Southwold enormously. I can't think of a better way to have spent my last August.

Victoria, I am sorry for our little deception. Simona insisted we had to know what you were getting up to, at every stage. It was fun, I admit, creeping up into the attic, copying your work on to my disk. We had to be very careful not to get caught reading it on Simona's laptop.

I am also sorry for losing your Day 12. The passage about the cannibal dinner party was very good, although I only skim-read it.

You are a very amusing writer and a very bad person. One day soon I hope you will realize that Simona, also a very bad person, is the only editor for you.

I would like to point out to the reader that Victoria has given herself every single one of the best lines, stealing mercilessly from all and sundry – including, more than once, myself.

That's enough.

X

X did not respond, having decided he wasn't going to read the manuscript.

TWO LETTERS

Polurrian Hotel
Mullion Cove
Cornwall
November

Dear Simona,

Firstly, I was devastated to hear of William's death. I am truly sorry for any hurt I may have caused him. Please let me know if there is anything I can do.

To business: Before you sent me this manuscript, this horrible thing, which I really don't know what to call, I was well on my way to forgiving you.

I decided not to reply straight away, because I was far too angry. I wouldn't have made any sense. It isn't necessary, I'm sure, for me to say I feel betrayed; there are too many people in my August diary (I'll call it that for the moment) saying and feeling that already.

It's one of its many faults – faults I would have corrected if I'd been able to turn the thing into a *proper*, finished book. I won't point out too many of the other faults, only to say that I don't really believe people's secrets are always and only sexual secrets.

As you see from the address above, I've taken your advice, or, if I'm to believe what you said in conversation (page 278), I've taken *my own* advice: I have checked into a nice hotel so that I – the heroine – can be luxuriously melancholy at the end of the novel. (This *is* the end of the novel.)

First we have to deal with *Finding Myself*. Please note I am still refusing to use the title which once I gave it. To my mind, no such book exists, nor will ever exist.

Your cuts to the text are quite atrocious. Some of your comments, I admit, are quite humorous; some of them hurt me deeply.

Your little account of the last afternoon, at the house and elsewhere, is quite wrong. I can't be bothered, though, to correct it – and it's so badly written, too.

I *did* go to the lighthouse, and I *did* get in. But what I saw there is private. It goes with the book that was never written; it is the climax – it was worth it.

Despite what the lawyers say I will not, under any circumstances, allow this book to be published. This is my final word.

Since the end of August, lots of things have happened. I was, of course, fascinated to read the others' responses; they were the first bit I turned to. I don't wish to comment on them. Some of the guests' news saddens me, some of it delights me – I'm sure you know which does which.

I came here to be alone, to think, to allow my regret the fullest scope to develop. I intended to take myself down to the beach – a very different beach from Southwold; a proper cliff-backed, fingernail-clipping-shaped inlet; black sandy, with wide breakers and rock pools and a sunset regularly hung above it. (I withdraw what I said in the Holiday Diary; some of the ones I've seen here have been entirely surprising in their ends; shocking; outrageous – so bloodthirsty.)

X had no idea where I was. Since the moment he walked out of the house, there has been no contact between us. I am desperate to see him but too proud to call him. What I hoped was that, when he read the manuscript, all of it, he would see – see how foolish I'd been, how soon I'd given up on seducing Henry, how much I wanted to be with *him*. This hasn't happened.

Yours sincerely,

Victoria

Polurrian Hotel
Mullion Cove
Cornwall
December

Dear Simona,

An arrival, an entrance, a motorbike! Here it was, ripping into the car park of the Polurrian Hotel, sounding like a petrol-driven thunderstorm. I had, as it happened, just come back from a freezing walk down on the said beach. If I hadn't, the whole incident would have been far less romantic.

'Hello, Victoria,' he said.

'X,' I said. (I really did say X – him having become that, in my mind.)

'Come on,' he said.

There was another helmet, a smaller one. He held it out towards me.

'Where are we going?' I said.

'Somewhere,' he said.

Luckily, I was wearing trousers. (Jeans, Breton jumper, hiking boots, navy-blue jacket – standard issue miserablism kit.)

I tucked my hair up, slipped on the helmet (which fitted) and climbed on behind him.

We were in St Ives in under an hour. Another lighthouse, but only in the distance.

I won't tell you exactly what X said to me, as we walked along the front, nor as we sat in the cosy restaurant eating lobster, nor as we stood in the moonlit car park beside the motorbike. What he said, it is enough for you to know, was exactly *the right thing*; and then, I admit, he took me masterfully in his masterful arms.

After we got back from St Ives, X moved into my room at the hotel – it was a luxurious double room, anyway.

I have just about worked out the chain of events which led X to come here. And you should *not* have revealed my whereabouts to Fleur – even when she begged. But I will always be grateful to her, for letting him know where I was.

And now I'm so happy I can't tell you. I don't care about the book any more. Reading through the whole thing again, in one go, I am reconciled to it coming out; it isn't finished, it isn't satisfactory in the way I'd like it to be; but it is, at least, alive. I think if I tried to novelise it now, my distaste for the whole idea would make it a stillbirth. I know you're going to print it, and that you think by doing that you're going to hurt me – but you can't. I'm beyond being hurt by it.

You may think this sounds naïve; I know already what sort of impression it might make, and how big. I know that people, after reading it, or just hearing about it, will view me in a different way; more negatively.

I don't come across very well; I come across uglily – morally. (You've made sure of that.)

Well, I have X. X loves me. There's nothing else in the world I care about.

Since he got here, I haven't thought of anyone but him – though there is, I have to admit, one waiter I'd had my eye on before: young, slim, cocky, and very cute; I'm fairly sure X has noticed him, too, and noticed my noticing. He (X) doesn't seem upset; in fact, I'm fairly sure he's thinking the same thing I am.

We intend to have fun.

Love,

Victoria

P.S.

If you beg and beg and beg me, I might tell you the brilliant idea I've had for my next book.